THE LOCKPICKER

DATE DUE	a/17
NOV 1 7 2017	
	PRINTED IN U.S.A

Books by Leonard Chang

The Lockpicker
Triplines
Crossings
Dispatches from the Cold
The Fruit 'N Food

The Allen Choice Trilogy:

Over the Shoulder
Underkill
Fade to Clear

THE LOCKPICKER

Leonard Chang

Black Heron Press
Post Office Box 13396
Mill Creek, Washington 98082-1396
www.blackheronpress.com

ISBN: 978-0-936364-18-3
ISBN ebook: 978-0-936364-19-0

BLACK HERON PRESS
Post Office Box 13396
Mill Creek, Washington 98082-1396
www.blackheronpress.com

For Toni Ann Johnson

PART I

1

Jacob Ahn saw blank faces around him. He walked along Van Ness, his feet hurting from trekking fifteen blocks up a long incline in tight shoes, and he stared at the faces of passers-by. Everyone was dead. Their eyes were hollowed out, decayed, their expressions zombified. He stopped at a furniture store window and examined his own face; he was still there. He existed. You can never be too sure. He shifted his backpack to his other shoulder, felt the stubble on his chin, then continued walking up the noisy street.

In his backpack was $8,755.00 in cash, mostly hundreds and fifties. Jake had counted it twice since he had left Seattle. There was also the jewelry. All stolen, of course. His back felt warm, the heat of money spreading to his body.

The zombies encircled him and chanted. They clutched mindlessly at his clothes. He waded through. Cars and trucks shuddered by, their roaring engines rattling the pavement and store windows; Jake inhaled diesel fumes, tasting oily soot. The smell of something rotting rose up from the gutters, garbage packed down and pungent from parked cars. He continued forward.

His destination: the white and grey building jutting up into the skyline, near the top of the hill, the windows brown-trimmed with narrow black balconies underneath. It was even uglier than he remembered, his last visit here about five years ago. He had dropped by Eugene and Rachel's unannounced, and they had made dinner for him. His brother Eugene kept saying, "Well, isn't this a surprise." When he told them he was in town to visit his girlfriend who had just moved here, his sister-in-law kept asking him to bring her over. But he left the city the next day, and had only spoken briefly to Eugene twice since then. Jake had trouble remembering what they looked like. He had broken up with that girlfriend shortly afterward.

His backpack was growing warmer. He wasn't sure, but he thought he saw a few zombies staring at it. He stopped, checked and tightened the straps, then moved on. Ignore them. Zombies were usually curious about the living. It was natural. Vestigal memories haunted them.

He approached his brother's concrete and stucco building, the white facade becoming more like laundry-water gray, the nearer he came, and he paused at the sight of a homeless man sitting on the curb with a "Supporting a family please help" cardboard sign. The man's jeans were torn off at the knees, his red sweatshirt covered with brown stains. Jake walked towards the man and looked into his eyes. The man blinked, then drew back. His dried out and stubbled face wrinkled in fear. "What?" he asked. Jake then saw that this man was a zombie too and walked back to the building entrance. He used the intercom system to dial Eugene's apartment on the twelfth floor, but no one answered. It was almost six o'clock. Jake could wait. He sat on the low brick wall that bordered a withering garden, and stared at the homeless man. Cars drove precariously close to the man's bare shins. He glanced back at Jake a number of times. He soon picked up his plastic bag, and shoved his sign under his arm. "Get off my back, Chinaman," he said.

Jake rose slowly from the wall, staring directly at the man. He took a step forward.

The man gave Jake the finger, and hurried away.

An elderly woman exited the building, her hands shaking as she pushed open the door. Jake slipped into the lobby before the door closed. Awful security. He took the elevator up to his brother's floor, and walked down the dark, quiet hallway. Number 12G was at the end. Jake knocked, then rang the doorbell. Nothing. Well, hell. He might as well wait inside. He pulled out his leather pouch. He kneeled down. He felt a small pull in his groin. He waited. Once the pain subsided, he leaned forward and inspected the lock.

2

Lockpicking is a dead art. Make no mistake about it. Those movies of gentlemen thieves, the Cary Grantish dapper tuxedoes leaning politely down and picking a lock one-two-three-zip-zap—those are full of crap. That's fantasy. Reality is brutal. Lockpicking has been shoved aside by crowbars and jacks that wedge open door frames, by messy saws and drills, by a meaty shoulder and a running start.

Doors are barriers, but they need not be broken through with stripped cylinders, sawed-off bolts, and splintered wood littered on the welcome mat. Doors and locks are puzzles to solve, mazes to navigate, questions to answer. It's the subtle touch, not the slamming fist, that provides access to a locked apartment, a quiet *click* freeing the secrets behind a small piece of metal from Medeco or Corbin factories.

Consider this door Jake appraised. He first made sure the door was in fact locked. Once he had begun working on a door only to discover that it had been open all along. This door, his brother's, was secure. He ran his fingers lightly across the stiles, feeling the grooves in the wood, until he reached the center. He pressed in, checking how much action there was—how tightly the door stayed sealed in the doorjamb. If the door was too tight, then he'd have trouble, since the latch assembly would be wedged against the jamb; he'd have difficulty feeling the nuances in his tension wrench. This door was snug, but not too snug. A small enough gap to work smoothly. He peered closer, smelling the greasy metal. There was a simple pin-tumbler, cylindrical lock in the door handle, and an additional tubular deadbolt above it, which might or might not have been engaged.

Jake sighed. Wasn't life much simpler when all he had to think about was opening a lock? He stood, stretched, and looked up and down the hallway. It was quiet. He thought he heard the TV news coming from an apartment a few doors down. He returned to the the task at hand.

These days, most gorillas trying to break through a door might try one of the common, cruder methods. They might drill into the cylinder, destroying the pins. This is akin to a blindfolded dentist using a claw hammer to get rid of cavities. Or a gorilla might use a high-grade screw to bore into the key hole, then yank out the entire cylinder with a pair of pliers. If the pliers are really strong, a gorilla could simply grasp the entire cylinder itself, violently twisting it until it broke. Even worse, and Jake really objected to this method, was the gorilla way of jacking or crowbarring the door frame apart, exposing the lock, then sawing off the lock bolt. Sawing! You might as well ram a truck through the house.

Jake tried to be neater. First, he took out his snapping wire, which looked like a large safety pin and was simply a shortcut first attempt before using his picks. He inserted the snapping end along with his tension wrench into the keyhole. Using the spring action of the wire— pulling it down and letting it snap up and lightly hit the pins inside the lock—Jake then tried to force the pins into place by applying pressure to his tension wrench, turning the cylinder. He was in effect jamming the pins up to their correct opening positions. It wasn't as pure as using his picks, but it was easy and fast, and worked about half the time. There were even pick guns that worked on the same principle, everything mechanized and loaded into a small pistol-shaped tool, and pulling the trigger snapped a small wire in the lock. But Jake never bothered with those. They were bulky and expensive. The snapping wire, just one long piece of thin metal bent into a curly "u" shape, was disposable, simple, elegant.

With the wire, it was still about touch, about feeling the slack in the cylinder, the tension wrench clicking into place. He worked quickly, snapping the wire, then checking the wrench. The tension wrench wasn't a "wrench" in the toolhead sense—it was another small piece of metal wedged into the keyhole and twisted while picking. It duplicated the turning action of a key. That was all. Very straightforward. Very easy.

Snap, click. Snap, click. After a few more snaps he felt the wrench give a little, and he slowly turned the cylinder, unlocking it.

Here we go, he thought.

Question: Which way do you turn? Clockwise or counterclockwise?

Answer: Doorknob locks almost always turn clockwise. As for padlocks, Master locks go in either direction. Yale locks clockwise. But here's a tip: before you begin anything, use the wrench to test both directions. You'll feel the pins engage when you turn the lock in the correct direction. In the incorrect direction, you'll feel solid metal resistance.

Jake tried to push open his brother's door, but the deadbolt was engaged.

Good for Eugene. Jake had always warned his brother to use both locks. The deadbolt was a wonderful invention. Security is very important, you know.

He tried snapping the deadbolt the same way, but was unsuccessful. The deadbolt looked newer than the door handle, with fewer scratches around the keyway, the brass shiny; there might not have been enough leeway in the shear line. No problem. He looked through his small pack of tools, and selected his rake pick, which used a similar principle as snapping. Here he used the jagged pick head and raked (or "scrubbed," as some people termed it) the pick back and forth, trying to force the pins up to the correct height. Yes, it was another rough and quick method, but he would be derelict if he didn't try these methods first. There was a procedure he liked to follow, moving from simple to intricate, quick to methodical.

The raking didn't work either. A decent lock. This was not

unexpected.

He unsheathed his diamond pick, one of his favorites. Unlike the zig-zagged rake pick, the sharp hook pick, or the bulbous ball picks, the diamond pick had a simple triangular head, and yet it opened so many different kinds of locks. Pin tumblers, disk tumblers, wafer tumblers, double wafers, warded locks, lever locks. You name it, the diamond pick—in the right hands—can open them all. Hell, he could even use the diamond to emulate other picks, such as the ball pick, by turning it upside down. Beautiful. He used to practice with this one, keeping his fingers in shape. He'd wear down the head so quickly that he'd always have a couple of spares.

Jake settled down in front of the deadbolt. He looked up and down the hallway. Where was everyone? It was past six. Possibly dinner. He set in his tension wrench and inserted his diamond pick, feeling the contours in the keyhole, pushing up each individual pin inside the lock, essentially imitating a key one notch at a time. He used the tension wrench to feel if he had clicked the pin above the shear line.

It was all about touch. A delicate, sensitive touch.

He couldn't see anything inside the lock, of course, and the only indication of progress was the tiny twitch of the individual pin "breaking" at the shear line, the point at which the pin allowed the lock to begin turning. He felt it in the tension wrench, a fraction of a fraction of a millimeter. The turning pressure helped keep the clicked, spring-loaded pins in place, so the slightest movement in the wrong direction could change their position and force him to start over. It was like balancing spinning plates. He couldn't forget the other plates as he spun a new one.

He worked on the five pins, moving from back to front, setting the pins in place while keeping the wrench at the right pressure. Then, after the last pin, Jake felt the wrench loosening as he turned the cylinder, now freed from the pins, and he slowly unlocked the bolt.

Jake always felt a pleasant rush when he picked a difficult lock, even if this one was his brother's. It was the feeling of satisfaction mingled with surprise, that he could actually do this, bypass locks meant to keep him out. He touched the deadbolt, then pressed his index finger over the keyhole, letting the small gap indent his fingertip. It was a superstitious gesture that he had started years ago—he wasn't even sure how or why he began doing it—but now, after a diamond pick job, he let the lock pinch his finger. Thank you. He put away his picks, and pushed open the door slowly, listening. He waited, but didn't hear anything, and slipped in. He immediately checked for an alarm control unit, and relaxed when he found nothing. The apartment was dark, silent. He stood still, and smelled beer. He heard a clock ticking. For the first time in days he felt relatively safe. He patted his backpack and stepped forward. Welcome, welcome.

3

Jake snooping in his brother's condo: Checking the bedroom bureaus and night tables. Finding software magazines and sleeping pills on Eugene's side, books of all kinds on Rachel's. *Faith and Philosophy.* Homeopathic fertility guide. *Resist the Clock.* Astroglide lubricant underneath Rachel's *NewStyle* magazine. A Bible on the floor. A Bible? Interesting. Jewelry box filled with fake pearls, tangled bracelets, and a gold herringbone set. Decoy box. More jewelry stashed in her stockings. Typical ploy. Ah. The good stuff. Sapphire and diamond bracelet, 14k gold. Diamond rings. Nice colors, ranging from one to three carats. Tsk, tsk. Ought to use a safe deposit box. Other drawers containing clothes, underwear—hm, black silk, open crotch, naughty kids. Microsoft boxers. Wait, a joke? Yes. *Microsoft Sucks* boxers. Eugene and his software company. Very funny. Closets filled with suits, slacks, shirts, dresses, ties—many, many ties—sport coats still in the plastic from the cleaners, belts, leather jackets. Too many clothes. Too many things. Weighing them down. Next room: guest room and library. More books. Software, computers, business, competition, *The Art of War, Management for Dummies, Fundamental Financial Analysis, Buffett's Way, Freeing the Fun Within You*, Fertility, Fertility, Fertility. Bought out the bookstore. Philosophy. *Why Are You Here? In Defense of God. Existentialism for Beginners. Presocratic Thinkers. The Meaning of This.* Photos of Eugene and Rachel. A rubber duck. The next room, an office. Two computers. A stereo system. Whoa. Nice. Must be new. Huge speakers. iPods. Tablets. TV stereo surround sound. Bastard. When did he get this? Satellite TV. The small dish on the balcony. Five hundred channels. Five hundred. DVD library. Movies, documentaries. X-rated movies.

Hello. Naughty kids. Wait. Home movies? Tsk, tsk. More framed photos. Strangers. Friends of theirs. Rachel's family. A few dying plants. The ones near the window turning brown. The ones in the kitchen already dead. Dust balls in the corners. Dishes piled in the sink. Stains and sticky brown spills on the counter. Old beer. Stinking up the place. Newspapers and magazines on the floor and coffee table. Unmade bed, dirty laundry overflowing the hamper next to the closet, mildew in the shower. No toilet paper. Box of tissues on the toilet tank. Toothpaste almost empty. Refrigerator filled with bottled water, beer, soft boxes of old Chinese food. Hardened pizza. Freezer filled with empty ice trays, frost spiking up at the edges. Starving. Finish the cold, tasteless pizza. Stay away from that Chinese food. Rest on the stiff, leather sofa. Watch a little TV. Five hundred channels. What a kick. Rest. Long day. Rest. Long week. Rest. Long month. Rest.

4

The sounds of someone opening the front door woke Jake. He grabbed his backpack, and sat up quickly. His brother Eugene stepped into the apartment, and stopped. "Jeez, what the hell are you doing here?" Eugene said.

Jake blinked. His brother's abruptness was familiar, comforting. He noticed that Eugene had put on some weight, thickening around his middle, his face fuller. He wore a business suit, though his tie was loosened and crooked, his jacket rumpled. There was a thin sheen of sweat covering his forehead. He looked green. Jake checked the clock; it was past midnight. He said,"Don't tell me you're just getting in from work?"

Eugene sighed and nodded, closing the door behind him. "Did the super let you in?"

"Uh, yeah."

The way Jake said this made Eugene look up sharply. He was about to protest, but shrugged it off. He pulled off his shoes painfully.

"Where's Rachel?" Jake asked. "And when did you get satellite TV? Five hundred channels, man."

"Rachel took off for a couple of days."

"Took off?"

"Took off." Eugene gave Jake a tired look. "She wanted a break from me."

"A break from you? You're kidding."

"Just for a few days. She wanted time to think."

"To think."

"Stop repeating what I say."

Jake nodded. He wasn't sure how to respond. "That's a surprise."

"Yes, well." Eugene took off his tie and threw it over a chair. He shrugged off his jacket and sat down heavily. "What're you doing here?"

"I blew Seattle and thought I'd stop by."

"Blew? Moved away?"

"Moved away."

Eugene saw the backpack. "Where are you going?"

"I'm not sure." He glanced down. "Yes, this is all I have right now. I got rid of most of my stuff." This wasn't entirely true. He had simply left his things in his apartment. It was a quick decision. A necessary one.

"What happened?"

Jake shook his head. "It's complicated."

"Are you in trouble?"

Still groggy from his nap, he said slowly, "Define 'trouble'."

"Oh, shit. Don't tell me that you've gotten—"

"Nothing is wrong. I just ran into a little, uh, complication up there."

"Does it involve the police?"

"No. A partner, a former partner of mine—we got into a little fight."

"All right. I don't want to hear this. Just tell me that everything's okay, and nothing down here is affected."

Jake nodded. "Everything's okay, and nothing down here is affected."

His brother walked into the kitchen. He asked if Jake wanted a beer.

"No thanks. So why did Rachel leave?"

"I'd rather not get into it now."

"Are you guys splitting up?"

Eugene popped open the beer can and drank deeply. He sighed. Finally he said, "I don't know."

"Christ." Jake had assumed their marriage was a constant. He remembered when he had first met Rachel when she and his brother were engaged, about ten years ago; they were renting a small one-bedroom apartment in the Richmond district. Eugene had recently changed careers and was working for a small software company. Rachel worked as a bank teller. They couldn't stop touching each other. They linked index fingers. Jake was embarrassed. Had that been ten years ago? He was startled by how quickly a decade had passed. He was even more startled to see that he had nothing to show for it.

"When did she go? Where did she go?" Jake asked.

"Two days ago. Staying with friends in Marin."

"No wonder this place is a mess."

"Thanks."

"So, what happened—"

"Look, I'm beat. I've got to sleep. I'm going back in at six."

Jake said, "Mind if I sleep here on the couch? I'll be out of the way in a couple of days."

"Take the guest room. Stay as long as you want. You'll have the place to yourself."

"Thanks," he replied, and stared at the top of Eugene's head. His hair was thinning, and Jake said, "Are you losing hair? Shit, does this mean that's going to happen to me?"

Eugene laughed, and squeezed the bridge of his nose. "No, that's my fault. Apparently I've been rubbing my head in my sleep. I have to wear a cap now."

"In your sleep?"

"You know, like this." He demonstrated, raking his fingers through his hair.

"Stress?"

"I guess."

"Euge, I've got to tell you. You don't look so good."

Annoyance crossed his face, but then he seemed to sag. "Yes, I know. It's been a rough six months."

"Sorry to hear that."

Eugene stared at Jake and said, "You've been touching that knapsack like it's a baby. What's in it?"

"You sure you want to know?"

"Yes. If it's something illegal I don't want it here."

"All right. I'll get a safe deposit box."

"Jesus. It's not drugs or anything—"

"Of course not. Just some jewelry, some cash."

Eugene's face tightened. Jake added, "I'll do it in the morning. First thing."

"All right. I don't care. I've got to rest. I'll try to get off early tomorrow. We'll grab dinner. You still like Korean food?"

"I do." Jake watched his brother pull himself up slowly, struggling with his own body. He finished the can of beer and said good night. Jake was alarmed to see the life flickering from his brother's eyes. Eugene was dying as well.

5

Jake's former partner, Bobby Null, pulled himself out of the dumpster, his rage so sharpened and crisp that he couldn't feel the bullet in his gut. He wouldn't get the full range of pain until after the surgery, when four inches of his small intestines would have to be removed because the bullet shredded part of his ileum and the abdomen muscle around his groin would have to be sutured and stapled. He would live because the bullet had first been deflected by his belt buckle, had torn through his intestines, travelled along his hip bone and had lodged into his left gluteus maximus. The surgeon would later tell him that had his large intestines or bladder been hit, he might have had to wear a colostomy bag for his feces, and a catheter for his urine. His prostate was safe, but he could have been impotent as well.

But before all that, Bobby had to live. Jake had shot him in the gut and left him in the garbage. Jake had made a mistake by not shooting him again, but Bobby had passed out inexplicably after the first shot, and perhaps he had seemed dead; it might have had to do with Jake's punches to his face while they were fighting for the gun. Jake was stronger than Bobby had thought. When Bobby awoke, he had no idea where he was. He knew he had been shot, though. He was surprised to be alive. His head pulsed so loudly, he felt the beating in his hands. He smelled rotting chicken and grass clippings, but then realized something was really wrong with his stomach. When he looked down and saw that his shirt and pants were soaked in blood, he felt his heart fluttering, and he moaned. He tugged at his shirt. He thought of germs, of maggots. He hated bugs. Bobby had been shot with his own goddamn gun. He slowly pulled himself up, his fingers scratching the rusty metal. He stopped. Something was moving in here. He yelped, and with a scrambling burst of energy he yanked himself out of the dumpster, the pain making him dizzy. He burned at the thought of Jake leaving him here to die.

He collapsed on the pavement, the pain ricocheting through his head and clouding his vision. The lust for revenge kept Bobby moving. No way he was going to let this end here and now, in a fucking dumpster with all that money and jewelry gone. Bobby had found the jewelers, had studied their routines, and had brought Jake in. It was Bobby's job. The fact that Jake improved it and did the actual stealing didn't matter. It was Bobby's job. He deserved more than half. He definitely didn't deserve this.

Bobby tried to stand, but he was too weak, and his legs buckled. He fell to the ground and let out a string of curses. He had lost too much blood. He was woozy. The street lamps in the distance blurred. He knew where he was—along Portage Bay in the U-District. He and Jake had chosen this place because it was so quiet at night. He needed to get to the road. He doubted their car was still there, but he needed help. He began crawling, dragging his legs behind him, his fingers scraping gravel. There was a marina a few hundred feet ahead. He had to find someone. He clawed himself forward a few feet at a time. He was growing weaker. His legs were cold. He saw bugs beginning to notice him, moving towards him.

He heard laughter and stopped. He listened for more. Nothing. Then he realized it was his own laughter he had heard. He was delirious. What the hell. He had tried to screw over Jake and it ended up like this: slithering on his fucking hands and knees, his guts spilling out. He laughed again. He was going to find Jake and make him crawl like this. He was going to shoot out Jake's knees and put a few bullets into his stomach, and watch him twitch on the fucking ground. The thought of this gave Bobby more strength. He inched closer to the road, but his arms were wobbly. His shoulders ached. Something was pinching him in his stomach. The bugs were circling him, readying for the kill. Fuck. Keep away.

He wasn't going to make it. He couldn't focus. His head grew heavier, and sank to the ground. The gravel dug into his cheeks, something long and sharp scraping his chin. He couldn't even turn his head. Fuck. He was blacking out again. He could really die. Not like this. Not fucking like this. The bugs began advancing. Get the fuck away. He tried to pull himself up, but his arms no longer worked. He was breathing hard. He heard footsteps, but thought he was imagining it.

"Hey, hey. You all right? Something wrong?" a voice said.

"Doctor. Help. Hospital," he whispered. He wasn't sure if he had said that aloud.

"Shit. Hold on. I'll call 9-1-1."

Bobby lost consciousness. He heard the bugs moaning in disappointment.

6

At the Yamachi Bank two blocks from Eugene's building Jake opened a checking account with two thousand in cash, and rented a safe deposit box. He offered his Washington driver's license for identification, but gave Eugene's apartment as his current address. Using a private booth, Jake catalogued some of his jewels, mostly diamond rings and gold wedding bands, again surprised by the amount. He really hadn't had time to examine all this carefully.

Look at this.

He hadn't expected the jewelers to bring home most of their store jewelry, just the important items they didn't want to leave at the store safe. It looked as if he might have cleaned out half their stock. He estimated the value of some of them, checking the hallmarks for the gold and the gemstone cuts, the mountings, the workmanship. Many of the diamonds were inferior—poor colors, flaws in the facet angles. He ignored the little white tags hanging from some of the pieces, the prices ridiculously high. But he stopped and studied a diamond, possibly one-carat, solitaire in white gold. A Tiffany setting. The lighting in this booth wasn't great, but the color seemed okay, maybe a G or H, and using his jeweler's loupe from his backpack estimated the clarity to be VVS2 or VS1—just a guess without any standard comparison stones and appraisal tools. Maybe four or five thousand retail?

The other pieces were crap, though. The 14-karat chains were machine manufactured with hollow links and high porosity. Some of the rings were just terrible: sloppy mountings with scratches, rough polishing, and even burrs on the cheaper wedding bands. Scrap. Cheap, imported shit. The diamond engagement rings were slightly better, though he found a few with glaring facet cut errors, and the colors looked off, possibly as bad as an M or worse. Still, there was an eternity ring, in which the diamonds were set partially around the band, that looked good, as well as that diamond solitaire in white gold that he would have to store for a while. He guessed that half of the jewels here would end up at a wholesaler as scrap. The rest he could sell on consignment as estate jewelry. If everything sold, he could bring in maybe thirty thousand total. That and the cash made this his biggest job. Especially since he was no longer splitting the proceeds. He stopped and thought about Bobby. Hell. He tried to tell himself that it hadn't really been his fault, that Bobby had tried to screw him over.

After packing most of the expensive jewels and keeping some samples to test the market, he buzzed the guard and returned his box to its slot. He stopped at a McDonald's and had some fries, sitting on a stool at the window. The street was crowded, dirty, and jammed with clothing and furniture stores, a few restaurants and coffee houses. He noticed a small group of homeless kids sitting on their knapsacks and rolled-up sleeping bags while asking for money from pedestrians. Large trucks double parked, their engines still running and puffing out black exhaust, clogging the already dense traffic.

He wasn't seeing death everywhere this morning. The banker who helped him open his account was alive, her eyes bright and pleasant. She was young, though. Maybe that had something to do with it. He knew all this death had to do with Bobby, and the fact that he had probably killed him. A gut shot like that was fatal, and he was out cold when Jake had left him.

He pushed this away. Focus on now. He'd have to check the Seattle papers to follow up what happened, see what the police did. The worst case: the police connect Bobby to Jake and start searching. But Jake had been careful. The only link was Chih, his fence, and even Chih didn't know Jake's last name, address, or anything too personal.

Everyone had been careful after the Malloy mess, something like a dozen guys going down because of one talkative asshole. Someone shot Malloy on his toilet. No one was surprised.

But all this taught Jake something. His father used to say there was a lesson in everything. He wondered if Eugene remembered that. Jake had avoided the police for this long and now he knew he couldn't depend on his luck. Bobby was a good example of this. No one had tried to doublecross him before. He thought he could read people. He thought he could sense subterfuge.

Part of the problem: Jake had been scaling back, and maybe this had dulled some of his skills. He had been doing fewer jobs, and actually was working part-time at an Italian restaurant on Capitol Hill. He was a cold-side assistant, slapping together cold pastas and salads. The pay wasn't great, but he had free meals and didn't mind the routine. In fact, he liked the change. He didn't have to worry about getting shot. He had moved from bus boy to buffet refiller to cold-side assistant chef. Not bad. Before that he had worked in the mailroom at InsurCo, and had quit after cursing out his manager. The restaurant was low-key, an extended family thing, and no one rode him. Christopher, the head cook, even mentioned more hours for him, if he wanted. The restaurant was a pit stop, a temporary oasis. He liked to think there.

That was all shot to hell now. He hadn't even given notice. Fuck it.

So what's the lesson here, he thought. Never trust anything handed to you. Never trust anyone who couldn't keep still. Work alone.

A black man smoking a cigar passed by Jake's window. He stopped, looked at Jake, and waggled his finger in a disapproving gesture. Startled, Jake turned around and checked behind him, unsure who the target of this was. But there was no one near Jake. He turned back. The man frowned, and continued walking. Jake stared, then laughed. Some people could read souls though the window of McDonald's.

7

Jake entered the apartment with Eugene's extra key. He saw someone who wasn't his brother slip across the hallway. Startled, Jake leapt for cover, rolling behind the sofa. He waited, listened. His back broke out in a sweat. His groin ached and he closed his legs. His thoughts scattered, flew away.

"Uh, Euge?" a woman's voice said.

Jake steadied himself. Rachel was peering at him from the bedroom doorway. When he stood up, her face froze. Jake quickly backed away and said, "It's me, Jake. Eugene's brother." He noticed that her hair—once long and silky—was now short. Although Rachel was Anglo, her hair had had that Asian gloss. "You cut your hair."

Rachel recognized him and stepped out. "Jeez! What the hell are you doing here?"

Jake smiled. "Eugene said the exact same thing when he saw me."

"Holy moly. I just had a heart attack." She was wearing a dark skirt and a wrinkled short-sleeved white blouse, the first few buttons undone, exposing a thin gold chain necklace. Her cropped hair made her neck seem longer, slimmer, and she squinted at him. She placed her hand over her heart. "You scared me."

"You scared me too." He moved out from behind the sofa. He fanned his shirt.

"You're a little jumpy," she said as she looked down where Jake had rolled.

"I thought you were in Marin."

She stiffened. "You spoke to Euge."

"Just briefly last night. Are you back?"

"Am I back," she said slowly, trying this out. She nodded. "For now."

Jake raised an eyebrow. He stared at her hair, cut so close to her scalp that it followed the contours of her head. Everything seemed sharper—the angles of her cheekbones, her jaw. Her small, wiry earrings matched her necklace. Threads of lit gold wrapped around her. He said, "Your hair."

"About a year ago. I needed a change."

"It looks good."

"Really? Most people don't like it."

"I like it."

She gave him a wry smile. Then it quickly disappeared. "What did Euge tell you?"

"About you? Visiting friends."

She took this in, then said, "And you're here."

"I am."

"Why?"

He told her he had left Seattle and was passing through. "Eugene offered me the guest room for a few days. I hope it's okay."

"It's okay. This place is a mess, though."

"It is. Eugene doesn't seem so hot either."

She turned to him. "Oh? How so?"

"He's pulling his hair out."

Smiling, she said, "That's been going on for a while. Did he wear his get-up?"

"I didn't see it."

"The head gear and the mouthguard—"

"The what?"

"Mouthguard. He grinds his teeth. He needs to wear a plastic mouthguard." She laughed. "When he goes to bed it looks like he's going into battle."

"That's kind of sad."

She stopped. "You're right. It is." She moved to the kitchen and began cleaning up the counter. Jake followed, and helped. He wiped the sink of grease stains. She said, "I'm just here for lunch. I have to get back to work soon."

"You still at that bank?"

"I am. Not for long."

"A better job?"

She shook her head. "I'm quitting and taking some time off."

He said, "I remember the last time I was here you talked about how much you hated it."

"I did? When was that?"

"About five years ago."

"Five years? Has it been five years?" She dumped the old pizza into the trash. "Now *that's* sad. What a waste."

"The pizza?"

"The past five years," she said. "My life."

"What're you going to do when you quit?"

"That's the big question." She turned to him and folded her arms tightly to her chest. "Are you sure you didn't talk to Euge about me?"

"He came in past midnight, inhaled a couple of beers, and went straight to bed. He left this morning before I got up." Jake noticed the sculpted muscles on her arms. She noticed him noticing. He said, "Have you been working out?"

She nodded. "You like?" She curled her arm and showed him a bicep knot.

"I like."

"Almost two years. Three times a week."

"Not bad."

"You still?"

"Yeah. You should show me the local gym."

"I'll bring you as my guest."

"Looks like Eugene could use a little working out."

Her face closed up and she turned back towards the counter,

running her hand over the edge of the sink. Jake wasn't sure what he had said. He cleared his throat and asked, "He's taking me out to dinner tonight. You're coming, of course."

"Sure. Like old times." She washed her hands.

"You okay?" he asked.

She shrugged. "Sure. I've got to get back to work. I'll see you later."

She dried her hands. Jake noticed that she wasn't wearing her wedding ring. An uneasiness rose up in his chest. Staying here wasn't a good idea. She put on a jacket and grabbed a purse. After a quick goodbye, she glided out of the apartment.

Jake remembered his brother and Rachel at their wedding, a big affair at Paradise Park in Tiburon, an outdoor wedding with a seven-piece band and a woman in a tight red dress who sang jazz, swing, and Sheena Easton songs. It had started out smoothly, most of the guests arriving on time, dozens of bottles of wine and champagne being opened and finished, and the ceremony itself on the grass overlooking the bay couldn't have been more picturesque. Rachel had cried when she gave her vows. Jake was moved by this.

The brief cloudburst during the reception didn't mar the event, but the mud caused a few problems. Two guests slipped after walking off the dance platform, their legs wobbly from the West Coast Swing. Shoes, pants cuffs, and dress fringes were splotched with dark spots. It grew cold very quickly, the breeze from the bay fluttering the decorations, and although nothing went really wrong, Jake sensed the anxiety in Rachel and her maid of honor, Julia. They hurried to the centerpiece candles on each table, securing the small vases against the wind. When it seemed that the guests were getting too cold, when fewer people went to the dance floor but stayed huddled at their tables, some hugging themselves and rubbing their arms, Rachel pulled Eugene onto the dance floor. Some mud had been splashed onto the platform, and Eugene pointed to her dress in alarm. Too late. Black streaks. Jake watched this from a table, where he was half-listening to another guest, one of Eugene's college buddies. Rachel looked down at her dress, bunched part of it in her hand and held it up above her ankles. Eugene's face was pained. Rachel said something like "Forget it," or maybe it was "Fuck it," and they danced. She whispered into his ear. He smiled. They hugged and slow-danced to the big-busted woman in red singing "For Your Eyes Only." Jake thought of James Bond. Rachel swayed back and forth in Eugene's arms, resting her head against his shoulder, and Eugene kissed her tenderly on her temple. She let go of her dress and held him with both arms, hugging him tightly. Jake stared at an edge of her dress dragging behind her.

Bobby Null heard his mother before he saw her. He was drowsing in and out of sleep, uncertain of time passing, hospital sounds of quick footsteps in the hallway, doctors being paged on the loudspeaker. Then a gravelly voice from down the hall said, "Where is room 214? Down here?" Bobby opened his eyes. Shit.

When his mother walked in, he pretended to be asleep. She said, "For Christ's sake. You've been out for two days." She shook his arm roughly, and this jarred his head.

"Hey!" he barked. "Stop that!"

"I've had it, you understand? I've had it." She was in her tan waitressing outfit, her hair pulled tightly back, and was carrying a small suitcase. She saw him look at it and said, "Yes, it's your stuff. I said you can visit as long as you stayed out of trouble. Look at yourself. This is staying out of trouble?"

"I was mugged—"

"Like hell you were. I know you too well. Don't you dare lie to me. You want to end up dead like your brother? Fine. I'm not going to watch it." She dropped the suitcase onto the linoleum with a slap. "Don't come back until you've cleaned up. I can't go through this again."

"Mom," he said, unable to stop the whine from leaking in. "I just got shot. You don't got to do this."

She pursed her lips, then shook her head. She turned to leave, but stopped. She said, "Oh, and those people from L.A. have been calling. You owe them money?"

The guy in the next bed looked over. Bobby said, "Fuck off." The guy turned away.

His mother said, "Did you hear me?"

"They called? At the house?"

"At *my* house. How dare you give them my number! Do you think I want some lowlife hoods knowing where I live? Do they seriously think *I* can pay them what you owe? Are you crazy?"

"They said that?"

"I'm changing my number, changing my locks. I don't want you in Seattle anymore. Do you understand me? Go back to L.A. I should've known you coming up here wasn't for your brother. You hated him."

"God, Mom, give me a break—"

"At least he was honest with me! At least he tried to clean up!"

Bobby said, "He was an asshole and deserved what he got."

His mother reached over quickly and slapped him. Bobby strained his stomach trying to avoid a second slap, and this sent a flash of pain so deep that he cried out. His mother said, "Don't you ever talk about him like that again. He loved you."

Bobby smiled, and turned away. He remembered the time Kevin slammed his face into the toilet, telling him to lick the rim.

"Do you hear me?" she said. "Go back to L.A."

A male nurse walked in and was startled by the sight of Bobby's mother. The nurse said, "Hey! Ma'am, I told you to wait. The doctor said the police have to interview him before any visitors."

Bobby stiffened.

"Don't you tell me when I can see my own son!" his mother said.

"Ma'am, I'm going to have to ask you to leave. Now that he's lucid I'll have to call the police—"

"What did he do?" his mother asked.

"All gunshot wounds must be reported."

His mother turned to Bobby and said, "Don't expect my help if you end up in jail."

"Leave me alone," he said, closing his eyes. "I won't bother you again." He was thinking about the police. What if that old guy he had beaten reported him? Witnesses? Bobby's head pounded, and he thought of all the shit around him. He knew Ron down in L.A. was adding juice to the ten grand Bobby owed. He had first hoped he could hit his mother up for some, but that was a laugh. Then the jewelry job looked good. Goddamn all this. Everything was fucked. He waited until his mother walked away, and he opened his eyes. It was time he got the hell out of here.

He pulled himself out of bed and dressed slowly, every small movement sending ripples of pain throughout his abdomen and midsection. He couldn't let himself cough, otherwise everything flared up, even his butt. His right buttock burned with any leg activity. Before the last round of painkillers, the doctor had told him that things were kind of churned up in there, the bullet doing a nice blending number. Four inches of his small intestines gone. How many did he have total? He had no idea. He had lost a lot of blood as well. No wonder he was so goddamn shaky. He was supposed to stay here for another night, but screw that. Not with the police around. Not with Jake humping his jewelry.

Bobby picked up his suitcase, and wheezed from the pain. He waited for the trembling to stop, then limped out of the room, knowing the man in the next bed was watching. In the hallway, he felt naked without his gun and looked for some kind of weapon. He grabbed an I.V. stand, and pulled off the top, a foot-long angled piece of hollowed out metal. He shoved it in the back of his pants. He always needed something in there. He always needed protection.

"Wait a minute! You! You can't leave yet!" a voice from down the hall echoed.

Bobby paused. He let out a slow, calming breath. Chill, he told himself. He practiced a smile. Then he turned, and said, "Yeah?"

It was the male nurse who had spoken to his mother, and he waved a clipboard at Bobby. The nurse was dressed in blue scrubs, and had the soft, fleshy look of an overfed frat boy, a blondie. Bobby concentrated on the guy's nametag, Thomas Stanley. "Hey," the nurse said. "You haven't been checked out yet. You have to stay in bed."

"I'm feeling okay."

"Yes, but still. Also, the police have to talk to you."

"I can drop by the police station if they want."

"No, that's not how it works. And I'm supposed to get your insurance company information."

"I don't got insurance."

The nurse sighed and shook his head. "Fine. You have to fill out some forms—"

"Thanks, but I got stuff to do." He turned and started to leave, but the nurse held his arm.

"Hey, you can't yet. Let me get a doctor."

Bobby felt the grip tightening. He'd have to try something else. He turned and asked if his mother had left.

"Yeah. I know she's your mother, but man she's pushy."

Bobby blinked, took this in. He looked around: a few other nurses and patients at the far end of the hall. There was an unmarked door next to the water fountain. He asked, "What's that room?"

"Supply closet. Come on. I'll help you back to your bed."

"What's in it?" Bobby asked, walking towards it and opening the door. Inside were shelves filled with sheets and pillows, neat stacks surrounding a small walk-in space. He smelled bleach.

"Hey! Jesus! Can't you listen?" The nurse came in behind him and tried to pull him out.

Bobby grabbed the nurse's hand and yanked him into the closet, quickly closing the door and turning on the light. A ribbon of pain threaded through his body, but he ignored it.

"What the—"

"Shut the fuck up." Bobby took out the piece of metal and swung it at the nurse's head, connecting over his ear. The nurse yelped, but Bobby covered his mouth and then shoved the tip of the rod into the nurse's neck.

"Shh, punk ass. I'll dig this into your corn-fed throat if say anything."

The nurse's eyes bulged. He stopped struggling. Bobby pulled his hand from the nurse's mouth and the guy said, "Please…"

"First of all, you little shit. No one ever talks about my mother like that, you got it?"

He nodded quickly.

"Second of all, don't be shaking your fucking head at me like I'm some little kid. You got that?"

The nurse nodded again. "Look, I'm sorry. I take it back. I didn't mean anything—"

"Who the fuck you think you are, you punk-ass piece of shit? Talking down to me like that? Your name is Thomas Stanley. I can find you. I can find your family. You say anything at all to anyone, I'm coming to visit."

The guy began crying silently, and Bobby thought, Give me a fucking break. Though it hurt his abs, Bobby took a quick step back and swung the metal rod into the nurse's head, hitting his ear and scraping down across his jaw and neck. Bobby opened a nice gash, and the guy went down holding his face. Bobby was about to bend over and hit him again, but the pain shot up through his stomach and forced Bobby back, holding his gut. Thomas Stanley kept crying as Bobby left him and closed the door. Bobby's insides blazed as he picked up his suitcase and shoved the rod back into his pants. He was getting soft. There was a time when he would've stomped the asshole until he stopped moving. He looked down and saw some spots of blood seeping through his shirt. He shouldn't have swung so quickly. Fuck it. It'll heal.

He had more important things to worry about. Finding Jake was his job now. Find Jake and teach him a lesson, and not some little punk ass lesson. Teach Jake a good lesson he will remember for his short and sad life.

9

They ate at a Korean restaurant in Japantown, across from Japan Center and the tall Buddhist tower that Jake thought looked like the muzzle of a cartoon ray gun aimed up into the sky. Jake felt the awkwardness all night between Eugene and Rachel, and considered skipping dinner, even cutting his visit short. But he was curious. There was that odd moment when Eugene had walked into the apartment while Jake and Rachel were talking; Rachel was telling Jake about a small gym two blocks away that had mostly gay members, and she didn't realize this for an embarrassing amount of time. "You know," she was saying, "men work out together. They spot each other. So I didn't think about it until I kept seeing a few men hugging. Now *that's* unusual at a gym."

Then Eugene came in. He stopped at the edge of the sofa and said he was sorry he was late. Then he looked directly at Rachel and said, "Hi, Rachel."

"Hello, Euge. How was work?"

"The same. Good to see you."

She nodded. "You mind if I tag along for dinner?"

"I wouldn't have it any other way."

They held each other's gaze for a moment, then Eugene broke it. "I should change," he said, moving towards the bedroom. "I was thinking of taking you guys to the New Korea place. Sound good?"

Jake noticed that Rachel's cheeks were flushed, and he thought, Do I want to be here?

Now, they sat in a booth and began picking at appetizers and condiments, the first stage of a large Korean meal with different kinds of radish and cabbage *kimchi*, pickled cucumbers, sesame leaves, fried bean curd, seasoned bean sprouts, and spicy zucchini—these were set out in a dozen small bowls around the sunken grill. Jake tried to fill the silence with carefully worded questions about Eugene's job. That seemed relatively safe. Jake had never grasped the concept of the company his brother worked for, and Eugene explained that they made software for managers to manage their clients. It had started out well, but competition nearly drove them out of business. They were now trying to make their program cloud-based. "They're integrating a central cloud add-on that will let companies stay in constant contact with clients," he said.

"How's the latest version of ManageClient doing?" Rachel asked.

Eugene said, "The reviews are coming out, and they're not good. The programmers are jumping ship."

"When's the new version coming out?"

Eugene shook his head. "TBA. We're sinking."

Jake still didn't quite get it, but asked about the job: "So what's your role there?"

"I'm head of customer relations. Basically sales and support."

"He started as tech support," Rachel said. "Clawed his way up."

Eugene quickly finished two beers, and ordered a third. Their main course was *bulgogi*, marinated beef that they cooked themselves on the small gas grill, a large vent directly above them. The smell of the strong marinade seeped into their clothes.

Jake said, "I haven't had this in years."

"No?" Rachel said. "Aren't there Korean restaurants in Seattle?"

"Sure, in the International District. But I hardly eat out."

"So you want to tell us what happened up there?" Eugene asked.

"I thought you didn't want to know."

"In Seattle?" Rachel asked. "Why, what happened up there?"

"My little brother has a tendency to get into trouble."

Jake stared at Eugene. "It's nothing."

"Yes, but where did the jewelry and cash come from?"

"Jewelry and cash?" Rachel said. "I missed a lot."

Jake used his chopsticks to flip the sizzling beef on the grill. "Come on. Maybe we should talk about something else."

"You said you had a fight with your partner," Eugene said. "About what?"

Jake shrugged.

"I guess what all partners fight about," Eugene said. "Right?"

"He tried to doublecross me," Jake finally said.

"How?"

Jake sighed. "He wanted it all."

"So what happened?"

"Why are you doing this?"

"Doing what?"

"You never wanted to know this stuff before."

Eugene stopped. He motioned to the waitress and ordered a fourth beer. Jake glanced at the empty glass, then said to his brother, "You know, it's not what you think. I've been working at a restaurant, a regular job. I was an assistant chef."

"You were not," Rachel said, smiling. "You cook?"

"Well, just salads and pastas. Assistant cold side chef."

"So then what was with the knapsack?" Eugene asked.

Rachel said, "What knapsack?"

"Temptation."

Eugene nodded.

Jake felt someone kick his leg, and he looked down. Rachel said, "Sorry. I meant to kick Euge. What's going on?"

Jake said, "Me and this guy did a small job. He tried to screw me over. I ended up taking everything, so I had to leave town. That's it." He wasn't going to reveal anything else. He imagined Bobby's dead body being lifted in the dumpster, then shaken into a garbage truck, pneumatic whirring and grinding packing him in with rotting vegetables. He had to admit to himself that he had killed Bobby. He was a murderer. It was self-defense, but he had never taken a human life before. There wasn't guilt or remorse, or even a hint of sadness; no, he was glad to get rid of the kid. But now Jake wasn't just a small-time burglar anymore. He wasn't someone who did an occasional job here and there to supplement his income. This was different.

He was losing his appetite.

"Eugene? Eugene Ahn?" called out a voice from across the room.

Everyone turned. A thin, bald man with a goatee, dressed in a sportcoat and jeans waved to Eugene. Jake saw his brother's mouth tighten, then smile. "Vincent," he said.

Vincent approached, shook hands around and was introduced to Jake, who learned that Vincent used to work with Eugene. "Got out in time, though, wouldn't you say?" he joked to Eugene. Rachel asked him what he was doing now, and when he said he retired, Jake took a closer look at him. He couldn't have been older than forty-five, and he had a trim, athletic build. No, early forties. No real wrinkles around his eyes. Retired?

"Retired?" Rachel said.

"Took some of my stock gains, invested and started a small company. It was just bought out, so I retired." He turned to Eugene. "Just read the *PC Insider* reviews of 4.3. How're things there?"

Eugene tried to grin, "You know. A little stressed."

"I told you to get out."

"I know."

"Well, live and learn. Catch you later. My son wants to see a movie." He said goodbye and left.

Rachel asked Eugene, "Did you know about that? What company?"

He nodded. "He started Blue Zone, a temp agency for middle managers in the tech industry. Manpower bought it."

"So, he's rich?" Jake asked. "That's why he retired?"

Eugene nodded.

"That bastard was rubbing your nose in it, wasn't he," Rachel said. "He told you to get out?"

"About four years ago. When the bugs began appearing."

"Smug little man." Rachel stabbed a piece of beef on the grill with her chopstick. "How much did he get for his company?"

"The papers said something like five million."

Jake looked up. "That guy was worth five million dollars?"

"Well, less, after taxes, but depending on how he was paid, maybe about three million."

Everything became a little fuzzy. His brother spoke of this as if it were nothing. What the hell was going on here? Jake asked, "Are you rich?"

Eugene smiled broadly, close to laughter. "Rich? I think not. We're working in negative territory right now."

"Negative? You mean debt?"

"I mean debt with a capital D."

"How much debt?"

Eugene and Rachel exchanged glances. Rachel shrugged. "He just told us about his problems. What's the big deal?"

Eugene said to Jake, "Debt is an interesting thing. There's big debt—the mortgage—which we don't even count. There's small debt—credit cards, car leases, payment plans for furniture—which hover over us. There's also leftover school loans—"

"Wait. You still have school loans?"

"Ah. Right. I guess the good thing about skipping college is you don't have to owe anyone money."

"You're still paying off school?"

"Almost done, but yes."

"So how much do you owe?"

"For school?"

"For everything."

"Not including the mortgage?"

"Sure."

He looked at Rachel again, and she frowned. She said, "There's also my own separate credit card debt. And yours."

"Right. In addition to the joint one."

Rachel closed her eyes for a moment, and said, "Something like sixty?"

"No, you're forgetting the Passat."

She opened her eyes wide and grinned. "Yes. That's a whopper."

Eugene said, "So maybe seventy?'

"Don't you know?" she asked.

"It's on the computer. That big red line."

She laughed. "It's so red it fills the room."

Eugene gave her a crooked smile.

Jake was confused. "So, how much?"

"Not sure," Eugene said. "About seventy thousand."

"Seventy thousand dollars?" Jake asked. "You two owe seventy thousand dollars?"

They turned to him, their faces unconcerned. "You don't have to yell it," Rachel said.

"Jesus Christ. Jesus. I can't believe it." Jake felt something twist inside him. They owed more than he had ever seen in his life. If he owed that much to anyone he wouldn't be able to function. He had never even applied for a credit card because he didn't like the idea of a company having something over him. He looked at his brother, then at Rachel, but they had already moved on, Eugene asking Rachel how work had been today.

The waitress brought another dish: marinated squid for grilling. Jake poked at the appetizers, sipped soup, but had already eaten more than usual. Eugene said, "Are you still thinking about our debt? It's common, believe it or not."

"Maybe."

"We were almost rich once," Rachel said to Jake. "Did he tell you about it?"

He shook his head.

Eugene said, "Never mind that."

"No, it's a good story," Rachel said. "Eugene's stock options of ManageSoft were worth close to a quarter of a million once, and if they had gone public, which they were planning to, his stake would've been worth maybe a million, probably more."

"Holy shit," Jake said. "Is she serious?"

Eugene said, "But then there was a lawsuit with some clients, the IPO was put on hold, and some bugs began appearing. It went downhill."

"You never told me this."

"You never asked."

Jake said, "So what's your share worth now?"

Eugene waved his hands in the air. "Who knows?"

"You know," Rachel said. "Don't they calculate it quarterly?"

"They do. The losses keep rising." He turned to Jake. "Debt with a capital D."

Rachel smiled. "But for a moment, it was really nice."

Eugene laughed. "We actually looked for a big-momma house in Marin. What a joke."

"Seventy grand," Jake said quietly.

"Stop that," Eugene said. "It's common."

"Common."

"Dad had tons of debt. Did you know that? He had a hell of a time getting out from under it."

Jake said, "I didn't know that."

"You were young. He filed for bankruptcy, went on a payment plan. It was harsh."

"How old were you?" Rachel asked Eugene.

"Twelve. This was right after our mother left. In a way that bankruptcy helped for college later. I was able to get a lot of financial aid. Big-ass loans."

Rachel turned to Jake. "You were how old when she left?"

"About eight."

"What was it like?" Rachel asked.

Jake shrugged. Eugene said, "After she left? Our father was really pissed for a while."

"Did he get more violent?" she asked.

Jake was startled. He looked at Eugene, who nodded and said, "Yes, our good mother sometimes took the brunt for us, and with her gone, it was a little tough."

"You told?" Jake said.

"Well, she's my wife," Eugene said. He hesitated, then added, "At least for now."

Rachel turned sharply towards him. Jake felt a headache coming on. He wondered how long he was going to stay. Probably not much longer. He just didn't understand this kind of thing. He knew locks. He knew jewelry. He knew pasta salads. He didn't know much else.

10

Three weeks ago Jake had received a note in his drop box from Chih, his fence and occasional appraiser of jewelry. Chih-seh Ing owned a jewelry shop near Westlake Center in downtown Seattle, the cash-heavy tourist trade helping him unload stolen jewelry. His store was a few blocks from Westlake Center and Pike Place Market, and Jake often stopped by the store when he went shopping. He dropped by on a Sunday afternoon, Chih selling upscale trinkets to some Chinese tourists and speaking a mix of Chinese and English. Chih was actually a Filipino American, his parents part of a Chinese contingent in Manila, and they had all emigrated to the U.S. when Chih was young. He spoke English, Tagalog, and Mandarin, and had managed somehow to get his store listed in a few foreign travel guides.

Chih, a short, squat man shaped like a barrel, saw Jake near the entrance and waved at him to stay. Jake heard him arguing in another language with a Chinese couple, but he kept adding in English, "Only if it's cash. You get a deal if it's cash." When he finished the sale, he bounced over to Jake, who was looking at the postcard racks.

"You got my message?" Chih asked, shaking Jake's hand. Chih's Rolex seemed too large for his wrist.

"Yeah. You know, I'm not really looking for a new job right now." Jake motioned to the postcards. "What's with these?"

"I need more tourist stuff. I'll probably get a few more displays like this."

"Do you always haggle?"

"The Asians like to haggle, especially if I speak the language."

"And you get cash."

Chih's moon face broke into a smile. "Of course."

"So what's this about?"

"There's this kid, a brother of a friend, who's setting up a jewelry thing, and needs someone good with getting into a home."

"A house? Private house?"

"Yeah."

"No one there, though—"

"Of course not."

"Who's the kid?"

"Remember Null? Kevin Null?"

"The guy that got killed?"

"Yeah, that's him. His brother."

"He had a brother?"

"From L.A. Came up to visit his mother after Kevin died."

"Null was an asshole."

"Yeah, sometimes."

"Didn't he pull a gun on some cops?"

"Yeah."

"I don't know," Jake said. "From L.A.? Is he in any gang? I don't want to deal with any of these gang kids."

"Why don't you talk to him? I can tell him to meet you here tomorrow."

"I gotta work tomorrow."

"Where are you working?"

Jake said, "Make it two days from now. Lunch time. I'll meet him here and see what he's got to say. What's your cut?"

"Depends on the take, but ten percent off the top."

"Plus shafting us on the jewelry."

"If there is any," he said, smiling. "But I'll give you a good price."

"I'll think about it."

"You're working a regular job now? Since when?"

"Since forever, it feels like. I gotta run. I'm still not sure about this, Chih."

"Just talk to him. See what you think."

Jake left. He had let it slip that he was working, but caught it quickly. Information about your life, any kind of information, was a crack in your shield; the more people knew about you, the easier it was to get at you somehow. When he was in high school and had broken into the principal's office, he was caught not because he had left anything behind, or had triggered any alarms. He was caught because he had told a friend he wouldn't have to worry about the disciplinary notices in his file. He would graduate. That was all he had said, and when he was expelled he knew what had gone wrong. A whisper here, a rumor there, and it all had led back to him. It was pride, wasn't it? He had managed to unlock a window using a knife, and had hurried straight to the registrar's files. He had found his flagged file, saw the five disciplinary notes with an attachment for a parental conference and a petition for suspension. He simply took the forms and two of the disciplinary notices, and unflagged his file. There was no guarantee this would work, but if his father didn't hear from the school, he was free.

His father did hear from the school, and it wasn't for a suspension; it was for expulsion. Although they couldn't prove it was he who had broken in and altered his file, and the school suspected inside help, Jake was kicked out six months before graduation. His brother wanted to appeal. Jake didn't care. He received his G.E.D. the following fall, fulfilling a promise he had made to Eugene. He attended a few classes at a community college, and soon drifted away from school.

But it was pride. He had circumvented the principal, and needed to tell someone. Even though he was careful not to reveal too much, the leak had exposed him. He had never let that happen again. The only people who were able to make any connections were Eugene and, by extension, Rachel. But their knowledge was sketchy at best. His brother's prodding at dinner had been unusual.

When they returned to the apartment, Eugene asked Rachel, "You cleaned?"

"I cleaned."

"Sorry. I didn't know you'd be back so soon. I was going to…" He trailed off.

"Damn. I forgot." She snapped her fingers. "We need toilet paper."

"I'll go back out—"

"No, it's okay. Tomorrow I'll do some shopping."

"No, I'll go now. I was planning to, but ran late—"

"Forget it. I'll go tomorrow."

Eugene cocked his head. "It's no big deal. I'll just run to the—"

"I said I'll go tomorrow. I always end up doing the shopping anyway."

Eugene's face tensed. He replied slowly, "That's not true. I do some of the shopping."

Rachel folded her arms, her jaw tightening. "You shop for beer and that's all."

Jake rubbed his eyes, then held his head. He sighed loudly.

This distracted both of them, and they turned to him. "What?" Eugene said.

"I came at a really bad time. I'm sorry. I'll get my stuff and go."

"No," Rachel said.

"No way," Eugene said. He grabbed his coat. "You're staying. We have the extra room. I'm going to get the toilet paper." He marched out of the apartment.

The living room became still in his wake, and Jake kept rubbing his temples. When he looked up he saw that Rachel's cheeks were red.

"This," Jake said. "This… You know, I should really stay somewhere else."

She frowned and shook it off. She said in a strong voice, "Don't be silly."

"What's been happening here?"

Rachel stared, tilting her head.

Jake said, "Never mind. None of my business."

She remained still, appraising him. Finally she cleared her throat. "Is it true," she asked, "that your father used to lock you two in the basement naked while he beat your mother?"

"Jesus." He stepped back. "You can't ask me that."

"Why not?"

He hesitated. "I don't know. You just can't."

"Don't you remember?"

"Of course I remember."

"Is Eugene screwed up because of that? I've been trying to figure it out."

"He's not screwed up. He's completely normal."

She snorted, then caught herself. "Well, I guess it's all relative."

Jake said, "I think there was an insult in there somewhere."

"No, no. I didn't mean anything." She waved this off. "Sorry. It's been a strange week."

Jake thought about Bobby Null dead in a dumpster. He let this image sit in his head and asked, "You going to work tomorrow?"

"Yes. Only three days left."

"Then you're out of there?"

"Then I'm out of there."

"I'll find a place by then."

"Why?"

"It might get cramped in here."

"No. It's okay. Wait until Euge and I figure out what we're going to do."

"Do? You mean about each other?"

"Yes."

Jake sat down, his stomach sour. He had eaten too much. He saw Rachel checking her face in the reflection of a framed print and noticed again the muscles along her arms. "I was just thinking about that wedding," he said. "How it got muddy and everything. You were great."

She nodded. "God, if that wasn't an omen, I don't know what is. Actually, it was fun. I didn't mind."

"Did you ruin that dress?"

"No. It got cleaned. It's in storage." She turned to him. "A cousin of mine was really curious about you after that. I think she wanted me to set her up."

"Yeah? Where does she live?"

"Santa Barbara. But she's married now. What about you? What happened to that woman you were seeing down here?"

"That ended."

"What was her name?"

"I never mentioned it."

"Okay, what was her name?"

"Mary. Mary Lim."

"Asian?"

He said, "Half Asian."

"How come you didn't bring her over?"

"I don't know."

"Were you embarrassed?"

"No."

"Were you embarrassed by us?"

He smiled. "No. Just two different parts of my life I wanted apart."

"Are you going to visit her? Does she still live in the area?"

"I think she still lives in Oakland. No, I'm not going to visit her."

"Why not?"

He wasn't sure. He said, "She dumped me. No reason to see her."

She glanced at the door; there were voices in the hall. She said, "I'm going to get ready for bed. Sorry about the drama."

"You'll take me to your gym soon?"

"Tomorrow night."

"Go easy on me."

She raised an eyebrow. "Easy? On you?"

"You're in really good shape. You'll wear me out."

She smirked and waved him off. "Goodnight, Jake."

He watched her glide down the hall. Jake wanted to wait up and talk to his brother, but he was tired and vaguely disturbed by Rachel's mention of their father. What else did she know? He went into the guest room and lay on the futon in the dark. Of course he remembered. He wondered if his brother claimed otherwise. Jake stared up at the darkened ceiling. He remembered huddling near the gas furnace to keep warm. That was one of the stronger images that had stuck with him. Naked and shivering, he had curled himself into a ball as he had squatted, hugging his knees, and had leaned against the dirty brown metal casing. His brother was usually crouched at the top of the stairs by the doorway, the thin line of light illuminating his curved back; the ridges of his spine reminded Jake of a lizard. The basement lights were controlled by a switch on the other side of the door, and their father usually kept it off. That was fine. The few times that he had left the light on, Jake and Eugene turned away from each other. Jake stared at the small pilot light buried inside the pipes and wires of the furnace. The insulation around the water heater was unravelling, held together by duct tape. He smelled dust, gas, and mildewed heat. Upstairs his father was beating the shit out of his mother. Eugene preferred to be close to the action, trying to see what he could from under the door. Jake always went down here, next to the heat.

Sometimes they would hear the sounds of their mother running from one end of the house to the other, her steps pounding across the floor. Doors slammed shut. Their father followed slowly, methodically; his steps were lighter, the floor simply creaked. None of the doors, except for the basement entrance, had locks (and that was from the outside; Eugene and Jake weren't going anywhere), so they usually heard a brief struggle at the doorknob. Their mother let out a high-pitched, frightened squeal that sounded inhuman. Jake and Eugene once tried joking about it. "Eeeeee," they mimicked, laughing. "Sounds like a bird call." But they never brought it up again.

If Jake stared long enough at the pilot light, then turned towards the darkness and let his eyes adjust, something happened to his vision. He could see in the dark. He saw movement, images, shapes. He saw the bugs crawling in the corner of the floor. He saw the ghostly ripples of trolls and goblins creeping along the wall. Sometimes they stopped, startled that he could see them. They looked at him. He looked at them. They tip-toed away.

He heard his mother sobbing, pleading in Korean. His father yelled something that he couldn't understand. Eugene knew more Korean than Jake did, though Eugene never translated the arguments. He did teach Jake some curses, and Jake recognized them when his father bellowed at his mother. Those were easy to understand.

11

Jake watched Rachel take off her sweatshirt, revealing her tight-fitting spandex two-piece suit, the black and yellow top hugging her chest, the black shorts painted over her.

He thought, Whoa.

Her calves and thighs were beginning to get the same sculpted look her arms had, and when she leaned to the side to drop her sweatshirt in a cubby reserved for members, stretching so that a curved line ran from her hand through her arm, torso, and to her foot, Jake thought of geometry. He wanted to run his hand along that curve. He tried not to think about the fact that he hadn't had sex in many months. The last time was with a waitress at the restaurant, an alcohol-induced fling that they both regretted immediately, but they had remained friendly.

Rachel motioned for him to follow, and he did. The muggy gym, low-tech and filled with old free weights and dirty Universal machines, was poorly ventilated, and he broke out in a sweat. He saw half a dozen Hercules clones glance up at them as they moved to a set of machines at the back. Then he remembered that this was a gay gym, and he felt self-conscious. Did they think the straights were taking over? Maybe they thought he was gay.

"How'd you find this place?" he asked Rachel.

"Accident, really. And it's the cheapest gym around."

"It looks old."

"Yes, but it has everything I need." She waved to the weights, then pointed to the treadmills and Stairmasters near the window.

"Can I say you look really good? Two years of this?"

"About two years."

"What about Eugene?"

She shook her head. "I brought him here once, but he never came back."

"Why?" Jake asked. "Not because it's a gay—"

"No. Look at how fit everyone is. He felt awful, really almost embarrassed."

Jake looked around. It was true, not one ounce of excess fat in this place. Suddenly Jake felt out of shape. He realized there were no women except for Rachel. He mentioned this to her.

She laughed. "There are a few regulars, but no, there aren't that many here."

"Why?"

"I don't know. But the women here are in better shape than I am."

"Really," he said too quickly.

Rachel smirked. "Down, boy."

Jake bowed his head contritely.

They began to alternate on the Universal, spotting each other and talking quietly. Grunts and heavy breaths from across the room punctuated the rhythmic whirring of an oscillating fan by an open window. There was no music. It felt religious. He stared at the sweat collecting on the back of Rachel's neck as she did lat pull-downs, the front of her top flaring out whenever she raised her arms.

He asked her politely about work, about how she was doing, and she answered with a shrug. They moved onto the shoulder press and switched off sets. Jake asked how bad things were for Eugene at work. She said, "He doesn't talk about it anymore. I think pretty bad."

"Maybe I'll drop by tomorrow. I've never seen the place."

"ManageSoft? It's just a big office."

"I know. But I never quite got what he did for a living. I mean, you're a banker—"

"I manage tellers. Just a pencil pusher. And not for long."

"But at least I understand it." They switched positions.

"I'm a glorified cashier," she said.

He began his set. "Whatever. For Eugene, I'm not sure." He felt a stitch in his groin, and paused. The pain subsided and he continued pulling down the bar.

"You should visit. Maybe you can scope out his girlfriend."

Jake stopped. "What?"

"There's a woman at work who's hot for him."

"No way."

She laughed. "Yes way." She mimicked a high voice, "Oh, Eugene, you know so much about everything."

"Eugene? Our Eugene?"

"Yes. He won't admit it. He pretends I'm imagining it."

"Are you?"

"Whenever I see this woman, she looks like she wants to slip a knife between my ribs."

"Wow. Eugene the stud."

"One of these days, he's going to take her up on it."

Jake glanced at the mirror, checking Rachel's expression. She was half-serious. They exchanged places, and Rachel continued her set. He noticed that she was hunching her back as she grew tired, so he pressed his palm against her spine. She straightened and thanked him. "I don't know if it'd be such a bad thing, with this woman," she said.

"No, you can't mean that."

"Why not? He claims to be so unhappy with me. Let him try someone else for a while."

"You want that?"

"Oh, I don't know," she said, slapping the weights down too hard. They moved to the chest press. As Jake lay down on the bench, Rachel laughed. "Don't listen to me. I'm just rambling."

"He says he's unhappy with you?"

"We shouldn't be talking about this."

He looked up. She didn't appear to mean this, so he pursued it with, "What could he possibly be unhappy about with you?"

"You should check his list."

"He has a list?"

"Well, we went to counseling for a while and were supposed to write down things that bother us about each other. Things that we said or did or just the way we were."

"And you kept one too?"

"I started to."

"And what was on your list?" he asked.

She grinned. "Oh, just small things, but we stopped going to counseling."

"Why?"

"Things got crazy at work for both of us," she said. "Though I suspect he's still writing his."

Jake nodded. His brother was always meticulous about homework, and of course Eugene would continue writing down Rachel's faults.

He mentioned this to Rachel, who said quickly, "Yes! No kidding! He has *everything* on his phone. I'm talking everything. Once he left it on and I saw a daily list. You know what was on it?"

Jake waited.

"Seducing me was on it. Getting me flowers, wine, all that."

"Why?"

"Something the counselor told us, but on the screen I was listed right after oil change. I'll never forget that."

"He probably didn't mean anything bad by that—"

"I know, I know. I'm sure it was time sequence, that he'd go to the oil place after work, then pick up stuff for me that night, but still."

"He needs that structure."

"I know. He tries to have everything in place," Rachel said. "Believe me, I know."

"Well, I'd have blocked out the whole day," Jake said, and winked.

She turned to him. "But you don't do that, keep lists."

"No. I'm not that organized."

"Where did Euge get it from? Your parents?"

Jake shrugged.

"Your mother?"

"Maybe. I didn't know her that well."

"How old were you again when she left?"

"Eight," he said, surprised that she brought this up again. He asked, "Your father died when you were young, didn't he?"

"Fifteen," she said, moving towards the freeweights and dumbbells. Jake followed. They were going to work on their arms. Biceps, triceps, deltoids. Rachel rolled her shoulders and stretched her neck. When she arched her back and stretched her arms behind her, one hand grabbing and pulling the other, Jake remembered she was an only child, and pictured her as a fifteen-year-old, lanky and awkward, her long, messy hair falling over her face.

She said, "Most of the men in my family died young. My father had a massive heart attack. My uncle was hit by a truck. My grandfather was killed in World War II."

"What about the women?"

"They live forever. My great grandmother is still alive. The women survive. The men blow up."

They used different weights, and worked out next to each other, both facing the mirror. After a few minutes of silence, Jake asked, "What did he tell you about our parents?"

She focused on her reflection, lifting her dumbbell unsteadily for a difficult set. Jake saw the sweat trickle down her chest. He leaned over and spotted her for the rep, helping her with the final couple of inches. She let the weight down slowly. "Thanks." Sitting down on the bench and breathing heavily, she said, "That your father was a little crazy. Some of this came out in the counseling sessions. It was surprising how we learn things from our parents' marriage."

Jake wasn't sure what that meant. What could Eugene and he have learned from their parents? Don't get married. Simple lesson. What else? Don't beat your wife. Jake turned to Rachel, startled. He said, "Eugene doesn't get...physical, does he?"

"What? God, no. I didn't mean that. No, I meant how our conception of marriage gets formed by what we see."

"Sounds like head-shrinking talk."

She smiled. "Maybe."

They did the triceps, flys, and forearm curls in silence. Someone went on the Stairmaster and the high-pitched whirring drowned out the other sounds. It was beginning to get crowded and Jake realized this was the after-work rush. He wasn't used to the schedule of commuters, since his job at the restaurant peaked during the evenings and weekend afternoons. Because of this, his gym was never crowded when he went there in the late mornings, and he never seemed to wait on lines at the grocery or the drug store.

Although he had been trying to find a normal routine in Seattle, trying cut down the number of jobs and not get greedy, he found that he also liked the excitement. He felt more present. More real. He liked being on the move. This worried him.

12

Jake met Bobby Null at Chih's on a weekday afternoon. First impressions: Bobby was too young—he had a restless look and couldn't seem to keep still, his leg shaking, his feet tapping. He kept running his fingers through his hair and looking around, never quite meeting Jake's eyes. They talked in Chih's back room; the front door chimes rang every few minutes as tourists walked in and out. Bobby took off his windbreaker and sat down. "All right," he said.

He was lean and sinewy, his skin pulled tightly over his face and neck. He stood up to turn his chair around, straddling the backrest and resting his forearms on the top. He searched in his jacket for his cigarettes and shook one out. "You mind?" he asked Jake.

Jake shrugged.

Bobby said, "Chih said you knew my brother."

"A while ago. Back when he was working as a security guard at the card club."

"Shit, that *was* a while ago."

"I didn't know he had a younger brother."

"Yeah. We didn't get along."

"Sorry to hear about the shooting."

"He was stupid." He inhaled deeply, and Jake heard the tobacco sizzling.

"What've you got?" Jake asked.

"Chih said you're not really doing much anymore."

"No. I'm not."

"Losing your nerve?"

Jake smiled. Man, this kid was young. He said, "Just being more careful."

"So what're you doing now?"

"Not much." This reminded him of the restaurant and he glanced at his watch. He said, "But I've got things to do."

Bobby nodded. "All right. Here it is. There's this old couple who run a jewelry store—"

"Where?"

"Next to the U-district. What is it, Laurelhurst?"

"Okay," Jake said.

Bobby told him how he had been checking out different jewelry stores downtown, but the security, like Chih's store, was really good. So Bobby looked towards less dense areas, more suburban-type neighborhoods, and found this one store, Good Luck Jewelry, that had expensive, upscale diamonds and gold, but was mom-and-pop enough for him to look closer. "So I watched the store for a while, checking out how busy it is, and what kind of security they have, and get this, every Saturday night when they close, they take most of the stuff and bring it home."

"That's not unusual."

"I know, but this is a couple of old people. So I wonder maybe I can hit them in the car, on their way home or something."

Jake shook his head.

"I know. Not smart. There are always a lot people around. So I follow them and check out their routines. Here's the thing. They go to church every Sunday. They leave their house empty all day. The jewels and stuff is there, with no one home."

"All day? Who goes to church all day?"

"I don't know. It's a Korean church further downtown—"

"Korean church? These are Koreans?"

"Yeah. That's how I know they'll be gone all day. I checked out the church."

"Is that why Chih set us up? Because I'm Korean?"

"Huh? No. I don't know. I don't give a shit."

Jake nodded. An old Korean couple. This bothered him more than it should have. He said, "Tell me the address of the store and the house. I'll check it out and let you know."

"I'll show you."

Jake said, "No. I want to check it out alone. We'll meet back here in a week—"

"A week? That's too long."

"I want to see what happens this Sunday."

"I told you what happens. Why you got to wait so long?"

"I don't know you, I don't know how much you missed. I need to check it out myself."

"How do I know you're not going to hit it yourself?"

"You don't. But if what you're saying is right, the house is probably loaded and it's a two-man job."

"And we're going half—straight down the middle, right?"

"Even though I'm going to do most of the work?"

"I found it all."

"We go half after Chih takes off the top."

"He takes how much off the top?"

"Ten percent."

"We'll see about that."

Jake turned sharply towards him. "Fucking over the guy who connected us isn't very smart, and he's the only fence I trust."

"He's gonna shaft us for the jewelry anyway."

"Not me, he won't. I've been working with him for a while."

Bobby frowned. His skin looked as if it might rip over his cheekbones—a skull with fragile skin. The skull said, "Whatever. You deal with him then."

Jake stared at the talking skull. Jake could never resist an easy hit. He had promised himself he would try to slow down, but this might be a gift. At the very least, he should check out the store and the jeweler's house.

13

There were no showers at the gym, one reason why membership dues were cheap, so Jake and Rachel walked home sweaty, chilled by the evening air. Jake felt his muscles tingling, the aches already setting in. He hadn't worked out this hard in months. He and Rachel had spent two and a half hours lifting. Jake didn't have the energy for the machines, so while Rachel had spent another twenty minutes using the Stairmaster, Jake had lain on the mats, exhausted, and had watched Rachel's butt through half-closed eyes.

Rachel bought a large pizza and carried it upstairs to the apartment. As they entered the dark room, she said, "Euge tells me you know a little about jewelry." She flicked on the lights.

"He's not home?" Jake checked his watch. Nine-thirty.

"Are you kidding? He won't be home for at least a couple more hours." She motioned to the pizza. "You can start. I'll take a shower first."

"Why do you ask?" he said.

"About the jewelry? Just curious. I found an earring a few days ago. It might be a diamond, but I'm not sure."

"Found it?"

"On the sidewalk."

"Show me."

She went to her bedroom and returned with a gold disk and pendant earring, possibly a half a carat in the pendant. He turned on more lights in the living room, and studied it.

"I was thinking about trying to scratch glass with it to test it," she said.

"That might work, but if it's a real diamond you might damage the facet, even if still scratches the glass."

"Ah."

"One quick test is to check if it's glass." He pressed his tongue to the gem, and waited. It remained cold. "Glass warms up pretty quickly. This didn't." He walked to the kitchen and she followed. He put the earring under the sink and ran water over it. "Another test is to drop some water on the gem—if it's real, the drop of water will hold its shape, but on glass the water drops spread out." He had trouble seeing anything on this small gem, and said, "I need my loupe. I'll get it."

"Your what?" she asked.

"My jeweler's loupe." He retrieved his loupe from his back pack and brought the ring under the light. He dipped his finger under the running faucet, then sprinkled a drop onto the earring. Through the loupe he saw that the drop was holding its shape. "It's definitely not glass," he said. "It has something to do with surface tension—the water drops not spreading out." But then he noticed the facets, now magnified. He looked through the stone to the back facets, and saw a double edge, a sign of zircon.

He looked up. "No. This is cubic zirconia, I think. You should bring it to a jeweler, but it's cut like a zircon."

"How much do you think it's worth?"

"The gold is real, but it says here it's only 10 karats. I'd say this single earring is about ten bucks, maybe twenty retail."

"That's all?"

"That's all."

"Where did you learn about all this?" she asked.

"A friend taught me about appraising jewels," he said, thinking of Chih.

Jake dangled the cheap earring and held it up to Rachel's ear.

"What do you think?" she asked, tilting her head towards him, posing.

"Looks good. But you need the other one." His hand brushed lightly across her cheek as he pulled away. He dropped the earring into her open palm, and said, "Thanks for taking me to the gym."

"Thanks for spotting me. I'm going to be sore tomorrow." She rolled her shoulders and neck.

"I'm sore now."

She said, "You can take a long shower after me. I won't use all the hot water."

"We can take a shower together, conserve water."

She smirked. "Ha, ha. I forgot about your sense of humor."

She walked down the hallway to the bathroom. He studied the whorls of his fingerprints with his loupe, listening to Rachel hum to herself as she closed the door and turned on the faucet. He whispered to himself, Careful, careful.

14

Jake was half-asleep in the guest room, his body aching, when he heard his brother come into the apartment. The gravity changed. His bed tilted towards the living room. He heard Eugene ask what there was to eat, and Rachel replied that they had saved him some pizza.

Pizza? Again?

It was late. We just picked something up after working out.

Don't we have anything real? I have to eat something real.

Pizza's real. You could've picked something up.

I was working.

So it's my responsibility to get food all the time?

Did you work out at the gym? Are you having fun? Did you get to watch a lot of nice TV? You couldn't pick up a goddamn salad for me?

Sh. Quiet.

Jake ignored this and rolled over, burying his head in the pillow. Their voices fell, but he still heard Eugene talk about work. Eon was spinning off a software division that would compete directly with ManageSoft. There was a leak in the company. Everything was falling apart, people were leaving.

So, you leave, Rachel said.

It's not that easy. I put in a lot of time there.

So?

If there's a buyout, though.

What's the likelihood?

I don't know. They're talking about that later this week with the bankers.

Why can't you tell Aaron off, get him to do something, for God's sake?

You don't think we've tried? Now there are rumors of me and Janine trying to undermine him. We have to be careful.

You're letting this happen.

Jake waited for his brother's response, but there was none. He heard the hiss and clip of a beer can opening and heavy footsteps moving towards the bedroom. Rachel stayed in the living room. Separate sleeping arrangements. Jake heard her raise the TV volume, then lower it. She changed channels.

Eugene was a brooder. Jake remembered as kids when their father finished a bottle of Southern Comfort and slowly began grumbling to himself, the prelude to a fight with their mother, or, after their mother had left, the prelude to telling Jake and Eugene how weak and stupid they were, sometimes deciding to toughen them up, Jake used to get scared, jumpy; he used to feel trapped. But Eugene seemed to shut down. His eyes drooped, his shoulders slumped. He reminded Jake of a turtle. *Chaddayut!* their father would yell. Stand at attention. He'd slap Eugene in the back and tell him to stop slouching. His father swayed drunkenly, his face red and sweaty, and Jake felt disgusted. Then his father would see Jake's glare and hold up his fists. You want to fight me? You want to show me how strong you are? On one occasion, after his father kept pushing and taunting him, Jake couldn't stand it and tried to punch his father. His father was a third-degree black belt in Tae Kwon Do, and even though he hadn't practiced since he was in the Korean Navy, and even though he was drunk, he was still fast. Jake ended up on the ground, the wind knocked out of him; he hadn't even seen the elbow strike.

Later, Eugene scolded him for letting their father get to him. That's what he wants, Eugene said. You can't give him what he wants.

Jake had stared at the blue and green bruise on his chest, and felt something inside him harden. His brother then took out the daily chart, and marked that night's fight. Eugene graphed their father's moods, trying to track the intensity of the fights. Tonight had been an eight, because he had hit both of them, though only once each. The rating stayed below five if there was no hitting. Eugene was meticulous about this log, and sometimes Jake would watch his brother flip to previous weeks and months, searching for patterns, always the technician.

15

The pawnshop was in the Tenderloin, squeezed narrowly between a second-hand clothing store and a corner bar open at eleven in the morning. It was dark inside the bar, a neon Miller sign and a weak wall lamp the only source of light. The clothing store next door had a large display window with a mannequin dressed in a wedding gown, a number of severed mannequin heads with wigs lined in front.

He entered the pawnshop, surveying the long glass counter and a back wall shelved with radios, small TVs, cell phones, and guitars. The other side of the room was stacked with computers and laptops, but Jake was interested in the counter, the display lights illuminating an array of knives, lighters, watches, and—drawing him—jewelry.

He peered down. The jewelry, as in most of the pawnshops, was limited to cheap, gaudy items without much melt value. A large, bearded man walked slowly towards him from the other end of the counter, taking his time. "Can I help you?"

"Are you accepting any jewelry right now?" he asked.

The man studied Jake, and said, "Depends on the jewelry."

He reached into his pocket and pulled out a few rings and the chain, first showing the man the wedding bands. "How much for these? They're 14K gold."

The man picked them up and squinted at the hallmarks inside. "I can give you twenty bucks for both of them."

Jake didn't react, but said, "They're over sixty bucks each retail."

"This isn't retail."

"They're brand new. I can get the receipt if you need it."

The man shook his head. "No. Can't give you more than that."

Jake said, "How about this?" and pointed to the gold herringbone chain. "Eighteen inch 14K gold. Also brand new. Three-fifty retail."

The man studied the chain, weighed it on a small scale, then checked the clasp. "You got the receipts?"

"If you need them. But I'd have to come back with it."

"Forty for this," the man said.

He held out the diamond ring. "And this? Last piece. 14K gold, with, I think, a one carat diamond."

"You think?"

"This one's estate. I just inherited it."

The man said, "Can I take this in back? There's a girl who knows more about diamonds."

Jake worried about a switch, but knew that this particular ring had a poor mounting, and he'd recognize it. "Go ahead," he said.

The man trudged along the counter and disappeared behind a black-curtained doorway. Jake heard voices. For a moment he had a paranoid thought that they knew the jewels were stolen and were calling the police. He shook this off. Impossible. He wasn't worried about the crappy pieces, the inferior rings and necklaces that he might even have to sell for scrap if pawn shops or jewelry stores weren't interested, but the more expensive pieces would probably have to stay in storage for a while. The jeweler's trade papers might mention them, warn jewelers of stolen diamonds resurfacing. It was a remote possibility. There was a column in one of the Gemologist newsletters, called "Stolen Gems," in which they profiled high-grade stolen jewelry, based on jeweler's reports and the Federal Stolen Goods Database. But even then the pieces he had weren't *that* good.

The man returned with the engagement ring and shook his head. "Mary in back said the diamond's not that great. Also it's less than one carat."

"How much for it?"

"Seventy."

"Seventy?" Jake wondered how much a wholesaler would give

him. Probably not much more. He said, "How about one-eighty for the whole lot?"

Looking down at the pieces and calculating, he shook his head. "One-thirty."

"I'll sell the chain and the wedding bands, but not the diamond." The man said, "Okay. Hang on. I'll write you a claim ticket." While the man did this, Jake pocketed the diamond ring. Maybe he'd find a big jeweler to consign the better pieces, but this was probably how he'd have to unload the crappy ones. He considered calling Chih. No. Sever all connections for now. He had no idea how much the police had found out about Bobby.

Jake walked out of the pawn shop with sixty dollars in cash and promptly bought an extra pair of jeans from the clothing store. He should check the Seattle newspapers to find out about Bobby. The prospect weighed on him; he just wanted to forget about the mess up there. He should blame Chih, really, for even thinking Jake could work with Bobby. Chih was getting sloppy.

16

When Jake studied the Korean couple's store that Bobby had told him about, Good Luck Jewelry, he found it wasn't as small-time as Jake had expected. It was in a mini-shopping complex on 45th in Wallingford, not Laurelhurst as Bobby had said, but in a good location with many shoppers. Jake watched the foot traffic in the area, then went into the store to look around. The clerk was a young man, not Korean, and when Jake asked about the Korean couple, the man said that they would be in later. Jake saw the infrared sensors near the door and front window, the contact breakers at each opening and mercury switches along the glass. There was also a pull-down aluminum gate which would bar the front door and window. The back was easily viewed from the street. They probably lit it up at closing. This place was secure. He glanced at the gleaming jewelry in the displays, felt the clerk watching him, and took off. He began to get interested.

He took a bus past University Village and got off in the vicinity of where the storeowners lived. He walked around a neighborhood of large, expensive houses. The address that Bobby had given him put the house towards Ravenna, and Jake eventually found it in a cul-de-sac off 55th. An occasional car drove by, then turned the corner into a tree-shrouded, winding neighborhood. He walked slowly, counting off the numbers on the houses, feeling relaxed.

Nestled between two larger houses with wooden front porches, the jewelers' house was stuck in a small hill, the lower half buried in the ground, the garage almost a cave, the upper half sitting as high as the roofs of the surrounding houses. There was a small front yard with a flower garden to the side, wooden blocks laid on the ground as steps leading up to the door. The front was too exposed, especially if this was supposed to happen during the day, and not just any day, but a Sunday. He saw the name "Chun" painted on the front mailbox, then noticed an ASA alarm sticker in the front window; this wouldn't be a problem since he already knew ASA's layouts, but it definitely meant he had to avoid the doors, which were wired with contact breakers impossible to alter from the outside.

He studied the surrounding houses, noticing how quiet it was. This was looking good. He decided to return later tonight to find the house's weak entry. Every house had a weak entry.

17

Jake returned to his brother's apartment and found a note from Rachel: "We're really sorry about last night. It won't happen again." She was referring to the fight, which Jake hadn't thought twice about. He had left this morning while Rachel was in the shower. Maybe she thought he was being discreet.

As he roamed through the empty apartment, Jake entered the main bedroom and found the bed crisply made, a book on the dresser table. He glanced at the title—*Ancient Philosophy*—and checked the bookmark. Rachel had been reading about presocratic philosophers. He stopped at one line which had been starred: "Most presocratic philosophers believed that there was a basic substance—either concrete or abstract—that was the foundation for all change." He puzzled over this for a moment, then put the book down.

He thought about Mary Lim, and Rachel's suggestion of calling her. Mary had accused him of being directionless, of not wanting enough. She didn't have time for dawdlers, she had said. Her move to Oakland had been for work, and she cut Jake loose pretty quickly.

He went to Rachel's panty drawer and pulled out a pair of her open-crotch black panties, holding it to his face and inhaling faint detergent smells. As he pictured Rachel in her tight spandex outfit from the gym, he grew excited, and unzipped his jeans. He pushed his erection through the open panties, trying to imagine what it would be like having sex with her. He stroked himself. He remembered watching her as she used the Stairmaster, her back to him, when he had to force himself to look away, thoughts of him entering her from behind flashing through his mind. She leaned forward and rested on her arms, her legs climbing and climbing. He was about to come, and looked for a tissue, but couldn't find any. He tried to walk to the bathroom but didn't make it. He soiled her panties, the rough lace scratching him. He leaned against the wall, and caught his breath. He examined the panties guiltily, and tried to clean them off with bathroom tissue. Hm. This wouldn't work. The tissue left white lint all over the black fabric. There were two basket hampers next to the small closet in the hallway. He decided to chance it, and shoved her panties deep into the colored clothes basket, amidst T-shirts, jeans, and a blue sweat suit. He closed the hamper. He was acting like an over-sexed teenager. He needed to get out more.

18

Bobby Null waited until Chih began closing up. It was six-thirty and the sun was setting, long orange shadows hitting the streets. Bobby was tired, and popped a couple of dexies to stay awake. He'd been watching Chih's store for the past four hours. He wasn't sure if Jake had already shown up while Bobby was in the hospital, but Chih was the only way Bobby would find out anything. His goddamn butt ached. His stomach felt mushy. The dexies and the bennies probably weren't that good for him, but he needed the juice. He felt soft around the edges. He felt blurry. The doctor had said something about eating only light foods and liquids. He didn't say anything about jump starts.

Bobby sat in the employee entrance of a furniture store. He chain-smoked out of boredom. Chih looked busy all afternoon. This was the dumbest jewelry store Bobby had ever seen, with postcard and map stands on the sidewalk, and a tray of ugly trinkets by the front door. Bobby had walked by the entrance a few times, to see what Chih was doing inside, and he had caught a glimpse of the black felt trays— tourist trinkets with "Seattle" and fake Indian necklaces. But people were buying the shit.

A cold breeze kicked up. He shivered. He hated Seattle. He was always cold. Lying in a dumpster for most of the night hadn't helped.

He thought about his mother. She never gave him a chance. Bullshit. The first thing she said to him when he showed up for Kevin's funeral was, What do you want? She could go to hell.

Chih put a "Closed" sign in the front window, though there were a few customers still inside. Bobby stood up. His head spun, and fuzz clouded his vision. The dexies were kicking in. He felt a hiss of calm and clarity. Fucking A. After a second, he walked across the street and into the store.

Chih looked up from the counter and started to say, "We're closing up—" but stopped. He nodded. Bobby waited by the counters. The tourists eventually left, and Chih locked the front door. "Where the hell have you been? Where's Jake?"

Bobby weighed his chances. Chih was getting old and fat; he was thick all over. Slow. "He didn't come here?" Bobby asked.

"No. I tried contacting him, and you, but couldn't. Your mother disconnected the phone."

"I've been in the hospital."

"Why?"

Bobby stared. "You don't know?"

"No."

"You're fucking lying. He's been here."

Chih frowned, and said, "I take it something went wrong. What happened?"

"He gut-shot me and left me in the fucking garbage is what happened."

"Jake?"

"Fucked me over."

Shaking his head, Chih said, "No. Something else. I know him. He wouldn't do that. What really happened? You try to pull something on him?"

This did it for Bobby. He took a few quick steps towards Chih, and then gave him a running kick to his groin. Chih doubled over and gagged, collapsing on his side. Bobby felt something pulling in his abdomen, but ignored it. He frisked Chih, then turned off the lights so people on the street couldn't see in. Chih kept coughing, his face purple.

Bobby went behind the counter and looked for a weapon. He found a small nickle-plated automatic, and checked the magazine. Full. He stood over Chih and pointed the gun at his temple, unlocking the safety. "Did he come here or not?"

Chih shook his head.

"If you're lying, I'll shoot off your balls." He lowered the gun towards Chih's groin.

"Not…lying," he said, and coughed. He covered his groin and squeezed his eyes shut.

"Where does he live?"

Chih said, "Don't know."

Bobby yelled, "You fucking with me?"

"No! I don't even know his last name!"

"How do you find him?"

"You're crazy. If your brother could see you now…"

Startled, Bobby pressed the muzzled against Chih's thigh and pulled the trigger. The shot was louder than he expected, and burned right through Chih's fat. The bullet came out and lodged into a cabinet. Chih howled, and Bobby slammed the butt of the gun into Chih's face. "Don't ever mention my brother again. How do you find Jake?"

"Mail drop. Don't shoot," he cried, covering his face.

"Address."

"In my book! On the counter! Under 'J'!" He began drooling.

Bobby opened the book and found Jake's name with an address on University Avenue. "He lives here?"

"No. Just a mail store. Give the kid a note or send it by mail. All you need is the box number. Jake will pick it up." He wheezed. "Ah, fuck. I need a hospital."

Bobby suddenly realized he was in a jewelry store. He looked around. Chih grew quiet.

Then, an alarm began shrieking all over the store. Bobby jumped. He glanced down at Chih and saw that he had a small remote in his hand, like a car alarm keychain. Bobby grabbed the remote and tried to shut it off, but couldn't understand the symbols. He threw it at Chih. "Turn the fucking thing off!"

"Can't. Only the police can."

"Motherfucker!"

He looked wildly around him. The police. He bent towards Chih and aimed the gun at his head. He said, "Too bad. Say hi to my bro." Chih's eyes widened, and he started to yell something but Bobby pulled the trigger and shot him through the temple. Chih's head kicked to one side. Bobby then leaped to the cash register and stopped. Fingerprints. He pressed the buttons with the gun, the tray popped open, and he grabbed all the cash he could. He then unlocked and opened the door, and wiped off his fingerprints. He remembered the light switch and wiped it clean as well. The alarm was still screaming in his ears. He pocketed the money, shoved the gun into the back of his pants, and walked out. The gun was hot, and felt like it belonged there, against the small of his back. He saw a couple across the street watching him. He turned away and hurried around the block. The wad of cash in his pocket dug into his leg. He had Chih's address book in his hand, and looked through it as he casually crossed the street, heading for the underground bus station.

19

Jake visited his brother at work. This, it seemed, was a mistake, because as soon as he told the receptionist who he was, and Eugene hurried down the hall, Jake sensed something was wrong. Eugene already looked harried and it was only noon. His tie askew, his hair mussed, Eugene blinked rapidly as he took in the sight of Jake standing there. Jake waved. "Hey."

"What's up? Something at the apartment?" Eugene asked.

"No. I just dropped by to see if you wanted to get some lunch." Eugene paused. "Lunch?"

"Don't you eat?"

"How'd you know where the office is?"

"Your business cards are all over the apartment. Should I leave?" He looked around. ManageSoft took up half the third floor of this office building in the Financial District, a couple of blocks away from the pier and down the street from Chinatown. Jake had found a bus that dropped him off across the street. He was standing in the main reception area, surrounded by stencilled glass and ultra-modern black furniture; the receptionist with a headset watched both Jake and his brother.

Eugene motioned him over. "I can show you around, but I don't think I have time for lunch."

Jake followed him down a narrow carpeted hallway, a few office doors closed, and Eugene waved him into a small office, the view from the window of a larger, grey office building. Eugene checked something on his computer, clicked his mouse, then turned his attention to Jake.

"No lunch?" Jake asked.

"No time. Hey, about last night—"

"Forget it. It's none of my business."

"Just that we might have been a little loud."

"I fell asleep."

Eugene studied him. "No, you didn't, but that's okay. As you heard, it was a stupid fight."

"Common?"

"Oh, very common."

Jake glanced at the bookshelves filled with computer manuals. "Nice office."

"This is where it all happens, where I lose the big bucks."

"You look tired."

"I've been here since six. My day's just started."

"I can go pick up something to eat and bring it—"

A knock at the door and an Asian woman poked her head in, long wavy black hair falling over her eyes. She stopped and looked at Jake. "Oops. Sorry—"

"No, it's all right," Eugene said. "Caroline, meet my brother Jake."

Caroline stepped inside and pushed her hair back. Small-framed and wearing a navy blue skirt and jacket, Caroline held out her hand and shook Jake's. "Hello! I heard you were visiting." She smiled broadly, and Jake was startled by her friendliness. Was this the one who liked Eugene?

"The houseguest from hell," Jake said. Her grip was strong, and when she laughed her nose wrinkled. She let go of his hand and leaned against the door. A strand of stray hair fell onto her shoulder. He stared at her legs, then covered this up by kicking imaginary lint off his shoe.

"Aw, shucks, he's shy," Caroline said.

Jake smiled, met her eyes. "I've never seen any of Eugene's co-workers."

"Never?"

"He never visited me before at work," Eugene said. "This is unusual."

"Well, here I am," she said, opening her arms. "The first co-worker. Honored by your presence."

"I should have visited you a long time ago, Eugene," Jake said, though he was still smiling at Caroline.

She blushed, and turned to Eugene. "You wanted to see me?"

"Later. Maybe this afternoon."

"It was nice meeting you," she said to Jake. "Are you here to see the office?"

"I was trying to take him out to lunch, but no dice."

"Eugene's on a diet," she said.

"I am?" Eugene asked.

"The stress and headache diet," Caroline said.

"Very funny," Eugene said.

"Eugene can't, but do you care to join me?" Jake asked Caroline. "Something nearby?"

She hesitated, then grinned. "Oh, really. Lunch? With you?"

"Uh, actually," Eugene said. "Caroline and I should probably do that meeting now."

She turned to him, puzzled. "Now?"

Jake looked at her left hand. No ring. Jake shrugged and said to his brother. "All right. I'll get going. Maybe we can all have lunch some day."

"That'd be nice," Caroline said. She turned to Eugene. "I'll be in my office. Come get me when you want to talk." She smiled at Jake and left.

Eugene closed the door behind her and said to Jake, "What are you doing?"

"What?"

"Were you hitting on her?"

"Yeah."

"You can't hit on my co-workers."

"Why not?"

"Because…because it'd look bad for me."

"Is she married? She's pretty cute."

"No, she's not."

"Not cute?"

He sighed. "Not married. Look, that was very inappropriate."

Jake studied his brother, and laughed. "Are you jealous?"

"Of course not. It's just not appropriate to do that kind of thing—"

"Wait a minute. Is this the one who has a crush on you?"

Eugene's mouth opened, then shut. He stuttered, "What?"

"The one who has the hots for you."

"What…Where did you…What are you talking about?" He glanced at the closed door, then back at Jake. After a moment he raised his head in understanding. "Ah. Rachel. Have you been talking to Rachel?"

"She mentioned someone had a crush on you."

"She was kidding. It's a running joke. Look, I have to get back to work. Maybe later this week—"

"I'm leaving, I'm leaving." Jake opened the door. "Sorry for the interruption."

"It's just that I have a lot going on…"

Jake held up his hand and slipped out. As he shut the door he remembered that graph his brother had made of their father's moods, and wanted to ask him about it. He opened the door again, and saw Eugene sitting at his desk with his head in his hands. Eugene looked up, embarrassed. "Yes?"

"Sorry," Jake said. "Just wanted to say goodbye."

"Goodbye."

Jake closed the door. He thought he heard his brother sighing. He hurried down the hall. This whole place reeked of zombies.

20

Jake and Bobby Null sat in the stolen car on the street adjacent to the Chuns' cul-de-sac. It was Sunday. They had just watched Mr. Chun engage the alarm, then drive his wife and teenage son to church. Jake had followed them last week to check Bobby's claims, and it seemed that everything he had said was correct. The Chuns drove to a Korean church in Bellevue, and stayed for over three hours. Bobby claimed that the second time he had followed them they hadn't returned home until eight o'clock that evening. Today Jake and Bobby waited for fifteen minutes to make sure the Chuns didn't return unexpectedly.

"Look at that fucking car," Bobby had muttered as they drove by in their Lexus.

It was too sunny. Jake didn't like having to do this without any cover. The only time day-hits were better were in large apartment complexes when everyone was at work and no one knew or cared if a maintenance man was in the building. Jake wasn't even bothering with a uniform. No one worked Sundays. He'd just have to slip into the backyard and see what happened.

Jake strapped on his waist pack with his tools and two-way radio. After fifteen minutes, he said to Bobby, "Turn on the scanner. You better keep me posted. And it looks like someone's home in the place next door. Stay alert."

"Don't worry about me. I'll do it."

Jake left the car, moving casually towards the house. He didn't have to rush, but he wanted to get in and out as soon as possible. He hoped there wasn't a safe. That would complicate everything. Bobby had seen the Chuns leaving their jewelry store with a portable strongbox, and was counting on this as the only defense.

He quickly hopped over the low, wooden backyard fence and began climbing the cypress tree closest to the house. Up here, he was well hidden, and had a direct route to a second-floor, double-hung window. The thick foliage of this tree and the smaller pine near the corner of the yard offered him concealment from the townhouses directly behind the Chun's house. Jake had considered coming into the back yard through the complex, but didn't like the large patio windows facing the Chuns' fence. He would have to walk by someone's kitchen and hop a fence in plain view.

When he climbed up to the target window, he saw the magnetic sensor on the inside sash; it would go off if he tried to open the window by force. But this was still the easiest way since the windows downstairs had anti-breakage magnetic foil as well as sensors, and the front door was exposed to the street and heavily locked. Both the front and rear doors were alarmed.

"Everything okay?" Bobby radioed.

Jake sighed. The kid was supposed to keep quiet. He picked up the two-way and whispered, "No contact unless there's a problem. Are you listening to the police scanner?"

"Yeah."

A thick limb extended up about three feet from the window, ending abruptly, apparently sawed off to give this window more light. But this truncated branch gave him a good position from which to work; he sat on the sawed off portion, his feet against the shingled wall for balance. All right. Here we go. Although he had gone over this dozens of times during the planning stages last week, he wanted to make sure he wasn't missing a simple solution, an elegant bypass. He reexamined the foil. Alarmed window. Quickest and quietest entry. Disable alarm. No other way. Get to work.

He pulled out his small roll of adhesive tape and, leaving a small strip hanging loosely, taped up a corner. He could've used a suction cup to hold the corner in place, but tape was cheaper. His surgical gloves squeaked on the glass. Using a glass cutter, he cut along the side sash in an "L," using the wood as a guide and pausing only when the grating sound became too loud. Then, while holding the tape, he finished the third side of the triangle, and popped out the piece of glass by pulling on the tape. He left this on the sill.

He took out his mini-electric screwdriver, and began unscrewing the sensor attached to the interior sash. This part of the alarm system was simple: half of the sensor was screwed into the sash, the other half into the frame, each of them next to the other when the window was closed. If the window was opened, separating the two halves of the sensors, the magnet in the sash would no longer be holding the switch in the frame closed, thus opening the circuit and setting off the alarm. He was simply unscrewing the sensor on the interior sash, which he would then leave attached to the switch, but freeing the window.

With the screwdriver he quickly pulled out the screws, and carefully taped the sensor to the switch. Though the window was still locked, opening the butterfly sash catch was just a matter of sticking a strip of sheet metal in between the upper and lower sashes and pushing the lock free. He had done this a number of times on other houses. Most windows weren't very secure, but second-floor windows were easy. He had even come across second-floor windows that were wide open, with no one home. Those and air-conditioners were a gift. He needed only to push the air-conditioner in, and most people rarely secured them with more than a few screws.

Unlatching the lock, Jake opened the window slowly, keeping an eye on the taped sensor. He wasn't certain if there were any mercury switches, or how sophisticated an alarm system the Chuns had upstairs, but he knew enough of the ASA first-floor perimeter system—thanks to Chih's specs—to guess that this was the extent of the security.

As he lifted the window high enough to slide through, he looked inside, checking for motion detectors, but, as he suspected, there was nothing. He turned up his walkie-talkie. Bobby, with the police scanner, had better contact him if there were any police dispatches sent here, just in case Jake had triggered a silent alarm.

He felt a small rush of adrenaline, and slid inside the house.

PART II

21

It was past midnight, and a line of light was still under Jake's door. Rachel was awake. Shadows moved back and forth—Rachel going to the bathroom, the kitchen—and the TV volume was on low. He heard pages flipping. He put on his pants and walked out, squinting in the light.

"I'm sorry. Did I wake you?" she asked.

He focused. She was curled up on the sofa in paisley silk pajamas. Her philosophy book was open, her pencil pushed behind her ear. He cleared his throat. "I was awake. What're you up to?"

"Reading. Can't sleep. Tomorrow's my last day."

"I visited Eugene at work."

"Downtown?" She smiled. "Was little Ms. Cutie there?"

Jake laughed. "Yeah, she was. She was cute."

Rachel drew back. "Really? Do I detect some interest?"

He said, "Who has time for that? Besides, you know you've always been my favorite."

"One of your many favorites, I'm sure."

"None like you." He smiled.

"Oh, dear," she said, but then her face fell.

"Did I say something? I didn't mean—"

"No, no. It's me," she said. "I was just thinking how I've become so serious these days."

"Must be all that reading," he said.

"This?" She held up her book.

"What's it about?"

She waved it away. "You wouldn't be interested."

"Tell me. Is that the book that's been lying around here lately?

Philosophy?"

She nodded.

"Tell me some philosophy."

Shrugging, she flipped a few pages back and read aloud, "Heraclitus postulated that the primary element was fire, making up everything in the world in its different forms through condensation and rarefaction. Fire, also a metaphor for change, reflected his view of the eternal flux occurring around him. 'We can't step into the same river twice,' he wrote."

Jake said, "Heavy."

"It's interesting how they kept searching for explanations, the key to everything."

"So, this guy thought fire was everything? Even the world?"

"Possibly. I like his idea of everything always changing, fire as a metaphor."

Jake sat down across from her and asked, "Do you do this a lot? Stay up and read?"

"Lately, yes."

"Why?"

She said, "Did you know that our cells continually regenerate so that in seven years all of our cells are new; everything has been replaced."

"Yeah?"

"So change is natural. It's biological."

"And you're changing?" he asked.

She smiled. "I'm so transparent, aren't I? Drug me if I start whining again." She put down the book and asked, "Why don't you keep in touch with Euge?"

"Not much to say."

"If I had a brother or sister, I'd want to stay connected."

"Maybe. Our family wasn't close."

"I thought when you two were younger…"

Jake said, "Yeah, but we weren't buddies. I mean, we had to deal with our father."

"So you move around and occasionally drop in."

"Occasionally."

"It must be nice."

"What?"

"To be so free."

Jake said, "You can do that."

"I don't think so."

"All you have to do is pack a bag. Bring what you can carry. What's stopping you?"

She shook her head slowly.

"You're free to do what you want."

She smirked. "Have you been reading my books?"

"Don't need books for that. It's obvious, isn't it?"

"You are so unlike Euge. You know that?"

"I know that."

"What really happened up in Seattle?"

Jake kept still. He tried not to show any expression, and wondered if she had been planning to ask him this all along. "Why?"

"I want to know."

"I don't want to talk about it."

Rachel leaned back and crossed her legs. She said, "The surest way to get me interested is not to tell me."

"Maybe I'll tell you once everything settles."

"Will you tell me something else?"

"What?"

"Tell me about your father."

Jake sighed. "Man. Don't you believe in small talk?"

She laughed, then said, "I'm tired of small talk. My whole life is small talk."

"You don't want to hear about that stuff."

"I do. Tell me how he came to the U.S. How'd he meet your mother?"

Jake told her that his father had been in the Korean Navy, enlisted for the Korean War and rose to become a captain. After the war he came to the United States to study engineering, but never finished his degree, and went through numerous jobs relating to nautical engineering, each one leading further away from his original goal. He ended up fixing boat engines for a small company in Marina del Rey. His marriage had been arranged by his grandmother back in Seoul. His new wife was not quite a new wife—she had been married before, but the marriage had ended in scandal when her new husband ran off. In order to start over, she had to leave the country. So she remarried, this time to a stranger in California.

"Why would she do that?"

Jake shrugged.

"What happened with the previous marriage?"

Jake shrugged again. "It's all murky. I don't know. I never asked."

"Then you two were born."

Jake said, "Yeah. Why do you want to know this?"

She shook her head. "Not sure. I've been thinking a lot about this stuff lately. Did you know that my father, for example, died in his mid-forties and did nothing he wanted to?"

"Like what?"

Rachel told Jake about her father's love of building things. He had a small workshop in the garage for woodworking projects, but Rachel knew he had only built a birdhouse, a spice rack, and a small bookshelf. He had the blueprints for dozens of projects, ordered from woodworking magazines, and had promised Rachel that he would build her a small playhouse out back. But his job kept him too busy.

His job? He was a salesman for a cardboard packager. He sold boxes.

She said, "That was his life, selling empty boxes. Whenever I think about it I get scared. I mean, what was the point? When he died, me and my mom had to clean out that garage, with all those woodworking plans with notes written on the back about how he'd modify everything. You know, 'add window' or 'use pine'. It scares the hell out of me."

"That's why you quit your job?"

"Partly. I mean, what's the point? What's the point of all this?"

Jake hesitated. He had never seen her like this, and wasn't sure what to say. He thought about her question, and it seemed clear to him. "The point is to survive."

She smiled. "Maybe you're not so different from your brother."

Jake was tired, and stifled a yawn. He said, "I'm going to turn in. I've got to run a bunch of errands tomorrow."

"What kind?"

"Errands," he said. "Can we work out again soon? That was great."

"I'm keeping you up. Yes, maybe tomorrow night. Hey, thanks for listening to me rant."

"I like listening to you."

He stood, and returned to the guest room. He heard Rachel start up her laptop, a chime ringing across the living room. The conversation had agitated him. He lay down and stared up into the darkness. For a number of years he had chosen not to think about it, not to stir it up. Their father beat the shit out of their mother. The few times early on, before his father began locking them in the basement, Jake had seen an entire fight from beginning to end, and it was beyond his comprehension. His father would punch his mother straight in the face. She would go flying back, the power behind the blow lifting her off the ground. She would crash into the wall, and crumple to the ground. His father would smack her a few times, then kick her a few times, hard, really hard, until she screamed. She cried and begged. His father would bellow in Korean and give her a few more kicks and stumble away. Jake and Eugene would wait until their father fell asleep, then go to their mother. She would try to hide her face, and push them away. "Go! Go to bed!" Her teeth were bloody.

One day she packed a suitcase and disappeared.

The world is fire. Strange, but it made sense to him. He saw flames flickering around him. Everything was bright and fiery. He slept, his skin burning.

22

Bobby Null found the Mail & Copy store on University, the place where Chih left messages for Jake. It was only four or five blocks from where they had brought the jewels and cash, where Jake had shot Bobby. Jake must live near here. Bobby felt his abdomen twinge. A few copy machines were lined up on one side of the room, and on the other side was a wall filled with mailboxes. He searched for number 400 and saw through the tiny window a few letters wedged inside. There was a young woman with a nose ring at the front desk, and he approached. He told himself to keep cool. When he asked how people got a mailbox, she said all you had to do was fill out a form and pay ten dollars a month for the smaller boxes.

"What if someone wants to contact me at my mailbox?"

"Mail it, or give me a note. I can put it in the box."

"Is the real address on that form?"

"Yes," she said. "Do you want an application?"

"Can I see the form for number 400?"

She hesitated. "Oh, I can't do that. That information's private."

Bobby studied her. She looked about nineteen or twenty, maybe a college student doing this part-time. He said, "I'll give you twenty dollars if you just show me the form. Just leave it on the table for a second." He pulled out the roll of bills he had taken from Chih. He lay a twenty-dollar bill on the counter. She glanced around the store, which was a good sign.

"I don't know," she said. "I'm not allowed."

Bobby smiled, and slowly peeled off another twenty. He dropped it on top of the other one. He said, "Just for thirty seconds. It's a joke on my friend. He bet me twenty bucks I couldn't find out where he lives."

"But you'll be down twenty," she said, motioning to the bills.

"It'll be worth it." He smiled again. He considered grabbing her hair and flashing his gun, but then he saw her eyes lock onto the bills. He relaxed.

She reached behind the counter. Bobby heard her opening a file cabinet. She pulled out a sheet of paper, placed it on the counter, and quickly took the two twenties. She said, "Thirty seconds." She walked to the other end of the counter.

Bobby turned over the form and saw the permanent address information. First he saw that Jake's full name was Jacob Ahn, which he jotted down on scrap paper. The address was 98785 Adali Lane. The college kid came over and pulled the sheet away. "Thirty seconds."

"Where is Adali Lane?" he asked.

She pointed to a Seattle map on the wall next to the copy machines. Bobby thanked her and looked up "Adali" in the index. He eventually found the coordinates. According to the map, Jake lived next to the University Bridge, again near where they had stopped to sort the jewelry. He walked out. He patted the gun in the back of his pants.

It took him fifteen minutes to find Adali Lane, but as soon as he saw how tiny the street was—with four houses, numbered 100, 200, 300, 400—he knew it was a fake address. He sat down on the curb and cursed. His insides hurt. Everything hurt. Even his goddamn butt hurt when he sat.

Now what?

He stood up slowly and began knocking on all the doors. Most people weren't home, but he asked two old folks who answered their door if they knew a Jacob Ahn. They didn't. He walked around the block and searched for any signs of Jake. He didn't expect to see anything.

He considered waiting at the mail drop for Jake to appear, since there were letters in the box. But that would take too much time.

Then he realized that those letters might reveal something—another contact, an address, anything. He headed back to the Mail & Copy store, his limp getting worse. He popped two bennies and waited for the rush.

23

Jake approached Pacific Gems off Van Ness, and was pleased to see the "We Buy Jewelry" sign at the bottom of the window. He had made a list of jewelers in the neighborhood, and wanted to start testing the market. When he walked into the store and noticed a small jewelry repair station near the back with mini burners, tool sets, and a large illuminated magnifying glass on a flexible arm, he knew they would probably want almost anything. They could fix or modify his poorer pieces. A young, heavily made-up woman in a blue blouse appeared from the back and asked Jake if he needed help.

"I just inherited some jewelry. I was wondering about selling it."

"Just a sec," she said, turning and calling out "Tom!"

They waited, and Jake looked up at the alarm system: motion detectors, and the control box was housed in steel with what looked like a cell phone antenna springing from the top. Remote connection to an alarm company, probably with a separate power source. He tried to see what was in the back room, but the repair tables and shelves blocked his line of sight.

When Tom walked in, an older, bald man in his fifties, he had a jeweler's loupe strapped tightly to his forehead. He blinked and refocused on Jake. The woman said, "Selling."

Tom asked, "Gems or gold?"

"Both."

"Let's see."

Jake pulled out the diamond ring and a few other newer pieces he had recently retrieved from the safe deposit box: a diamond pendant, gold and diamond earrings, and a blue and white sapphire bracelet. He said, "I actually will be getting more. They're coming to me in small shipments."

Tom began examining the pieces, starting with the ring and pendant. His long, thin hands flipped the ring deftly. He said, "These look new."

"They are. My mother was always buying. I don't think I'll sell the old stuff yet."

Tom nodded, pulled the loupe over his eye, and peered down. He clucked his tongue. "The fire's bad. The mounting's bad. Oh, no, this is cheap stuff. The facets look off."

"Yeah," Jake said. "And the colors too. You can tell."

Tom checked the earrings. "These are better. I'll need to check the color and clarity more closely, but it's clean in there." He examined the bracelet and shook his head. "This is cheap stuff." He looked up, pushing away the loupe. "You want to sell all this outright?"

"Do you consign?"

"Yeah. The cheap stuff," he motioned to the bracelet and diamond ring, "might do better consigned. We take fifteen percent."

"How much for the ring outright?"

"I'll give it a closer look, but no more than a hundred, max."

That was thirty more than the pawn shop. Jake said, "The earrings?"

"Maybe three hundred? Not sure yet. I want to check the cuts too."

Jake said, "Can you handle a lot? Consigned or buying?"

"We have three stores in the Bay Area. We can handle it. Also, we know wholesalers and designers interested in junk for melting."

Jake nodded slowly, pretending to consider it. But he was thinking, Bingo.

24

Jake climbed through the Chun's window, making sure that he held onto his tools and that no clothing snagged, and he found himself in a teenager's room. A computer with a screensaver—a woman in a bikini—caught his eye. Clothes and lacrosse equipment lay all over the floor. He moved quickly out into the hallway, and searched for the master bedroom. He smelled a familiar scent: Korean food. A hint of spices and soy sauce marinade. He had never hit a Korean house before.

Entering the master bedroom, he quickly opened and searched the drawers, the bureaus, and stopped when he found a small jewelry box in one of the night tables. He emptied it on the bed and scooped up the gold necklaces, diamond rings and earrings, depositing them into his waist pack. The rest—fake costume junk—he returned to the box and returned to the night table. But where was the strong box?

He went through their closet, but there were only a few gold tie clips and a pair of silver cufflinks. Nothing. He began sweating. It had to be here somewhere. He thought back to last night when he had watched the Chuns return home from the jewelry store. The living room lights went on first. Then the kitchen. Then the lights upstairs. Maybe it was in the living room.

He stepped carefully down the stairs into the living room, keeping his eye on the alarm control unit next to the door, a red light blinking slowly. He checked around the room again for motion detectors, and stopped when he saw two wires running out from underneath the front mat. He stared. Shit. An alarm on the floor mat? Had he underestimated them?

Moving slowly across the carpet, steering clear of the front mat and checking his path for any other pressure-sensitive alarms, he saw another room next to the kitchen, a small office, separated by a bookshelf and a doorway without a door. He cocked his head. He hadn't seen this room in his surveys, since it was hidden from the windows. It looked like a converted walk-in closet. As he approached this small office, he checked the doorway, the carpet, and the interior for any extra alarms, but there were none. He stepped in and headed straight for the metal desk, tugging on the file cabinet drawer. It hissed smoothly opened. The strong box lay there in the center, amidst papers and a few files. He held his breath, and thought, All right.

He pulled the box out slowly, weighing it, and checked the latch. Locked, as he expected. He shook it and felt the weight of jewelry.

"Fuck," Bobby radioed. "The neighbor is watching me. He keeps looking out the window."

Jake whispered into his unit, "Drive away. You look suspicious. Go around the block. I'll radio you when I need you."

"Okay."

Jake closed the drawer and began retracing his steps upstairs, thinking ahead of what he had to do now: bring the jewels to Chih, and split the money. He had to work at the restaurant tonight.

Before he climbed out of the window and shut it, he drew the curtains, certain that this would give him more time, hiding his small hole in the window. The son would probably change out of his clothes and then spend the evening in the living room, watching TV, as he had done the last Sunday night. If Mr. or Mrs. Chun didn't check the desk drawer right away, it would be twelve hours before anyone even suspected a theft. He radioed Bobby. "Come and get me. Everything okay?"

"Yeah. I'm around the corner."

Jake shimmied down the tree, the strongbox clipped to his belt, and once he hit the ground he stayed behind the fence, waiting.

Bobby pulled up in front of the house, but before Jake could walk out, there was a voice from the other yard. "Excuse me, can I help you?" A man in a sweat suit was walking onto the sidewalk, directing his question at Bobby.

Jake fell back and stayed hidden. He knew this had been too easy. He held his breath, and hoped Bobby didn't screw this up. Bobby stayed inside in car, and the man looked through the open passenger-side window. "Can I help you with something?"

Jake thought, Keep calm. Bobby, cornered in his car, said something that Jake couldn't hear, something about waiting for a friend. He climbed out of the car and looked around. He said, "I was supposed to pick him up ten minutes ago."

The man said, "Oh, are you friends with Roger? You mean Roger Chun?"

Bobby nodded.

Jake thought, Good. Roger Chun must be the teenage son.

"You might have just missed them." The man turned and motioned to the house. "You have the right place, but they always go out on Sundays…"

Jake saw Bobby pulling out a gun from the back of his waist, and something caught in Jake's throat. He yelled, "No!"

The man and Bobby turned to Jake, and Bobby jumped towards the man and slammed the butt of his gun into the back of his head. The man stumbled forward, letting out an "Ah" but he didn't collapse. Bobby brought the gun down again, this time harder, and the man groaned and fell onto his hands and knees. Bobby quickly grabbed him by the collar and pulled him towards the yard. "This way, asshole." The man tried to get up, but lost his balance.

"What the hell are you doing?" Jake said.

"What the fuck else do I do?" Bobby turned to the man, who was sitting on the ground, stunned, rubbing his temple. Bobby ran up to him and kicked his head. There was a thump when he connected, and the man's head snapped back, and he slumped on the ground. "Please,

God," he managed to say.

"Stop," Jake said. "Take it easy." He saw Bobby's gun, a .38. He hadn't known Bobby was carrying.

"You got it?" Bobby asked, nodding to the strongbox.

"I got it. Let's go."

Bobby glanced at the man on the ground, and gave him one more kick to the head. The man passed out. Jake was already moving towards the car. It was the middle of the day and they were in full view of the other houses. Jake climbed into the driver's seat, and Bobby jumped in, shoving the gun into his pants. Jake glanced at the gun but didn't say anything. As he drove off, he knew there was going to be a problem.

25

Jake awoke from a nap, and heard rustling in the living room. When he walked out, he saw Rachel in her sweats, packing a water bottle into a gym bag. She turned to him, smiled, and said, "Good evening."

"Gym?" he asked.

"Yes. Care to join me?"

He hurried back into his room to grab shorts and T-shirt. While they were in the elevator, Jake said, "Today was your last day."

"It certainly was."

"Congratulations."

She nodded slowly, her attention distracted. They left the building and walked down Van Ness, but it seemed more crowded than usual, so they soon veered onto the side streets, winding their way towards Laguna. Jake was still groggy from his nap, and they were quiet the entire walk to the gym. At the doorway she said, "I think the guest pass expired."

"I have cash. How much?"

"Eight."

He pulled out a small wad of bills, and handed her eight dollars. She looked down and said, "Is this good money or bad money?"

"You mean counterfeit? I don't have counterfeit."

"No. Stolen money or earned money?"

"Does it matter?"

"No."

"Earned money."

They walked upstairs, and at the front desk she filled out a form and paid for him. They separated to change in the small locker rooms. When he came out, she was already at the free-weight bench press, loading the bar with twenty-fives. She wore a different Lycra outfit, this one navy blue with a silver stripe running down the side, interrupted by her bare midsection. Jake stared. As he approached, he noticed that every Stairmaster and treadmill was taken, the cacophony of differently pitched whirring and buzzing as oppressive as the heat. There were more women tonight, and Jake saw Rachel wave to an Asian woman on a treadmill. He waded through the muggy air, and Rachel said to him, "Spot me. I'm trying for twelve." She lay down.

"Is everything okay?"

She paused and looked up at him. "What do you mean?"

"Are you okay?"

"Today was my last day at work, and I'm feeling odd."

"Why?"

"It's a bit of a let-down. I'm not sure what I expected." She inhaled deeply, exhaled, and lifted the bar up. She began her set, and started having trouble at seven. The bar tilted and swayed, so Jake came in and steadied it. At eight she couldn't lift it and cursed. Jake helped push the bar up. She said, "One more." She struggled, and her arms shook. The bar froze a few inches above her chest. Jake began lifting it off her, and when he slipped it into the hooks, she sighed. "Damn. I'm getting weaker."

"Maybe you're tired."

She sat up and turned towards him. She stared.

He waited. "Yeah?"

She cleared her throat and asked, "Did you have to beat an innocent bystander?"

Jake kept his face blank and said, "What?"

"The hardware executive. He lived next door. You two beat him."

"What are you talking about?"

"In Seattle."

Jake blinked, then said, "What hardware executive?"

"Did you beat someone when you were stealing the jewelry?"

Jake shook his head slowly, trying to figure out how she could know this.

"There was only one big jewelry burglary reported in the newspapers recently. It wasn't you?"

"This was in the newspaper?"

"Online," she said. "So why did you do that, beat him?"

Jake said, "Is he okay?"

"Hospitalized, but he'll recover."

"What else did they report?"

"Why did you beat him?"

Sighing, he finally said, "I didn't do that. My partner did it. Ex-partner."

She drew back in surprise.

He said, "What newspapers?"

"*The Seattle Times* and the *Post-Intelligencer*."

"What did they say?"

"A jeweler's house was burglarized. The next-door neighbor came across the two men and was beaten."

"Could he describe them?"

"Not really. He was confused."

"Any other witnesses?"

"No."

"The police have anything?"

"No. Nothing it seems," she said. "So it *was* you."

Jake didn't reply, and added ten pounds to each side. They switched positions and he began his set. He did ten reps. He asked, "There was nothing else?"

She shook her head. "About the burglars? No. Why?"

"Can I take a look at those articles?"

"Tonight, but I want to know more."

"Like what?"

"Like what happened."

They switched positions, and Rachel reduced the weight back to the twenty-fives. She lay down and began her set. She had trouble with the second rep, and Jake helped her. They didn't talk, and moved onto the other weights. Jake wanted to ask her more, especially about police leads, but knew she would demand his story. He could wait. They did shoulder presses, curls, tricep raises, and lat pulldowns. Then they moved onto leg exercises. By the time they finished, Jake had trouble lifting his arms, his back and shoulders aching. His calves were cramping up. They moved slowly to the mats, and began stretching. Rachel winced as she tried to touch her toes, and she pointed to her hamstring. "I strained it."

"Here," he said, moving towards her. "I can put some pressure on it."

She turned over, and he slowly lowered the heel of his palm onto the back of her thigh. She nodded. "Ow. Yes." She was lying on her stomach, resting her head on her clasped hands. She turned towards the mirror and said to him, "Near the knee. Ow."

Jake stopped.

"No. That's good."

He rolled his palms across her leg, pushing and kneading. He glanced at her butt, then looked at her reflection, and saw her staring at him. His hands were unsteady. He let his fingers touch her bare calves lightly, then returned to her hamstring. He massaged the area behind her knee, and went up near her butt. He could feel his heartbeat quickening.

"Shouldn't you two get a room?" the Asian woman said as she walked over from the treadmill.

"Hi, Marie," Rachel said. She quickly rolled away from Jake.

"I'm next," Marie said, smiling and pointing to her legs.

"Marie, this is Jake, my brother-in-law."

He shook her hand.

"Brother-in-law?" Marie said. "I thought this might be the mystery husband."

Jake glanced at Rachel, who said, "She's never met Euge."

"I'm sure he doesn't exist. She tells people about him so no one will hit on her."

"He exists," Jake said. "I'm his brother." To Rachel he asked, "People hit on you here?"

"She's kidding." Rachel smiled at Marie.

"It looked like you two were killing each other on the weights," Marie said.

Rachel laughed and sat up, rubbing her arms. "I forgot how spotting can really work you."

"You certainly look good," Marie said to her.

Rachel waved her hand dismissively. "Not there yet."

"I've got to go, but one of these days I'm going to meet the mystery man." She waved to Jake, then walked towards the locker room. Jake watched her.

"She's a lesbian in a fifteen-year relationship," Rachel said. "Can you believe it? Fifteen years. And stop looking at her ass."

He laughed and felt himself redden.

"Busted," she said, laughing too.

They stood up slowly, preparing to leave. Jake felt his hands tingling.

26

When Bobby Null returned to the Mail & Copy store, the nose-pierced college girl wasn't there anymore. Now there was a tall, goateed kid with glasses. Bobby looked through the small window of box 400, and saw the envelopes still there. He pulled at the knob, but it was secure. The goatee glanced up at him, then went back to sorting mail. Bobby tried to figure out how to play this. He approached the counter and asked where the girl was.

"Shift ended," he said, barely looking up.

"Could you get my mail in box 400? I left my key at home."

"Got ID?"

"Not on me. But I can tell you my name, address, all that."

Goatee shook his head. "Nuh-uh. Need ID."

Bobby saw that the mailbox slots were around the wall, and all he had to do was step behind the counter and grab the mail in 400. Goatee looked up. "Can I help you?"

"Will you get me my mail? I'm not going to walk all the way home and then come back just for ID. Get me box 400."

"No can do. Sorry."

Bobby stared at him and thought, Everyone in my fucking way. He shrugged and acted as if he were leaving, walking towards the door. When Goatee returned to mail sorting, Bobby turned and walked directly behind the counter and towards the boxes. Each open cubby had small labels above it, light filtering in from the tiny windows on the other side. Cardboard boxes were piled along the other side of the wall.

"Hey, man. What the hell you doing?"

"Getting my stuff." Bobby had trouble finding the box. There. The hundreds towards the right. He scanned the labels.

Goatee walked towards him. "Hey! You can't be here!"

"Fuck you." Bobby kept looking, overshooting the numbers at 500 and backtracking. There. The 400's. He found 400 and pulled out the envelopes. Goatee grabbed his arm.

"Put that back. You can't do this."

Bobby looked down at the kid's hand touching him. "Get the fuck off me."

"I'll call the police. You're stealing mail." The kid suddenly looked uncertain. "Put it back."

"Get your hand off me."

"Put the mail back."

Bobby reached into his waistband and pulled out the automatic. The kid let go and moved up against the wall. Bobby aimed the gun at the kid's chest and said, "Do you get paid enough to die for your job?"

The kid's mouth moved but nothing came out. He shook his head quickly.

"Let me see some ID," Bobby said.

"What?"

Bobby raised the gun to the kid's face. "Let me see some ID."

The kid scrambled for his wallet, and pulled out his driver's license, holding it up. Bobby grabbed it and said, "Taylor Brown. Is this your current address?"

He nodded.

"Taylor, I'm going to take this license. If you call the police or tell anyone what has happened, I'm going to visit you one night. Do you get it?"

He nodded, his eyes on the gun.

Bobby then hammered the gun into the kid's ear. The kid cursed and fell down, holding his head and crying, "Please don't…"

"Remember, Taylor. You talk, and I'll visit." Bobby walked out from the behind the mailboxes, and shoved the gun back into his pants. He heard the kid whimpering.

Walking down the street and opening Jake's mail, Bobby threw out the junk mail, a few bills, but stopped when he saw the letter from SeaTac Bank. It was a form letter, but it had Jake's social security number at the top. The letter thanked Jake for his patronage at SeaTac Bank, and they were sorry that he was closing his accounts. They hoped Jake would consider them in the future. That was all, but the social security number was important.

Bobby and his friend from L.A., Jules, used to steal mail and look for credit card applications. They'd fill them out, and when they needed the social security number—if it wasn't already in their other mail—they'd call Jules' sister, Lavelle, who worked in the financing department of an auto dealer. She had access to anyone's credit report. All Bobby needed was a full name and address, and she'd pop up a social security number.

Bobby immediately called Jules, who said, "Where the fuck have you been and when the fuck are you going to get Ron off my back?"

"I'm working on it."

"He's getting serious. He and his asshole friends are beginning to bother me. Where the hell are you?"

"Seattle. I'm coming back down soon. I'll have the money."

"I hope so. He'll come after you if he thinks you're fucking with him."

"I'm not. My brother was killed. That's why I'm up here."

"Oh. Didn't know that."

"I need Lavelle's number."

"Why?"

"I want to do a credit thing."

"You're not getting ten grand from a credit—"

"Just give me the fucking number. I'm not doing that credit card scam. What's her number."

Jules gave him the phone number, and Bobby hung up on him in mid-question. He then called Lavelle.

"I don't know. I can't keep doing this. I can get in trouble. They list inquiries," she said.

"We haven't asked in a long time. Just this once more."

"All right. Spell me the name, and give me the social security number."

"What can you get me?" Bobby asked.

"The address, credit cards, debts, things like that."

Bobby spelled out Jake's full name, then read off the social security number. She said she'd call back in fifteen minutes. He thought about Ron bothering Jules. Ron had his asshole army, and Bobby might have to call him soon. Tell him the money's coming. Then again, who gave a fuck? He'd get his money. Once Bobby found Jake, everything would be okay.

When Lavelle called back, she told him that this guy had no credit history. "He doesn't have credit cards, has no debt, and looks like he goes under the radar."

"Address?"

"A few of them. He's moved around Seattle a lot."

"The last address?"

She read off an Eighth Avenue address in Seattle, which was a few blocks from University. Jake wrote this down with a smile. "Lavelle, you're great."

"When you coming back down here?"

"Just as soon as I finish up my business. I'll take you and Jules out on the town."

They hung up and Bobby walked towards Eighth. He tasted bile in his throat, and spit a few times onto the sidewalk. He had trouble ridding his mouth of the sour taste. Backwash from too many bennies? He spit again. He hoped Jake was there. His abdomen flared as he adjusted his gun against the small of his back.

27

Jake came out of the bathroom, and saw his brother and Rachel at the small dining room table. They looked up. Rachel's hair was still wet, slicked back from her shower. The tense look on Eugene's face made Jake stop. "Everything okay?"

Eugene said, "Just some problems at work."

"You want me to go out and buy you two dinner?"

"Thanks," his brother said, "but I'm going back to work in a minute."

Jake nodded. Rachel's laptop computer lay on the table. He went to the guest room and changed, hearing Rachel's questioning tone followed by Eugene's somber answers. By the time Jake came back out, Eugene was putting his coat on, and told Jake, "I'll just be a few hours. Sorry I'm being such a terrible host."

"No, it's fine. You're busy."

"Tomorrow night we'll take in a movie or something. I promise."

Jake shook his head. "Don't worry about it."

His brother left, and Jake turned to Rachel. She said, "It's complicated. People stabbing each other in the back."

"In *his* back?"

"Possibly. That's why he's meeting his supervisor outside of work. They're going to talk strategy."

"Will he be all right?"

Rachel looked up at him and shook her head. "I don't think so."

"Shit."

She smiled sadly. "He'll be fine. He's a plugger."

"A what?"

"Plugger. Plugs away. He's like my mom."

"He *is* a plugger," Jake said.

"I know."

"What does your mother do? Is she still working?"

"Oh, yes. Hotel administrator. Started out in janitorial. Same hotel company for twenty-three years." Rachel said, "The sight of hotel-sized soaps and shampoos make me ill. That's all we used when I was growing up."

"I didn't know that."

"She's a soldier. When my father died, she had never had a job. Married young, that kind of thing. We had no money and she had to support me. She went out and plugged away."

"Do they get along?"

"Euge and my mom? Sure. She had a little trouble with the Asian thing at first."

"Really."

"She didn't know any better, but once she got to know him, it was fine. You met her at the wedding."

He did? Jake then recalled a short, squat woman bossing the caterers around. "She was the one who made everyone dance."

"That was her."

Jake pointed to her laptop.

"Yes?" she said.

"How about showing me what you found."

She smiled. "We have a deal."

"What deal?"

"I show you, but you tell me what happened."

Jake was about to contradict her, but then said, "Let me see what you have."

She lifted up the screen and turned the laptop on. It chimed. Jake sat down next to her. She said, "I didn't save the first one, because it was just about the hardware guy reporting the beating. They didn't discover the burglary right away."

She clicked on a file and text filled the screen:

SEATTLE - The Seattle Police Department has new leads in the assault of Gregory Hanson, the hardware executive beaten in a neighbor's yard. At first believed to be a mugging gone awry, the beating is now seen as connected to a burglary of a neighbor's house, Won Sil Chun, owner of Good Luck Jewelry in Wallingford. Mr. Chun hadn't noticed jewels missing until the next morning, at which time he called the police. The investigators found evidence of a sophisticated burglary. "We now believe the beating victim must have surprised the burglars," said Sergeant Jim Keller, Seattle PD spokesman. "We have a description of a car, a navy blue or black Ford Escort, in the vicinity at around that time, and a preliminary description of the two attackers. Our sketch artist is working with Mr. Hanson, and we're following every lead." Sergeant Keller asks anyone with relevant information to contact the Seattle Police Department.

Jake stared at the names, and found it jarring to connect people with what he had done. He said, "What about those sketches."

She pulled up another story, which said the sketches were inconclusive, and there were no real leads. The estimated value of the stolen jewels and cash amounted to over sixty thousand dollars. Rachel said, "That's it."

"That can't be it," he said.

"That's all I found."

"Can you search more?"

"I have to get back online."

"Just a few more things."

She logged back on. "One sec." It took a minute, and she found her way to the newspaper site. "What do you want to do?"

"Check for more follow-ups."

"I did."

"Check again."

She shrugged and began typing in keywords, setting the dates to search. The screen came up with no articles.

Jake said, "Try 'Bobby Null' or 'Robert Null'."

"Same dates?"

"Yeah, up to today."

She typed this in, and nothing came up.

Jake said, "How about 'U-district' and 'shooting'?"

She hesitated, then typed this in. Nothing.

"How about 'Dumpster'?"

She typed, then shook her head.

"How about 'gunshot'?" .

A few articles came up. She said, "A gunfight in Denny Park. Self-inflicted suicide in First Hill. That's about it."

Jake wondered if Bobby's body had ever been found. Maybe not. Maybe it had been taken to the dump and buried as garbage.

Could he have survived? Wouldn't there be an article about it then?

Rachel turned to him. She said, "You shot him."

He nodded.

"Why?"

"He was going to shoot me."

"And you left him in a dumpster?"

"I did."

"So he's in some landfill somewhere."

"Probably."

"Is that why you came down here in a hurry?"

"It is."

She stared at him, making him uneasy. She said, "I just can't see you doing that."

"I didn't want to. He pulled his gun on me."

"God, Jake. I don't know what to think."

He stood up. "I don't know either. I've never done that before. He was an asshole, but I didn't want to kill him."

She turned off her computer and pushed the screen down. "How'd you get involved with him?"

"Why?"

"Why what?"

"Why do you want to know?"

She said, "I already know a little. I want to know more."

Jake sighed and gave her a quick version of meeting Bobby, leaving out most of the details. He ended it with, "I guess I was out of practice. I should've never worked with him."

"You've never been caught?"

"I came close a few times. I was once actually shot at."

"No."

"Some grandfather was living in the basement of a house. I didn't know he was there. He surprised me with a gun."

"And shot you?"

"Tried to. He was shaking so much he couldn't aim. I was out of there before he could try again. It was a while before I did another one." Jake felt odd, telling her this. It felt risky, but at the same time a small bubble of relief welled up inside him. He let out a small sigh.

"Does Euge know about this?"

"No. Early on, he wanted to know how I was getting my money, but he didn't want to know much more."

"Is it a lot of money?"

"No."

"But sixty thousand—"

"That's an exaggeration, I think. The jewelers inflate it for insurance." He checked his pockets for the keys, and began heading towards the door. "I'll see you later."

"Where are you going?"

"For a walk."

"A walk?"

"I need some air."

"Want company?"

He said, "Not right now."

She gave him a crooked smile. "All right. You don't have to worry about me, Jake."

"I don't?" he said.

"No, you don't."

He said, "Okay." He left, his hair still wet and cold.

28

Bobby found Jake's apartment building, which was only a few blocks from the dumpster where Bobby had been left to die. Smart. Jake was able to lose the car, walk home and hide out. In the front doorway, Bobby read the names on the intercom slots. There. "Ahn, 2D." Bobby felt wired. Gotcha, you motherfucking piece of shit. He had to calm himself. He wanted to rush up there and beat the crap out of him. But no. He had to be careful.

Second floor. Bobby circled the building, trying to get a sense of the layout. It was an eight-story building, and he counted six balconies or patios per floor. He had no way of knowing which was Jake's, so he returned to the front entrance. He took out his keys and stood a few feet away from the glass doors. As soon as someone entered the small foyer, Bobby wanted to appear as if he were about to open the door.

He waited. He was tempted to buzz Jake and check if he was home. Bobby hoped the jewels and cash were in the apartment. Then everything would be so easy.

He heard voices approaching from the sidewalk, and he dropped his keys. As he reached down to grab them, a young couple stopped and waited. He moved aside, fumbling his keychain, and said, "Go ahead. Too many keys."

They smiled politely and went to the intercom system, pressing a button on the fifth floor. A static-filled voice answered, "Yeah?"

"It's us," the man said.

The front door buzzed, and the woman pulled it open. She walked through, then the man held it open for Bobby, who thanked him. The couple waited at the front elevator while Bobby found the stairs behind the corner. He climbed to the second floor, his palms sweating.

He entered the narrow hallway, and looked around. Apartment "A" was right next to him. He pulled out his gun and walked down the hall to "D." It was cramped in here, and he worried about the neighbors. He knocked on Jake's door, and turned around so that Jake couldn't see his face through the security hole. He knocked and pressed his ear against the door. Nothing. He checked the doorknob. Locked. There were two deadbolts in this door and he doubted he could break through.

The balcony. Bobby counted apartments from the stairwell, estimating the location of Jake's balcony. Then he hurried downstairs and outside, making sure to shove a piece of folded junk mail into the latch. He walked around the building and counted off four balconies from the stairwell. There. That must be Jake's.

The patio beneath Jake's balcony was filled with potted plants and plastic furniture. He went back to the front foyer and buzzed 1D. No answer. Perfect.

He walked to the side of the building, checked the patio again, then climbed the chain-link fence separating the property from the sidewalk. Jake's balcony jutted over the patio, but in order for Bobby to reach the base he had to climb up the low brick wall surrounding the patio, then pull himself up. He scrambled onto Jake's balcony, ignoring the sharp pains throughout his abdomen. When he looked through the glass doors, he saw that the interior was a mess, clothes and books all over the floor. He tried the door, but it was locked and latched. There was also some kind of double lock along the floor. Christ. Fucking Fort Knox.

Bobby examined the small window next to the sliding doors, and decided the only way in was to break it. He took out his gun, and tapped the glass lightly. Thick. He saw some old newspapers on the ground, and opened one up, spreading it over the glass. He tapped the glass again, this time closer to the latch. Then, in one quick motion, shattered the glass. He kept still, listening. He then pulled out large pieces, laying them on the ground, and unlatched the window. He climbed through.

Inside, he immediately knew that Jake had left. Drawers were open and empty, clothes piled and separated on the floor and mattress. Bobby searched everywhere for anything that would've clued him in on where Jake had gone. Nothing. The apartment had been cleaned out, and there was nothing even with Jake's name. He checked the garbage. Nothing.

"Fuck!" Bobby yelled. He looked around. Jake had packed fast. Left no evidence. The whole place looked as if Jake was ready to run at any moment. No real furniture. A cheap black and white TV. Why was the place a mess? Because he was in a hurry. He had packed and cleaned this place out.

Bobby saw a large ball of rolled-up old plastic bags. Safeway supermarket. Jake was probably using them to throw out things. Wait. Jake had bagged everything then had thrown it all out...where?

He unlocked the deadbolts, and went into the hallway. There was a small broom closet at the end, and when Bobby opened the door, he saw the garbage chute. He slammed it shut and ran down the stairs, finding two dumpsters in the underground garage. Both dumpsters were overflowing. He saw a man starting his car, and hurried over to him. He knocked on the window and asked, "Do you know when they pick up the garbage?"

"They were supposed to a few days ago, but the super forgot to unlock the gate. So the garbage is doubling up."

Bobby thanked him, and returned to the two dumpsters. Shit. He'd have to go through this mess and find the Safeway bags, which were probably at the very bottom, the garbage from last week. Even then, he might find nothing. He cursed loudly, and began pulling down wet plastic bags. The smell of something foul eased over him. He looked out for bugs. He always seemed to end up in a dumpster.

29

Jake walked by a small jewelry store as the owner was closing up. He recognized the name from the yellow pages—Franklin & Sons Jewelry—but he hadn't planned to visit until he had first checked out the Pacific Heights stores. He was in the Cow Hollow neighborhood, the Union Street shops still active with early evening customers. He watched the owner pull down a skeletal grilling, and lock it with a large padlock. There was an empty storefront to the right of it with a sign "E-Zone Café Coming Soon!" On the left was a women's clothing store, brightly lit with a few customers inside. Above the jewelry store were what looked like apartments and offices, two stories up. The owner checked the lock, then walked away. Jake backtracked and stood in front of the jeweler's window. The front displays had been cleared, and he saw break detector foil along the windows. He glanced at the padlock, and knew he could open that in five minutes.

The empty storefront next door had sheets of drywall piled in a corner. Still a long way to go. The buildings were crammed up against each other, and Jake searched for the rear. He walked around the block and found a narrow, crooked alley that led to the back of the stores. Beyond a few recycling containers, he found the clothing store, then the jewelry store back exit. Both had heavy iron doors. But when he looked closer at the lock on the jewelry store door, he recognized an old Yale deadbolt; dirty and worn, it could probably be snapped open quickly. He stepped back. There must be an alarm, but what kind? He felt a quickening in his chest. He heard classical music coming from a third floor window. Violins sang into the alley. Jake closed his eyes, wondering about the security system, and rose up with the music. He felt his body floating away.

Jake returned to the apartment and found Rachel and Eugene drinking champagne in the living room. They both turned to him, and swayed. The bottle on the table was empty. He laughed. "Well, I leave you two alone for a minute and you get wasted."

They smiled. Rachel said, "I forgot we had this. It's to celebrate my last day."

"Where were you?" Eugene asked.

"Just walking. Went along Union."

"Join us," Rachel said.

"It looks like I'm too far behind."

"We also have beer," Eugene said.

Jake said, "You're celebrating nicely."

Eugene held up his glass. "I'm celebrating my demise."

"Get some beer. Toast with us," Rachel said.

Jake grabbed a can, and sat down with them in the living room. He asked his brother how his meeting went.

Eugene shook his head. "I'm sure you don't want to hear the nitty-gritty, but there's some maneuvering going on with the board."

"The VC and the head are going to sell their stake to Eon," Rachel said.

Jake smiled. "I didn't understand a word you just said."

"The Venture Capital firm holds a twenty percent stake," Eugene said. "The guy on the board is teaming up with Aaron, the guy who started the firm, who has thirty-one percent. They're selling their shares to Eon, a competitor."

"What does that mean?"

"It means Eon will then take whatever it wants from us, then close the company down."

Rachel said, "And the VC and Aaron will walk away with Eon stock."

"And you?" Jake asked his brother.

"Zip. If they shut down the company, there's no parachute, there're no equity to sell. Nothing."

"I thought you were worth a million bucks—"

"No. I could've been, if everything went well, which it didn't. But what little stock I have, if all this goes through, is worth nothing."

Jake looked at his beer. "I don't want to open this."

"Open it," Eugene said. "It doesn't matter."

"What're you going to do?"

"Forget about it," he said. "Drink up."

Jake eyed his brother, then pulled back the tab. Rachel said, "Woo-hoo," and held out her glass. Jake filled everyones', and Eugene made a toast: "To a wasted eight and a half years."

Rachel said, "To being unemployed."

Jake shook his head, but smiled. They clinked glasses and drank. Jake checked the champagne label.

"The expensive stuff," Rachel said. "Only the best for us."

Eugene leaned back into the sofa. "I'm getting a little dizzy."

"That's it? Just dizzy? You had most of the bottle," Rachel said.

Jake said, "I didn't know you drank this much."

Eugene groaned. "I shouldn't have mixed it."

"Euge is pretty good with alcohol," Rachel said.

"Not tonight," Eugene said, covering his face.

"Just don't get sick," Jake said.

"What I should do is go to Aaron's house and get sick all over his door."

They laughed. "That'll show him," Rachel said.

"And his car," Eugene said.

"And his dog," Rachel said. "Get sick on his dog."

Eugene laughed harder. Rachel cackled and covered her mouth. Jake stared at them, then said, "Man, you two better slow down."

"Come on," Eugene said. "This is nothing."

Jake kept quiet, and put his glass aside.

"It's not like some people we know," Eugene said, snorting.

"Like who?" Rachel asked. "Oh, you mean your father?"

"Maybe after that second bottle of Southern Comfort he'd get bad," Eugene said. "But that first bottle was okay."

"What about your mother?"

"Nah. She never touched the stuff."

Jake said, "I think I'm going to turn in—"

"Nooo," Rachel and Eugene said together.

Rachel said, "You two are so funny. You never want to talk about her."

"About who?" Eugene said.

"About your mother."

"Nothing to talk about."

"But she left. Isn't that bizarre?"

"What's so bizaare?" Eugene said. "She got sick of getting beaten up and left."

Jake thought, Get me out of here.

"Not a word to anyone?" Rachel asked Jake. "She just disappeared?"

"Not to me," he said.

Rachel turned to Eugene. "What about you?"

Eugene hesitated.

Jake caught this and sat up. "She said something to you?"

Waving this off, Eugene said, "It's nothing. Let's drink to unemployment again."

"No, wait. Did she say something to you?"

He frowned. "Just something about looking out for you."

Jake said, "Wait a minute. You knew she was leaving? She told you she was leaving?"

Rachel raised an eyebrow and said, "Uh-oh. Did I do something?"

"No," Eugene said. "It's nothing. She just said one thing."

"But she must have told you she was leaving then," Jake said.

"Not really. It was the night before. She just said to look out for you."

"How come you never mentioned this?"

"It didn't seem...I don't know."

"So what did she say *exactly.*"

"You don't have to interrogate me—"

"I want to be sure you're not leaving anything out. What did she say? When was this, what time?"

"Does it really matter?" Eugene asked.

Jake nodded.

"It was late," Eugene said. "I got up to go to the bathroom."

"Where was our father?"

"Out."

"Where was she?"

"In the living room."

Jake said, "So what were her exact words? No, you were going to the bathroom. Then what?"

"I saw her in the living room. She saw me. She told me to come over there."

"And?"

"She said I was the oldest one, and I had to look out for you."

"And?"

"And that's it."

"No, what did you say then?"

"I don't remember. I said 'Okay' or something like that. I had to go to the bathroom."

"What was her expression? What did she look like."

Eugene sighed. "We don't have to go through—"

"I want to know."

"I just told you—"

"Tell me more," Jake said, lowering his voice.

Rachel cleared her throat. "Easy, boys."

"Tell me," Jake said.

Eugene nodded. "She had been crying. It was after a huge fight. Her face was messed up It was that night she went to the hospital."

"Hospital?" Rachel asked.

"What else? Did she say where or when or how? What about reaching her? She didn't say anything?"

Eugene shook his head. "She never mentioned anything except taking care of you."

"Why didn't she say anything to me?" Jake asked.

"Maybe she thought you were too young. Maybe it was too hard."

Rachel said, "She probably wasn't planning to tell anyone, but Euge just happened to be there. So, she left that night?"

Eugene nodded. "The next morning she was gone."

Jake tried to absorb this. He stared at his brother, whose cheeks were flushed, his expression glassy. Jake said, "Have you ever tried to find her?"

He said, "Once."

"When?"

"I didn't know this," Rachel said.

Eugene shook his head. "In college. My roommate's uncle was a private detective. I thought I'd try."

"And?"

"Nothing. They never legally divorced, she wasn't dead, and there was absolutely no paper trail. She might have gone back to Korea."

"Hell," Jake said. "How come you never told me?"

"What's the point? It didn't work."

"Why didn't she say anything to me?"

"You were too young."

Rachel asked Eugene, "Have you ever thought of trying again?"

"Sometimes."

"Really?" Jake said.

Eugene sighed. "I don't know. Sometimes I feel like I need to learn more."

"Well, this doesn't change anything," Jake said. "She left us hanging."

Eugene didn't reply.

"You just don't do that," Jake said. "Leave us alone with him. What the hell was she thinking? Pretty damn cold."

Eugene looked down at his empty glass.

"Whatever." Jake stood up. "I'm going to get some dinner. You guys want anything?"

"It's kind of late," Rachel said. "We have some Chinese in the fridge."

"I'll find something." He left the apartment and heard Rachel murmur to Eugene as he shut the door. Jake wanted to lose this restless feeling, and watching his brother get drunk wasn't going to do it. He took the stairs down, his thighs weak from the earlier workout. He liked the faint pain. His footsteps echoed around him.

31

Bobby Null realized the sour smell was coming from the mound of diapers that wasn't in any bags, and he began cursing people who didn't bag and tie their garbage. He was knee deep in shit, and kept muttering, "Goddamn fucking Jake." He was in the second dumpster; he didn't find anything of Jake's in the first one, but judging from the newspapers and the smell of the garbage, the first dumpster was more recent. This second one was disgusting and putrid, and he gagged as he lifted bags that crumbled apart—unrecognizable, disintegrating chunks of moldy, slimy food fell everywhere. He imagined worms and slithering things moving near his feet. He climbed out every few minutes to make sure nothing was crawling up his legs.

When he found a clump of Safeway bags at the bottom, he opened one up and saw ripped up papers and receipts. The other bags had clothing, magazines, newspapers, and piles of junk mail. Bobby took the bag of receipts and scrambled out of the dumpster. Ignoring the black liquid all over the bag, he tore it open and emptied the contents onto the ground. More junk mail. But Bobby saw the name Jacob Ahn on a label, and he went through the pile more carefully. Jake was trying to tear up all this, but didn't have time to do a complete job. The junk mail had his name and address, and he had even left a bank statement only partially torn in half. Four thousand in a checking account. Then, Bobby found a pay stub, a half of a paycheck receipt, with Jake's name, social security number, and a list of taxes withheld. At the top was "Molino Restaurant" with an address and phone number. He saved this and continued searching through the papers. Nothing personal in here.

"Hey! What the hell are you doing?" someone called to him.

Bobby looked up. It was the same guy he had seen here a few hours ago. Jeez, was he here for that long? "I lost something," Bobby said.

"I hope you're going to clean that shit up."

"Who the fuck are you?"

"I live here. You're making a goddamn mess."

Bobby stood up slowly, taking the guy in. He said, "I'll clean it up. Keep your pants on."

The man walked away, and Bobby re-read the pay stub. All right. Jake worked here. There must be someone there who'd know where to find him. Bobby looked down at his sneakers—brown mush was oozing around the shoelaces. First he had to clean himself up. Then he'd visit this restaurant. He was getting closer.

He left the garbage as it was, torn and dripping bags on the ground. He was staying in a cheap motel in Pioneer Square, paying weekly, and wondered when the hell he was going to get out of this place. The smell of baby shit followed him down the street.

32

Jake had left the apartment and had gone straight to a small dive on Van Ness. He ordered a beer, though he had no desire to drink, and sat at the bar. He ate some peanuts. He listened to the conversations around him. He tried to think about Franklin & Sons Jewelry, but his brother's revelation bothered him.

The images of his mother's departure that had formed and hardened in Jake's mind were ones of ghostly disappearances, magical acts of invisibility. A blink and his mother was gone. Smoke swirled up where she had once stood. He had imagined her walking out of the house as a zombie, stiff-legged, shuffling, arms rigid and extended, her body slowly blending into the night. She had taken very little of her clothes and belongings—so little that his father hadn't realized she had run off until that evening. And even then he had seemed certain that she would return.

Eugene's revelation required a shift in Jake's memory. He couldn't even recall what she looked like. His father had destroyed all the photos of her shortly after her desertion. He had raged all night, burning her clothes, breaking—tearing apart, really—anything of hers she had left behind. Jake and his brother were in the basement when this was happening, the thumps and crashes upstairs confusing them, since their mother wasn't the target.

As Jake grew older he entertained more possibilities of what had happened to his mother: his father had murdered and buried her; she had been kidnapped; she had amnesia; she committed suicide. But with all these scenarios, she, in his mind, was shell-shocked, mute, blank. Definitely not aware or fully conscious of her decisions.

So he had been wrong. It caught him off guard. His mother really had abandoned them, leaving them exposed to their father; she really hadn't wanted to take them with her. It was a calculated act, a mathematical equation of options, and in the end Eugene and Jake simply didn't have a high enough value. Maybe she was living right now with a new family. New sons.

Sometimes his mother used to hide in his and Eugene's room when their father started drinking. Jake remembered Eugene holding a pair of homemade nunchucks by his pillow as they went to sleep, as if he would actually use them on their father. But if their father came storming in, the brothers would get sent to the basement, and Eugene would leave his nunchucks under his pillow.

Jeez. Nunchucks. He hadn't thought of that in years. His brother used to be really into kung-fu. Not tae kwon do, which is Korean karate and which his brother probably avoided because their father knew it, but kung-fu, the Chinese art form. Eugene practiced in the back yard and would sometimes show off for their mother. This is the Crane style, he would tell her, and do some sweeping, arching movements that actually did remind Jake of a crane. Their mother would clap lightly with her fingers, and say, Very good.

Once when they were in the basement, naked, the fighting going on upstairs, it was so cold that Jake couldn't stop shivering. Their parents were screaming at each other in the kitchen, right next to the basement door, and Eugene backed down the steps as the fight grew closer. Their mother was trying to get to the door, it seemed, and their father was pushing her away. A few times someone would crash against the door, and their mother would scream out in pain. Jake stayed crouched near the furnace. He heard the familiar spitting Korean curses filtering through. He didn't know what *shang* meant, but knew it only came up during the fights.

Then he heard his brother near the middle of the room, breathing hard, with the sounds of his bare feet sliding over the cement. In the darkness, Jake could only make out shadowy images of his brother moving across the floor. Jake saw the goblins creeping along the wall suddenly stop and watch his brother as well.

What're you doing? Jake whispered.

Dragon meets Tiger, his brother said in a normal voice, which sounded too loud. The goblins scurried away.

Upstairs, their mother was crying, begging, and a few loud slaps silenced her.

Eugene exhaled slowly; the sound of his steady breath calmed the goblins. His feet stepped, skipped, then brushed against the ground. Jake heard the air around his brother whoosh. It was too cold to move, so Jake remained crouched, hugging his knees.

For an instant he saw through the darkness. His brother was balanced on one leg, his arms stretched out and sweeping around him in graceful circles. He then lowered himself, still on one leg, his hands becoming claws, his extended leg transforming into a sweeping tail. Before blinking back into complete darkness, his brother arched his back and strained his head towards the ceiling, opening his mouth and baring his teeth as if to breathe fire.

33

Jake found Rachel dozing off in front of the TV. The champagne bottle stood next to four crumpled beer cans, an open bag of potato chips, crumbs and wet spots on the coffee table. Rachel stirred and sat up. "Hello," she said, rubbing her eyes.

"Where's Eugene?"

"Sleeping it off."

"You're okay?"

"Waiting up for you."

This stopped him. "For me?"

"You seemed upset."

"No. I'm fine." He glanced at the TV. Business news with the closed captioning on. He watched the words jerk across the screen.

"Are you angry?"

"No."

"I checked the newspapers for more articles," she said, pointing to her laptop. "There wasn't anything."

He thought, Articles? Then he realized she was talking about Seattle. "You don't have to do that."

"Don't worry. I'm not going to say anything—"

"I know."

He sat down in the recliner; everything smelled of stale beer. "How is Eugene holding up?"

"He needed to blow off steam," she said.

"Does he always drink like this?"

"Lately, more."

"Why?"

"He might seriously lose his job." She made a circling motion with her hand. "His ordered life is screwed up."

"He can always get another job."

She nodded. "True, but from what I understand, the CEO has been badmouthing him and his supervisor, who's a board member, to make the selling-out look more justified."

"Badmouthing?"

"Quietly, of course, but his reputation might be tainted. He's not sure."

"Sounds like a nice business to be in."

She shrugged.

Jake had nothing else to say, so he moved towards his bedroom. She stopped him with: "Can I ask you something?"

He sat back down. "Okay."

"How did you start doing it? I mean, what happened?"

"Doing what?"

"You know, burglarizing places."

He smiled.

"Tell me about the first time."

"The first time?"

"Did you just decide to do it?"

Jake leaned back, sighed. Rachel was still a little drunk, and it was loosening her up. He said, "The first time, I think I was stoned and broke, and had just lost a job. I walked by a house and decided to break in."

"Just like that?"

"Just like that. It was stupid, and I'm amazed I wasn't caught, but it suddenly seemed like a new career path."

"How old were you?"

"Around nineteen, twenty. I was living in L.A."

"Where was Euge?"

"Working, I think. When he was still with that telephone company."

"And you were never caught?"

"No. But if I had continued using the same method, I would've been caught. Most break-ins are druggies looking for a quick sell for cash. I got smarter."

"How?" She leaned forward, her forehead creased.

Jake sat back. "You don't want to hear this."

"I do."

"Why?"

She said, "I don't know."

He thought about this, and said, "It started with lockpicking."

She waited.

"There was this guy at the department store I was working in. He was a locksmith apprentice before getting fired. He taught me how to pick locks." His name was Michael, and they used to smoke outside on their breaks. Michael was only a few years older than Jake, but had already spent a couple years in juvie and a year in Folsom for drug possession and burglary. Before Michael was fired from the locksmith's, he had learned the basics of raking, snapping, and picking, and after a few months of working together in the stockrooms, he showed Jake.

The idea was simple: picking locks was the act of imitating a key. Practicing was difficult. Jake's first tools were a bent screwdriver and a heavy-duty paper clip. The clip was straightened with a curved tip at one end, and wrapped with electrician's tape as a small handle on the other. The screwdriver was his tension wrench, which was heavier and bulkier than actual tension wrenches locksmiths used; he had to be gentler, and use more of a twisting than a pushing motion. Following Michael's advice, Jake had practiced on his own locks, studying his keys as a guide on how high to push the pins inside, but even with this learning aid, he had struggled with the locks for almost four months before he began to get a feel for the technique. That had been the hardest part. He conditioned his hands by tying knots with sewing thread, by touching his radio and turning the volume down lower and lower until he could feel more than he could hear. He disassembled and reassembled old locks, taking out springs and loosening shear lines to make his practice picking easier. Later he would learn that his crude tools had hampered his picking, making the fragile process more difficult. He hadn't minded because when he made himself his first set of real picks (from grinding down hacksaw blades to the right size and shape), opening locks became startlingly easy.

Once Jake had learned how to pick pin-tumbler locks, he began concentrating on other kinds: wafer tumblers, double wafers, the easier warded and lever locks, and finally the more complicated tubular-cylinder locks. He hadn't actually picked any locks for his burglaries at that point, since he hadn't been confident enough. He had only just begun his attempts at small burglaries. Here, Michael helped him out again, introducing him to his fence, and showing Jake what items to steal. But Michael wasn't very careful and he was eventually caught breaking into an expensive home in Newport Beach. He spent two years in prison and Jake never saw him again.

"I liked how it became a puzzle: find the best way into a house, usually through a lock," he told Rachel. "It wasn't just about breaking in. It was about breaking in cleanly."

Rachel smiled. "I don't think I've ever heard you say this much about anything."

He was startled, and shut up. She was right. He had kept quiet about this for so long that it had come out too suddenly, unrestrained. He wondered if the two beers at the bar had lowered his guard. He said, "I should get some rest. I'm beat."

"What are you going to do with the jewels you have now?"

"Why?"

"I want to know."

"Hold on to most of it. Sell some slowly."

"Where?"

He shook his head. "Here and there." He needed to get her off this.

He asked, "So I guess you and Eugene are okay?"

She hesitated. "Why do you say that?"

"You just got drunk with him."

"But that means nothing."

"Oh."

"We were commiserating. That's not a good foundation for a marriage, but that's all we seem to do."

"So what's going to happen to you two?"

Her face slackened.

He said, "Never mind. It's none of my business."

She looked up at him. "Honestly? I have no idea what's going to happen."

Jake stood up and said he was going to get ready for bed. She nodded and tried to pull herself out of the sofa, but fell back. She touched her temple and winced. Jake held out his hand, which she took, and pulled her up. He didn't let go, and said, "I hope you don't mention any of what I said—"

"No. I won't."

He moved closer to her, said quietly, "You know more about me than anyone else in the world."

Her eyelids fluttered as she tried to focus on him. They were inches apart. He let go of her hand, and he remembered massaging her leg at the gym, how he was tempted to move further up her thighs. He wanted to touch her now, reach out and run his finger over her cheek, her throat. He moved away. "Goodnight, Rachel," he said, and went to the guest room.

34

Late, late night. Jake moving in and out of sleep. His back and arms sore from working out, his stomach acidic from the beer. Blinking awake at sounds from the living room. Rachel still awake. Reading her books? A dim line of light underneath his door. Rolling over and feeling his erection ache. Thinking, She is right out there. Right out there and all he has to do is go out and walk up to her and touch her like at the gym, massaging her leg and moving slowly up until he'd push his hand underneath her shorts. Stop. Not an idiot and knows what's wrong and why. Knows his brother is in the room down the hall and that even thinking this is wrong. Knows that. Knows it and tells himself and repeats it in his sleep. Sitting up and stretching, everything hurting. Bed creaking. Strange shadows on the ceiling from the light outside. Night eyes adjusted and sharp. Remembering his night eyes as a kid, looking out in the dark basement and seeing, really seeing everything. Superhero powers. Night boy. See everything in the dark. Darkness his friend. Shrouded, protected. Swimming through blackness. Watching the ghosts move across the floor, ignoring him and his brother, but stopping when they saw him seeing. He saw them all. The goblins passing through his basement while their father kicked their mother across the floor, their ceiling, and everyone pretending they heard nothing and Eugene practicing kung-fu naked. His mother knew. Knew she was leaving, knew she was abandoning her kids and said nothing to him, didn't even say good night if he remembered but wasn't sure. Shouldn't let it bother him. Take care of your brother, she said to Eugene. Yeah. Right. Take care of yourself and run off in the middle of the night. Stop. Stop. Doesn't matter. Nothing matters. Think of the dead. Bobby dead and buried under tons of garbage, sea gulls poking out his eyes and pulling on his tongue. Bobby going to haunt him. Should call Chih. Find out what to do, maybe save some of the stuff for him, find out what happened. Got to find a new place, new gig, miss the restaurant but don't want to do that right now. Loaded. Am loaded with cash and rocks and don't have to work, but can't just sit around and do nothing, what about that Franklin place? Whoa. Stop. But that padlock's a fucking joke. Got to check out the alarm system. Stop it, shithead. Eugene was a millionaire. Goddamn million dollars. What to do with a million dollars? No idea. Buy a house, buy a car. Then what? Get a nice TV. Satellite TV. Buy books. Catch up. Then what? What a sorry piece of crap can't you think of anything? Help Eugene. Help Rachel. Rachel. What's the point? The point is to survive. She knows too much. He blabbed like a fucking school kid. Just like in high school and got nailed for it. Mistake, mistake, mistake. Hell with it. Going to have to trust—

Creak, creak.

Outside the door. Rachel walking quietly towards the door. Stopping. Two feet in the line of light. Waiting, listening. Was he making noise? Stop. Quiet. Touching the door? Shit. Coming in? Shit. No. Stopping and listening. Listening for what? Listening for him. Come in. Come in right now. I'm waiting for you. Come in right now. Come in. Open the door. Walk in. Come to the bed. Sit down. Put your hand on me. Rest. Touch. Lean in.

Line of light brighter. Feet gone. Creak, creak. Sounds of settling in the sofa. TV on, then off. Light off, then on, then off. Shhhh. Quiet. So close.

35

There were no problems selling the jewelry. Jake was surprised by how fast the consigned pieces went at Pacific Gems. He had called ahead and learned that everything, even the cheap bracelet and the diamond ring, had sold. He had four hundred and thirteen dollars waiting for him, and Tom, the man in charge of buying and consigning, had told Jake to bring more rings, if he had any.

Jake had plenty. He decided to bring one important piece to be appraised. It was a round brilliant cut diamond set in platinum, maybe three carats, with two quarter carat bagette diamonds on either side. He had missed it earlier because it was untagged and unwrapped, thrown in with what looked like a cubic zirconium ring, but as he spent more time in the safe deposit examination room, sorting and categorizing, he realized this wasn't a cheap imitation. The cut was near perfect as far as Jake could tell, the table facet and crown height looked to the naked eye beautifully proportioned. He needed an appraiser to check the actual proportions as well as the crown angles, but he suspected this was a GIA-certified Class One diamond. If that was the case, he was looking at twenty grand easy. But it worried him that the ring was so carelessly mixed with the cheap stuff. Maybe he was mistaken. Maybe he was reading it wrong. He needed a second opinion, but had to be careful. This was the kind of ring that was listed in stolen jewelry alerts.

He'd also bring the tiffany-setting, one-carat ring, the eternity ring, and a couple of the cheap engagement rings. He wouldn't sell or consign them all; he wanted a better sense of value. This job was larger than he had thought—maybe that newspaper article was accurate about the value of the take—and as he left the bank and walked towards Pacific Heights, he thought about the Korean family he had taken this from. He had cleaned them out, and even with insurance they were in serious trouble—jacked up premiums, bad publicity, coming up with new inventory. Chih had a friend who had been robbed, and the insurance red tape had gone on for years. By the time the friend had received a check—and it wasn't even for replacement value—he had gone out of business.

Jake stopped walking. He was one block from the jewelry store and looked around. He had the feeling of being noticed. Cars drove by, cutting each other off as they raced through yellow lights. Pedestrians across the street waited at the corner for the Walk sign. Jake scanned the area. Maybe someone had seen him a few days ago heading to the jewelry store, and noticed him again. It was possible. He never ignored his instincts. Jake had learned that a feeling—even a fleeting one—of something amiss was usually grounded on a perception not fully registered, a glimpse of a familiar figure, even a sound of a voice or a cough that barely reached his ears.

The rings in his pockets were sending out signals. They were singing an aria of money, and Jake was an easy, unarmed target. He should be wearing a "Rob Me" sign. The paranoid get no rest.

He turned a corner and headed in the opposite direction. No need to see the jeweler right now. He'd go for a nice long walk. He saw movement in the shadows, and thought, Zombies wait and watch.

36

Bobby took a bus to Capitol Hill and walked along Broadway, searching for Molino Restaurant. Everything seemed cleaner here compared to his dumpy hotel in Pioneer Square, and he did a double-take when he saw two men holding hands. He thought, A homo neighborhood? Then it made sense: if Jake was hiding out, here would be a good place.

Bobby found the restaurant, part of a small brick building, and stopped at the front window. It was open for lunch, most of the tables filled, and he was getting hungry. Rather than go in and possibly expose himself to Jake, Bobby decided to locate the rear entrance. He walked around the building until he saw parking spaces with the sign "Molino Restaurant and Capitol Video Employees Only!" He walked into the restaurant and found himself in a hallway next to a small locker room. A man was putting on a waiter's uniform. Bobby said, "Hey, is Jake working today?"

The man, a young guy about Bobby's age, with silver glasses, said, "I don't know. I haven't seen him in a while."

Bobby thanked him and continued down the hall until he came into the kitchen, white-aproned cooks at the stove and counters, a row of different pasta and meat dishes heating under red lamps. A few people hurrying by glanced at Bobby, but didn't say anything. He kept alert, expecting to see Jake any moment. A waitress ran in and said, "The specials are popular. Get ready for more."

A cook at the stove raised his spatula.

Bobby didn't see Jake and asked one of the chefs adding whipped cream to a dessert, "Is Jake here?"

"No, that flake hasn't shown up in days. Where the hell is he?"

"I don't know," Bobby said. "Where's the manager?"

"He's helping in front. The guy in the suit."

Bobby left the kitchen and walked out into the dining area. He saw the man in the suit on the phone and writing in a reservation book at the front counter. Bobby waited until the man hung up. Bobby approached and said, "I'm looking for Jake."

The man answered. "You and me both. That guy left us shorthanded."

"He hasn't been in at all?"

"No, not since last week. He's not answering his phone either. Who are you?"

"He owes me money."

"Can't help you. If you do find him, let him know he's in trouble."

"Did he have any friends here? Someone I can ask about where he might've gone?"

"Don't think so. He was a quiet guy."

"What did he do here?"

"Cold side chef—"

"He was a chef?"

The man shrugged. "Cold side is different. He just put together pastas."

Bobby said, "Do the other chefs know him?"

"Why don't you ask them?"

So Bobby did, but none of the chefs knew much. He realized that Jake had been very careful, and for the first time since all this had happened, Bobby wondered if he might not find him. Then it occurred to him that Ron might not get his money. Bobby could never return to L.A. Everything was fucked. His abdomen flared, the pain pulling down into his butt. He cursed quietly.

He saw a waitress going out the back for a smoking break and he followed her. He asked her if she knew Jake.

"I saw him around. He did long night shifts."

"He didn't have any friends here?"

"Not really."

"He didn't talk to anyone?"

She shrugged. "I think he had a brief thing with Arlene, but that was a while ago."

"Who's Arlene?"

"Another waitress."

"Is she here?"

"Uh-uh. She'll be in tonight, though."

"What does she look like?"

"Short, thin. Long dirty blonde. Kind of mousy."

"You got another cigarette?"

"Yeah, sure." She tapped one out of the pack and handed it to him. She stopped and pointed to his stomach. "You're bleeding."

He looked down. Spots of blood were seeping into his shirt. "Shit," he said.

"What's wrong?"

"Nothing," he said, walking towards the street. "Thanks for the smoke."

"You want me to tell Arlene?"

"I'll come by tonight," he said.

Bobby hurried down the street, trying to fan his shirt to keep the blood off it. He ran into a Starbucks and pulled out a wad of paper napkins from the dispenser, and blotted the stitches. The pain worsened. He grimaced and limped out onto the street, ignoring the stares of the customers. Arlene, he thought. Mousy Arlene.

37

"Branded" diamonds are labelled and advertised as such in order to guarantee a specified proportional cut, insuring that the diamond you buy is of the highest quality. This was new to Jake. As Tom, the buyer at Pacific Gems, analyzed the four-carat diamond ring Jake had brought in, drawing a diagram that showed the Eppler proportions of a 56% table width, a 57.7% crown height, and the bezel area at 14.4%, Jake realized that he hadn't been keeping up with new developments in diamonds. He asked, "So is this a Class One?"

"It falls within Class One specs, but it's also 'branded' as an Eppler cut, and is worth even more."

"When did people start doing this branding business?"

"A few years now."

"The body color looks great," Jake said. "Is it 'E' or 'F'?"

"I'd say maybe even 'D'. The clarity is VVS2. I can have another guy confirm all this, but this is a really good diamond. I'm not even talking about the baguette diamonds on the sides."

"How much?"

"You want to sell it?"

Jake shook his head. "Not now."

"We can do a professional appraisal, have it documented. You should get this insured."

"Give me a ballpark figure."

"The entire ring? At least thirty-five thousand."

Jake let out a slow breath. "You'd give me thirty-five grand for that?"

"No. I'd give you twenty-five maybe, but I'd want to see proof of ownership, documentation, everything."

Taking the ring and staring at it, Jake shook his head. "I don't want to sell it. It was my mother's favorite ring, but now I know why."

"It looks new."

"She had it redone, added the baguettes. The big one came from another ring."

"What about these?" Tom said, waving to the other rings Jake had shown him.

"Which do you want to buy, which would do better consigned?"

"Sell me the tiffany and the eternity. Consign those cheap ones."

"How much?"

"Three thousand for the tiffany, fifteen hundred for the eternity."

"What would you price the others?"

"Those two," he said, pointing to the gold engagement rings with quarter carat diamonds, "might go for a couple hundred each. The others are lousy. I couldn't charge more than sixty or seventy for them."

"All right. I'll sell you the eternity, consign the cheap ones, but hold onto the tiffany and my mom's favorite ring."

"You sure? I like the tiffany. I might offer you more if I can get a second opinion on the diamond."

Jake shook his head. "Not yet. I'm in no hurry."

"Let me draw up the paperwork. Be right back." He went into the back room, and Jake pocketed the two rings he wanted to save. Thirty-five thousand dollars for one ring. His take for this job just doubled with this one ring.

He examined again the security: infrared motion detectors, two small video cameras, a wireless link with a private patrol company, but this time he moved behind the counter and saw what looked like a huge one-ton safe with an escutcheon plate as large as the door itself in the back. There was also security grilling along the back room, probably pulled down at closing.

After signing the paperwork and receiving two checks, one for the previously consigned jewelry and one for the eternity ring, he headed to a check-cashing store, where he would use one of his fake driver's licenses and social security card. The jewelers knew him as a "William Han," his ID courtesy of Chih. He was making good progress and wondered why he had never done this before. Time had been a factor. It was also easy with Chih offering to buy everything. The low-balling and the 10% cut must have made Chih's percentage more than Jake's each time. No wonder Chih was always eager to get Jake involved.

Then it happened again: the feeling of being noticed. He stopped and turned around: a man in a business suit hurrying across the street; a teenaged couple holding hands; an elderly Asian woman with a shopping bag; another man in a jacket and tie; cars driving by. Jake sat down on the steps of an apartment building and waited. More pedestrians walked up and down the street. Jake didn't see anything out of the ordinary. No one stopped or dawdled. Jake remained sitting for another fifteen minutes. He decided not to return to this store for a while.

He stepped into a doorway, took out the branded diamond ring, and held it close to his eye, letting the sparkles fleck his vision. Rainbow colors flashed around him, then disappeared. This was life viewed through thirty-five grand, through his "mother's" ring.

His mother had only one diamond ring that Jake knew of. It had been stolen off her finger when she had been rushed to the hospital. Before that, though, he remembered feeling the cool metal on his cheek once, when she told him to sleep. He had been very young. She touched his cheek with her palm, and said, Please sleep. He hadn't thought of that in over twenty years. He pocketed his ring and wandered down the street.

After a half hour of walking, he stopped, confused. He was standing in front of Franklin & Sons Jewelry. He had intended to return the two rings to his safe deposit box, but instead found himself in a different neighborhood, walking into this store, doing a quick scan of the interior. There were wall displays, glass cases with angled felt mountings, small lamps shining down onto the gleaming gems. One long display counter in a U shape filled the room, and Jake saw the alarm control unit, an old one, that was deactivited with a key. This wasn't a combination coded alarm, and he traced the wires to the door—a simple magnetic break sensor—and the windows.

"Can I help you?" a large, beefy man asked as he entered from the back room. His puffy cheeks were ruddy, his forehead shiny.

"Just looking around," Jake said.

"For anything in particular?" The man folded his arms and stood in the doorway. He looked Jake up and down. "We have some nice men's rings that came in last week."

"Oh, yeah? Let's see them."

The man pointed to the end of the counter, and began taking out two displays. Jake saw immediately that they were cheap machine-manufactured rings, the gems glued on without any prongs, tiny burrs on the one he examined. The price, $85.00, was about triple what it was actually worth. Jake smiled.

"What's the matter?" the man asked.

"A little overpriced, don't you think?"

"No. That's fourteen k gold and a good sapphire."

"Man-made sapphire?"

"No," he answered quickly.

Jake suspected he was lying. He said, "The gold spot price is pretty low these days."

The man frowned. "This isn't a negotiation. That's the price. Take it or leave it."

"Then I'll leave it. Let's see your diamond engagement rings."

The man put away the displays and said, "You going to buy something?"

"Depends."

"You're going to waste my time?"

"Depends on the rings."

The man looked him over again, and said, "They'll probably be out of your range. I mean, if that sapphire was too much for you—"

"Are you joking?" Jake looked down at his jeans, his scuffed shoes. He was wearing an Oxford shirt, and thought he looked fine. "I want to see the engagement rings. Are you going to show them to me or not?"

"They're right there," the man said, pointing to the other end of the counter. "Look for yourself."

"What's your name," Jake asked.

"Why?"

"Are you Franklin or one of the sons?"

"Neither. There is no Franklin and sons."

"Are you the owner?"

"I am."

"Are you an asshole to all your customers?"

"Just the cheap ones."

Jake smiled, shook his head, and walked out the door. He heard the man mutter, "Cheap bastard."

Jake stopped. He was tempted to go back in, and almost turned around. But instead, he swallowed this and continued. Jake patted the rings in his pocket and told himself to keep cool.

38

On the way to the check-cashing store, he felt it again. This time he was worried. He began looping around the block, unsure if he was becoming paranoid, and kept stopping to look around. Nothing registered. Nothing, that is, until he began searching the cars driving by, and he noticed a black car a block down that had pulled to the corner, parking illegally. He thought it might be the police, but then, after a moment, recognized the car: it was Eugene's. He cut across the street, and saw Rachel in the driver's seat. She sunk lower when their eyes met. He knocked on the passenger side window, and she unlocked the door. He climbed in.

"Damn," she said.

"What's going on?"

"How'd you know?"

He turned to her. "Have you been following me all day?"

"Yes. How did you know?"

"I felt it. I sensed it."

"Sensed it? Like Spiderman?"

He shook his head. "I wish. No, just paranoia."

She put the car in gear and merged with traffic. "Where to?"

He was about to tell her, but didn't want to show her any more of his activities. "The apartment."

"Already?"

He nodded, then asked "Why are you doing this?"

"I'm not doing anything."

"You were following me all morning."

"When did you know?"

"On my way to Pacific Gems."

"I was running errands in the neighborhood and happened to see you walking. I decided to check what you were doing."

"Why didn't Eugene take the car?"

"I don't know. He said he didn't need it."

"He's at work?"

"Of course."

"What's happening with that?"

She shook her head, keeping her eyes on the street. There was something about her expression—defeat—that prompted Jake to ask, "Is it ending?"

She glanced at him. "Is what ending?"

"Your marriage."

Quiet for what seemed like a full minute, she eventually said, "I think we're giving up."

"What about last night?"

"What about it?"

"You two got along."

She smiled sadly. "There's more to marriage than getting along."

Her patronizing tone bothered him. "What about a counselor?" he asked.

"I told you we tried."

"How come you guys never had kids?" he asked, then remembered too late her books on infertility. He added, "I guess it's a good thing. Kids would complicate it."

"No. We wanted children. I can't seem to have them."

He kept silent.

There seemed to be a traffic jam ahead, and she let out an annoyed breath. She said, "So what were you doing? Selling jewelry?"

"Something like that."

"How do you choose which place to burglarize?" she asked.

This startled him, and he said, "What?"

She repeated her question.

"What do you mean?"

"Do you just choose a house? Do you do some kind of lookout?"

Jake said, "It depends."

She waited, and when he didn't continue, she asked, "On what?"

"On the situation."

She said, "Look, it's not a big deal. I'm just curious. It's not brain surgery."

He was stung by this, and knew his questions about her marriage had annoyed her. He said, "When I first started with a partner, it was systematic. We'd drive around in a nice neighborhood at night, and looked for any signs of an empty house." He explained the checklist: No cars, no lights. Piled newspapers, mail, or restaurant leaflets. Michael had already done this at least a half dozen times, and talked Jake through it. Was it worth the job? If there was a car, was it nice? Any clues to what might be inside?

"Then what?"

"Michael knocked on the door with some magazines in his hand." If someone was home, he would try to sell them magazine subscriptions. But since the lights were off, and there was no movement, they guessed there was no one there. Then: a visual check of the windows for alarms. Were there any alarm control boxes, switches, stickers? Just to make certain, they knocked on the back door, the windows, ready to run. They were looking for people, dogs, anything.

"It was methodical," Jake said. "We chose an emergency escape route before anything else. If someone showed up, if the cops appeared, we'd have a way out. Then we went in." Michael's favorite entry had been the sliding patio doors. Most nice houses had them. And many homeowners didn't lock them, or if they did, it was with a tiny hook in the handle. A joke. A crowbar could yank it open. Sometimes he would use a screwdriver, and pry the entire door off its track.

Rachel said, "What about alarms?"

Jake nodded. "This guy Michael got me scared of alarms. At the very first house we hit, as soon as we got in, he picked up the telephone and listened. I asked him why. He was checking for an alarm signal going out."

"A signal?"

"A hidden alarm automatically calls the police or alarm company. But at that house there was nothing." Michael left the phone off the hook. It was simple. They went through the closets, the drawers, looking for jewelry and cash. Maybe a few small electronic items, but nothing big. They were in and out within twenty minutes. They had jewelry, some cash, a notebook computer, and Michael had found a little coke. A small bonus.

"You don't do drugs, do you?" Rachel asked.

"No."

Jake's take for those twenty minutes, after fencing the jewels and the computer, was two thousand. Not bad for a night's work. The next day, they were back at the department store, unloading and unpacking crates.

Jake told Rachel how he had soon developed his own methods. He would watch a place for a few days, and would target it only if he knew there was something worth taking. He'd carry a police scanner and try not to leave any evidence of his theft. Michael could pick locks, but didn't have the patience on the job. Jake never understood that; he had taken the time to teach Jake, but rarely used this skill himself.

Rachel listened, and when Jake finished, she said, "I always imagined it to be more haphazard."

"It usually is."

"Doesn't it bother you that you take all these things people saved for?"

"A little."

"But it's every man for himself, I guess."

"Something like that."

"Is that your outlook? You watch out for number one?"

Jake heard her biting tone, and said, "Who else would I watch out for?"

"It seems kind of selfish."

He felt the jab, and turned to her, wondering if she was trying to start a fight. He said, "My life would suck if I didn't try to make myself happy. You do whatever it takes, that's *my* philosophy."

"No matter what the consequences are."

He found himself unable to get angry at her tone; she couldn't rile him. He smiled and said, "There you go."

"No responsibility."

"None at all."

A sports car was trying to cut in front of her on the left, and she accelerated to keep it away. The sports car then sped up as well, zipping by her but she wouldn't let it in. "Goddamn him," she said. She swerved around the car and kept ahead of it. The car honked. Jake gripped the door handle, surprised by her driving. "Uh," he started to say.

Rachel had accelerated too quickly, and the cars ahead had stopped for a red light. She was approaching too fast, and Jake said, "Slow down."

She slammed on the brakes, and the sports car thumped into the rear corner of her car, the crunch throwing them back. There was an explosion of white and dust, and his face was slapped, his body pushed back. He realized then it was the airbag, and his neck hurt. For a confusing moment he heard honks, a few screeches. A man was cursing and yelling as he came towards Rachel's side.

Jake managed to push away the air bag, coughing out some of the white dust, and asked if Rachel was all right. She turned to him, her face streaking with tears, and she nodded slowly.

He jumped towards her. "Are you hurt? What's wrong?"

"I'm okay," she said, shaking her head. "Nothing hurt."

"Why're you crying?"

She wiped her face. "I don't know." She stared at him, her forehead creased, her eyes locked on his. White dust sprinkled through her hair and eyebrows, turning them grey. She said quietly, "I think... I'm sinking."

39

Jake drove Bobby Null and the stolen jewelry out of the cul-de-sac, away from Chun's house, and sped down 45th. He soon turned onto Roosevelt, working their way towards the area near the University Bridge. A few marinas and boat repair shops lined the streets along Portage Bay, and Jake had chosen this spot to split their take because it was quiet during the weekends. The fact that he lived nearby was a factor too. Once they abandoned the car, Jake knew they would be exposed on foot, and wanted to be able to stash the jewels quickly.

"Why the hell did you hit him?" Jake asked. "You could've just said you'd wait for the son, and the guy would leave."

"Fuck that. He was getting a good look at me and he was talking too much."

Jake saw out of the corner of his eye that Bobby still had the gun in his hand. He thought of everything that was going wrong: the man had seen Bobby, and probably had gotten a quick look at Jake. Maybe some neighbors had seen the car out in front. Although they were both still wearing gloves, Jake knew they were leaving all kinds of forensic evidence behind—hair, clothing, dirt on their shoes—and the identification with the car would be a problem.

"Did you get it? What's in it?" Bobby asked.

"I haven't opened it yet."

"What? How do you know anything's in it?"

"I know."

"Let me see. I'll open it now."

"It's locked."

"So, I'll break it."

"Not now. What if I get in an accident? What if we get pulled over?"

"Shit. Hurry up, then."

"Why'd you bring a gun?"

"Insurance."

Jake was fucked. He thought of ways out of this, maybe driving straight to Chih's, but the change in plan would make Bobby suspicious. He said, "What if we go to Chih's right now?"

"What? Fuck no. I want see what we got before telling him."

"Whoa. He's getting his share—"

"I didn't say he wasn't."

"Then why not go straight to him?"

"Because that wasn't the plan. We got to dump the car."

"I'm still setting aside Chih's share."

"Let's see what's in the fucking thing first."

Jake drove along the one-way side streets and eventually parked across the street from a parking lot on Northlake. The lot was hidden behind some trees and well off the road, and adjacent to the lot was a large building with a loading dock and a garage. There was never activity here on weekends. Jake wasn't sure what kind of business it was, but had noticed it a few times as he passed it on his way to one of the bus stops along Boat Street. He parked the car and unhooked the wires underneath the dash—Bobby's handiwork—then climbed out with the strongbox.

As they walked across the street and into the lot, Jake saw Bobby shoving the gun into the back of his pants. They headed behind the dumpster. They knelt down, and Jake inspected the lock. He recognized the "V" keyway immediately: a Schlage wafer-tumbler. He pulled out his picks, and Bobby said, "What the hell? Just break it."

"No. This is faster." Jake inserted his tension wrench, then used his lifter pick, counting to the eighth wafer, retracting it, then pressing the wrench a little more to keep the wafer in place. He went through the other wafers easily, since they require less play, and he turned the wrench smoothly, unlocking it. He opened the strongbox, and immediately saw the wad of cash held together with a rubberband.

"Oh, baby," Bobby said.

Jake put aside the cash, and then saw the jewels—some in small plastic bags, others lying there in a black felt container. "There's a lot," he said. "Chih will want to buy all of this."

"How much cash?"

"These are hundreds."

"Fucking A."

"All right. We can split the cash, leaving 10% for Chih, right now. If you want we can try to split most of the jewelry."

Bobby nodded, and pulled out his gun. "All right. I'll take it all."

Jake sighed. "You're so goddamn predictable, it's sad."

"You carrying? Get away from the box."

Jake shook his head and tried to appear calm, but his mind was racing. "I don't think so."

"I'm not fucking around. Get away from it."

"Why'd you think I chose this spot?" Jake said. "You don't think I have a partner here, waiting?"

Bobby froze. "What?"

"You stupid asshole. Put your gun down before he blows a hole in your head."

Bobby glanced around quickly. Jake closed the box, locking it again, and said, "I'm taking this to Chih's. Put your fucking gun away."

"Hey! Fuck that. Where's your guy then?"

Jake picked up the box and began walking to the car. "You coming or what?"

"Stop! What the fuck you think you're doing!"

Jake kept walking. He heard Bobby running up to him, his steps quickening, and Jake knew Bobby was going to hit him. Jake spun, throwing the strongbox at him, then leapt forward. Bobby tried to block and catch the strongbox at the same time, and Jake grabbed the gun, aiming it away. They fell together onto the ground, and Jake grabbed Bobby's throat with his free hand. He said, "Don't be stupid." He squeezed hard. "We split it like we agreed. I'll take the gun. It's either that or you lose it all."

Bobby struggled, and tried to twist the gun free, but he was choking now, unable to breathe. Jake held him tightly. But then Bobby used his free hand and grabbed Jake's groin, and Jake cried out in pain, letting go of Bobby's neck, and they began rolling, Bobby gripping his testicles harder and yanking, which made Jake howl and as they rolled Jake began punching Bobby's face frantically, hammering his nose and eyes, and Bobby's grip loosened. Jake wrenched the gun away and aimed it into Bobby's stomach and pulled the trigger. The shot lit up both their midsections, and Jake felt the burning heat from the muzzle. Bobby rolled back and let go of Jake's groin.

Jake scrambled away, the pain so penetrating that he felt like vomiting. He was breathing hard, trying to stand, and kept saying, "Goddamn this... goddamn this..." His body had broken out in a warm sweat, but his teeth chattered. He spread his legs and tried to keep everything still. He glanced over at Bobby, who looked unconscious. Jake didn't believe it. He aimed the gun, but then realized another shot might bring attention. One shot could be a car backfiring; another was suspicious. Jake had to get out of here. Maybe take the car somewhere else.

Slowly, he stood, keeping the gun aimed at Bobby. He limped over to him and stomped him in the stomach, which sent shooting pains through Jake's groin. He almost whimpered. Jake kicked Bobby again right where he had shot him. Bobby's head jerked back, but he didn't make a sound and he didn't open his eyes. With the gun still aimed at him, Jake grabbed Bobby's hair with his other hand and dragged him to the dumpster. He lifted the lid. The smell of rotting food blew out.

The pain in Jake's groin and stomach pulsed. He gritted his teeth and dropped Bobby's head to the ground. Still no response. He kicked him again. Nothing. Blood had seeped through Bobby's shirt and pants. Jake quickly lifted Bobby and shoved him into the dumpster, closing the lid. If Bobby stayed unconscious for a little longer, he'd bleed to death. That was that.

Jake limped to the strongbox, picked it up, and stopped for a moment. The pain reached through his groin and into his chest. He walked slowly out of the lot and to the parked car. First he'd have to take the car somewhere else, maybe park at a meter and let it get ticketed and towed. Then he'd dump the gun, the clothes, the strong box. He doubted Bobby would live, which meant things would get messy. The old man would connect Bobby to Jake. Chih might not even want the jewels since it would then be linked to murder. No. Everything was too messy. Jake had to get out of town for a while. Let things settle. And that was when he thought of his brother.

40

Bobby wasn't feeling so good. First he hung out in a small shopping center on Broadway, eating fast food and trying not to do any more walking. Something was wrong with his wound, and he needed to rest. Then he sat outside and smoked all afternoon. He needed a benny, but didn't have any more, and wasn't sure where to get some around here. He felt things shifting inside his stomach. He shouldn't have had a burger.

By early evening he was dizzy, queasy. He wanted to go back to his hotel and sleep, but he needed to talk to mousy Arlene. He walked to Molino's, and entered through the back. He passed the locker room and asked a waiter if Arlene was in yet. The waiter nodded.

Bobby walked through the kitchen, and saw a small woman with large eyes and stringy hair. Mousy. Her head seemed too large for her body. He waved to her, and she stopped, trying to recognize him.

"Arlene?"

She nodded. "Do I know you?"

"I'm a friend of Jake's and I'm having trouble finding him."

"Yeah, he seems to have disappeared." She tightened the small white apron around her thin waist.

He thought she was cute, and said, "You went out with him?"

She wrinkled her nose. "Not really. Everyone thinks that. We were friends, had a short thing, and that's it."

"You talk to him recently?"

"Two weeks ago. I talked to him a little."

"Does he have family in the area?"

"No, I don't think so."

"Family anywhere?"

She looked up, thinking. "He's got a brother somewhere. He

might've mentioned that once."

Bobby tried not to seem anxious and leaned against the wall. "You're cute. You want to go out sometime?"

"Oh, jeez, another smooth one. No, I don't want to go out sometime."

"All right. Do you remember where his brother is?"

"Bay Area, I think. Jake said something about his brother being a techie."

"San Francisco?"

"Something like that."

"A name? Did he mention a name?"

"He might've, but I don't remember."

"Nothing?"

"Nope. He didn't talk much about family."

"What about other friends? Anyone else around here?"

"Not really. He was pretty quiet."

"What about friends in the Bay Area?"

"Why?"

"Jake owes me money."

"A lot?"

"A lot for me."

She narrowed her eyes. "Are you really a friend?"

"Yeah. I was just at his place. He left me a key. But the thing is, he hasn't been home in a while." He smiled. "You sure you don't want to get a drink after work?"

"I've got a boyfriend."

"You don't know if he had other friends, someplace he might go?"

"Nah. He didn't tell me much about—" She paused. "He did talk about an ex-girlfriend once. We were hanging out here late and drinking. Something about him getting dumped."

"Around here?"

"Nuh-uh. Bay Area. I guess he's got connections down there."

"Remember a name?"

She nodded slowly. "He had a picture of her I saw. Nice looking. I don't think he got over her. Maybe it was the beers talking."

"Name?"

"Hold on. Yeah. Plain name. Mary something. I thought the whole name was her first name. Like Mary Ann. Or Mary Lou."

Bobby waited.

"Mary Lin. Yeah, something like that. Mary Lin—no, wait. I thought it was Mary Lin, but it was Mary Lim."

"Mary Lim? That's her name?"

"Think so. You could tell he was still a little hung up on her."

"Why?"

"Just the way he acted."

"You sure it's Mary Lim?"

"Pretty sure. I gotta get back to work. You find him, you say 'hey' for me."

"I will. Thanks." He watched her hurry off to a table, pulling out a pad and pen. He stared at her for a while, wondering if he had time to get her into bed. Probably not. Jake covered his trail pretty good, and if Bobby didn't move fast, he might lose him. The thing was, Jake probably didn't expect anyone to get this far.

Bobby limped out of the restaurant, searching for a bus stop. He'd grab his bag, and head down to San Francisco. Hell, it was on his way back to L.A. anyway. He still had a small wad of cash from Chih. Nice of him to give it away so easily.

An ex-girlfriend and a brother in the Bay Area. Jake had to have run down there. Bobby could do a little looking around. If Jake wasn't there, at least Bobby might get a better fix on where he might be. His brother would have to know something. Bobby felt, though, that he was getting closer. Jake had run far and fast, but Bobby wasn't about to give up. You shoot me, he thought, you better finish the fucking job. You shoot me, I better be really dead.

PART III

41

Throughout the week Jake continued selling and consigning jewelry to stores around the city, the best sales going to Pacific Gems. He now had nearly eighteen grand at the bank, some in his checking account, most as cash in his safe deposit box, and he still had three-quarters of his jewelry left. This was much slower and more complicated than dumping everything with Chih, but at least he knew he was getting market prices.

He had just returned from an afternoon in North Beach, where a large jeweler owned by Asians had bought everything he showed them except a 14K gold bangle bracelet with three small mediocre diamonds set on the top. Besides the fact that the diamonds were inferior, bracelets apparently didn't sell, so Jake had this in his pocket when he walked along Union street, turned a corner, and headed to Franklin & Sons.

The jewelry store was still open, two customers inside. The alarm that he had seen before, the old-style broken circuit kind, was a relic, and he suspected the store must have something else. He had recently heard about auditory alarms, microphones stationed around the store with a listener at a central office, but he hadn't seen anything along the walls. It was also possible that the alarms were contained in the back room, part of a storage system that didn't require anything sophisticated in the show room.

Jake crossed the street and sat on the steps of a two-story Victorian. The E-Zone Café next to the jewelry store was still under construction, the windows sheeted off but the glass door exposing the interior. The molding and paneling along the door and windows had been removed. Swatches of blue and yellow paint were streaked along the frame. It was dark and quiet in there, and he wondered if he could enter the back room of the jewelry store through the café.

He turned towards a group of teenagers approaching. He hadn't even sold off most of the jewelry from the Chun job, and he was already looking at this new place. He had never overlapped jobs before, and he wasn't sure why this store seemed so ripe. The teenagers—a mix of boys and girls—glanced at him as they passed. He stood up and moved away; he still had twenty minutes before the store closed.

Jake entered a bookstore on Union and wandered through the "Philosophy & Religion" section. He found an introduction to ancient philosophy with two chapters on the pre-Socratics, and promptly bought it. When he returned to the side street, he saw the owner of Franklin & Sons pulling down the security grilling. Jake checked his watch. The owner was closing early. Jake had missed the other security measures. He noticed, though, that the man wasn't carrying anything with him—no briefcase, strongbox, not even a small satchel. Nothing. The man secured the padlock, then walked in the other direction.

Jake began walking as well. He stayed a half block behind.

The man moved slowly, his gait heavy and labored. He stopped often to look in store windows, catching his breath, and Jake thought he saw the man talking to himself. After walking for another two blocks, the man climbed into a silver sedan, and drove off. Jake caught the first few letters of the license plate.

Back at the jewelry store, Jake examined the padlock again, and peered through the main windows. A security light shone on the glass counter, the contents empty. So, every night the displays were taken out and stored in the back room somewhere. A safe, of course, but what kind? What sort of security?

Jake looked up at the telephone lines, and realized that only the Union Street shops had their electricity and telephone lines piped underground. These side streets had everything on poles, perfect if he needed to cut off a central alarm system. He moved to the café door window. The stacks of drywall were still on the bare concrete floor. He was tempted to survey the back alley again, but he didn't want to linger in this area.

He flipped though his new book and skimmed the opening pages. He walked leisurely to the apartment, a lightness in his step.

Rachel was on the phone. She had the classifieds open in front of her, scribbling in the margins. She glanced up at him and waved hello. She said into the phone, "Two months' rent is your fee?"

Jake sat down and watched her take notes. She listened, pressed the pen against her lip, then asked the person on the other end to fax her an application. She hung up and told Jake, "This is going to be tough. I had to hire a rental agent."

"A rental agent for what?"

"For finding an apartment."

"You're moving out?"

Rachel said, "I'm looking into it."

Jake didn't know what to say. "So you two are splitting up?"

"Separating. A trial."

"When did this happen?"

"Recently."

"I see," he said. "How are you doing?"

She stopped, and turned to him. "Okay."

"Car stuff all taken care of?"

"Euge said he'd handle the insurance. It should be fine."

"You never told me what you meant."

"What I meant?"

"You're sinking."

"I'm what?"

"In the car. You said you were sinking—"

She grimaced and waved this off. "God, I'm sorry about that. I was weepy and disgusting. Never mind."

"No. It's okay."

"It was dumb," she said.

"Right after that you and Eugene decided to separate."

"I decided," she said. "Everything became clearer."

"After the accident?"

"After talking to you."

"Me? Don't say that."

"It's true. Look out for number one. Damn the consequences. You said it."

Jake nodded. "I did."

"I have to think about me." She shook this off. "All this is so depressing. Must we talk about it? Where were you?"

"Selling."

"Successful?"

"Yeah," he said. He pulled out the bracelet. "Except this."

"Let me see."

He threw it to her and she caught it. She slid it on her wrist and held it up. "Not bad," she said.

"You like it?"

"It's nice."

"It's yours," he said. "A birthday gift."

"You're late by a few months."

"Happy Car Accident?"

She frowned. "I don't know if I like that."

"How about it's yours because I like you?"

She studied him for a moment. "I don't know."

"Oh, come on. Take it. It's a gift."

"Does this mean we're going steady now?" She held up her arm again.

"I would never be so lucky."

She laughed. "All right, Jake," she said, shaking her head. "I'll take it. Thank you."

"Let's work out again one of these days."

"You got it." She pointed to the phone. "I have to make more calls."

He went to the kitchen. As Rachel began talking on the phone again, Jake listened to her voice fill the living room. He watched her over the kitchen counter, the bracelet still on her wrist, sliding down with each of her telephone movements. He liked the way her voice lowered when she asked a question. She nodded into the phone, her expression focused. She seemed to glow. Everything around her melted away.

42

Bobby Null was taking the bus out of Seattle. After a few dozen long-distance phone calls, he found a Mary Lim in Oakland who had known Jake. The conversation was strange, because Bobby realized that they must have had some kind of fight. She didn't want to talk about him. She had said, Yes, I knew a Jake Ahn, and then clammed up. He asked if she had heard from him recently, and she said No. He asked if she knew where he could find Jake, and she said No. Finally, he asked if she knew anyone, like Jake's brother, who could help Bobby, and she said No. When he told her he'd be in the Bay Area soon, and asked if she wouldn't mind talking to him some time, she said, What's this about? He said, I need to find him. She said, I haven't heard from him in years. Then she hung up.

It was always tough doing things over the phone. Bobby knew that meeting her in person would be better. He could tell if she was lying, if she was protecting him, and he could then get the truth out of her. He could be very persuasive.

Bobby stared out the window. He was so goddamn glad to get out Seattle. It stunk of family.

His stomach hurt. He was beginning to feel like he had to piss more, even though when he went to the bathroom, not much happened. He just stood there, waiting, maybe a small sting inside. He knew it had something to do with his wound, and it just added to his urgency. He wanted to get Jake and he wanted it soon.

Everything was easier when you knew what you wanted.

He had tried to break into his mother's house before leaving town. She kept a pretty good stash of money in her bedroom, but it was harder than he thought. First of all, she *had* changed all the locks. He was shocked. Changing the fucking locks on your own son! What the hell kind of mother did that? And he wasn't any good at the picking, so he went to the bathroom window in back, the translucent one that slid to the side and which he knew his mother kept partially open to let shower steam escape. The window was higher up, so he had to use a lawn chair to boost himself, then he had to rip the screen open.

The problem was that his neighbor, Mrs. Hathaway, an old woman who had lived there ever since Bobby was a kid, saw him through her kitchen window. She came out of her back door and yelled, "Hey, you! What are you doing?"

"It's just me, Mrs. Hathaway," he said. "I forgot my key."

"Oh no, you don't! Your mother said she changed the locks! You stay away! I'm calling the cops!"

Bobby cursed and climbed down. He said, "It's my house."

"Your mother told me about you. Why can't you give her a break? She's still upset over Kevin—"

"Don't worry," Bobby said, climbing back up the chair. "I just want to check—"

"I'm calling the cops, then I'm calling your mother," she said, hurrying back into her house and slamming her door. Bobby sighed, since she probably would call. The old witch. He ran off.

So he left Seattle with a ratty suitcase and less than a hundred bucks in his pocket, the other three-fifty he had taken from Chih blown on more bennies, food, and his hotel bill. He should've been leaving with a shitload of cash and jewelry, but Jake had beaten him to it.

The bus was too warm and Bobby felt queasy. This was one of the newer buses with an air nozzle above him, but when he opened the nozzle, nothing came out. He shifted back and forth in his seat, kicking the foot rest. What did Hathaway say? His mother was still upset over Kevin? That bothered Bobby, since Kevin had them all snowed. You act nice and polite, you smile and pretend you're interested in someone, and you're suddenly a good guy. When Bobby lived at home throughout his teens, Kevin used to sucker punch him whenever he walked by. Hey, Bro, he'd say, and then give Bobby an uppercut to his ribs or kidneys. Whap. Bobby was no match for Kevin's steroid freak strength. Sometimes Kevin liked to hold Bobby by his throat, closing his fingers slowly, watching Bobby grow red and choke. Bobby didn't even have the arm or leg length to hit his brother. One of his brother's bulging arms could hold Bobby up onto his toes, stretched out beyond kicking reach.

Even the thought of his brother made Bobby uneasy. Kevin's acne-covered face was disgusting to look at—steroid side-effects— and those tank-top T-shirts he always wore, even in the winter, showing off his chemical muscles, stretch marks on his arms from the abnormal growth. What a loser. A dead loser.

"Excuse me, will you stop kicking?" a man in a crew-cut asked, peering over the back of his seat.

Bobby looked up. He hadn't even realized he was doing it. He didn't stop, though, and said, "Bothering you?" The man, about Bobby's age, narrowed his eyes, and Bobby thought, I can take him.

"Yeah it is. Cut it out."

"Move, if you don't like it." Bobby continued kicking the footrest with his toe. He stared at the man with a blank expression, and waited to see what the guy did.

"Are you fucking with me?" the guy said, raising up further.

Bobby pushed aside his jacket, revealing the handle of Chih's automatic in the side of his pants. Bobby said, "Move or shut the fuck up."

The guy stared at the gun, then grabbed his duffel bag from the seat next to him. He walked to the back of the bus. This didn't make Bobby feel any better, though. He stopped kicking the seat. He had to use the bathroom again, and was tired of all that was happening to him. He stood up slowly, feeling the pain in his stomach, his mood growing darker, and walked down the aisle. Kevin was killed by a bunch of bullets tearing into him. Some kind of robbery gone bad. Not much all that muscle could do against the cops. He must have thought he was Superman. All those steroids probably pumping up his brain as well as his muscles. What a stupid move.

Bobby passed the guy with the crew-cut, who looked quickly away. Yeah, that's right, Bobby thought. To hell with you all.

43

Jake was watching a PBS documentary when Eugene walked in with a box under his arms. Sweat stains darkened his armpits, and a glossy film covered his face. He dropped the box onto the ground, and something inside clattered. He kicked it aside and asked, "What's on TV?"

"Something about jungle cats," Jake said, staring at his brother.

"Why?"

"It's relaxing."

Eugene sat down at the dining table and yanked off his tie. He flicked it away.

"What's in the box?" Jake asked.

"Office stuff. I was fired today."

Jake sat up. "Fired."

"Canned. Kicked out. They had a fucking security guard watch me."

"You're kidding."

"It's standard procedure ever since a guy got fired and he knocked over shelves and cursed everyone out."

"You didn't do that."

"No. I knew it was coming. All my friends are gone."

"What about Caroline?"

Eugene looked up. "Yeah, she's gone too. She jumped to a start-up."

"Sorry to hear that."

"Where's Rachel?" he asked.

"Went out. I think looking at rentals."

"Christ. Already?"

Jake nodded.

Eugene turned towards the darkened window. "She must be in a hurry," he said. "So she told you."

"Told me what?"

"That she's leaving."

"Not really," Jake said.

"She says she has to look out for herself. She says she has to be selfish."

Jake found it strange to hear his words echoed through his brother. He said, "What does that mean?"

"The hell if I know. I've been walking around all day thinking about it."

"All day?"

Eugene said, "I was fired this morning."

Jake was about to ask why he hadn't come straight home, but Eugene sighed and said, "Shit. I thought there was still a possibility, but I guess we're both tired of it all."

Jake said, "Tired."

"I seriously feel like everything is going to hell. I mean everything. I'm pulling my hair out, I'm grinding my teeth, my career is fucked." He looked up, and raised his voice. "My marriage is over. Jeez, is this a joke? Is someone playing a joke on me?"

"Hey, it'll be okay. Maybe this is something good—"

"What?" Eugene said. "What the fuck are you talking about?"

Jake kept still.

"Good?" his brother said. "Are you joking? My life is falling apart and it's good? Do you have any idea what you're talking about? Do you have any idea what I'm going through?"

"No."

"Of course you don't. You've never held a real job, had a real relationship. What the hell do you know about anything? You just steal things and live off them while you can."

Jake said, "Okay, maybe I'll go out now—"

"Wait. No. Sorry, Jake." Eugene advanced quickly, holding up his hands. "I'm sorry."

"No, you're right. I don't know anything."

"Forget it. I'm just not feeling too good right now." Eugene walked into the kitchen. He opened the refrigerator and said, "Damn. Did I drink all the beer?"

"So, what will you do?" Jake called to him.

His brother was pale, drained. He leaned on the counter and said, "I guess find another job. Jeez. Eight years at that place, and I started when there were only six of us. I got fucked over big time."

"Let me buy you a drink."

"You're on. How about dinner?"

They left the apartment, and in the elevator Eugene said, "We were actually going down in this elevator to look at the car. I was trying not to get mad about the accident, because it sounded like she was driving aggressively."

"She was almost cut off," Jake said. "It wasn't really her—"

"And then, she just tells me that it's over."

Jake was quiet for moment. "Oh. Just like that?"

"Exactly like that: 'It's over.'"

"What did you say?"

"What could I say? It took me a minute to absorb it, then I said fine."

They walked out of the elevator and through the lobby in silence. Eugene motioned towards a small steakhouse two blocks away. Jake saw his brother hunching over, shoving his hands deep into his pockets and sighing. He reminded Jake of a turtle. As kids Eugene would turn inward like this after being yelled at by their father. Jake suddenly had an image of his brother as a twelve-year-old, standing stiffly with his arms at his sides, his head hanging forward, as their father leaned over him and threatened him in a low voice. Eugene was crying. Then his father turned to Jake, who started running.

Jake said, "Do you remember Dad chasing me around the house at one point?"

Eugene was gazing down at the pavement as they crossed the street. He nodded slowly. "Yes."

"What did I do again? I forgot."

He turned to Jake. "You did?"

"I talked back to him?"

"Yes, but that wasn't it."

"What then?"

Eugene stared out onto the street. "You lost one of his tools. One of his gauges that you thought looked like a space ship. You took it out to play with somewhere and left it. He told you to find it, and you couldn't. One his engine gauges."

"Really?"

"You stayed out all day, trying to avoid him, but eventually you had to come home and say you couldn't find it. He was drunk by then."

"Oh."

"Then you talked back. You told him it was just a tool." Eugene smiled. "I think Mom fainted when you talked back."

"Wait a minute," Jake said. "Was that when I was yelling the nursery rhyme?"

"Yes, that was so weird." Eugene let out a small laugh. "'Jake be nimble, Jake be quick.'"

"Right. 'Jake jump over the candlestick.'" Jake remembered letting out a deranged high-pitched laugh as he ran from his father, who was screaming at him. The world had blurred around Jake as he slipped out of his father's grasp and made a mad dash for the back door, chanting the nursery rhyme to himself, but that seemed to enrage his father even more. At one point his mother tried to intervene, but his father smacked her away. What had happened next? Jake said,

"Oh, wait. That was when he started beating the shit out of me. Mom was there too."

Eugene nodded.

Jake had managed to reach the back door but before he could open it, his father had slammed it and grabbed Jake by the arm, lifting him up easily. Jake twisted and kicked the open air, like a snagged fish, flopping and arching; his shoulder socket seemed to wrench loose. He let out a yell as he ducked his head and tried to be a moving target. He was twisting so wildly that he didn't see the first punch coming. He heard his mother shrieking.

Jake said, "Mom was still there."

"That was right before she left." They walked another block and passed a homeless man on the sidewalk. Jake recognized him from his first day here, the guy who had called him a chinaman. The man now pointed his crooked finger at Jake, who held up his middle finger. The man cackled.

Eugene said, "You know that guy?"

"I've seen him around here before."

They entered the Ribeye House, and took a table near the window. Eugene ordered a pitcher of beer, and Jake, squinting at the menu in the semi-darkness—the lights above them dim and unsteady—asked for an appetizer platter. Jake turned towards the window and watched cars driving by.

Jake then noticed in the reflection Eugene staring at his hand. Jake turned back to his brother.

Eugene looked up. "Do you ever feel like you screwed up your life?"

Jake said, "No. I don't think about things like that."

"About your life?"

"About doing well or not. Measuring things. I just go along."

"Yeah, you're like that."

Jake cocked his head. "Like what?"

"You just move along, even-steven."

"I survive."

Eugene looked down at his hand again and said, "Did Mom ever tell you that story about the clay kid?"

Jake shook his head.

"The story about the bad kid who never listened to his parents, so they turned him into clay?"

"No."

"So the kid became this soft clay, but he went outside into the sun, disobeying his parents again, and he began hardening and drying. Then he began crumbling."

Jake smiled.

"That story scared the hell out of me," Eugene said. "I kept picturing this kid's arms falling off."

"That *is* scary," he said. "Mom told you that?"

"When she was mad at me once. I forgot why."

Jake asked, "How come you never told me that stuff about Mom leaving?"

Eugene glanced up at him, then shook his head. "I don't know."

"Do you think she's still alive?"

"Yeah, probably."

"Do you think about her?"

Eugene didn't answer for a while. He eventually said, "Yeah. A lot lately."

"You do? Like what?"

"I miss her."

Jake was startled. "After all these years?"

"Yeah," Eugene said. "It's strange, isn't it."

Jake didn't know what to say. He ran his fingers along the gouges on the table. "Sorry about you and Rachel."

Eugene shrugged.

"What happens next?"

"We'll separate, eventually file for divorce."

"Already?"

"I guess this has been brewing for a while." Eugene continued looking at his hand. He said, "I'm turning to clay. I feel it."

"You're not turning into clay," Jake said.

"I'm solidifying. Soon I'll start chipping off into pieces."

"Stop."

Eugene looked up. "What've you been doing the past couple of days?"

"Raising a little cash. Thinking about my options," he said. "Is it time for me to move out?"

"No. It's fine. You're not planning on anything illegal, are you?"

Jake tilted his head. "Why do you ask?"

"It's when you keep a low profile that I worry."

Jake didn't reply.

Eugene said, "You're not, are you? What did I say about staying with me—"

"Take it easy. I'm not doing anything—"

"But you're acting like, I don't know, something's—"

"No." Jake shook his head. "I'm just weighing my options."

Eugene studied him, then waved this off and said, "What the hell. I don't care. Maybe you should do something big and let me live off you."

"You can be my partner," Jake said.

"Does it pay well?"

"A few days ago I had one ring appraised. It's worth thirty-five grand."

"Thirty-five grand?" Eugene asked. "How many rings do you have?"

"Plenty, but none as good as that one."

He shook his head. "I'd rather not go to jail."

Jake sat back as the waitress brought their pitcher of beer and two glasses. He said, "Yeah, there's always that downside." He smiled.

Eugene hunched over and drank his beer. He sank into the booth, and Jake saw with surprise that his brother was solidifying. A spider web of cracks appeared in his arm as he reached for the pitcher.

44

Jake accompanied Rachel to view apartments the next day, since he might soon be doing this himself, but he grew bored after the second one, a studio in the Sunset district listed at $1200 per month. The apartment was clean and roomy with hardwood floors and large windows, but he told Rachel as they left that it certainly wasn't worth $1200 a month. She smiled at him. "That's not as high as you think."

"It's not?"

"Poor Jake. If you do stay down here, you're in for a shock."

He wasn't sure if she was serious until he saw her face, and he said, "No wonder you guys are in debt."

"You're right. I should be looking at cheaper places." They climbed into the car, which hadn't been repaired yet. They had stuffed the deflated airbags into the steering wheel and dashboard, but the compartments rattled open. Eugene had said he didn't need the car, and would try to take care of the repairs soon. Rachel added, "When we split up, I'm going to be taking on more debt. Boy, my life is getting rosier and rosier."

"How're you going to pay it off?"

"Simple. I'll have to get another job."

"What about your time off?"

She sighed. "That's pretty much over."

"That was short."

"Unless you have thirty grand to give me, I have no choice."

He asked, "Why don't you live in a cheaper area?"

"Maybe, but if I want to get a good job, this is the place."

"So you're kind of trapped."

She was about to start the car, but stopped. She thought about this, then rested her head on the steering wheel. "Holy moly, what am I doing?"

Jake watched her.

"I can't afford these places. I can't afford anything. I'm in trouble." She raised her head. "Maybe I should go live with my mother for a while."

Jake smiled. "You don't want to do that."

"No, I don't." She turned to him. "I had to do this, you know."

He nodded.

"I was...losing myself."

"Sinking," he said.

She glanced at him. "All right. I guess so."

Jake asked, "Still?"

"I don't know. But at least I'm doing something. Moving ahead."

Jake nodded.

"You know, sometimes I wonder if I knew this all along. Him, too."

"Splitting up?"

"From the beginning, we knew it might not work. We were so different, and it was obvious from the beginning. Our personalities, our interests."

"Like what?"

"We never do the same things. He doesn't like to read, he doesn't like the gym. I hate watching TV and movies, and I hate centering my life around work."

"So why'd you get married in the first place?"

She was quiet for a while. She finally said, "Because we were in love."

Jake visited them once when they were still dating, when Eugene lived in the Richmond district. It was true: they had been in love. He had noticed it then, their giddy attention towards each other, the way they held hands in an unembarrassed way and she leaned her head on

Eugene's shoulder. He said, "I remember. You two were all lovey-dovey. It was strange seeing him like that."

"That's right. You came by before we got engaged. We were so young." She stared out onto the street. "Young and stupid. We had all these plans, but nothing went quite right."

Jake heard the wistfulness in her voice, and said, "You mean your jobs?"

"That and other things."

"Like what?" he asked.

She shrugged. "I think I mentioned it. We tried to have children."

Jake remembered that yes, she had told him. "Can I ask why?"

"Why we wanted children?"

"Why you couldn't."

She frowned. "It's complicated."

Jake waited.

Rachel said, "Euge wanted kids more than I did." She explained that Euge wanted the clichéd family, with two kids, a house in the suburbs, and Rachel driving an SUV to take little Robert and Sarah (no chance of them being teased for their names, unlike him, he had said) to soccer practice and music lessons. When they thought they were going to be rich and were scouting towns in Marin, they stumbled across a public park in Mill Valley where there were three simultaneous soccer games—girls', pee-wee, and boys'—on adjoining fields, the parents clapping from the sidelines and the parking lots filled with gigantic four-wheel drives sparkling in the sun. Rachel had watched Euge take this in, his gaze sweeping across the fields, stopping at Mt. Tam, the sky deep blue, the yells and whistles and clapping surrounding them, and she could've sworn she saw his eyes watering. He had turned to her and said, "Pretty nice."

Jake said, "I think he's into that whole thing. Family."

"Of course. He's never had it. A normal family, stability. Who has? I understand."

"And you?"

"I didn't feel the same need, no. I'm not sure why."

"But you went along."

"Sure. It could've been nice."

"But…?"

"Endometriosis."

"What's that?"

Rachel told him it was an abnormality—a disease, really, that screwed up the lining of her uterus—and it soon overwhelmed their lives. She agreed to the laser surgery. She agreed to the drugs, the clomiphene citrate, the Pergonal, Humegon, and Fertinex. She handled the nausea, vomiting, bleeding, headaches, bloating, rashes, and all those lovely side effects. Of course their health insurance didn't cover this. Of course it didn't work. At one point they were going to induce false menopause with even harsher drugs to stop the endometrial cells from producing. Then they'd try implantation (again), and she said, You know what? Forget it. I'm done. We're done. You want a kid? We'll adopt.

But Euge didn't want that.

"Why not?" Jake asked.

"He just didn't. But then things started going wrong anyway. And we were at each others' throats."

"I didn't know all this."

"Why would you?" She checked her planner.

"Come on, let's blow off the apartments," he finally said. "Let me take you out to lunch."

"But I have appointments—"

"More $1200 studios?"

Nodding, she started the car. "You're right. Screw those. Where to?"

"How about Cow Hollow? There are some nice places to eat on Union."

She said, "Sure, why not. Let's eat out. Let's spend more money."

After a quick lunch at a soup and salad restaurant, Jake and Rachel walked around the neighborhood. When they approached the corner near Franklin & Sons Jewelry, Jake guided them up the side street and glanced through the store window. A different person at the counter, a young man with gold-rimmed glasses, was wiping the display cases. Jake said, "Can we go in here?"

Rachel eyed him. "Okay."

They stepped inside. Jake looked quickly at the alarm unit again, trying to see what kind of keyhole it was. Tubular cylinder. Shit. Those were a nightmare.

"Good afternoon," the young man said. "May I help you?"

Jake smiled. "My wife is looking at diamond rings."

Rachel began to turn towards him, but stopped herself.

"We have a great selection," the man said. "Over here, you'll see, are our gold and platinum rings, all set with very high-grade diamonds."

Jake looked for cameras, but saw none. He said to Rachel, "Honey, why don't you check those out? I'll just look around."

She nodded. The young man met her at the end of the counter and began pointing out different rings and telling her what they were. Jake took inventory: six floor display cases with varying amounts of jewelry, two wall-mounted displays behind the counter with diamond and pearl necklaces, a small display of watches in the corner, and a window display with a mixture of gems and jewelry. If the owner didn't take these home, then the back room held it all. He checked the line of views through the window. He couldn't see anything on Union; cars and people on that main street couldn't see anything in here. It would be hidden at night from police drive-bys.

Jake heard Rachel playing her part, telling the man that she hated gaudy rings, but liked the diamonds large.

The back room was separated by a wooden door with a simple

pin and tumbler, but Jake needed to see everything behind it. He approached the young man and asked, "May I use your bathroom?"

The man hesitated. "Sorry, customers aren't allowed in back."

"Just for a minute? It's a little…urgent."

"There are bathrooms at the restaurant across the street."

"I'll be really fast."

"Sorry. My boss would kill me."

Rachel watched Jake, and he smiled. "That's fine. We should go then, honey."

She took his arm as they walked out. They moved down the street, out of sight of the store, then Rachel asked, "What are you up to?"

"Just looking."

"I hope you're not thinking what I think you're thinking."

"Oh, and what's that?"

She gripped his arm tighter. "I thought you were done with all this."

"Did I say that?"

"No, but you implied it."

Was this true? The mess with Bobby had scared him, but whatever fear or regret he had felt was wearing off quickly. He said, "Can I borrow the car tonight?"

"Why?"

"I want to follow the owner, find out where he lives."

"What are you doing?"

He turned to her. "My job." He liked the feeling of her arm linked with his and pulled her closer. Their legs touched, and he said softly, "I'll be careful. Very careful."

"But why? Do you need the money?"

"Not yet," he said. Though he liked the idea of having a cushion, something he had had only once before.

"Then why?" Her cheeks were pink, and she blinked rapidly, trying to focus on him.

"Because, it's...it's what I do." He gave her arm a light squeeze, then pulled away. Her perfume mingled with the smell of coffee. As his fingers brushed down her arm, he felt the bracelet he had given her and smiled. "You're wearing it?"

"I like it."

"So, can I borrow the car?"

"I'll drive you. What time?"

"*You* will drive me?" he asked.

"I will. What time?"

"Six. You don't have to."

"I know," she said.

"Are you sure about this?" he asked.

"No, of course not."

45

Bobby watched Mary Lim's place on Park Blvd. He waited in a stolen Mazda directly across from her house, among other parked cars. No one noticed him. He went through two packs of cigarettes, fought the urge to piss all afternoon, and sat in a haze of smoke, his eyes stinging. He had some trouble finding this place—he had thought he could take the subway—but ended up stealing a Ford truck, checking into a large parking garage downtown, then stealing this old Mazda and switching the plates. He preferred taking cars from garages, especially long-term ones, since they usually weren't noticed right away. But he'd have to dump this car after tonight. He'd drive it to his hotel in the city, a crappy place in the Mission, and leave it. From the looks of the neighborhood, the car would probably get stolen again.

He itched to get back to L.A. He was always cold. He was always getting lost. He just wanted to find Jake and get this goddamn thing over with. When he returned to L.A., the first thing he'd do would be to get a doctor to check him again. Something didn't feel right.

He half-hoped Jake would be hiding out here, but a quick look around the house showed nothing. She was probably at work. He wasn't sure how he'd play this. He went over the possibilities while he smoked his throat raw.

He hadn't eaten all day, and also had refused to drink because he didn't want to piss. He kept tasting something sour in his mouth, adding to the ash flavor.

A small sports car—a low two-seater—sped by, slowed at the center divide, made a U-turn, then signalled in front of the house. It pulled into the driveway. Bobby sat up. The signal light was still blinking when a woman shut off the car and climbed out. She activated her car alarm. Bobby had trouble seeing anything except long hair and a large, bulky grocery bag, as she walked to the front door and let herself in. The lights went on inside.

He waited fifteen minutes. He gave her a chance to put away her groceries, change out of her work clothes. He didn't want her annoyed by his surprise visit. The other houses around hers were still quiet. More cars drove by, rush hour in full swing.

Bobby limped across the street. A car was approaching, and he had to run, which immediately sent shooting pains through his stomach and groin. He stopped at the other side, panting. The fresh air felt good. Some of the wooziness left him.

The house was dirty white, the shingles cracked near the front door. He knocked, then rang the door bell. After a moment the porch light went on, and he stood back in the light and waved. The door opened, and through the screen he saw that she had changed into a sweat suit. She said, "Yes?"

"I'm Bobby. I called from Seattle about Jake Ahn?"

Her face immediately lost its curiosity, hardening. She frowned and said, "So?"

Bobby saw that she was a mix, a little bit of Chinese and white— her eyes were set wider than Jake's, but she still had long straight black hair, and there was something about her cheekbones that made him think of Chinese people. He said, "I was passing through and wanted to ask you about him."

"How'd you get my address?"

"Information. You're listed."

"I haven't seen him in years."

"I know, but I'm trying to find him, and don't got any leads."

"Why are you trying to find him?"

His bladder seemed to bubble up and he suppressed a wince. He said, "He owes me money and just took off."

She nodded. "Too bad."

"All I'm asking is maybe you know where he might go, who he knows, that stuff."

"How'd you find out about me?"

Bobby said, "A girl he used to go out with said he mentioned you."

"Jake mentioned me to another girlfriend?"

He shrugged. "Just a couple minutes, that's all I need." He felt another pain in his bladder and he stiffened.

"Are you all right?" she asked.

"Yeah. It was a long ride down here."

She studied him, looking him up and down. "I don't know. Maybe tomorrow, during my lunch break."

He said, "Yeah, that's fine. I was just passing through..." He paused. The pain in his bladder got worse, and he inhaled sharply. Shit. Something was wrong. He said, "Tomorrow at lunch? Where are you working?"

"Are you sure you're okay?"

"I just need to rest. So, maybe twelve tomorrow? You work around here?"

"Downtown. Right next to City Hall. The Fedco building. Rodale Insurance. I can meet you in the downstairs lobby."

He said, "Okay. I'll see you tomorrow." He needed to piss badly, and was going to run into the bushes, but he slipped on the steps and stumbled backwards, hitting his head on a flower pot and crashing against the edge of the brick steps. He bounced off the corner and fell heavily onto the ground. The wind was knocked out of him and he couldn't move. He stared up at the porch light above. A moth kept flying into the bulb.

"Jesus! Are you all right?" She opened the screen door and hurried down to him.

He lay still, blinking. He slowed his breath, and waited for his lungs to recover. His skull throbbed. He had landed flat on his back, and for some reason it hadn't hurt. But his bladder burned. She leaned over him, blocking the light, and said, "Hey! Should I call an ambulance?"

He shook his head.

"Oh my God, can you move? Are you okay?"

He turned his head towards her, looking at her upside down. Her hair fell around her face, the edges glowing from the light directly above her. He stared. "You're very pretty," he said hoarsely.

She drew back, and the light hit his eyes, blinding him. He heard her say, "Oh God, you're delirious."

"I'm okay." He sat up slowly. The pain in his bladder softened. "I just slipped."

"Do you need help?"

"I'm okay." He pulled himself up, rubbed the back of his head, then saw the broken flower pot littered along the steps, black soil clumped around him. "Sorry about that."

"Are you sure you don't need a doctor?"

"Yeah, yeah. I just need to get back to my hotel. I'll see you tomorrow."

"Wait," she said. "Shouldn't you rest a second? Do you need anything?"

He said, "I'd really like to use your bathroom, if that's all right."

46

Rachel drove Jake to the jewelry store in the early evening. He asked her to circle the area as he looked for the silver sedan with the 3TCN license plate. They had time to search up and down the many blocks. It was possible the owner had used one of the parking garages, though Jake suspected otherwise. Parking was free on these side streets, and if he came in early enough, the owner would find a spot.

"There's a silver one," Rachel said, pointing up the road. The car was wedged in between two SUV's. She stopped next to it, and Jake climbed out to check the license plate.

"This is it," he said. They were on Vallejo, two blocks from Union. "We need to wait back there, ready to go when he goes."

"Get in. I'll circle."

They drove around the block, and, unable to find a space, Rachel parked across someone's driveway. She said, "When will he be showing up?"

"It should be in fifteen minutes. That's if he goes home."

"And why are you doing this?"

"I want to know where he lives."

"Why?"

He thought about lying to her, then said, "The more information I have about him and the store, the better off I am."

"You're going to burglarize that store?"

He liked the word "burglarize." It sounded so polite. He said, "I'm in the information gathering stage. I might not do anything." He realized with a small jolt that this wasn't true, and was startled by the ease with which he had slipped into this mode, a natural progression from seeing an opportunity and preparing to take advantage of it. His mind was clicking, his vision sharp and wary. He thought about their parking in a no-parking driveway as a possible danger. He was glad for the descending darkness.

"Are we still going to the gym later?" she asked Jake.

"Maybe."

"I really should. I'm feeling soft."

He said, "You look good to me."

"Thanks," she said. "There was a time when I was in better shape."

He turned to her. "When? I don't remember."

"In high school. I did sports: track, swimming, a little gymnastics."

Jake imagined her as a teenager, and smiled.

"What's funny?"

"Just thinking about you in high school."

"Oh, no," she said, shaking her head. "Don't do that. It wasn't a good time for me."

"Why?"

"You know about my father dying. My mother started working two jobs, I was feeling really lonely. I was pretty unhappy." She stopped. "Good God, I haven't changed that much, have I," she said.

"Didn't you date a lot?"

"Me? Are you kidding? I was a misfit."

"Not one of the jocks?"

"I did those sports for me, for college. I didn't say I was any good at them."

"You, no boyfriends?" he said. "That can't be true."

"Oh, it's true. I didn't start dating until the end of college."

He said with disbelief, "Come on. But you're so…right now, you're so—"

"So?"

"You know," he said. "You know what I mean."

She grinned. "Boy, where were you in high school when I needed you?"

He said, "Getting kicked out."

"Right. Euge mentioned that."

Jake said, "So I was one of the losers in the school. I doubt you would've talked to me."

"I would've," she said.

A light over the garage door flickered on, and they turned towards it, waiting. After a moment, Jake said, "Automatic." A slice of dim light passed across Rachel's face as she sat back in the seat. She pulled up the sleeves of her sweater, exposing the bracelet. She turned to him, smiled, then noticed something. She stared, and said, "Is that thin line a scar?"

He touched his cheek. "An old one. Very old one."

"From what?"

"Long story," he said. He traced the line with his index finger. "I cut myself with a knife."

"Tell me."

"Some other time."

Rachel glanced at the mirror and perked up. Jake turned. He saw a large, heavy-set figure trudging up the other side of the street. He whispered, "It might be him. Stay down."

The man walked slowly and crossed the street, heading for the silver sedan. Jake said, "Okay. Get ready to follow him."

She started the car, but kept the headlights off. The sedan took a while warming up, then had trouble getting out of the tight space. It only had a foot or so to maneuver, so they waited for five minutes as the car inched back and forth, angling out onto the street. Jake asked, "Do we have enough gas?"

"For what?"

"He might live far away."

"We have enough."

The sedan finally eased out of the space and drove away. Rachel turned on the headlights. "How close should I get?" she asked.

"Fairly close. It's getting dark and I don't want to lose him."

She followed him off Vallejo and onto Van Ness, heading south. There was one car between them, a small compact. She said, "I hope he doesn't hit 101. It's a mess this time of day."

Jake was watching the sedan. He hadn't been able to tell whether or not the man was carrying a strongbox, but he suspected not. He was also clocking the drive, determining how long it took the man to return home. Rachel said, "It looks like we're going to pass Market. It gets a little tricky here. I might have to get closer."

Jake said it was fine. He doubted the man would notice. Most people don't expect to be followed. Rachel sped up, changed lanes, then cut in right behind the sedan. He said, "Just don't let his taillights show our faces."

She nodded. They passed Market, but then the sedan turned off, and Jake no longer knew where they were. Rachel said, "He's not taking the freeway. He must live around here." They drove up and down one-way streets and alleys, keeping the sedan at a further distance.

"Where are we?" Jake asked.

"This is the SoMa neighborhood, South of Market."

"Residential?" Jake asked, seeing the warehouses and store signs along the buildings.

"It's becoming more so. Wait. He's turning into that gate. It looks like private parking." She pulled up to the curb, and they watched the gate roll back slowly. The sedan pulled in, and the gate began closing.

Jake said, "Drive past it and park."

Rachel did, and Jake saw that the sedan was in a small lot for five or six cars, adjacent to a warehouse building. She said, "He must live in a loft."

"In there?"

"A converted warehouse. The apartments are sectioned off as big rooms."

"You can wait here. I just want to see where he goes," Jake said, opening his door.

Rachel climbed out of the driver's side. She said, "I want to see too."

Jake waved her over. They walked along an uneven and crumbling sidewalk, and turned the corner. The lower level of the warehouse had a high concrete wall shielding the building from the street, but beyond and above the wall Jake saw the large, multi-paned windows, over six feet in height. He couldn't find any evidence of an alarm system, though it was dark. A man with a sleeping bag draped over his shoulders pushed a shopping cart along the street. Jake looked around: decrepit storefronts and boarded-up windows along the street. He asked again, "This is residential?"

"A mix."

They found the front entrance with a gated entryway, securely locked. No cameras. The intercom was covered with heavy, scratched plexiglass and listed six names. Jake turned to Rachel and said, "You go back to that side, I'll go over here. See if any lights are going on now."

They separated. Jake moved towards the street and looked up at the windows. He saw two sets of windows on the second floor, and a partial set on the ground floor, hidden beyond the brick wall. There was a dim light already on the upper left loft. Jake waited. After a moment he heard Rachel call out his name sharply.

He ran around the corner and saw two men facing Rachel. She was shaking her head, and backing up slowly. She glanced at him and said, "Jake?"

The two men turned towards him. They were teenagers. One scrawny white kid in an army jacket, another muscular Latino with an arm band around his flexing bicep. Jake said, "What's up?"

They looked him up and down and then turned to each other. The Latino kid shrugged, and they walked away.

"What did they want?" Jake asked.

"They kept asking if I wanted to buy drugs."

"You okay?"

She nodded.

"Let's go," he said.

"But I saw a light go on."

"Which one?"

"This one," she said, pointing to the second-floor windows. "Just a minute ago."

"All right. Do you have a pen and paper?"

"In the car."

Jake retrieved some scrap paper and a pen, then wrote down the names and apartment numbers listed on the intercom system. He said to Rachel, "That's it for now. Let's go."

Inside the car, Jake watched her fumble with her keys; her hands were shaking. He said, "Do you want me to drive?"

She said, "Yes. That'd be great."

He climbed out and circled as she scooted over to the passenger seat. He drove away.

47

Rachel didn't want to return home yet, so they went to the gym. Jake stayed on the free weights, while Rachel spent thirty minutes on the Stairmaster, rolling her shoulders and increasing the speed until the machine was whirring loudly above the others. Jake planned. He needed to make sure the owner of the store in fact lived there, and he wanted to correlate the name on the intercom system with the owner's name, then watch the loft again to double check. Jake still wasn't certain how he was going to do this, but the more he thought about it, the more it seemed like an easy target: one owner, poor security, all the jewels locked up, a side street. If the owner brought his jewels home, that might've made Jake's job easier, but he had to check the back room of the store before deciding anything.

He also had to stop bringing around jewels to sell or consign. He needed to withdraw from everyone's memory. Three stores currently had his rings and necklaces for consignment, but he'd take them back within the next two weeks. Maybe everything in Seattle had cooled, and he could return there soon, give Chih new business.

He glanced at Rachel, who was climbing off the Stairmaster slowly, painfully. She limped over to him and said, "I think I'm done."

"You were pushing yourself."

"I know," she said. "I'm trying to figure out why everything's going to hell."

"No, it's not."

"I realized something just now."

Jake waited.

"I realized that my life is defined by fear."

"How so?"

"I'm afraid of everything."

"Like what?"

"Poverty, loneliness, death."

"Who isn't?" Jake started to smile, but then realized she was serious. He said, "What about working out, exercise? That's so you feel and look better."

"Fear of fat. Fear of weakness."

Jake had to laugh. "Oh, come on."

She shook her head. "I can trace all my decisions to that one emotion: fear."

"What about me?"

"You?"

"You drove me today. What were you afraid of?"

She stopped. "I'll have to think about that."

"Don't think too much."

She sat down next to him on the bench. "Tell me more."

"About what?"

"About the other kinds of places you've…broken into."

"I've already told you a little."

"Tell me more," she said.

"Why?"

"I want to know."

"Here? Now?" he asked.

"No. Let's go."

"I'm not finished." He pointed to the weights.

She leaned forward, her eyebrows furrowed. "Please." Sweat beaded along her neck, and Jake saw a vein near her throat pulsing. He smelled her faint muskiness and it excited him.

He said, "Okay."

They left the gym. As they drove away he told her about following a man in a Mercedes for over two weeks, learning his routine and daily schedule. The man, Olsen, as Jake would learn, worked at a Merrill Lynch, and lived in an expensive Newport Beach townhouse. This was when Jake lived in L.A. and was getting better at burglaries. He no longer did easy hit and runs, no longer worked with anyone if he could help it, and he was always careful, always deliberate in his plans.

Olsen was going on vacation. Jake wasn't sure of this until Olsen had taken a cab to the airport. Jake watched for the usual morning newspaper deliveries, which never came. Jake waited for the mailman, who left Olsen's box empty. He watched the lights inside Olsen's house go on and off automatically every evening. His garbage can remained empty. The clincher was the outgoing phone message, in which Olsen's low voice said to call his cell; he wouldn't be checking his landline messages for a couple weeks.

Olsen had an alarm system, of course. Jake had already watched Olsen activate and deactivate the system from a control panel next to the door, but this didn't concern him. He was more concerned about the neighbors, and the possibility that Olsen had given the keys to a friend to water the plants and check the house. What Jake should have realized was that no one knew their neighbors anymore, and Olsen depended too much on his alarm to keep everything safe.

After watching the empty house for three days, Jake decided to act. At midnight, he climbed the telephone pole in front of Olsen's house, and quickly cut the telephone line. This landline was the link to the alarm company—most companies still weren't using cell service. When there's a break-in, a fire, or any major disturbance in the alarm field, the control panel calls the monitoring station, and tells the computer what's going on. Jake simply prevented the call.

But there was more to do. He had his police scanner on, and plugged in his earpiece, then checked the frequency. He was also worried about triggering an audio alarm, and wanted to turn off the power just in case. He knew from the placement of the electrical wires and the meter that the main fuse box was somewhere on the right side of the house, possibly the basement. He needed to get there first as soon as he broke in.

He walked to the back door. He picked the door locks quickly. He opened the door, and, as he suspected, he heard the control unit beeping. He probably only had fifteen seconds or so to disable the alarm. He ran downstairs, turning on all the lights, and immediately saw the fuse box. He tried to pull open the door and thought for a panicked moment that it was locked. But it was simply stuck. He yanked it open, and quickly turned off all the switches. The lights around him went off. He turned on his flashlight and hurried back upstairs.

The alarm unit was blinking an alert, trying to call the monitoring station about the break-in and power outage. He cursed. The unit was being run by a back-up battery. The audio alarm burst on, a loud siren. Jake quickly pried off the control face, and snipped all the wires. The siren died.

He walked out the back door, re-locked the door handle but not the deadbolt, closed the door, and walked through a neighbor's yard. He circled the block, then hid behind a large set of shrubs across the street from Olsen's house. He turned up his scanner. And he waited.

He could never be certain if he had tripped a second silent alarm, if Olsen had a separate, buried phone line, or if the alarm company had installed a new cell unit. He doubted it, but he needed to be certain. If he heard anything on the scanner or if he saw security cars pulling up, Jake would quietly disappear.

But after forty-five minutes, there was nothing.

He re-entered the house through the back door, closed it behind him, and thought, All for me.

"And what did you get?" Rachel asked. They were driving towards their building.

He pulled into the underground garage, and said, "I ended up with a stack of Kruggerands, three really nice Rolexes, and some bad jewelry."

"Kruggerands? Gold coins?"

"Yeah. Those coins let me stop for over a year. I bought a motorcycle with two coins."

"How many coins did you get?"

"Fifteen," he said. "We going up?" He opened his door.

"I guess so," she said. They walked to the elevators. "What did you do with all that money?"

"Eventually spent it."

"All of it?"

He nodded. Now that he thought about it, he wondered where all that money had gone. He had moved to a nicer apartment, had eaten out every night, and had taken a number of trips, the last of three visits to Seattle convincing him to leave L.A. As they rode the elevator up, he thought about the restaurant, his life up there, and said, "Have you ever been to Seattle?"

"Just once, on business." They walked down the hallway.

"I think you'd like it. In the summer you can look out towards Mt. Rainier—" Jake opened the door and stopped. There was someone lying on the floor. "Eugene?" Jake said. The overpowering smell of stale liquor wafted from his brother's dirty suit.

Rachel said, "What the…"

Eugene lifted his head off the floor, his face shiny and streaked with dirt. He burped and said, "Good evening, ladies and gentlemen."

48

Bobby relieved himself in Mary's bathroom, the sharp sting running up through his penis and into his bladder. He gritted his teeth. He gulped down water from the sink tap, and felt less shaky. He looked quietly through her medicine cabinet and drawers, finding dozens of bottles of contact lens solution, but not much else. He felt the bump on the back of his head, but it didn't seem to hurt. The pains in his gut had raised his threshold for discomfort. When he returned to the den, he thanked her, and said he'd meet her tomorrow.

"Well, you're here anyway. You might as well ask me what you want."

Bobby got a better look at her in the light, seeing again her long, shiny, black hair, and wondered how Jake kept finding such good-looking women. He said, "You dated him?"

"Yeah, off and on for almost a year."

"Why'd you break up?"

"I wanted to live down here. I hated Seattle."

"Me too. It's always so goddamn wet."

She said, "My allergies were killing me." She pointed to a padded bench. "Have a seat."

He did, and let out a small sigh.

She said, "He owes you money?"

"He owes me a lot of money."

"I'm telling you, I haven't seen or heard from him in years."

"When was the last time?"

She looked up at the ceiling, calculating. "Over five years. He came down here to visit."

"I hear he has a brother in the area."

"He does, but I never met him."

"Why not?"

"Beats me. No reason to. Jake didn't really keep in touch with him. I don't think they're a close family."

"What about parents or other brothers or sisters?"

She shook her head. "No idea. He never talked about it."

"Never?"

"Nope. Just mentioned a brother in the city."

"Do you have a name?"

She said, "He might have mentioned it once, but I don't remember."

"How'd you two meet?"

"He worked in the mail room at a company where I was a secretary."

"You mean you two went out for a year and you don't know anything about his family?"

"What, we weren't married or anything. We were just dating."

Bobby was suddenly suspicious. She was being helpful, or pretending to be, but just the other day on the phone she had hung up on him. He tried to read her, but couldn't. He asked, "What do you do?"

"Still a secretary. Actually, 'administrative assistant' is what they call it now."

Her eyes flickered to the hallway, and Bobby suddenly jumped up and whirled around. He was expecting an ambush, but instead he saw a cat freeze, then walk towards Mary. Bobby eased up, let out a slow breath. Mary was watching him with alarm. Bobby said, "Sorry about that. I'm a little antsy." His quick movements had hurt his stomach. He pressed his hand over his abdomen, but didn't feel any pain.

"A little," she said. "It's just my cat."

He sat back down. "Now, are you sure you can't remember the brother's name?"

The lines around her mouth deepened as she frowned. She shook her head. "I'm telling you, I don't remember."

"This other girlfriend said the brother was a techie."

She said, "I don't know."

Jake had probably scared her, and now he had to make a decision. Hard or soft? He said, "Look, sorry about all this. You gotta understand that Jake shot me and now I'm all jumpy. The reason why I don't look so hot is that I just got out of the hospital."

"Jake shot you?"

Bobby pointed to his lower abdomen. "Pretty bad. I'm all cut up in there."

"Shot you with a gun?"

"Yeah. I almost died."

She started to say something, then seemed to change her mind.

"I need to find him," he said.

"For revenge?"

"For my money. He took my money."

"Your money?"

"Yeah."

"He robbed you?"

"Yeah."

"This doesn't sound like him. Shooting and robbing? Are you sure you have the right guy?" Her voice had become unsteady.

"I'm sure."

"It just doesn't sound like him."

"Maybe, maybe not. Alls I know is he took my money and I want it back." He watched the cat leap onto her lap, but after a few seconds, unable to settle in as Mary kept shifting her legs, it jumped back down onto the floor. Bobby leaned over, held his hand out, and whispered, "Pssss, pssss, pssss." The cat looked towards him.

Mary sat up and said quickly, "I wish I could help but I don't know anything."

"Pssss, pssss, pssss." The cat began walking towards him.

She stood. The cat stopped. She said, "You should go now. I don't think I can help."

Bobby sighed. Hard or soft. It was going to have to be hard. He pulled out his gun and placed it next to him on the bench. "Will you sit down, please?"

"Oh, no. Wait... I just..."

"Please, Mary. Sit down."

She did.

"Pssss, pssss, pssss," he said to the cat. He leaned over, and the cat walked lazily towards him.

49

Jake and Rachel managed to drag Eugene to the sofa and pull off his jacket and tie Rachel brewed coffee. Eugene collapsed back, his head lolling from side to side as he whispered, "I'm so screwed. I'm so screwed."

"What the hell's the matter with you?" Rachel said. "You've got work tomorrow. Are you trying to mess things up?"

"I'm so screwed."

Jake turned to her. Work? Didn't she know?

"Drink this." She held up the cup of coffee to Eugene.

"Does he do this a lot?" Jake asked. He stared at his brother's blotchy face, and said, "He's always drinking."

Rachel shook her head. "He's never done this."

"Sure he has," Eugene said, trying to lift his head but giving up. "He got wasted at Louis Egglesworth's bachelor party. Remember? He was sick for a whole day."

Rachel smiled sadly. "Why are you doing this?"

"You're leaving me. After all we've been through."

"Goddammit, don't," she said. She stood up.

"I'm claymation. I'm Mr. Bill. Oh no, Mr. Bill. Come get me, Mr. Bill. Jake? Jake? Did you ever see that? Mr. Bill?"

"No."

"Right. Past your bedtime."

"Have some coffee."

"There was this Kung-fu movie on one of the satellite channels. Man, it's been so long since I saw one of those. Remember that, Jake?"

"Yeah. You used to watch those a lot."

"Last month. At three in the morning. Man, what a kick! This poor

boy sweeping out the temple for lessons. You know what happened?
He was the only one who could take on the bad guys! Oh, it was
great. He was the only one. He was even fighting off the bad guys
with a bowl and chopsticks! You should've seen it. All those villagers
cheering and thanking him. Chopsticks! Can you believe it? I got all
weepy." He sniffed and wiped his eyes. "The little guy was fighting
the odds."

"Just like those movies when we were kids," Jake said, smiling.
"Those dubbed ones."

"You remember them?"

"Of course. You used to want to practice on me."

"Oh, yeah. Right. Rachel, Rachel, I used to practice Kung-Fu on
Jake."

"I heard."

"Rachel, Rachel, I really screwed up big time—"

"No. I told you it's not just you. It's everything. We have to—"

"No, no, no. Not that. You don't get it. You don't get it. Jake, she
doesn't get it."

"Jesus," Jake said to Rachel. "He's gone. We should just put him
to bed."

"Do you remember me doing Kung-Fu?" Eugene asked. "I was
pretty damn good at it."

"I remember," Jake said, motioning to Rachel. They began to lift
him up. "You did it in the basement."

Eugene was quiet as they hefted him against Jake. Then he said,
"That fucking basement. I hated that goddamn fucking basement. Do
you remember the basement?"

"How could I forget?" Jake said. He then recalled the charts and
asked, "Hey, you don't still have those charts, do you?"

"Charts? What charts?"

"You used to graph the fights."

"Charts? Stock charts? More money I'm losing?"

Jake walked him slowly towards the bedroom, his clothes smelling of alcohol and sweat. Rachel helped on the other side. Eugene lurched forward, then back. "Whoa there," Jake said. "No, you used to chart the fights. You know, give it a number and graph it out."

"He did?" Rachel said.

"I did?" Eugene said.

Jake wondered if he had imagined it, then shook his head. "Don't you remember? You kept it hidden behind the Bruce Lee poster? The night she left must have been a really high number."

"Ah, Bruce Lee was a hack. A hack, I tell you. His stupid Jeet Kune Do was just a hodgepodge of half-assed forms he made up 'cause he couldn't handle the real stuff. A hack!"

They brought him to the bedroom and Rachel said, "Wait. Let me take off these dirty pants before putting him down."

"Woo-hoo," Eugene said. "She's taking off my pants!"

"Euge, I'm very disappointed in you," she said, unbuckling him and yanking down his slacks. "Why'd you do this? How are you going to handle work tomorrow?"

"You don't have to worry about my work. You're leaving me. You're not allowed to do that anymore."

"That's not fair," she said. She motioned for Jake to lay Eugene down, which he did, and she peeled away the slacks.

"Jake, little brother, how about slipping me some cash," Eugene mumbled. He crawled up to the pillows and curled into a ball.

"What?"

"Some cash for my stash. Running low for the hash."

Jake and Rachel glanced at each other. Then Eugene said, "Uh, I don't feel so hot."

Rachel said, "Wait! Don't throw up on the bed! Let me get a bucket!" She raced out of the room as Eugene groaned.

Jake watched his brother hold his stomach, panting. Rachel came running back in with a small plastic garbage container. She said, "If you have to throw up, do it in here."

"I'm okay, I'm okay, I'm okay," Eugene said, as he rolled his head back and forth.

"Get some rest" Jake said.

Eugene nodded. "Sleepy."

Rachel shook her head and motioned Jake out of the room. She turned off the light. They moved intot he living room, and Jake said, "Not too pretty."

"He's just blowing off steam."

He said, "Do you know why?"

She hesitated. "I guess everything."

She didn't know about Eugene losing his job. He said, "Maybe you should talk to him. Find out what's happening."

"I'm leaving him," she said. "I'm not allowed to do that anymore."

50

Jake waited until the owner of Franklin & Sons left for his lunch break. The young clerk with the gold-rimmed eyeglasses stayed in the showroom, helping a woman choose earrings. Jake walked in, and pretended to examine the watches. The clerk approached and asked Jake if he needed any help.

"Do you buy jewelry?"

"Sometimes, but it's up to the owner."

"Can I talk to him?"

"He just went out. He should be back in an hour."

Jake nodded. "Maybe I'll call later. What's his name?"

"Tony."

"Tony what."

"Tony Lomax. He should be here all afternoon."

The clerk didn't seem to recognize him from his visit two days ago; the guy had been too interested in Rachel, ignoring Jake. This could be helpful. Jake left the store and checked the list of names he had copied from the intercom system. He found a match: Anthony Lomax, #6. He ripped up the sheet of paper and threw it away.

Entering the side alley, he looked up at the buildings. The residential windows on the second floor had a direct view of the rear doors, so this could pose a problem at night. A small sign on the iron door had the store name and "Please use our front entrance." He saw corrosion around the deadbolt. It could be rusted shut, which would require a forced entry. But he needed to know if there was an alarm system in the back room.

He spent the next hour lingering near the store, monitoring the customer traffic. Moderately busy. Six walk-ins. Jake expected alternate lunch breaks. He needed to get a look at that back room, and wondered if he could use Rachel's help.

Last night, after putting his brother to bed, Jake and Rachel spoke about Eugene's drunkenness. That apparent loss of control was unusual, and Jake couldn't remember a time when his brother seemed so unhinged. She asked him about the chart and how it had looked.

"It was just a graph: date and level of fighting."

"And the night she left?"

"A doozy. He broke her nose, sent her to the hospital."

"You witnessed this?" she asked, her voice rising.

"No. We were in the basement. We figured it out later."

As Jake watched Lomax's store now and took in the activity, he relaxed. He thought about the night his mother had left. He and Eugene had been locked in the basement for almost the entire night, something that hadn't happened before, though would happen much more once their mother was gone. The fight upstairs had long since ended, and they were waiting for the sounds of the jiggling doorknob. Sometimes their mother would unlock the door and hurry to the small second bathroom near the kitchen, disappearing before they'd emerge from the basement. That night it was taking a while. Jake curled up near the furnace, a chill in the air. Eugene crouched on the steps and waited. It was silent upstairs. Jake drifted in and out of sleep, often waking up with a start, shivering. He wasn't sure how long he had been here, and was confused. He squatted down into a ball. He noticed that the goblins were trudging along the walls, hunched over and sullen. They seemed to be working on something, occasionally stopping to stare at Jake, but otherwise distracted. Then Eugene suddenly yelled and banged on the door. Let us out! Jake jumped at the sound. The goblins scattered.

His brother continued yelling and hitting the door. Frightened by the panic in his brother's voice, Jake stood up and asked what was wrong

His brother yanked on the doorknob, and banged against the door. He said that no one was home, that they had been left here. He banged again, his voice unsteady.

Jake saw some of the goblins return, watching him curiously. One of the goblins pointed to the paint cans in the corner. Jake saw through the darkness: hard-dried paintbrushes lay on the cans. Next to these were a roller and a screwdriver with a white painted tip. Jake walked across the room and picked up the screwdriver. He climbed the steps.

His brother asked what he was doing, and Jake replied, Maybe we can use this. He saw that his brother was reaching out blindly, and Jake realized that Eugene couldn't see in the dark, which surprised him. Jake grabbed Eugene's hand and placed the screwdriver in it. Eugene asked where Jake had found this.

When Jake replied, In the corner, his brother blurted, You idiot, why didn't you tell me before?

I'm not a idiot.

His brother inserted the screwdriver into a small hole in the doorknob and jiggled it. He turned the screwdriver slowly, and then turned the doorknob handle. The door opened. Eugene said, Finally. Jake asked how he had done that.

Everything can be opened with the right tools, his brother said. He told Jake to return the screwdriver, or their father might notice it misplaced.

Jake left the screwdriver on the paint cans, and saw the goblin who had helped him. Jake waved. The goblin waved back. Jake hurried upstairs. His brother had wrapped himself with a bathroom towel. His pale skin was goose-pimpled. He was examining the floor. As Jake approached, Eugene held up his hand and told him to stop.

Why?

There's a little blood here.

Jake backed away. Eugene said, Get some clothes on and go to bed.

Whose blood?

Who do you think, his brother said. Go to bed.

When Jake awoke the following morning, his mother was gone.

51

The next day at noon, during Lomax's lunch break, Jake and Rachel sat in the car two blocks down from the jewelry store. Jake wasn't sure if Rachel would back out. She said, "What if it doesn't work?"

"Then I try something else."

"And all you want is for me to look around?"

"Yeah," he answered. She had already asked this.

"What if I can't recognize an alarm?"

"That's fine."

"You think he'll let me?"

"Possibly."

She frowned.

Jake said, "You look good." He pointed to her short skirt and cropped black leather jacket. "If I was the clerk and you came in, I'd let you take all the jewels."

"Ha. Ha. I feel slutty."

"Is that a bad thing?"

She smiled.

"Should we go over it again?"

"No. I'll do my best." She kept pulling on her skirt. When she saw him noticing, she said, "I haven't worn this in ages. Now I know why." She sat back. "You were out late last night."

"I was watching Lomax's apartment."

"Euge told me about losing his job. You knew?"

Jake nodded.

"I don't know what to do."

"Why should you do anything?"

She sighed.

"Last night," Jake said, "while I was watching Lomax's place, I read more about Heraclitus."

Her eyes, puzzled, stayed fixed on him, and she said, "Since when are you reading that?"

"Since you told me a little."

"What do you think?"

Jake saw in the mirror that Lomax was leaving for his lunch break. He said, "Not a lot of it makes sense, but it sounds good. Sleeping is being close to the dead. He just left."

"What?" she asked. "Oh, him. Lomax. Should I go?"

"Go."

"Where will you be?"

"Waiting here."

She took a deep breath and said, "I'll do my best, but don't be disappointed if I can't—"

"I know. Don't worry. Just see how it goes."

She left the car and walked with short steps down the block. He watched her in the rear-view mirror, her tight skirt riding up her long thighs, and she pushed her hands against her hips, sliding the skirt back down. She had slicked back her hair with mousse, and it still retained that wet look, so he didn't really recognize her in this outfit. He stared at her legs. Her well-defined calves tightened and relaxed with each step.

He had tried to devise ways of glimpsing the back room—all he needed was a few seconds to see what the layout was—but nothing short of a trial break-in seemed possible. He was certain Lomax would recognize or at least remember him if he "accidentally" walked into that room, and the clerk had now seen him twice. Jake knew that as an Asian, especially in this neighborhood where there didn't seem to be many, he would be remembered.

Last night, as he watched Lomax return to his loft after work, Jake knew that everything hinged on how secure that back room was;

again Lomax didn't bring any jewelry home. Jake also took more time looking over Lomax's building. In the conversion to residential lofts, the builders hadn't changed any of the windows. Not only did the windows seem to lack any real insulation, but they were held shut with simple swivel latches, easily opened with a knife. The only problem was access, but he could probably climb down there from the roof.

But he needed more information. He wouldn't think of doing anything until he felt he could anticipate all of the contingencies.

After ten minutes, Rachel left the store. She climbed into the car, and Jake drove away.

"Did you see any of the back room?" he asked.

"See it? He let me in to use the bathroom."

Jake turned to her, impressed. "You went in?"

"I went in. He even left me alone for a few seconds while he checked the main room."

"And?"

"And what?"

He sighed. "And what did you see?"

She gave him a sly smile. "What do you mean?"

"Very funny."

"I bet you're dying to know what I saw."

"I am."

"I bet you'll do anything for my information."

"Almost."

"Really? Well, I'll have to think of something good."

"I'm at your disposal."

She winked, then said, "The back door to the alley has an extra metal bar across it, locked with a padlock."

"Across the whole door?"

"Yes. It looks like one of those dungeon bars, fitting into slots on the wall and on the door. The padlock is over one of the slots."

Jake thought, Forget that entry. "What else? Alarms?"

"I didn't see anything you told me to look for. No control panels. No wires near or around the door, or anywhere. It was just that wooden door."

"What about a mat?"

"No. Bare concrete floor."

"Skylight?"

"Oh, rats. I didn't check. I don't think so. The only light was the fluorescent."

"Bathroom?"

"What about it?"

"Windows, vents, anything?"

"I think a fan on top."

"Okay. Describe the room."

"Everything?"

"As much as you can remember."

She closed her eyes. "I walk in and I see the dirty concrete floor, a folding table with two chairs, and a desk with an office chair. There are metal shelves along the walls with books and small boxes. At the desk are a couple of lamps and something that looks like a magnifying glass on an arm. Next to the desk is a safe, a big one."

"How big?"

"Higher than the desk and about three feet wide. Pretty deep because it was sticking out."

Jake cursed silently. Too big to steal. "Can you describe the safe?"

"It's brown, has a big dial on the front, and looks kind of old. I didn't get a chance to see much more because he kept talking to me, and after I used the bathroom, he turned off the lights and waited for me to get out."

"When he closed the door, did he lock it?"

"I don't think so."

"Did you see any small green or red indicator lights, anything near or around the door?"

"Nothing. I looked."

Jake was pleased with this, but the safe would be a problem. He said, "You did great. I can't believe you saw all that."

She punched the air. "Piece of cake."

Jake heard it in her voice, that juicing up inside, the flash of adrenaline. He said, "You're feeling it."

"What?"

"The charge," Jake said. "From the risk."

"Yes."

"How do you like it?"

"I like it."

52

The front alarm was the biggest hurdle. Jake would have to disable it quickly, but wasn't sure how, not with that tubular cylinder lock. He would need maybe thirty minutes to pick it, and that was unacceptable. Cutting the power was a possibility.

He also had little experience with safes. He had stolen an entire safe from a house once, and it had taken him two days to break it open. The one that Rachel had seen was too large; he needed to bring someone in.

Jake had spent the afternoon checking the status of his jewelry, collecting checks and withdrawing unsold items. He decided not to bring out any more new jewels. If he was going to consider Lomax's store seriously, he couldn't be appearing in jewelry stores all over the city. He cashed the checks and stored the unsold jewelry at the bank, then walked back to the apartment. He remembered that Chih had once mentioned someone who handled safes. What was the name? It was familiar to Jake through stories of a big bank job, though Jake wasn't sure if Chih had been vouching for him. Hunt was the name. Something Hunt. But after Bobby Null, Jake wasn't so sure about Chih's judgment. It was time to check in, find out what had happened up there after he left. Chih probably thought Jake and Bobby had shut him out. Jake would explain, then maybe sound him out for someone who knew safes.

Rachel was home. She was packing books into U-haul boxes. The split-up was truly happening. He said, "Did you find an apartment?"

"Possibly. I applied for one that looked good. A studio in the Marina. I should hear from them in a couple of days."

"How much, or do I want to know?"

She shook her head. "You don't want to know."

"And you're packing already."

"I have to sooner or later."

"Well."

She skimmed the titles of one stack, and said, "Look at all these stupid books on fertility."

"Where's Eugene?" Jake asked.

She shrugged. "Job hunting, I guess. I really hope he's not out drinking."

Jake thought of his brother face-down on this floor, right where he was standing. He said, "He's been like this before?"

Rachel didn't reply, and put more books into the box. She rolled up her sleeves and wiped her forehead with the back of her hand, sighing. "No. You should talk to him," she said.

"Me."

"He'll probably listen to you."

"What should I say?"

"Just that he might be drinking too much and you've never seen him like this."

Jake nodded. "All right."

"Have you had dinner?"

"Not yet."

She stood up, her knees cracking. "I'll pick something up." She looked down at the boxes. "If Euge shows up while I'm gone, don't say anything about my apartment. I'll tell him."

When she left, Jake looked through the open boxes, reading the covers of the books. He walked down the hall and saw the empty bookshelves, which depressed him. He closed the door.

He had Chih's number in his wallet, and called the store in Seattle. A woman with an indistinguishable accent answered, and Jake was confused.

"Uh, is Chih-seh there?"

A pause. "Who is this?"

"Who is this?"

"This is his wife."

"His wife? I thought you hated his store."

"Who is this?"

"It's Jake, a friend of Chih's. Is he there? Can I talk to him?"

"Oh, no. You don't know."

"Know what?"

"Chih...Chih was killed in a robbery."

Jake wasn't sure he had heard her correctly, but her voice cracked and continued with, "He was shot and they took his money. I...I'm closing the store. They killed him."

53

"Relax," Bobby said. "I just want information, then I'll never bother you again."

"I told you. I don't know anything." Mary's face was deep red, her cheeks splotchy. Her eyes kept flickering towards the cat in his hands.

"Thing is, I don't believe you. You went out with him for a year and you don't know anything? Maybe you want to protect him? Maybe you know where he is right now. Maybe you're going to call him as soon as I leave." He scratched the cat's head.

"Please, you're scaring me. I swear I haven't heard or seen him in five years."

"What was it like, going out with him?" he asked.

She sat stiffly at the edge of the chair. "We had an okay time."

"Why'd you break up?"

"I moved down here for a job, and he didn't follow."

"What's his brother's name?"

"Something nerdy. Dexter or something."

"Ah. So you do remember."

"No. I'm not sure. He mentioned it once or twice, but it never stuck in my mind. It was a name that I thought was nerdy."

"Dexter."

"Something like that."

"Where did he work?"

"The brother? In the city. He worked at some kind of techie place."

"Name?"

She shook her head.

"What kind of techie place? Computers?"

"He didn't know."

"Jake didn't know what his brother did for a living?"

"Just that it was tech-related."

He sighed. "What about other friends?"

"He had no friends, really. He always kept to himself."

"What about other family? Parents?"

"He told me his parents split up when he was young, and he hadn't spoken to either of them since he was a teenager."

Bobby stared at her, then said slowly, "Have you ever watched a cat choke to death?"

She began crying. "Please, I swear I don't know anything else."

"My brother, who's dead by the way, used to do crazy things like that, just to freak me out. Once there was this neighborhood cat that I liked." He stroked Mary's cat, and it purred, settling into his lap. Bobby said, "He saw that the cat liked me better. You know, it came to me when I called it, but not to him. You know what he did?"

She shook her head and wiped eyes.

"He grabbed it around its neck with both hands, lifted it into the air and began squeezing." Bobby had tried to stop him, but Kevin had kicked him viciously in the leg and Bobby went down. He said, "My brother's arms were getting all scratched up. I mean really bloody, but he just smiled and squeezed harder and harder. He was really strong, and the cat was trying to fight back. You know, clawing and trying to hiss at him. It was one of the worst fucking things I've ever seen."

"Your brother did this?"

Bobby nodded. "I don't know why he hated me so much. I was just a kid. Anyway, the cat stopped moving, and he flung it at me. He said, 'Now call it and see if it comes.' I'm not kidding you. This really happened."

"What did you do?"

"His arms were all scratched and bloody, and I was completely shitting in my pants. The cat just lay there. I went screaming for my mother."

"And?"

"And he told her that they cat went wild, and he was trying to protect me. The story I told was just so bizarre. She didn't believe me. She never did. He was her favorite."

She covered her face with her hands, and said, "Please go."

"You can't help me?"

She shook her head.

"Do you love your cat?"

She nodded, her face still covered.

"All right. I'll go."

She looked at him.

"What, you think I'd hurt this cat? After what my brother did? Hell, I'd sooner choke a person to death than a cat. What the fuck did the cat ever do to me?" He pushed the cat gently off his lap. It hopped onto the floor. Bobby said, "Let me ask this: If you wanted to get in touch with him again, what would you do?"

She waited until the cat left the room. She said, "I'd call his number in Seattle."

"And if he wasn't there anymore? If the number was disconnected?"

"I'd send a letter to his address and hope it got forwarded."

He said, "No forwarding address."

"I'd try to find his brother."

"How?"

"I'd call every Ahn in San Francisco."

Bobby nodded. "Yeah. I guess that's what I'll do." He stood up slowly, wincing. His head now ached from the fall. He grabbed his gun, and said, "I'll go now. You're not going to call the police or anything, are you?"

She shook her head quickly.

"I know where you live. I know who you are."

She nodded.

"All right. Sorry about scaring you. I had to know if you were lying."

"Please go."

He walked out of her house, hearing her lock and bolt the door, and he limped towards his car. It bothered him that his mother never knew the real Kevin. Even getting shot by the police hadn't changed her mind. She wanted to sue the police. She believed that it was all a mistake. Bobby had missed the funeral, but saw how his mother had moped around the house for days. She would drift into Kevin's room, fixing his bed and cleaning his windows. Bobby knew she'd keep it a goddamn shrine, and the thought of it pissed him off. Kevin once smothered Bobby with a garbage bag, seeing how long Bobby could survive without breathing. Bobby, a kid at the time, saw the world through white plastic, his lungs squeezed, his body convulsing, and when Kevin pulled off the bag, Bobby cried. Kevin smiled.

Bobby wished Kevin was still alive, if only to show their mother what a true piece of shit he was.

54

Jake didn't stay on the phone with Chih's wife for long, but learned the essentials: it was a daylight robbery, and they had only taken the cash in the register. Chih's handheld panic button—something that Jake had once laughed at—prevented the robbers from getting the jewels. His wife said no one had seen anything, and no one had been caught, even questioned. Jake said he was sorry, and after a moment asked about getting Hunt's number. Chih's wife looked up the name in an address book and gave Jake two numbers of two different Hunts. Jake then asked if he could do anything for her, and she said, "Do you know who could've done this?"

Jake said, "No."

"Then there's nothing you can do." She said goodbye and hung up.

He was suspicious of Chih's death occurring so closely after the Chun job. The worry grew when he considered that Bobby's death had never been reported in the news. He needed to check the Seattle newspapers again. All this could be a coincidence, but the vague feeling that Bobby might be alive turned his mood grim. A bullet in the gut, kicked a few times in the head, and left in the garbage. Could Bobby have survived?

He pocketed the two Hunt phone numbers, and found himself rattled for the first time since coming down here. Chih was dead? They had only taken the cash. It might have been a hit and the stolen cash just a way to make it look like a botched robbery. Chih had more cash in a safe, and Jake couldn't believe that none of the jewels, not even the ones openly displayed, were taken. The alarm had possibly thwarted that, but he didn't know.

Maybe Chih was into something that Jake didn't know about.

Maybe this was a coincidence.

He sat down on the sofa. Poor fucking Chih. He was a cheat, a liar, and, as a fence, screwed everyone over, but Jake had liked him.

Jake saw a philosophy book Rachel hadn't yet packet, and he flipped it open to the Presocratic section. He read some of the translated fragments. *War rules everything, and it's through the conflict and strife of opposites that we find harmony. Death and life are one.*

Tell that to Chih, he thought.

55

Jake woke up when his brother entered the apartment. He heard Rachel stirring, the sofa bed creaking, and she said in a loud, crisp voice, Not again.

We desert people have eyes in the back of our heads, Eugene said.

What?

The sounds of the kitchen faucet mingled with Eugene gurgling.

Jesus, Euge, you've got to get your act together.

You're packing?

Shh. Yes.

Look what you're doing to me.

Don't blame me for this, Rachel said, her voice low.

My limbs are falling off.

You're drunk. You need help.

I need a sculptor.

What?

I need Michelangelo.

God, you can't even hear me, you're so drunk.

I hear you. I am drinking because I lost my fucking job and my wife is fucking leaving me, and I have no fucking money, and I'm drowning in fucking debt. Is that all right?

Jake sat up.

Don't talk to me like that—

I hear you all right. I hear you because my ears haven't fallen off and my head is still attached for now—

Keep your voice down—

And you're leaving me because you haven't gotten what you wanted. Well let me tell you something, you think I wanted all this bullshit? Do you?

Eugene, please...

You think I wanted to live in an overpriced piece of shit apartment and bending over for an asshole boss and not have a family? You think this is what I wanted? You think I'm fucking happy with the way we live? Do you! Do you! Do you!

Jake listened. Rachel was quiet.

Eugene muttered, My arms fell off. Leave them there. I'll get them in the morning.

He walked heavily down the hallway.

Jake heard Rachel crying.

56

Jake and Rachel took a bus to Lomax's building. It was late afternoon, and for the previous two hours Rachel had been checking online for any stories about Chih or Bobby. She and Jake had found a brief story of Chih's murder in *The Seattle Times*, but that was it. There was no follow-up, no stories of leads or investigations, and Jake wasn't surprised to find other news, such as a Greenpeace demonstration and arrest, getting more coverage. Chih was a small-time jeweler. It was just another robbery and murder. There was also nothing about Bobby Null, about any dead bodies found in a dumpster, about a gunshot victim in the U-District. The crimes of petty thieves seemed irrelevant. During the crowded bus ride, Jake was certain he had shot Bobby squarely in the gut, a slow, but fatal wound. Bobby had been unconscious and the only way he could've survived would have been if someone had found him in that dumpster. That was impossible, yet why wasn't there any news of it?

"Thanks for not mentioning last night," Rachel said.

"No big deal," he said. He noticed that she had changed into black sneakers and black jeans. "You have on a creeper outfit."

She shrugged. "This is comfortable. Did you talk to him this morning?"

"He asked me if I thought he was drinking too much."

"What did you say?"

"I said yes."

"Good. What did he say?"

"He said I should start looking for a place because after you leave, he's going to sell the condo."

"What? He said that?"

"He did."

"What else did he say?"

"Something about getting the car repaired."

She nodded and stared out onto the street. "You think he's going to go drinking again?"

Jake shook his head. "I don't know."

"What are you thinking about?"

"About Chih. He was a friend."

"The guy in the paper. I'm sorry. I didn't realize."

"We go back a while."

"You didn't mention it."

"I know. I'm still a little surprised."

She said, "Do you know who could've done this?"

"No," he said. "Probably a random crime. I think."

After a moment, she said, "You were close to him."

"Close?" He realized he didn't need to be so secretive. "He was my fence and a guy who taught me a lot about jewelry."

"Oh, I see. Are you going back up for the funeral?"

He hadn't even thought of that. He should've been more consoling to Chih's wife; instead he had pumped her for Chih's contacts. Nice. He told Rachel, "I don't think so."

"Do you think his death is connected to what you did?"

"No," he said.

"Are you sure?"

"No." A line of people filed off the bus. Jake thought of Chih bouncing around the store, overcharging tourists for cheap jewelry. He said, "There was a moment, once I began visiting his store more, when we both realized at the same time that we were dealing with stolen jewelry. It was funny."

"Why?"

"I was doing what I'm doing here, selling jewelry, and after I brought in some diamonds, we began talking. It was just the way we were careful about where I got the diamonds, and how he liked to deal in cash. All these clues. Then I said something like I had more, and then he looked at me, and we both knew." There was that moment when their eyes met and Chih gave him a slow, knowing smile. They had continued to speak indirectly about the jewels-for-cash deal, testing each other, until Jake knew he was a fence.

"So he was a legitimate jeweler?"

"Yeah. Didn't start out that way, but soon had a pretty good store."

"Was he married? Kids?"

"Married. I don't know if he had kids."

"You don't know?"

"We didn't talk about personal things," he said, and felt a tinge of regret. Personal tidbits leaked out from time to time, and Jake suspected Chih did have kids from something he had once said about the lousy schools in Seattle.

Rachel pulled on the cord over the window, signaling the driver. She said, "We get off next."

They left the bus, Jake disoriented and following Rachel as she moved briskly through a crowd of people waiting to board. They walked for three blocks in silence, their steps in unison. At one point Rachel linked her arm in his, and Jake tightened his elbow around hers. She smiled, but stared ahead. The side streets were darker with more homeless settling in for the night in doorways and alleys by the larger warehouses. They approached Lomax's block, and Rachel asked where they should be.

"Let's check if his car is here yet."

The parking lot was empty except for one pick-up in the corner. Jake wanted to watch the front entrance, so he and Rachel hid across the street by an office supply building. They found a spot beside a garage door, a high concrete curb as their seat. Except for the darkening dusk sky, there wasn't much lighting on this side of the street, so Jake wasn't worried about being seen. Most of the traffic ran on Howard and Folsom. The smell of cheap wine and motor oil seeped into their clothes. They settled in.

During the next thirty minutes, as they watched the sparse traffic in silence, Jake kept thinking about Chih getting killed. The newspaper report said only that he was fatally shot; it didn't report how. In fact, most of the details had been left out. Did he suffer? Jake didn't want to consider this.

"There's someone leaving," Rachel whispered.

They watched a man in a white T-shirt and jeans hurry through the front door and out the security gate, letting it slam loudly on its own. He jogged around the building. Soon, the pick-up pulled out of the lot and turned a corner. It was quiet again. Jake asked, "What day is it?"

"Friday."

"Where is everyone?"

"Friday night. People going out."

Jake said, "Without work I'm losing track of the days."

"Me too," she said. "You mean the restaurant?"

"Yeah."

"Tell me what you did there. How'd you get to be a chef?"

Jake told her about starting as a part-time bus boy. He had wanted a crappy job just to keep busy, and to supplement his income. When the owner needed a volunteer to come in on Sunday morning at five a.m. to help prepare the brunch buffet, Jake was the only one interested. He spent all morning filling the carts with ice and arranging them in the dining room, then setting up the Steno burners and hot trays. He refilled the food trays throughout the day, and by the early evening, he'd pack it all down, empty and wash the carts. He liked the solitude of the job—he didn't have to deal with customers or waiters. He liked waking up at dawn and moving through the restaurant when it was quiet and empty. He liked cleaning up after everyone had gone home. The owner was surprised, since the other busboys hated that job, and either quit or refused to do it any longer, but Jake stayed with it.

Soon, instead of bringing the empty trays and serving bowls to the kitchen and asking for refills, the cooks began telling him to refill them himself. Then they asked him to prepare the easier pastas by himself. Within a few weeks the owner moved him off the bus boy schedule and he began working the cold side during the week. He continued manning the Sunday brunches, and still liked that the best.

"You sound like a farmer, getting up at dawn and all that," Rachel said.

"It was so simple. You have to do certain things, and you do it. I liked that. When I was working the mail room at a company, I had to deal with all kinds bullshit."

"Like what?"

"Petty supervisors taking credit for what you did, people asking for special favors for their mail, people messing up the postage meters and then blaming you." He shook his head.

"Why even bother with a regular job?""I needed something regular, something different. I still do. Keeps me out of trouble."

He saw Lomax's car drive by, and he nudged her. This time, however, the car didn't pull into the parking lot, but stopped by the curb. Lomax climbed out and then a woman opened the passenger door. They were talking.

"A date?" Rachel whispered. "Well, well."

The blonde woman was tall and fleshy, her dress a little too tight; her arms squeezed into the sleeves. She had a shiny black pocketbook she swung as she walked with Lomax through the front gate. They entered the building. Jake said, "He can't park there for long. They must be going back out soon."

"Damn. If we had the car we could follow them."

Jake calculated the length of a date: dinner, maybe a movie or a club, maybe drinks. Would they come back here or would Lomax drive her home? A few hours at least. He felt the adrenaline beginning to whisper through him, the quiet hiss of excitement. He modulated his breathing, exhaling slowly, and focused on the building. The second floor loft had its lights on, but that was it on this side. What was Lomax doing? Maybe changing, getting cash, looking for something. He picked the woman up right after work, but needed to drop by his place first. It'll be just a second, Lomax told her. Why don't you come in.

A police car turned the corner and drove down the street. As it passed Jake, he stared at the cop driving. He felt Rachel tense next to him, but Jake wasn't worried. They were just sitting around. The cop continued down the street, unaware of them. Routine patrol. He turned to Rachel, who said, "I feel like a criminal and I haven't even done anything."

"Guilty conscience."

"Not you?" she asked.

Lomax emerged from the building, holding the front door open for his date. The woman walked under the yellow light above the entrance and paused; her face was warped by the shadows, then blinked into darkness as they passed through the gate and moved to the car. Lomax wore a leather jacket, and held open the passenger door for her. Jake and Rachel watched them drive away.

He pulled out a pair of surgical gloves and snapped them on. Rachel watched him, startled.

He turned to her and said, "You ready to try something a little risky?"

"What do you mean?"

"It's my 'poking around' phase. I look around a little bit."

"Where?"

He pointed towards Lomax's building.

57

Bobby found a phone book in the lobby. The stale carpets stank of mold. The overstuffed chairs near the front desk were crimson and green; small tears had been sewn with differently colored threads. Old men with crumpled newspapers filled every chair. There was a wrinkled Chinese guy in one of the chairs, reading a Chinese newspaper. A sign near the front desk read, "Welcome to the Bishop Residence Hotel. Weekly and Monthly Rates."

Bobby had called only a dozen Ahns in San Francisco. The phone book had over forty listed, and he knew that Jake's brother might not even have a public number. It was possible, too, that the brother lived outside of the city, since Jake could've said "San Francisco" as the general area. Wasn't Silicon Valley south of San Francisco?

Bobby slammed the phone book shut. Everyone looked up.

He had to start over. Jake was careful, but not careful enough. Bobby had his social security number, bank numbers, a Seattle address, and pay stubs. There must be something here, but he needed help. He looked through the Yellow Pages for "private investigators" and searched for an office nearby. He found one on this same street, 16th, memorized the name and address, and returned to his room to get Jake's paperwork. With these in hand, he left the hotel and walked six blocks to an old brick office building. He checked the listings near the stairwell—immigration lawyers, bailbondsmen, a dentist—and saw that Underhill Investigations was on the fourth floor. The elevator had an "Out of Order" sign on it. Someone had scribbled "Fuck you LandLord" underneath.

Bobby was growing tired, and looked glumly up the long flight of stairs. He had spent the entire night in pain, going to the bathroom every two hours and trying to piss. He had been feverish until this morning, and he still was a little shaky. He touched his cheek; his face was clammy. He began climbing the steps slowly, figuring that he was here and he ought to check this guy's rates. A flash of burning pain crackled deep inside his stomach. He stopped walking and cursed. Something was really wrong, and he knew he'd have to find a doctor soon. This was all Jake's fault. He gritted his teeth and said Jake's name with each step up. His back was slick with sweat.

Underhill Investigations was a small room with a desk and a computer. The door was wide open, but no one was there. Bobby sat down in the hard wood chair across from the desk and waited. He thought of a cover story, practiced it, then looked around. His hotel room was bigger than this office, and he also had a window. Here it felt like a jail cell—dark, cramped, and cold. He glanced at some of the papers strewn on the desk, and read what looked like letters to lawyers and businesses, trying to sell Underhill Investigations' services. Bobby read the line "We specialize in background checks and employee screening" but then saw in a different letter that Underhill specialized in "worker's compensation cases and insurance fraud." He snorted.

"Find anything interesting?" a voice said.

Bobby turned slowly and saw a small, skinny man with a brown bomber jacket that hung too loosely. He had a cup of coffee in his hands. Bobby said, "How can you specialize in all those things?"

The man walked behind his desk and pushed the letters aside. He shrugged off his jacket. Underneath he wore a shirt and tie. He sipped his coffee, and took off his glasses, rubbing his eyes. "You shouldn't be looking at my personal mail," he said.

"You shouldn't leave your door wide open with your mail lying around," Bobby answered. He felt another stinging pain in his stomach and grimaced. The man noticed this, but didn't say anything. Bobby asked, "Are you Underhill?"

"I am. What can I do for you?"

"I need you to find someone, but I want to know your rates."

"Depends on how much information you have."

Bobby told him what he wanted, Jake Ahn's brother, and what he had: Jacob Ahn's former address, bank statement, pay stubs, and former girlfriend. "But the catch is I don't know this guy's—Jake's brother—first name."

"Why don't you ask this Jake?"

"He's disappeared."

"But you don't want me to find him?"

"I need to find the brother, not Jake."

"How'd you get all that information?"

"I got it," Bobby said. "How much to find this guy?"

"The guy with no name? That's tough. They have the same last name?"

"Yeah."

"He's in the area?"

"Supposedly. I have some background, like the guy's a techie, has a geek name like Dexter or something."

"Why do you want to find this guy?"

Bobby said, "Doesn't matter, does it?"

"No. Why'd the brother disappear?"

"Doesn't matter."

Underhill leaned back in his chair and touched his fingertips together. "You said you have a bank statement?"

Bobby nodded. His back was sweating again, a chill running up and down his spine. "So how much?"

"I can charge you a flat rate. $1000 for a week's work. Expenses included."

"You got to be shitting me. A grand to find a guy?"

"You're not giving me much to go on."

"Forget it," Bobby said, standing up. He was dizzy. "I'll do it myself."

"If you tell me more, it might make it easier. Hey, you okay?"

"Yeah." He sat back down. "What do you want to know?"

"Why do you want to find this guy?"

Bobby felt a heaviness pushing down on his chest. He was getting sick of all this. He just wanted to go back to L.A. to his old life. Fuck Jake for doing this. He said, "This guy, Jake, owes me money. He's gone. The only way I can find him is through the brother."

"Why don't you hire me to find Jake?"

"You won't."

"How do you know?"

"That's what I've been doing. He's pretty slippery."

"How much does he owe you?"

"None of your fucking business."

Underhill held up his hands. "Hey, I'm just asking—"

"And I'm telling you it's none of your business."

"You don't look so good," he said. "You want some water?"

This made Bobby think of pissing, and then he suddenly felt the need to go to the bathroom. Not again. He said, "You know, never mind. I gotta go." He stood up, wavered, and held the door as he tried to leave. His vision suddenly went fuzzy, his head swimming, and the pain that travelled though his stomach now sharpened and buzzed into his groin. He cursed, and doubled over, but this gave him a head rush, and he started to black out. He felt himself hitting the ground, heard Underhill saying "Yo, what are you doing?" and then everything went quiet and dark.

58

The first lock: Lomax's security gate. Standard pin tumbler, worn from overuse and probably could be snapped open, but Jake only had his picks. His snapping wire was back at the apartment. Plenty of leeway and action here, though, but spring-loaded for one-handed unlocking and opening. With a key, a resident only had to twist it an eighth of the way and push the door open. The key sprung back into position. This made it a little difficult because Jake had to keep the tension wrench firm—any loosening would jar the pins out of place. The latex gloves felt wrinkled and warm from being in his pocket. He knelt. He was able to rake the pins up, and opened the gate in about twenty seconds.

"Jesus," Rachel said.

"Keep watch," he warned.

She looked up and down the street.

He moved to the front entrance, yellow light spilling around him. Rachel stayed by the security gate, holding it open and checking for pedestrians, cop cars. He crouched and inspected the second lock: another pin tumbler, spring loaded. He inserted the diamond pick and felt inside for the last pin, found it, then twisted in the tension wrench. He began raking quickly, forcing the pins into place. He felt the wrench turning, loosening, and then, after the tenth rake, *click,* the pins lined in place, and he turned the wrench. "Okay, come on," he said to Rachel, who followed quickly behind, the security gate slamming shut. They entered the building, and Jake kept the tension wrench in his hand, warming it, keeping it flexible.

He glanced at Rachel, whose jaw was tense, her face pale.

Apartment one was on his right. He examined the doorknob and deadbolt; they looked fairly new. There was a second door mid-way down the hall, and he guessed number three was at the end. Lomax's apartment was number six, and Jake pointed to the ceiling. They took the stairs at the end of the main hallway. The walls were painted a shiny pale yellow, the floors rust red. Everything was concrete. He looked around for cameras, security panels, anything problematic, but found nothing.

On the second floor the layout was the same, apartment number four next to him. He walked quickly, passing number five, and saw Lomax's door around the corner, recessed from the hall. None of the doors were in the line of sight of the other doors, a good privacy measure, but also making it safer for Jake. He knelt down.

"Wait," Rachel whispered. "You're going in?"

He stopped. "What did you think?"

"I thought you were just going to look around in here."

"No. I want to look inside. The more I know the better off I am." He examined the door, pushing it in to feel how snug the lock was, and said to Rachel, "You can stay out here, warn me if you hear someone coming." He started on the doorknob lock, knowing this might take a bit longer. Newer doorknobs always had more rigid shear lines. He wasn't certain from the action, but the deadbolt might not be engaged. With both doorknob and deadbolt locks in the jamb, the door would be tighter. Also, he was guessing that Lomax, in a hurry to start his date, might have simply left one lock on. He tried raking the doorknob lock, but that didn't work. As he worked the pick into the back of the lock, and felt in the tension wrench the first pin lining up and breaking easily, he thought about the possibility of alarms inside. From the poor set-up of the windows, he doubted this—there wasn't much point in securing the door if the windows were exposed, but he wanted to be prepared. There was always a ten- to twenty-second delay from the door opening to the alarm, and if, once he entered, he saw any alarms, he and Rachel had time to get out.

Click. Another pin slipped into place. Three more. He moved through the next two pins quickly, but the last one gave him some trouble. He couldn't find the shear line. Rachel fidgeted. He tried to concentrate. He raised and lowered the pin, searching, and was careful to keep the tension on the wrench even. If he moved the wrench in either direction just a millimeter, he'd have to start over.

"Jake?" Rachel whispered.

He didn't reply, searching, searching, then felt the last pin click into place. But when he tried to turn the wrench, the cylinder wouldn't give. He let out an annoyed breath, and eased the wrench very slightly, hoping that it was just one pin overextended, and with the right touch it might fall into the breaking point.

"Jake," she said. "I don't like this."

"Hold on," he whispered, feeling the wrench give. Then, reapplying the pressure as soon as he felt another click, he turned the cylinder and unlocked the knob. All right. He pulled out the pick and wrench, and pinched his finger over the keyhole. He said to Rachel, "If I say 'Go' I want you to hurry out of here as quickly as possible."

"What?"

Jake turned the doorknob and pushed in the door. The deadbolt wasn't engaged, and he slipped in, looking quickly at the surrounding foyer. Control panels? Blinking lights? Contact plates? He scanned the walls, then ran towards the kitchen, also scanning. Nothing. No alarm. He hurried back to Rachel, who was crouched, ready to run. "It's okay," he said.

"What the hell is going on?"

"Just in case there was an alarm."

"Alarm?"

"I'm going to look around in here. Keep watch. If you hear anyone coming in downstairs, let me know."

"What if it's Lomax?"

"Then let me know fast. I'll have time to get out."

She nodded. "I'll wait near the stairs so I can hear better."

Jake hurried back into the apartment. It was a large concrete room with high ceilings and a small open bedroom area up a set of narrow stairs. He checked the windows; a long aluminum pole hung next to them, required to unlatch and pull open the upper sections. He saw in the corner a desk with a computer, and approached the file cabinet. He was about to open it, but stopped. He again checked for alarms. Nothing.

Lomax's files were organized by personal, business, and home sections. Jake wasn't looking for anything in particular, just information about the store, the alarm, the kinds of jewelry perhaps, a deeper kind of surveillance. He flipped through the business files, finding old tax forms, expense and income reports, and jewelry newsletters and magazine clippings. He had trouble with his gloves, his fingers awkward with the papers. He paused when he saw brochures and warranty certificates for jewelry repair equipment. Then, when he saw "Lifetime Warranty for Harding-Bower Safes," he stopped. He pulled it out. The safe was guaranteed for fire and water damage. At the bottom was a space for the make and model number of the particular Harding-Bower safe, and Lomax had filled it in. Could be very important. Jake folded this and shoved it in his pants. He continued flipping through the files, looking for alarm or security information. Nothing.

He closed the filing cabinet, and turned his attention to the desk. The main drawer was filled with pens and office supplies. The top drawer on the right had Franklin & Sons stationary, envelopes, and business cards. The bottom drawer was locked.

Examining the small keyhole, he thought it might be one of the older lever locks. He needed a light, though. He turned on the desk lamp, and saw the lever mechanism. These were easier than pin tumblers because there were no pins. The key simply fit into certain grooves, and once it turned, the lever was released, opening the lock.

All Jake had to do was use his hook pick, search for the moving parts—the levers—and push them back by twisting the pick in the right motion. He did it on the first try. The shackle spring clicked, and he pulled the drawer open.

A small wad of cash bound with a rubber band, two boxes of checks, and more files. In the corner, though, there were three keyrings, each with five or six keys. He pulled them out and lay them on the desk. One set was labelled, and he almost laughed when he saw "Xtra Store Keys" written on the small plastic tab. The other two weren't labelled but they looked like more back-up or old, unused keys. He didn't want to take the whole ring, because Lomax would notice. There was only one tubular cylinder key, a small key with a half-inch notched cylinder at the end. This had to be the alarm key. He thought, Today is my lucky day.

He saw another tubular cylinder key on the ring with a set of older, worn keys. He compared the two cylinders, and they didn't match. The older one could've been for another alarm, a coin box, even a Coke machine. Jake unhooked the store alarm key, pocketed it, then replaced it on the chain with the older tubular cylinder. Unless someone tried to use this key, the switch probably wouldn't be noticed. Then he examined the other store keys, identifying the warded padlock key for the security gate, the door and deadlock keys, and possibly the back room key. There were two more he wasn't sure about, but it didn't matter. He was tempted to take them all, though the only one he really needed was the tubular cylinder.

Rachel burst into the door and closed it quickly. "Someone's coming!"

"Lomax?"

"I'm not sure. They just ran in. I didn't have time—"

"Sh." Jake turned off the light, replaced all the key chains as he had found them, and closed the cabinet. He had to re-lock it, but there wasn't time. He ran to the door. "How many voices?"

"At least two."

"A woman?"

"I couldn't tell. They were in a hurry."

The voices came up and rang through the second floor halls. Laughter. Jake didn't recognize Lomax's voice, but he couldn't be sure. He slowly engaged the deadbolt, and locked the doorknob.

"What are we going to do?" Rachel asked, her voice tight.

Jake glanced up at the windows. Could they climb it? He heard more laughter as the voices neared. He held the deadbolt latch and said, "Can you get out through those windows?"

"Up there? Are you kidding? And we're two floors up! How will we get down—"

"Quiet."

She grabbed his arm tightly. "Jake—"

"Sh." He held the deadbolt tighter, hoping that it would seem jammed. His breathing quickened, and he held it as he listened.

The voices stopped. He heard keys jangling, but they weren't at this door. He let out a small sigh. "It's the neighbor. It's number 5."

Rachel made a fist and pressed it into her other palm. "Jake."

"I need one more minute—"

"What? Let's get out of here—"

"One minute. Stay here." He unlocked the door and opened it a crack. "Stay here and listen. One minute."

"What if Lomax comes—"

"He won't."

"How do you know?"

He motioned to the room. "Don't touch anything. Fingerprints."

She stiffened. He hurried back to the desk, crouched in front of the bottom drawer lever lock, and picked it again. Locking it was the same as unlocking it, but because he was a little rattled, it took him a full thirty seconds. He finished, checked the desk, and noticed that he had moved the lamp. He moved it back.

"They're leaving again," Rachel said.

She was resting her palm on the door. He went to the kitchen, ripped off a couple sheets of paper towels, dampened them in the sink, then motioned her away from the door. He wiped it down. He opened the door, did the same with the exterior. Crumpling the towels, he said, "Let's go."

He relocked the doorknob and shut the door behind him. They walked casually down the stairs and out of the building. He threw out the paper towels and his gloves in a garbage can near the bus stop. As they waited for the next bus, Jake felt the key in his pocket and suppressed the rising excitement within him. He turned to Rachel, who had been staring at him. He mouthed the words, Are you okay?

She nodded slowly, leaned towards him to whisper in his ear. Her cheek brushed against his, and she said, "That was crazy." When she pulled away she continued to hold his arm. He moved closer to her, pressing his palm against the small of her back, drawing her to him, and said into her ear, "That's just the beginning." He lingered a moment, pressing harder, and then withdrew. She blinked rapidly, then gave him a puzzled smile out of the corner of her mouth.

59

Jake and Rachel came home to find Eugene watching TV. They stopped, studied him, and Eugene said without turning, "I'm fine. The car won't be ready for a few days. Rachel, you got a call from Truman. Call him at his home."

"What did he want?"

Eugene shrugged. Rachel picked up the cordless phone and walked to the bedroom. Jake sat down next to his brother, who asked, "Where were you two?"

"Rachel was helping me with something."

"With what?"

Jake said, "With checking something out."

Eugene glanced at him, then turned back to the TV. He flipped through the channels. Jake heard Rachel murmuring in the bedroom. Eugene cleared his throat. "You wouldn't happen to have some extra cash to lend me, would you?"

Jake wasn't sure he heard his brother right. He said, "What?"

"I'm liquidating my IRA, but it'll take a few days. I need a few thousand. I can pay you back next week."

"What's an ira?"

"I.R.A. My retirement account."

"Are you having money problems?"

Eugene said, "A little."

Jake sat back. Eugene was asking him for money? He had trouble digesting this. "How much?"

"This car repair's going to be more than I thought, and I've maxed out most of my credit cards—"

"How much?"

"Thirty-five hundred."

"For the car?"

"Also for some smaller bills." Eugene waved his hand. "Look, it's no big deal. Forget I asked—"

"I can write you a check now, or get you cash tomorrow."

"A check is fine. I can pay you back next week."

Jake nodded and went to the guest room to find his checkbook. These were still the temporary checks the bank had given him, and he wrote one for four thousand dollars. He returned and handed it to his brother. Eugene glanced at it and said, "It's more."

"I like even numbers."

"Thanks." He folded it and slipped it into his breast pocket.

"Who's Truman?" Jake asked.

"Guy at her old job. I think they want her back."

"The bank?"

Eugene nodded. "Maybe she'll go back now that things are different."

"You mean splitting up," Jake said. He glanced at the boxes. Rachel hadn't made much progress since yesterday. "Where will you live?"

"I don't know."

"How soon do you need me out?"

"A month."

"All right," Jake said. "How's your job search?"

"What job search?"

"Aren't you looking?"

"No."

"Why not?"

Eugene said slowly, "I'm not ready."

"Don't you need money?"

"Are you going to get on my case?" Eugene said.

Jake shook his head.

"Let me worry about my problems. You worry about yours."

He said, "Sorry."

After a minute, Eugene said, "I remember the charts. I had forgotten about those."

"The ones about Dad?"

"Yeah. I'm surprised you remembered them."

"I liked that you did that. It was somehow steadying."

Eugene nodded. "I did it until high school, and by then I had a pretty thick book. But I never tried to analyze them. It was too much data."

"What'd you do with them?"

"I think I threw them out when I left for school."

"Threw them out? All that work?"

Eugene said, "There was no pattern."

"How do you know if you didn't analyze them—"

"There was no pattern."

"If you say so."

Eugene nodded. "I say so."

Jake glanced at the clock. He thought about calling the numbers Chih's wife had given him. He pulled out his cell phone. "Gotta make a call."

Jake began to walk out. He felt Lomax's warranty certificate still folded against his waist.

"You know," Eugene said. "You can always go straight. Maybe I can help you find a decent job."

Jake stopped. "And make me a millionaire like you were?"

He shook his head. "I wish she hadn't mentioned that."

"I'll be fine."

Eugene said, "Are you sure about that?"

"No, but I'm doing okay."

"If you say so."

"Of everyone I know, and that includes you and Rachel, and even

Dad, I seem to be the only one not hating what I do."

This made Eugene pause. "Maybe." He was quiet for a moment, then asked, "Did you ever visit Dad at work?"

"No."

"I did once."

"Yeah? When?"

"When I was doing the messenger job with Vid-Pro."

"When you biked all over town?"

"That's right. I had to deliver something to a production company near Pacific Point Boat Repair."

"One of the places he worked at," Jake said.

"I thought I'd look in," Eugene said, shrugging. "He had a small corner with a water tank for outboard engines. When I went in the other guys there were looking at a hull. Dad was in the corner working. They called him 'Chinky' and asked him to check out the hull."

Jake tensed. "Did they," he said evenly.

"Dad looked pleased and went over there. He looked at the hull and the guys asked him what he thought. They said, 'So what's your big engineering degree tell you?' And Dad said something I couldn't hear but the others laughed. One of them said something like 'You'd sink the boat, you idiot.' Another one told him to go back to his jap engines. He was just a big joke." Eugene shook his head. "No wonder he hated his goddamn job."

60

Jake called the first number Chih's wife had given him. When a man answered, Jake asked for Mr. Hunt, then introduced himself as a friend of Chih's, needing some help for a job. After a confusing interchange, the man said he was a travel writer and wasn't sure what Jake wanted. Jake thanked him and tried the second number. This time, as soon as Jake mentioned Chih-seh, the man became quiet.

"Can you help me?" Jake asked.

"With what?"

"A job."

"How'd you get my number?"

"Chih's wife."

"How is Chih-seh?"

Jake hesitated. "Haven't you heard?"

"Heard what?"

"He was killed in a robbery."

"Yeah, I heard. How'd you hear about me?"

"Chih mentioned you in the past."

"Who are you again?"

"Jake. He might not have mentioned me."

"He didn't. I don't know you. And Chih can't vouch for you."

"Can I ask you a question?"

"Go ahead."

Jake pulled out the warranty, and glanced at the safe name. "What's the best way to get at a Harding-Bower safe?"

"I wouldn't know."

"All right. I get it. I've known Chih for almost eight, no, nine years. I knew him before that rinky store starting doing well. All I want is some advice for a job."

"What kind of job?"

"Jewelry store."

Hunt was quiet. "How big a store?"

"Not big."

"Alarm?"

"Taken care of."

"How big is the safe?"

"Big. It's at least four feet high."

"You can't take it?"

"No."

Hunt said, "How much time you have in there?"

"All night."

"You'll need to bring someone in."

"I need someone local."

"Local? Where are you?"

"San Francisco."

"Shit. You called me from down there?"

"I told you. I just need advice."

"You don't know anyone there?"

"Not for this."

Hunt sighed. "You get me interested, then you tell me that. I ain't going down there for a small job."

"You know anyone?"

"No. Wait, yes. An old-timer. He might know someone."

"What's his name?"

Hunt paused. "What's Chih-seh's rate?"

"What?"

"Chih-seh's rate. You say you knew him. What's his rate?"

"It was 10% off the top, plus screwing you over for the jewels."

Hunt laughed. "Which you had to sell him. Okay. The guy's name is Dormer. Doug Dormer. He's old and out of it now, but he'll tell you who to talk to down there."

"How do you know him?"

"I met him in San Quentin. He taught me loads of shit."

"He's going to ask me about you. What should I say?"

"Tell him I ain't never going to forgive him for that tattoo. He's in the book. He lives in some shitty place in San Rafael. Retired."

"Thanks."

"You still talk to Chih's wife?"

"I might."

"Tell her to stop giving out my fucking number." He hung up.

61

Bobby awoke in a hospital, and for a moment he thought he was in Seattle. He wasn't sure if he had dreamed the entire trip to San Francisco, and this gave him some relief. All that painful pissing hadn't happened. A curtain was drawn on either side of him, but directly ahead he saw nurses pushing patients on gurneys, orderlies rushing by. A nurse noticed him, and called a doctor, "He's awake."

A baby-faced Asian man in a white coat approached, and said, "I'm Doctor Fong, the attending. Are you allergic to penicillin or any other antibiotics that you know of?"

"What happened to me?"

"Your wound seems to be infected. We need to test for a nosocomial bladder infection. The nurse will take a urine sample. Are you allergic to antibiotics?"

"I don't think so."

"Have you had pain when urinating? Blood in the urine? Lower abdomen pain?"

"Shit, yeah. No blood, but my piss looks different."

"How?"

"Sort of cloudy?"

"Definitely a bladder infection. How long ago did you have surgery?"

"Not long. Just a couple of weeks ago—"

"All right. We'll run a urinalysis." He motioned to a nurse, spoke to her quickly, and left.

Bobby was confused, and said, "Am I in Seattle?"

The nurse shook her head. "San Francisco Mercy. Your friend brought you in. You passed out from the pain."

"Friend?"

"He's still waiting for you outside. Here, I'll help you up. We need a urine sample, but it has to be mid-stream. Urinate for a second or two, then fill this cup. Do you understand?"

"What friend?"

"A man with a leather jacket?"

Underhill. Bobby reached down into his pants, but then realized he wasn't wearing any. "Hey, where are my clothes! Where are my jeans—"

"Take it easy. We had to cut them off. Your wound had reopened."

Jake's papers had been in his pockets, and he sat up quickly, "Where's my stuff!" Then he swooned and lay back down.

"You lost a little blood, and your infection was pretty advanced. You have to rest."

"My stuff?" he said.

"Right here. We just put them in a bag."

He turned and saw his keys, wallet, but he didn't see Jake's papers. He said, "Where's Underhill, the guy?"

"Outside."

"Can I talk to him?"

"In a second. Give us a urine sample first."

Bobby nodded and let her help him out of the bed. He was trying to figure out Underhill's angle, and limped to the small bathroom off to the side. He pushed away his paper robe, and stared down at his stitches, now crusty with dried blood, but swabbed with some orange stain. He pissed into the cup, the sting dulled, and then returned to his bed. The nurse took the cup away and asked him to fill out some forms. He waved them away and said, "I don't have insurance."

"All right," she said. "But you still need to fill these out."

He did, but used different names and made-up information. He then lay there, exhausted. When the nurse finally returned, she told him he had an infection possibly picked up at his previous hospital, a severe strain of bacteria, and he'd have to take more powerful antibiotics. She gave him one week's worth of pills, and a prescription for two more weeks, and handed him his clothes and belongings. His pants had been thrown out, and she told him he could find another pair at the lost and found at the nurses' station. He dressed, pocketed his wallet and keys, then realized that his gun was missing as well. Underhill. He shuffled out of the emergency room area and towards the waiting room. He shook the vial of pills in his hand.

He was wearing a pair of jeans that was a size too large; he had rolled up the cuffs, and had to keep hiking up the waist. He saw Underhill sitting in the back, leafing through a magazine. Bobby sat down next to him, and said, "Where is my gun and those papers in my pocket?"

"The gun I left in the office. They have metal detectors in some hospitals, you know. And they might have called the police."

"My papers?"

"Right here." He pulled them out of his jacket.

Bobby grabbed them and checked. They were all here.

Underhill said, "They fell out when the ambulance guys took you away."

"Did you read them?"

"Yeah," he said. "From that bank statement you could probably find out the brother's name."

"How?"

"This guy Jacob have any other relatives?"

"He might have parents, but I don't think he's seen them in a while."

"Any ex-wives, kids, anything like that?"

"I don't know," Bobby said. "How can you find out the brother's name from this?"

"Hire me and I'll show you."

62

Jake studied the stolen tubular cylinder key. These ingenious locks were difficult to pick—the pins were arranged in a circle, rather than straight like a pin tumbler, and the key depressed seven pins simultaneously, allowing the cylinder to turn. To pick this, Jake needed to find the shear line of each pin, but the problem was that the cylinder relocked after each small turn. So Jake would have to pick the lock eight separate times to turn the cylinder the full unlocking diameter. He could buy a keyhole saw with a cylindrical bit, and drill out the lock, but that still took time, especially with the alarm engaged.

Without a key, he'd have to shut off the electricity somehow, or maybe rip off the alarm casing and disarm it with a gorilla method.

It was late, and Jake was in bed. He hadn't been able to reach Dormer yet, but he'd try again tomorrow. He thought about ways to take the entire safe, but it was too complicated. A safe like that could weigh five hundred pounds. Moving it would draw too much attention. He needed to get in quietly, take what he could, then leave. That was all. He didn't want to bring anyone in, but until he learned more about that safe, he had no choice.

He hid the key in his shoe, and read his philosophy book. The section on Heraclitus was short, and contained a list of fragments. Jake puzzled over them. "We never step into the same river twice. We are and we are not." What was the appeal for Rachel? She liked the contradictions of it. She liked the movement of opposites.

Closing his eyes, the book resting on his chest, he drifted. He thought about his father being called "Chinky" by his co-workers, and knew his brother's feelings for their father were complicated, a hint of pity edging his words. Yet Jake's hatred was so clean and simple. It was founded on violence, on the memory of being punched in the face by a man three times his size and strength. He thought his brother was a sap. And it had gotten worse once their mother had left. Within a week, when their father realized that she had in fact left him, he began drinking more, demanding to know from the boys where she had gone. Once he had thrown them down the steps of the basement, Jake managing to grab onto the bannister to stop his fall, but his brother tumbling down onto the concrete, twisting his knee. Eugene rocked back and forth, cursing and sucking air through his teeth. Jake moved near the furnace. Their father was destroying the kitchen, shattering glass and plates, resting, then throwing pots and pans across the floor. The sounds reverberated through the house, and Jake hunched his shoulders at each crash. Their father yelled in Korean to his missing wife.

Jake remembered hearing his brother trying not to cry, whispering to himself, Goddammit. Goddammit. Jake hadn't quite grasped yet that his mother was actually gone. How could that be? He pictured her smiling, but then he saw her bloody teeth. He remembered the way she clapped with her fingers. He wished he had learned Kung-Fu to show off to her.

Their father was running back and forth between the kitchen and the bedroom.

Eugene kept whispering, I can't take this anymore. I can't take this anymore.

Later that night, when things upstairs had quieted, Jake helped his brother up the steps, and used the screwdriver to pick the lock. Eugene limped towards the refrigerator and opened the freezer. He took out the ice trays.

Jake smelled smoke and burnt chemicals. He searched the house and found their father passed out on the bathroom floor, puddles of vomit near the toilet; he turned away, sickened. The bathtub was filled with his mother's clothes and pictures, smoldering in a half-burnt pile. The window was open, but the chemical odor stung Jake's throat. He turned back towards his father, whose cheek was pressed into the linoleum, saliva dribbling from the corner of his mouth. Venom burned inside Jake as he watched his father twitch, a tremor in his stubbled cheek. He hoped his father would die right there, just stop breathing. He wondered what would happen if he shut the window, relit the clothes, and then closed the door tightly.

He tried to close the window, but he wasn't strong enough. It was stuck high in the frame. He then tried to light the pile of clothes, but everything was wet. His father must have doused it before it flared too high. He threw the matches down angrily. He turned to his father.

He unzipped his pants, his neck prickling with fear, and leaned back. He began pissing on his father's shirt, the sound of the hissing strange without the accompanying splashing in the toilet. His father's shirt was soaked in one spot, so Jake moved and spread his piss around.

What the hell are you doing? whispered his brother.

Jake finished, shook himself, then zipped up. He said to Eugene, I'm pissing on him.

Eugene hopped back, his eyes frightened. Are you nuts?

Jake saw the ice bag in his brother's hand. He said, *I'm* not nuts. *He* is nuts.

Their father began coughing, and Jake leapt out of the bathroom, almost knocking his brother over. They waited and watched, but their father just rolled against the bathtub.

You can't do that, Eugene whispered.

I hope he dies. I hope he dies right there.

Eugene shook his head and limped to their bedroom. Jake continued staring at his father. He knew one day he would be stronger than his father, so he wouldn't have to wait until his father was passed out to piss on him.

Eugene called him from the bedroom, Leave him alone or he

might wake up.

Jake closed the door tightly, trapping in the smell of piss and vomit and burnt clothes.

Jake woke to the sounds of movement in the living room, Rachel making up the sofa bed. It was midnight. He stared at the dark ceiling and listened to her brushing her teeth as she walked through the living room, then back to the bathroom. The line of light under his door clicked off, and he heard her settling in. He had liked the feeling of her close to him, of her holding his arm, of him pulling her close. The thought of this aroused him.

He sat up, listening. He heard her shifting restlessly.

He stood up, and glided across the room. He opened the door. She stopped moving. In the darkness he could see her frozen, listening. He waited a few moments, then moved quietly towards her. He saw her lying back and closing her eyes. His senses were heightened. He could hear her soft, shallow breathing. He smelled the mint toothpaste on her breath. She rested her hands by her sides. He stood over her, watching her through the darkness, her eyes opening, blinking, then closing. He leaned over, and softly touched her hair, his fingers tracing her ear.

Her breathing quickened, but she pretended to be asleep. He let his fingers trail across her cheek, her neck. He moved over the sheets, and his fingers brushed over her breasts, and down her stomach. She was breathing faster. He stopped and waited for some kind of response. When she remained still, he leaned over, kissed her lightly on her forehead, and walked quietly back to his room, glancing back and seeing her open her eyes, searching the darkness. He thought, You are and you are not. He returned to bed.

Dormer wouldn't talk much. He grunted affirmatives and negatives, asking how Hunt was, and when Jake relayed Hunt's message about the tattoo, Dormer let out a wheezing, hollow laugh. Jake tried to ask questions, but Dormer said, "Not over the phone."

Jake took a bus up to San Rafael, a hassle because he had to use a different system—Golden Gate Transit—which he had trouble distinguishing from the city-based Muni. Two hours after setting out for Marin, he finally arrived at San Rafael, irritable and tired. Downtown San Rafael was crowded with traffic, small restaurants and stores along Fourth, where Jake was supposed to meet Dormer. It was lunch time, and office workers streamed onto the sidewalks. Fenced construction sites appeared every few blocks. Jake saw more Hispanics here than in the city.

Dormer had told Jake to meet him at a bar off Fourth, a tiny dump with red tinted windows and only two tables. A few men sat at the counter, drinking shots. They looked up at him when he walked in, their faces shaded red, their eyes blank. Jake sat at one of the tables, and the bartender asked him from behind the bar what he wanted. "Any beer on tap is fine," Jake said.

One of the men at the end of the bar turned toward him and said, "You Jake?"

Jake saw through the dim room a gray-haired, scraggly man with hollowed-out cheeks. Jake nodded.

"You're late," the man said. He stood up and shuffled over. His hand trembled and Jake thought, No way.

"I took the bus up," Jake said.

Dormer held out his bony hand, which Jake shook. Dormer's

fingers were cold and lifeless. Dormer sat down with his empty shot glass. He looked at Jake more closely and said, "You're an Oriental fella."

Jake blinked. "Yeah."

"From China?"

"From L.A."

"Chinese?"

He said, "Korean. Hunt says you're retired."

"Yup. What you think of them Hyundai's? I'm thinking of buying one."

"I have no idea. You used to work safes?"

Dormer motioned to the bartender for another shot. He said to Jake, "That was a long time ago."

"How long ago?"

"Haven't touched a safe in ten years."

"Why?"

Dormer shrugged. "I got busted, quit the life."

"What do you do now?"

"You sound like a cop."

Jake laughed. "I'm no cop."

"You're looking to do a job or something?"

"I am. Do you know anyone?"

"What kind of safe?"

"It's a Harding-Bower."

Dormer looked surprised. "They went out of business years ago."

"So?"

He shook his head, "You don't know nothing about safes, do you."

Jake said, "That's why I'm here."

The bartender brought over Jake's beer and Dormer's shot. Jake could only sip his drink, since it was still too early for him. He waited for Dormer to explain. It took a while as Dormer brought his shot glass unsteadily to his lips. He gulped down the whiskey. He said to

Jake, "When they go out of business, there aren't any more secrets."

"About the safes."

"About the safes. The templates go out, and everyone knows."

"Templates?"

"Drilling templates."

"There are drilling templates?"

Dormer sighed. "Every safe company got templates for locksmiths to drill their safes. In case the owner forgets the combination, or the Feds need to open it. It's a paper that you put up over the dial. Shows you where to drill and the angle."

"It shows you?"

"Yeah. Little holes pointing where to drill, telling you the angle. They never lend them out, and when they do they record everything."

"But if they go out of business—"

"Yeah, no one's keeping records. No one cares. The templates get around."

"Is this common knowledge?"

"For locksmiths, yeah."

"Do you have the templates for Harding-Bower?"

"No. I don't do that anymore."

"Do you know anyone who can do this?"

"Hell, anyone can drill a safe if you got the templates and tools."

Jake asked, "Where do I get the template?"

"I can ask around, but every model got a different one. You got to find all the templates—"

"I know the model and make of this safe."

Dormer smiled. "How the hell you get that?"

"I did my homework."

"I can ask around. It's going to cost you."

"How much?"

"What kind of job is it?"

Jake didn't reply, wondering if he even needed him. He said, "That doesn't matter. How much for the template?"

"Five thousand."

"If what you say is right, I might be able to get it for free."

"Five thousand, plus I show you how to use it."

"Five *hundred*, and you show me how to use it."

"Five thousand, I show you, and I give you tools."

"You have tools?"

"The best, with carbide and cobalt drill bits."

Jake thought about this. If he could do this himself, he'd feel safer. He said, "One thousand, plus the tools."

"Three thousand, plus a percentage."

"No percentage. I'm not sure how much there will be."

Dormer said, "Three thousand. Cash."

"Twenty-five hundred cash, tools, template, and you show me everything?"

"Cash in advance. A bonus if everything goes well."

Jake said, "How soon can you get the template?"

"Depends on the make and model. But it shouldn't take me more than a week or so."

"You'll show me everything?"

"We can practice on an old safe. Twenty-five hundred plus a bonus afterwards. You decide how much."

Jake nodded. "Deal."

65

When Jake walked into the apartment, Rachel looked up and brightened. "Hey, stranger," she said. She put the roll of packing tape down and wiped her forehead. More boxes lay against the wall.

He met her eyes, and remembered how soft her skin had felt, his fingers running over her warm cheek and neck. She was looking at him differently, a puzzled smile on her lips, and he wondered why she had pretended to be asleep.

He asked her if she was getting her old job back.

"They want me back, but I'm not going."

"They couldn't live without you."

She folded her arms. "Most people can't."

He smiled.

"What were you up to?" she asked. "I can't stop thinking about what we did."

He hesitated. "Lomax's apartment?"

"His apartment. His things. You just walked right in there. Does that happen often?"

"Not often. It was risky, but it paid off."

"You mean the key?" she asked.

He had shown her on the bus ride home what he had taken, and had explained its importance. He said, "And the information I got from his files will be helpful."

"The safe?"

"The safe."

"Tell me: where were you?"

"Making preparations. I was pricing police scanners and two-way radios."

"So, you're actually going through with this?"

Jake said, "I am thinking about it."

"But why? Do you need money?"

"Not right now."

"So, why risk it?"

He said, "The opportunity presented itself." He added, "Depending on how this goes, I might be able to stop for a long time."

"Is that the goal?"

"Goal?"

"Your ultimate goal, your plan."

He was about to agree, but then recalled a previous conversation.

"My ultimate goal is to survive."

"Tell me what you learned."

"About the safe?"

She nodded.

"Nothing to tell."

"No, tell me," she said.

"Why?"

"Because I want to know. I want to know everything."

Jake said, "The more you know, the more you're involved."

"I'm already involved."

"I mean *really* involved."

"How so?"

"I'm going to need help."

Her expression froze. "What do you mean?"

"I mean, when it comes time to get in there, I'm going to need help."

"Oh."

"So, the more I tell you, the more I'll expect your help."

There was a long silence while she struggled with this. He cleared his throat, waited, then walked towards the kitchen.

"Just out of curiosity," she said slowly.

He stopped.

"If I were to help," she asked, "would I get a share?"

66

Bobby sat in Underhill's office again. Underhill pulled out the gun from his desk drawer. Bobby tensed. Underhill slid it towards him. "Relax," he said to Bobby. "When you fell, this thing stuck out. I figured you didn't want the hospital to ask questions."

Bobby checked the magazine. Loaded and ready. He said, "So you still want a grand for doing nothing?"

Underhill shook his head. "You gotta understand that I'm running a business. I just can't help you for free."

"Look, I got like fifty bucks on me right now. If I had the cash on me I might pay you, but I don't. When I find the guy I'm looking for—"

"Jacob Ahn."

Bobby stopped. What the hell was this guy up to? He said, "Yeah, Jake Ahn. When I eventually find him I'll get my money back and we can work something out."

"How much will you get from him?"

"That's none of your fucking business. You help me now and if it works out, you'll get your grand."

"If you find the brother. If you then find Jake. A whole lot of 'ifs' there."

"What you got to lose? You just tell me what you know, and that's it. I'm not asking you to lift a finger, for crying out loud."

"How do I know you'll pay me?"

Bobby was exhausted. He had an infection inside him. He had bacterial bugs running all over the place around his bladder and he felt sick. He needed to buy more antibiotics and he was down to his last fifty dollars. He looked across the desk at this guy who was trying to hustle him, and Bobby just didn't have the patience anymore. He pulled out the gun and aimed it at Underhill. He said, "Why you fucking with me?"

"You're not going to kill me," Underhill said calmly.

"Why not?"

"Because I can help you."

Bobby lowered the gun. "I'm tired. I'm really tired. I'm going back to my hotel and sleep this off. Maybe we'll talk tomorrow."

"We make a deal now, I can start working tonight."

"Doing what?"

"Making a few calls. Checking the Internet."

"What kind of deal?"

"How much he owe you?"

"You don't need to know that."

"Give me a cut, and I'll help you find him."

"Oh, motherfucker. You got to be kidding me!"

"You're stuck, otherwise you wouldn't have shown up here. I can help."

"How do I know that?"

"Tell you what. I'll show you how to get the brother's name right now. You make one phone call. Actually, the bank's closed, but tomorrow morning you make one phone call and you get the name."

"From the bank? It's Jake's account, not the brother—"

"I tell you this. You bring me in. You give me a cut."

Bobby thought, Everyone trying to fuck me over. He said, "If this works, we'll see."

"For a cut?"

"For one grand and a piece of Jake's share."

"Which is how much?"

"Depends on how much he spent."

"Give me a ballpark."

"A few thousand."

Underhill's face was expressionless. He said, "I don't believe you, but we'll start with that. One grand as my fee, three grand as a commission."

"Tell me how to get the brother's name."

Underhill said, "When you open a bank account you have to list a beneficiary in case you die. It's called a 'payable on death' clause. So the bank knows who to give the account to if you die."

"And Jake probably listed his brother?"

"Who else would he list?"

Bobby thought about it. Even if it wasn't the brother it would be someone close, and that could lead Bobby to Jake. He said, "So I call up and ask?"

"No. That'd be suspicious. You call up as Jake and ask to change it. You call up and say you want to add someone, but first tell them you're not sure if you put your brother already. And they should tell you. They might ask for Jake's social security number or address, which you got."

"Wait a sec. He closed the account."

Underhill shrugged. "So, you say you want to reopen it. You changed your mind. They still got the paperwork. You say you want the same things, but maybe a different beneficiary. You tell them to send you the paperwork, but tell them to spell the name."

This sounded complicated, and Bobby wasn't sure he could pull it off. He said, "Tomorrow morning I'll come back here and you do it."

"So we got a deal?"

"You find the name, then we'll talk deal."

Underhill smiled. "All right then. I'll find you the brother, and I'll find you this deadbeat."

Bobby limped down the steps and back to his hotel. Everyone trying to get a piece of him. But screw it. He did what he had to. He was getting closer. He could smell Jake.

67

Late, late night. They sat on the floor, their empty wine glasses resting on the coffee table, the lamp on the end table dimmed. Jake was telling her his schedule—at the end of the week he'd see Dormer and buy the tools and template; he'd figure out how difficult it was to use them; he'd watch Lomax a couple more days, until after the weekend was over. He hoped to hit the store early next week.

"So soon?" she said.

"Yeah." He hadn't included her in any of this yet, though he needed a lookout. He didn't know anyone else around here and wasn't about to ask a stranger. He had learned his lesson with Bobby. He said, "Lomax closes earlier on Mondays and Tuesdays."

"And this guy in San Rafael is going to show you how to open the safe?"

"So he says."

"What if Lomax notices the missing extra key?"

"I doubt it."

"But what if?"

He nodded. "Anything's possible. I'll have to abandon the plan."

"It's all so risky."

"Not that bad. The locks are easy. I have the alarm key. I'll have the template for the safe. We know Lomax's schedule. I'll probably want to make sure Lomax doesn't return to the store that night."

"How?"

"Slash his tires or something like that."

Her forehead wrinkled, and she shook her head. "I don't think I can help you."

"All right."

"It's just too dangerous."

"I know," he said. He tried not to seem disappointed, but this would complicate things. He'd have to monitor the police scanner himself, as well as periodically check the street for people, all the while working on the safe.

"Did Euge tell you where he went tonight?" she asked.

Jake shook his head.

"I don't know what to do," she said.

"Maybe he's job hunting."

"I doubt it," she said.

Jake was quiet.

"He's losing it," she said. "He's messing up."

"What should we do?"

She shook her head. "I have no idea."

Jake stood up and told her he was turning in. "I've got a bunch of things to do tomorrow."

"Like what."

"Get back all my jewelry. Buy supplies."

"I have to find an apartment," she said.

Their eyes met as they said good night, and Jake felt the pull. She watched him, then turned away, and they drifted in different directions. She turned off the lights as he went into his bedroom. He closed the door, but listened to Rachel's movements as she made up the sofa bed. Jake stripped off his clothes, aroused, and climbed onto the futon. He was wide awake, knowing that they were alone in the apartment.

He heard her lying onto the sofa bed, and he waited. He was warm; he removed the top blanket, keeping the sheet on. He touched himself lightly. Rachel was just a few yards away, just ten steps from this door. He pictured her in her work-out clothes, stretching in front of him, and remembered massaging her legs. He inhaled slowly, ready to stand up and walk out there. He thought of his brother coming home and catching them. This made him more excited. No, he shouldn't think like this.

Movement. The floor outside creaking. The apartment settling or Rachel approaching? Jake rolled onto his stomach. He liked the pressure, and rubbed himself some more. His door opened slowly. Rachel's shadowy figure closed the door behind her and moved towards him. She stood over him, wearing a sheer nightgown, her hands by her sides.

She touched the back of his neck, her fingers cool. She grabbed the edge of the sheet and peeled it away slowly, exposing his bare back to the air. Sitting down at the edge of the futon, Rachel ran her fingers down his spine, circling. She used her fingernails, then brushed down over his bottom, his legs. Jake's heart beat loudly in his ears. His erection was hurting him. He turned onto his side, facing her.

Rachel hesitated, then ran her fingers along his waist, up along his stomach and chest. Her nail trailed over his neck, then lingered back and forth on his cheek, along his scar. Jake watched her through the darkness. Her mouth was slightly open, her gaze directed at his body. He reached forward and rested his hand on her thigh. She continued touching him, letting her fingers trace down his stomach and brush against his penis. The contact sent a shiver through him, and he moved his hand up her leg. She stopped his hand, placed it on the bed. She pushed him gently onto his back. He lay still.

Her fingers brushed his skin in circles, nearing his groin. He had to resist pushing up his pelvis, the need for contact was so strong. She finally touched him there, slowly, gliding her fingernails over him, and he closed his eyes. She held him, moving up and down, and then leaned forward and put him in her mouth. The sudden warmth and wetness startled him. He let out a quiet groan. She stopped, pulled away. He saw her shrugging off her nightgown and couldn't believe that Rachel was sitting right next him, naked, touching him. He worried about his brother.

She climbed over him, reached down and guided him as she lowered herself. He tensed as he entered her, pushing up higher. She was warm. She exhaled sharply and shifted positions, moving left and right, forcing him deeper into her. He ran his hands up her leg again; she stopped him, grabbing his wrists and sliding them to his sides. She moved slowly, back and forth, the weight of her body resting on his pelvis and thighs. He saw her hands touching her breasts, running her fingers over her nipples and chest, and she leaned back, quickening her pace.

He was close to coming, and held his breath. She moved faster, and she cursed quietly, leaning forward and pressing her hands into his shoulder as she thrust hard against him. She made three long, deep thrusts and grabbed his shoulder hard, her nails digging into his skin, and locked her arms, then arched her back. She inhaled deeply, then stopped.

Jake kept pushing up, and when he grabbed her thighs, she didn't stop him this time. When he came, his body broke out in a sweat, and he whispered her name.

They stopped moving, both of them panting. Rachel leaned forward, kissed him lightly on the lips, then climbed off him. He shivered as he left her, and she lay down with her back to him. He wrapped his arms around her, their skin cooling, and they soon fell asleep.

PART 1V

68

At Dormer's apartment, Jake studied the Harding-Bower template. It was just a piece of laminated paper, roughly five inches square, with a large hole that was supposed to fit over the safe's combination dial. Light lines running across the template helped position it on the door plate. There were two smaller holes, one above the dial with the numbers "3.75 18'" printed next to it, the one to the left with "4-1/8". Jake asked Dormer, who was sitting across the small table, "Why two holes?"

Dormer explained that there were two ways to drill a safe. The first way, the hole on the left, was to drill through the locking bolt, removing the point of contact between the cam and the bolt. This would allow the handle to swing open without hitting the bolt.

Jake asked, "But one drill hole would do that? Isn't the bolt large?"

Dormer nodded. "That's why you got the template. It should show you the exact place where the bolt and cam meet. Without it, you'd have to keep drilling to get chunks of the bolt out."

"Just one drill hole."

"More or less. You should be able to force the handle open after the drilling."

Jake found this way messy and imprecise. He worried about slipping, about getting the angle wrong, about his inexperience. He saw it parallel to the gorilla method of drilling the pins out of a pin tumbler lock.

Jake glanced at the demo Harding-Bower safe Dormer had found for him, just a small two-cubic feet home safe. Next to it on the dirty carpet were the metal briefcases containing the tools Jake was buying. The studio apartment had the same worn look as Dormer, the furniture scratched and peeling, the linoleum in the kitchen bubbling up. They were above a barbershop. Jake smelled stale beer and butter coming from the sofa cushions. He asked, "What about the second hole?"

Dormer told him it was the "peephole" method, where the drilled hole didn't affect any of the locking mechanisms; rather it was used for the person to peer inside the wheel-pack to see the combination plates. "Once you see inside, you can tell what numbers are set for the wheel slots," he said. "Then it's a matter of figuring out what the actual combination is."

"Wait. You can't just open it by looking?"

"No. You look to see what the dial ratio is. So, let's say you look inside and start turning the dial. You'll see the slots appear, and you can match them to numbers on the dial. Let's say it's 30-20-10. The thing is, the slots are aligned to open the safe on the side of the dial, not where you're looking, so the actual combination is probably not 30-20-10, but three sets of numbers in the same ratio. So maybe it's 35-25-15."

"Why can't you just look to see what the exact combination is?"

"The mechanism blocks your view near the handle."

Jake examined the hole in the template, trying to imagine what the slots in the wheel pack would look like. "Won't it take a while to find the combination?"

"Maybe. You just start with the numbers you find, then begin adding one, and move up. You can estimate faster by knowing where the gate and fence is." Dormer described the locking mechanism: once the combination plates were lined up, the "fence" clicked into the slots, and the "gate" allowed the bolt to be opened. "If the gate and fence are towards the handle, which it is for these Harding-Bowers, then start adding twenty to the ratios you find. Then twenty-one, twenty-two, twenty-three, and keep doing this until you hit it."

Jake said, "Because the slots that open the gate are a quarter turn to the left, and the dial is a hundred notches, so it's roughly twenty-five notches away?"

"Exactly."

"So, if the ratio begins near the hundred mark, you just start the count over at one."

"Yup. You got it."

"But how do you see through that small hole?" He held up the template. "The safe wall is pretty thick."

Dormer nodded and opened the first metal case. Inside was a cylindrical object that looked like a short flashlight with narrow tube-like connections. He said, "This is a fiber-optic scope. It's an older one—the newer ones are smaller and brighter—but this does the trick."

"You use that to look into the hole."

"And you get a perfect view of the combination plates."

"So you like this way better."

"If you got the time. If you're really careful, you can putty up the hole, make it look like part of the metal. They might not even notice anything for a while."

"What about picking the combination?"

He shook his head. "There are some things, like using electronic sensing equipment, but it's mostly TV bullshit. That James Bond crap doesn't really work."

"Why not?"

"Think about it. Even if you have a really sensitive gadget that can hear the clicks, you don't think your breathing will affect it? Cars on the street? Someone walking in the apartment next door? Come on, that's bullshit. And some of the new safes have false sounds."

Jake wondered if there was new equipment Dormer wasn't aware of, developments since he had quit. He watched Dormer's unsteady hands put together the scope for Jake's benefit, screwing on the eyepiece, the connecting light, and demonstrating the flexible arm. Jake noticed a framed photograph on the kitchen counter, and a child's finger-painting taped to the wall by the refrigerator.

"Why'd you quit doing this?" he asked.

Dormer shrugged. "Got busted and did five years. My wife took off, and when I got out, I didn't have the stomach for it."

"You have a wife?"

"Had. And a daughter. No idea where they are. Sure they like it that way." He turned on the scope and peered through it. "Get new batteries just in case. This looks a little low."

"Where'd you get this?"

"Lab supplier," he said. "You got family?"

"No."

"No? What about a girlfriend?"

Jake was about to say no, but thought of Rachel. He wasn't sure what she was. They were having sex in the middle of the night, and never talked about it. In the morning they pretended nothing had happened. It was the strangest affair he'd ever had. Yet in the evenings, Jake waited. He stripped and closed his eyes and listened for her footsteps.

"Girlfriend?" Dormer asked again.

Jake finally just shook his head.

"Guess that's better. Sooner or later this catches up to you."

"What does?"

"This life." Dormer scratched his stubbled chin and winced when he pushed his chair back. "How long you been doing this?"

"About ten years."

"And never been caught?"

"No."

"Well, you're either lucky or good."

Jake shrugged. "How'd you get caught?"

"Stupid fucking mistakes. Thought I could break down an alarm. They caught me with some tools and pinned a shitload of other local jobs on me."

"Which you didn't do?"

His face wrinkled up into a smile. "I did, but it shouldn't have been pinned on me."

Jake heard people in the apartment above walking heavily across the floor.

"Want a drink?"

It was noon, and Jake shook his head. He watched Dormer shuffle to the kitchen area and pull out a bottle of brandy. He poured himself a shot, and brought it to the table.

"Show me the drill."

"You're getting a good deal for this equipment. This drill here is a portable drill press, something you just can't find in stores." He opened the second case and showed Jake the hand-held drill with clamp attachments. "This strap goes around the safe, and this small platform goes over the template."

"So you can get the right angle."

"Yup. This thing never let me down. You'll wear out the bits really fast though, so you should buy more."

Jake counted the bits already in the case. "There are over a dozen here."

"Yup, but different sizes. You'll need one size, and maybe ten to fifteen of them. A fresh three-eighths-inch, carbon-tipped bit will go for a couple of minutes, then you'll need a new one."

"And I go three and a quarter inches deep, at this eighteen-degree angle?"

"Yup. Let me show you how to rig this drill." He motioned to the small, old safe on the floor.

"The same as the one I'll be working on?"

"Yup. It's smaller, but the wall's the same." He began setting it up, showing Jake how to strap on the portable press, position the hand drill, and find the correct angle. "Use these guides. They're marked every five degrees, so for the in-between angles, use your eye."

"What about the hole on the left? The drill goes straight in?"

"Yup. Ninety-degrees."

"Should I try?"

Dormer began unstrapping the drill press. He said, "Try it from scratch. You gotta make sure it's really tight, otherwise you'll slip it."

Jake stood. "Let me try to open the safe. You have a template for it?"

"Yup. Let's see how you do. You ready?"

Jake examined the test template, and then sat on the ground in front of the small safe. He said, "Yup," and began to work.

The only problem Jake had was with the initial drilling—he hadn't expected it to require so much finesse. He broke the first drill bit trying to force the hole faster. Dormer had told him that it wasn't just strength that did it; Jake had to ease off at the beginning in order to set the hole, then slowly begin applying more force. The small safe had required eight bits to drill the peephole, and Dormer warned him that the actual safe might be higher rated. If Jake had seen the UL tag on the safe itself, they could've figured out how strong it was. Underwriters' Laboratory tests every model of safe and rates it. Dormer gave Jake a listing of the codes. "If the metal UL tag has a rating of TRTL-60 or TXTL-60 then it's the highest protection and drilling might take a while," Dormer said. Once Jake had drilled the hole, using the fiber-optic scope and determining the combination was easy. Jake saw the combination plates—though he had to get used to the warped perspective of the lens—and found the notches, quickly determining the corresponding combination ratios. He then began the combination sequences, unlocking the safe after the fifth series.

Dormer said, "Not bad. You done this before?"

"No," Jake said. "But I have a feel for locks."

69

Bobby Null had a few days to recuperate. The antibiotics and bed rest had helped. He saw everything clearly now. It no longer hurt to piss. Two nights ago he had become delirious, the infection breaking, and he had lain on the hotel bed, staring up at the ceiling that rippled like water. He heard bugs in the mattress, plotting to lay eggs in him. He saw the ghost of his brother Kevin, laughing at him for being such a wimp. His brother's face was shot up, holes in his cheek and forehead. His chest spouted blood. Bobby didn't know all the details of his brother's death, but he hadn't realized that Kevin had been so mutilated.

He had blown off Underhill because he had been so sick, but now it was time to deal with him. He telephoned Underhill and told him he'd come by the office. Underhill said, "I was wondering when you'd call."

"I was sick."

"I figured."

"You got the name and stuff?"

"Oh, yeah."

So, Bobby was getting closer. He bought a burger and fries at a dingy Mom and Pop grill, ate them standing up by the window, then looked up and down the street for a dealer. He saw one, a pale, scrawny junkie leaning against a wall, trying to catch the eye of people walking by. Bobby crossed the street, and the man, dressed in an oversized denim jacket with his sleeves rolled up, his forearms bone thin, said, "Weed, rock, crystal?"

"Bennies. Uppers."

The man smiled. Two of his lower teeth were capped with silver.

He said, "All right, my friend. You wait here. I can get diamonds, dexies, and black beauties. How much you want?"

"How much for dexies?"

"How much you got?"

"Enough."

"A nice baggie with ten dexies—hundred bucks. Top, man."

"Ten bucks a pop? Fuck no. Twenty for the bag."

"I gots to run down the street for them. It's labor. Top shit."

"Get it and let me check it out."

The man walked down two blocks, stepping over a homeless guy under a cardboard blanket, and turned a corner. Bobby hated buying off the street like this, but he needed that kick. He just wanted to get all this shit over with and then go back to L.A. where he could lie out on Venice beach and soak up some heat. He was always cold up here, even colder than Seattle. This sucked.

He worried about Ron wanting his money. He owed juice on the juice, and it was getting higher every week. But with the stash Jake had stolen from him, Bobby would be fine. He'd pay it all back and then some. And he'd swear off card rooms and swinging-dick poker games forever. He'd get a tan. Bobby looked at his white arms and hands. You could almost see through him right now. It was from Seattle and now this place. Where was the goddamn sun? Why was it always so cloudy and grey?

He rubbed his arms and thought about how he'd deal with Underhill. Bobby knew the asshole would try to squeeze him, and he had to think of a fast and easy way to get what he needed.

The junkie with his dexies turned the corner and approached. Bobby looked around for cops, but saw only a bunch of panhandlers. The man said, "Got you a dozen. Check it out." He slipped Bobby a plastic bag.

Taking out one pill, Bobby read "10 mg" on the side, and said, "This is lightweight. I'll give you twenty for these dozen."

"Fuck no. A hundred for the bag."

"Thirty."

"Fifty, or you can take a fucking walk."

Bobby thought about it, then said, "All right. Here's fifty. But I'm taking one now. If anything's wrong, I'm coming back for you." He pushed aside his jacket and showed him the gun.

"Don't be showing me that bullshit." The man held up his hands. "I'm just a businessman. It's good. We're cool."

Bobby swallowed the pill and nodded. Everyone was trying to fuck him over. He turned and walked up the street towards Underhill's building. He considered waiting until the pill kicked in, but wanted to get this over with. He saw his ghost brother watching him from across the street, shaking his head. Fuck you, Bobby thought. You're so smart, you got shot in the face.

Jake waited in the darkness, his vision playing tricks on him. He saw white static superimposed over the shaded and murky objects in the room. He had probably concentrated too much tonight on watching Lomax's store in the semi-darkness, and now his night vision was off. He closed his eyes. He listened for Rachel.

The apartment was settling into the late night stillness, Eugene in the bedroom, Rachel on the sofa. His mind buzzed with too many thoughts, too many things he had to do tomorrow, and too many concerns. He tried to push them away. He wanted Rachel to come in now. He touched himself, expectant.

He began drifting, but jolted awake when he heard movement in the living room. Rachel crept quietly towards his door. Jake's breath quickened. He rolled onto his side to watch her. She opened the door, looked inside, then slid in, closing the door quietly behind her. She was in a sheer robe, and let it drop as she approached. Naked, she stopped by the side of the futon. She leaned over and touched his arms, dragging her fingers down, onto his hip, across his legs. She touched him, then grabbed him tightly. He turned onto his back. She sat down on the mattress next to him, leaned further down and slowly kissed him there. She flicked him with her tongue, and Jake smiled.

When she put him in her mouth, he pushed himself deeper into his pillow and reached down to hold her head. He felt her warmth, her tongue swirling, and he ran his fingers across her short hair, her scalp hot. She moved up and down slowly, stopping when the futon creaked. She continued even more slowly, and it almost made Jake come. He stopped her. She pulled away, wiping her mouth, and climbed over him. Instead of positioning herself on him as she usually did, she turned, crawled backwards, her knees straddling his head, and began to lower herself against his mouth. He tasted her saltiness. She put him in her mouth again. They swirled against each other, pushing and pulling, and he felt her digging her fingers into his legs, curling her hand underneath his thighs and grabbing them tightly. Her breasts pressed against his stomach.

She pulled away quickly, turned, and held him in place while she lowered herself, then she let out a small sigh as she sat on him. This was what he liked the most, when they were connected tightly against each other, and she rocked slowly against him.

His door didn't lock, and he knew that this was dangerous. It excited him more, and he began thrusting up, and she turned her head back and forth in rhythm, breathing through her teeth. He knew when she was close, when she tightened her legs around his, and tensed. As soon as she did this, he thrust harder and let himself come. Her breath came faster and she pressed down deeply against him, then slowed, shuddering, and lay down on top of him, her body cold with sweat. They panted heavily, quietly. They rested like this, their breathing in sync. She ran her finger along his scar and whispered, I'll help you.

71

The next night Jake and Rachel parked near Franklin & Sons, and observed the street and apartments for activity. He was driving a tiny '82 Honda Civic that he had just paid eight hundred in cash for, and it seemed to be holding up. He just needed it for the job. Giving a fake name and address for the owner's DMV paperwork, Jake had made sure he could dump the car without a trail.They had timed Jake driving to Lomax's and back, and were now trying to determine how quiet it was. Except for a car every five or ten minutes turning off Union, it was almost deserted. He began telling Rachel the plan in a low voice: "Once I get in, you have to keep me informed of everything that happens out here. If people walk by the store, if a car slows, if a light goes on."

"And the scanner?" she asked.

"Listen in and you'll hear this street mentioned if they're sending a cop car here. If you do, radio me, make sure I know, then you take the car and go."

"Without you."

"I'll be fine. I don't want you anywhere near trouble."

"Let's say it goes well. Once you get everything, you'll come out and…"

"And get into the car. I'll drive. We'll go to the apartment, and you'll get your share."

"My share."

"Of course. You don't think you're doing this for free, do you?" he asked.

"No, but we never decided…"

"How much? It depends. We'll try to split it evenly, but I think I'll give you more cash than jewelry. It's easier for you."

"How much do you think?"

"I don't know. Total? From the looks of the inventory, I can guess maybe forty grand."

She turned to him. "We'd get twenty each?"

"Possibly. Maybe more. It all depends."

"Jeez," she said. "And tax free."

Jake glanced at her. "Tax free?"

"Income without paying taxes," she said. "You pay taxes, don't you?"

He shook his head. "Never filed."

"What?"

"The restaurant takes a chunk out, but I've never filed a return."

Rachel said, "You could be getting some money back."

"I don't want them to know me."

"Them."

"The government."

She stared. Jake shrugged.

"You don't think they know who you are right now?" she asked.

"They have an idea, but I've never lived in a place for more than two years. Never had a bank account for more than three. It's tough to get a fix."

"You don't mind living like that?"

"Mind? I prefer it."

She nodded to herself and settled back. Jake felt the distance between them. He said, "Tell me about the philosophy you're reading."

After a few moments she replied, "One thing I've been trying to figure out is Heraclitus' belief that all things are filled with souls and spirits."

Jake turned to her. "I saw that."

"What do you think it means?"

"I don't know. I thought it was just superstition."

"It feels religious, but it could also mean that spirits are like fire, a metaphor for change."

"I don't get it," Jake said.

"Maybe he just saw everything with a kind of awe. You know? Everything is amazing to exist. A rock exists, and its formation is a kind of miracle."

"The way it's shaped?" Jake asked, watching the street. He noticed a streetlamp flickering a block away.

"Yes," she said. "It was made through strife and change. Millions of years of pressure and volcanoes and whatever."

"Like diamonds," Jake said.

She nodded. "Yes. Diamonds have spirits. They didn't just appear out of nowhere. They were formed through change." She nodded. "That's what I'm missing."

"Change?"

"Awe. That sense of awe. Nothing moves me. Nothing affects me."

Jake turned to her. "Nothing?"

"I'm getting a divorce and I don't care. I'm never going to have kids. I don't care. We're going to steal diamonds. I don't care."

Jake was about to ask if she cared about him, but already knew the answer. Instead he said, "So how do you get it? This awe?"

"Beats me."

"How did Heraclitus get it?"

"I'm not sure. Maybe he needed a lot of time. To think. You know he was so sick of people that he went off to live in the mountains? He ate grasses and plants, and lived by himself." She turned to face him. "Doesn't that sound nice?"

72

Bobby sat across from Underhill, and felt the bennies humming through him. They were coming in faster, smoother. Everything was sharp, and his mind was quick, calculating his future with each word Underhill said. Bobby needed only to listen with half his attention. He measured the risks of a fight, of other people hearing them. Most of the offices were closed; the hallways and rooms were quiet except for Underhill, who was trying to cut a new deal with Bobby.

Bobby stared, his face blank. He didn't want to hear this shit. He watched Underhill lean forward on his desk, point his finger at Bobby and say something about Bobby needing help.

Bobby said, "Give me the name. Give me what you got."

"I got the name, I got an address, I got a phone number, and I even got a picture."

Bobby focused on him. "Of the brother?"

"Yeah."

"How?"

"Website of his company."

"Let's see."

"I told you. I want to talk about guarantees."

"Fuck guarantees. Just give me what you got." Bobby heard the buzzing in his head, the bennies and the antibiotics mixing. His germ fighters were jazzed.

"I did some work for this. I want to be sure I'm going to get paid."

"You made a few calls. I can do the same thing."

"Not anymore. The bank's not going give out that information again." Underhill leaned back in his chair and folded his arms. "I told them not to."

"What?"

"I told them to get rid of all the paperwork."

Bobby tried to keep cool. He fingered the gun against his waist. Angles. How to play this guy. How to get the brother. He said, "What do you want?"

"I want to go with you as you look. That way, I know you can't screw me over."

"I'm not looking for some goddamn partner. That's how I got into this fucking mess in the first place."

"I'm not asking you. I'm telling you the way it is."

"The way it is, huh." Bobby felt his brain electrified, crackling and zipping. He rolled his neck and stretched his arms. "The way it is." He stood up and closed the door behind him. He laughed to himself. Everyone wanted a piece of him. Everyone wanted to fuck him over. Did he have "dumbshit" printed on his forehead? Did he look like some stupid son of a bitch that didn't know his ass from his knee?

"What're you doing?" Underhill said, annoyed. "Don't play tough with me."

Play tough. The way it is. This motherfucker had a way with words. Bobby laughed again. His fingertips tickled him. When he looked down at his splayed hand, he saw lightning bolts shooting out and fizzing into the air. He turned to Underhill, who was saying, "I'm warning you…" and Bobby pointed his fingers at him. The lightning bolts zigzagged towards Underhill and went through his body, lighting up his hair.

Underhill said, "What the hell's wrong with you?"

"You're warning me?" Bobby said, his voice rising. "You little piece of shit, you think you can tell me what to do?"

Underhill reached into his desk and pulled out a small automatic. He pointed it at Bobby and said, "Don't fuck with me."

Bobby looked down and laughed. "What, you're gonna pop me? You're gonna 'play tough'? You stupid motherfucker. I've been shot,

I've been dumped in the fucking garbage can. I've got bugs crawling inside me. You can't kill me. I'm a fucking god."

Underhill's eyes flickered with doubt. "You're crazy."

"Go ahead. Shoot me. Shoot me in the heart. Right here." Bobby leaned forward and stuck his chest out. His groin hurt for a moment. "I've got electricity instead of blood. You shoot holes in me and I'll light up this fucking office."

Underhill backed away. "Maybe I'll call this guy, tell him there's a maniac after him."

Bobby stopped. "What?"

"Maybe I'll call him. Tip him off."

Bobby waited for a moment. "Did you just call me a maniac?"

Underhill's gun hand faltered. Bobby felt giddy, a release of tension that made him suddenly realize that this guy didn't have the balls to use the gun. Big mistake. Bobby pretended to relax and wave this off, easing himself against the desk, and said, "What's it gonna be? You give me the information or not?"

Underhill lowered the gun a bit more, and Bobby lunged forward, grabbing it and yanking it out of his hand quickly. He checked the magazine—nice and full—and switched off the safety. He aimed it at Underhill. "You're in the wrong business, shithead."

"Look, never mind all this. Just take the stuff and go."

"Where?"

"In here," he said, reaching for the side drawer.

"Whoa. Stop. Don't move."

Underhill stopped.

"Get away from the desk."

Underhill pushed his chair back a few feet. Bobby kept the gun on Underhill and reached for the drawer. He pulled it open and saw another gun, a .38. "Motherfucker. Sneaky little bastard, aren't you."

"Listen—"

"Shut the fuck up." Bobby pointed the gun at Underhill's shoulder and pulled the trigger. It was a babyshot flesh wound, but Underhill went down like it was cannon. He screamed and rolled on the floor. Bobby jumped back, startled.

"You shot me!" Underhill yelled.

Bobby kicked him in the gut, and pointed the gun at his head. "Quiet. Understand? Quiet. Shhhh."

Underhill nodded, holding his arm. His face was red and sweaty. He tried to sit up but Bobby kicked him again. "No. You stay right there. Where are the papers?"

"If I give them to you, you'll kill me."

"Asshole, you did this, not me. Alls I wanted was a name. You pulled this other shit on me. Where are my papers, and where is the stuff on the brother?"

"How do I know you won't kill me?"

Bobby was getting tired of this. He looked around and saw Underhill's bomber jacket on a hook. He took it down and wrapped the gun and his hand with it. He needed to muffle the sound. Underhill watched with confusion, until Bobby aimed the bunched-up leather wad at him. Underhill began shaking. "Wait wait wait. I'll tell you! I'll tell you!"

Bobby aimed the gun at Underhill's knee, and pulled the trigger. The gun's crack was softer, but still loud. Underhill's knee exploded. He opened his mouth to yell but nothing came out. Bobby watched, amused. He smelled burnt leather, and wrinkled his nose. He felt his nose hairs tickling him, and wondered if he should trim them. His hand was warm. He lowered the gun to Underhill's other knee, and smiled.

"Please," Underhill gasped. "Please."

"Where's my stuff?"

"In the safe," Underhill whispered, pointing to the file cabinet by the window. He looked down at his bloody knee and whimpered.

Bobby shook off the smoldering leather jacket and opened the cabinets. The lower one had a small combination safe inside. "What's the combo?"

"Left 29, right 39," Underhill answered, his voice faltering. "Left 20, right 30."

Bobby spun the combination, then opened the safe and found some cash, Jake's papers, and the notes Underhill had taken about the brother. He read the name and said, "Eugene Ahn? That's the brother's name?"

"I. Need. A. Hospital..." Underhill looked like he was going into shock. He was holding his bloody shoulder with one hand, and clutched at his knee with the other. His eyes were glassy. Bobby walked over to him and kicked him again.

"Eugene Ahn? This is his address?"

Underhill nodded.

"Where's that picture of him?"

"Printout."

Bobby searched the safe again and pulled out a piece of paper with a dark black and white printout of Eugene Ahn. There were large dots that blurred the image, but Bobby could make out the guy's face, which did remind him a little of Jake. "Not bad," Bobby said.

"Please. Let me call an ambulance."

"The thing is, how do I know you're not going to call the police or worse, call this guy Eugene and warn him, like you said?"

"I promise—"

"See, I don't believe you. You fuck me over, you blackmail me, you lie, you try to shoot me. I mean, I just don't trust your motherfucking ass."

"Please."

"And now that you said it, I can't stop thinking that maybe you will call this guy. Maybe you'll try to shake him down too. You know? You say, I know some guy coming after you. Give me money and I'll tell you more. Something like that. No fucking morals, you."

"...I won't..."

"What about guarantees? You're big on those. What are my guarantees?"

"I promise—"

"Oh, bullshit. You want to know my guarantee? This is my guarantee." Bobby leaned forward, pushed the gun into Underhill's chest. Underhill tried to twist away, but Bobby pressed harder. He stared into Underhill's eyes. He said, "If you see my brother, tell him he's a son of a bitch."

Underhill raised his arms, about to say something, but Bobby pulled the trigger. He felt the bullet jolt Underhill, who stiffened, and blinked rapidly. "You b-b-bastard..." Underhill said, his voice cracking. Bobby kept his eyes locked on Underhill's, looking for the moment when Underhill died. Blood bubbled up from the bullet wound as he tried to breathe. He raised his head, then fell back, still trying to gulp air. Then he stopped. Bobby leaned forward, staring. Underhill blinked. He moved his lips and tried to speak. His mouth hung open. He became still, but Bobby saw something in his eyes. A gleam. But then slowly, the gaze faded away.

Bobby was disappointed that this was all he saw. He had expected more. What? A clue, a glimpse into death. He stood up, looked around. He'd clean off his prints, take all the cash, and make this seem like a late night robbery. He was getting good at this. He popped two more bennies and got to work.

The afternoon before the Lomax job, as Jake tried to relax in front of the TV but kept thinking about the timing—disabling Lomax's sedan, then returning to Rachel—Jake's brother appeared at the apartment with empty boxes. Eugene began taking apart his stereo, tinkering in the back, behind the shelf system, and distracting Jake, who turned off the TV.

Eugene looked up from behind the shelves. "You can leave it on."

Jake saw the sweat beading on his brother's forehead. "I'll help you."

"Can you pull this speaker out slowly?"

Jake did, and thought the speaker looked like the small safe at Dormer's.

Eugene looked up. "And I have your money."

"My what?" Jake said.

"Your check. To pay you back."

"Already?"

"I liquidated my IRA. It was less than I thought, but enough."

Jake said, "No hurry." An image of Rachel flashed through his mind. He was sleeping with his brother's wife, and felt a strange disconnect. Nothing was real. He dreamed his nights with Rachel. His days were filled with planning and practice. Jake stared at his brother as he bent down and unconnected the wiring in the back of the stereo. Eugene scratched his head, then looked up. "I can write you a check whenever you want."

"You look better," Jake said.

"I'm not drunk on the floor. I hope I look better."

"Are you looking for work?"

Eugene stiffened. "Did Rachel tell you to ask me that?"

"No."

"I'm not. Not yet. I just can't bring myself to."

Jake kept quiet and pulled the second speaker out of the cubby. Dust floated down onto his hands. Eugene sneezed.

"It doesn't matter," Eugene said, wiping his nose. "I'd just end up a grunt somewhere else. Why rush into it? You know what happens to grunts? They get shot. They get left behind. They get fed to the enemy." He shook his head. "I need to take a break. I need to plan. I need to start over."

Jake nodded. He understood planning.

"I mean, what's the goddamn point of taking a job you hate and that you'll end up getting fired from anyway?" Eugene stopped. "Shit. I sound like Dad."

"You are not Dad."

Eugene smiled. "That bothered you, didn't it? The story I told you about his work."

"Being called 'Chinky.'"

"I don't think he even knew it was an insult."

"He must've known."

Eugene shrugged. "Maybe." He pulled out more wires and said, "Did I ever tell you that he wrote me after I got married?"

"Wrote you? How'd he know where you lived?"

"No idea. Kept tabs on me, maybe."

"What'd he say?"

Eugene rolled his eyes. "He was hurt that he wasn't invited to the wedding. He said everything he did was for us."

A flush filled Jake's cheeks. He didn't know what to say. "You're joking."

"No. He even signed it 'Jesus loves you'," Eugene laughed. "I thought I was misreading it. I thought, Does that really say 'Jesus'? It was bizarre."

"I think you once mentioned that he got religion."

"Did I?" Eugene said. "Yes. He's getting close to kicking off, so he makes friends with the Big Guy."

Jake frowned. "I hope it's not that easy."

"What?"

"Making friends with the Big Guy."

"Why?"

"Because if it is, then the Big Guy is a chump."

Eugene laughed. "I wouldn't have pegged you as such a skeptic."

Jake lifted out the tuner and laid it carefully on the ground. Eugene emerged from behind the shelves. He crumpled up newspapers, lining the cardboard boxes. Jake watched in silence. He knew that his father could never have found his address since Jake was so careful, but he wondered if his father had tried. He doubted it.

"Did you say anything about me?" Jake said.

"To Dad? No."

"Good," Jake said, "Let's keep it that way." The thought of their father still out there made him uneasy.

By the time Jake turned nine, a year after his mother left, and he accepted that she wouldn't be returning, the vague, hopeful thoughts of her being on a short trip, a break from their father and from the family, such that once she returned she'd be refreshed and ready for more—once he understood the finality of her departure, he began to turn mean. He viewed his goody-goody brother with contempt, though Jake tolerated him because Eugene dealt with their father; he viewed his classmates in school as victims, losers, and worse of all, as weaklings.

He stole lunches. Of course his father never made him a bag lunch, and Eugene could buy lunches at his junior high school cafeteria, but Jake was still in elementary school, and was supposed to bring a lunch. He would start his day at school by slipping into the coat closet where everyone kept their bag lunches, and stole a sandwich from one, a drink from another, a dessert from a third, and sometimes an extra dessert from a fourth. He had an old wrinkled and smoothened brown paper bag he reused, and filled it with other kids' goodies.

Some of them had really good lunches: roast beef, smoked turkey, even meatloaf. He didn't have time to choose carefully—he usually just shoved his hand into a random bag and groped for a sandwich— so sometimes he got stuck with peanut butter and runny jelly. He'd laugh to himself when he heard someone say, "I can't believe my mom forgot my drink again!"

He thought, Sucker.

Eventually it caught up with him. Enough complaints made his teacher, Mrs. Weintraub, wary, and one day towards the end of the year he was in the closet, his hand in someone's bag, and he felt someone grab his neck. "Got you!" Mrs. Weintraub said.

His father had to leave work early for a conference with Mrs. Weintraub and the principal, then had to return for a second shift at the boat shop. But when he came home that night he dumped his bag onto the floor, and immediately rolled up his dirty sleeves. He said, You make me look bad, like I have bad morals.

Eugene tried to calm their father down. It's just a lunch, Eugene said. He won't do it again.

But Jake thought, Yes I will.

You dirty beggar stealer, his father said. You think I like them talking like I stupid?

Dad, Eugene said. Dad, come on. He's sorry.

But Jake thought, No I'm not.

You sneaky beggar. *Shang nom. Michin nom.*

Jake looked at his father curiously. He recognized the curses.

Shang nom.

Speak English, Jake said.

This stopped them. His father backed up in surprise. Eugene's mouth opened. His father said, What?

Speak English to me if you're going to use curses, Jake said. He was nine years old, but he knew how to piss off his father.

What! His father said, his expression darkening.

Eugene hung his head.

Jake yelled, Speak English! Speak English!

Now, as Jake watched his brother packing his stereo, he pointed to the faint scar on his cheek and said, "Do you remember the time I was caught stealing lunches from school?"

Eugene stopped crumpling newspapers. He remained quiet for a minute, staring at his inky hands, then nodded slowly. He looked up at Jake and said, "Yes. I remember that."

74

And so it began. Jake drove past Lomax's building and circled the block, checking for differences, inconsistencies. Lomax's sedan was parked in the same spot, the building and neighborhood quiet. Jake pulled over across the street and waited with the engine running.

It was two in the morning. The stream of cars moving along a busier street two blocks down was thinning, and Jake checked the area for cops. He had to be careful with burglary tools in the trunk. His neck pulsed, his breathing slowed. His night vision was sparkling. He saw auras around streetlights.

He turned off the engine and listened. There was a crispness to the evening air that carried noises farther—he heard the pulsing rhythm of a distant nightclub. Although he had prepped for this many times, he wanted to be sure nothing had changed. What was different? There was a car missing in the parking lot, four slots away from Lomax's sedan. The lot was usually full by this time. He couldn't wait much longer, though. Rachel was watching the store, checking the activity in the area.

He climbed out of the car. He had a thin hunting knife in his sleeve, and walked towards the lot. Looking up at the building windows, he saw only darkness. He approached the automatic gate and quickly scaled it, flipping himself over it and landing on the ground quietly. He hurried to the wall, where he would be shadowed from the security lights, and ducked down in front of Lomax's sedan.

Voices across the street. Jake waited. He heard two men talking loudly as they passed his parked car and moved slowly down the block. He worried about Rachel. If he took too long she might think something happened, and he knew she was already nervous. When they had separated earlier, he had seen the paleness in her cheeks, her flickering eyes. She had said "Good luck" in a tight, unfamiliar voice. He peered over the hood and saw the men turning a corner. Crawling to the side of Lomax's car, he pulled out the knife and pressed the tip slowly into the tread of the front tire, which smelled like dog shit. After an initial resistance, the blade eased in. A soft hissing surrounded him. Jake pressed harder and twisted the blade. More air. He heard the car's suspension groan as the front end angled to the ground. Pebbles dug into his leg. He watched the rim ease to the pavement.

The front gate clicked, and Jake sat up quickly. A car approached, and he knew it was the missing one. The gate began scraping open, the automatic motor huffing. Although Jake was hidden between Lomax's car and a pick-up truck, he couldn't risk being seen, so he rolled underneath the truck and shimmied his way towards the front axle, drawing his legs close to him. His elbow rested in a thin slath of motor oil.

Headlights flashed across the lot as the incoming car turned and drove past Jake. The brakes squealed as the car pulled into the empty space. The driver shut off the engine. The front gate closed, shuddering as it locked into place. A door slam. A sigh. Jake knew the person would be walking by the truck to get to the front entrance, and he remained still.

The person's shoes clicked on the pavement and passed the truck, the pace unbroken. Once Jake heard the front door close and lock, he rolled back out towards Lomax's car and began working on the rear tire. This one he sawed back and forth, the air hissing out. The left side of the car now leaned into the ground. This was enough. Lomax could replace one tire with a spare, but with two down he'd need to call a tow.

Jake crouched and listened. When it seemed quiet enough, he stood up and approached the gate. He again climbed over it and jumped to the sidewalk. He walked across the street, brushing himself off, not looking back. Once in his car, he glanced at Lomax's sedan, and saw it tilting towards the truck, as if it were whispering a secret. Jake drove away. Showtime.

75

Bobby took a cab to Jake's brother's apartment building. He used Underhill's money and gave the cabbie a five-dollar tip, something he wouldn't do if he weren't so pleased with his progress. He stepped onto the sidewalk and checked the address in Underhill's notes. Apartment 12G. His bennies were fading, a dullness setting in, clouding his vision. He popped two more and walked around the building, searching for an easy entrance. Since it was late, he wasn't sure if there'd be enough foot traffic in front.

A panhandler in a red sweatshirt was rocking back and forth near the building's ventilation grill, his hands shoved deep into his sweatshirt pockets, his hood pulled tightly over his head. Bobby asked, "Is there a back entrance to this building?"

The man looked at him with bloodshot eyes. "They are guarded over by benevolent wraiths," he said.

Bobby stepped back. "Huh?"

The man grinned and turned back to the ventilation grill. Bobby took a step forward and said, "Hey, is there another way into the building?"

The man nodded. "Look for the cars."

"Cars? A garage?"

The man said, "But the wraiths are crafty."

"Yeah, whatever. Here, buy some booze." Bobby flicked him a few dollars. The bills sprinkled to the ground. The man stared at them. Bobby walked away, but stopped when he realized that the guy wasn't going to pick up the bills. "Hey, you don't want them?" he said.

The man continued staring at the bills, which were fluttering in the breeze.

Bobby said, "Fuck that. I'm not wasting it." He walked back to the man and picked up the bills. "Asshole."

The man pointed his finger at him and laughed.

Bobby called him a nutcase and left. He found the underground garage entrance and checked the metal gate that rolled to the left on small wheels. A keypad on a concrete stand was stationed to the left of the entrance driveway. Bobby tried to squeeze underneath the gate, the space for the wheels about six inches high, but he didn't fit. He didn't want to wait out here for a car, so he returned to the front entrance and started pressing the the intercoms buttons. When someone answered he would say, "Sorry to bother you but I locked myself out accidentally. Could you buzz me in?"

The first five responses were of annoyed, sleepy residents telling him no. The sixth one said, "Christ, it's two in the morning!"

"Sorry. I didn't know I left my keys upstairs—"

But the door was already buzzing, and Bobby leapt to it, yanking it open. He stepped into the warm lobby, stamped his feet and rubbed his hands. The new set of bennies were revving him up, and his thoughts flew quickly by, too fast to stop. The polished marble floor reflected the bright lights from above, and he squinted down at the shiny gloss, happiness filling him. Everything looked so clean here, and coming from his shitty hotel, he knelt down and touched the floor. Smooth.

He entered the elevator and whistled quietly, watching the numbers light up. At the twelfth floor he stepped out into the hallway and approached apartment G. He checked the gun in his waistband, and took deep breaths. Jake could be here. He could be sleeping. He could be hugging the fucking jewels right now.

Bobby's hands shook. He knocked on the door and covered the peephole with his fingers. He knocked again. Through the door, someone said, "Who is it?"

"I'mafriendofJake'sandIwonderifhe'shere?" he said, his words tumbling out. Whoa. He worked his jaw up and down. Everything moving too fast.

"What? Who is it?"

"I'm a friend of Jake's. Is he here?" Bobby said slowly, over pronouncing his words.

The locks clicked, and the door opened. A thick-faced man who Bobby recognized from the picture peered out. Bobby stepped back.

"You Eugene?"

The man looked surprised. "Do I know you?" he asked.

"Jake mentioned you. Is he here?"

"You know it's two-thirty in the morning," Eugene said.

Bobby nodded. "Sorry, man. It's an emergency."

"Well, he's not here right now. He went out earlier and hasn't come back."

"Oh, so he is staying here?"

Eugene nodded. "Not for long, but yes."

"Maybe I can wait for him?"

"Look, it's late. I've been packing all night. Why don't you come by tomorrow?"

Bobby studied the brother. He looked soft, flabby. Too many doughnuts. Some yuppie shit. Bobby pushed the door open and shoved his way past the brother. He said, "No, I think I'll wait for him."

"What the hell do you think you're doing?"

Bobby pulled out his gun. "Close the door, doughboy. We're gonna wait for Jake."

76

After puncturing Lomax's tires, Jake drove to Cow Hollow and parked his Honda in a driveway, diagonally across the street from Franklin & Sons. He saw Rachel approaching. She was wearing black clothing; her face and hands glowed in the semi-darkness. He moved to the passenger seat, and waited until she climbed in and closed the door. "How's it look?" he asked.

"Quiet, like the other night. You?"

"Fine," he said. "Ready?"

She nodded. He handed her the police scanner, set to the San Francisco P.D. frequency, and told her to use the earpiece, since the frequency would be active. He slipped on a pair of latex gloves. His backpack with all his tools was at his feet. He asked, "You have a good view of the street and the store from here. Keep me posted."

She said, "I will."

He saw how pale she was. He was about to try to calm her, but she said, "I'm okay. Go. Let's do this."

He left the car and walked to the jewelry store. He turned up his two-way radio, checking the street around him. At the pull-down security grilling, he knelt and inspected the padlock. Warded. It was easy, but he didn't want to get lazy. He examined it closely. A warded padlock is held shut by a locking spring, and the key simply fit through the notched wards and turned to unhitch the locking spring. He pulled out a special double-headed "T" pick that enabled him to go past the wards and hit the locking spring. He didn't even need more light. He could do this just by touch. He inserted the pick, pressing against the lock shackle, and felt the first set of retainers binding. He pushed the pick to the second set, spread them, and it clicked; he opened the lock.

He unlatched the grilling, and raised it a few feet. He crawled under it, dragged in his backpack, then closed the grilling behind him. He glanced up at the windows across the street. Everything was quiet and dark.

He knew he looked suspicious, and hurried with the deadbolt first. He took out his snapping wire, inserted his tension wrench and then slid in the wire. He began snapping lightly, carefully, then increased the tension when he felt a pin aligning. After a few more snaps, he aligned all the pins, and opened the deadbolt.

Then he worked on the regular lock. He snapped it open on the second try, surprising himself. Before opening the door, he pulled out the alarm key.

Okay. He took a deep breath. After this point, everything was uncertain.

He looked up through the display window and saw the old alarm unit. He wasn't sure about the delay, so as soon as he opened this door he had to disable the alarm. He quickly considered the worst-case scenario: the key didn't fit. If there was a long enough delay, he'd try destroying the alarm. If it began ringing immediately, he'd get out of there.

He felt his heartbeat quickening. He took a slow breath. This was what it was all about. He opened the door, made it to the alarm control in three steps, and pushed in the key.

It didn't fit.

He heard his eardrums pulsing as he counted off seconds, still trying to force the key in, ready to try to knock the whole console out of the wall, but when he turned the key one-eighty degrees and tried again, it fit. He shook his head, rattled, and quickly twisted the key in the lock as the bell began ringing. He switched it off in mid-ring. A loud, frustrated clang echoed down the street. He hurried to the door, pulled in his backpack, checked to see if the Honda was still there, then headed to the back room. He could hardly hear anything—his eardrums were pounding. He let out a small laugh and thought, Calm the fuck down.

He pulled the key out of the alarm console, and pressed the keyhole with his finger. Goddamn you little sucker.

His two-way radio squelched, and Rachel said, "What was that?"

"My fault," he said into the radio. "Anyone notice?"

"I don't think so. It scared the hell out of me."

"Me too. Keep listening to the scanner."

"I am."

He clipped the radio to his belt and examined the door to the back room. Rachel said she had seen no evidence of another alarm. He knew that a second alarm here was impractical, but he had to be ready. He tested the door handle. Unlocked. He opened the door slowly, listening for the beeps of an armed alarm, but didn't hear anything. He looked into the darkened room, and searched quickly for LED's, any alarm indicator lights. Nothing. He closed the door behind him and turned on the lights.

The room was as Rachel had described it: a cold concrete room with metal shelving, a jewelry repair station, a desk, and a safe. Before checking the safe, he slipped out of the room, closed the door, and checked how noticeable the lights would be. A thin outline of the door glowed, but he didn't think anyone on the street would see this. He went back in.

The Harding-Bower was four feet high, and three feet wide. Jake searched for the UL tag, and found it on the side: "The Harding-Bower Safe Co. Underwriters' Laboratories Inspected Safe. Class A Fire. Class T-20 Burglary. No. TRTL-60." There. TRTL-60.

So it had a "high degree" of protection. The lab people had done a sixty minute test on the door and body.

He checked the iron door to the back alley, and realized that in addition to picking this lock, he'd have to break the rusted padlock outside to open this. Too much time and trouble. He lost his emergency exit. He turned back to the safe.

He searched through the adjacent desk and looked among the books on the shelves. Dormer hadn't mentioned this, but Jake knew that often someone would write the combination down nearby, just in case. He would be negligent if he didn't at least do a cursory check. He flipped through the jewelry repair, design, and appraisal books on the lower shelf, and looked over the customer files and store receipts in the desk. Nothing.

Now, as he began unpacking his tools, he felt a tinge of apprehension. Dormer's fee, the car, the extra equipment—Jake had already invested quite a bit in this, and he had no way of knowing exactly how much was in here. He hadn't followed Lomax home tonight, so it was possible that Lomax had decided to take everything out of the safe. Or perhaps Lomax had a second, hidden safe.

Jake fit the drilling template over the dial and escutcheon plate. Perfect fit. He colored in the wheel-pack peephole with a magic marker, and removed the template. He'd find out soon enough. He strapped on the portable drill press, the flexible metal bands held together with mini-clamps, and positioned the press over the black dot. He locked in the first drill bit, masking tape marking the depth required on all the bits, though he'd probably go through many of these. He then set the angle, using the notches next to the joint, and tightened the swivel handle. Almost ready.

He unrolled the electrical cord and crawled to the outlet on the other side of the desk, and to his surprise he found that the cord didn't reach.

He stopped. The cord to the drill was five feet long, and he hadn't considered this hitch. He looked for another outlet closer to the safe, but there wasn't one.

He thought, Shit. Why hadn't he prepared for this possibility?

He tried to move the safe. It wouldn't budge.

He sat down, thought about this for a moment, then began

looking along the shelves for an extension cord. There weren't any. He laughed. This was how you knew the difference between an experienced safecracker and an idiot.

Grabbing a small flashlight, Jake slipped out of the back room and searched in the display room for an extension cord. Finally, with some relief, he found one connecting a light in the wristwatch display case to an outlet further along the wall. He unplugged this and returned to the back room.

Once everything was plugged in, he doublechecked the clamps, tightened the drill bit in the jaw, and tested the trigger; the drill buzzed to life.

He radioed Rachel. "You read me?"

Static. "I do."

"Let me know if I make too much noise."

"Everything okay?"

"Fine."

He got to work.

77

Bobby told Eugene to sit down. Eugene didn't. Bobby said, "Doughboy, I don't care if you're alive or dead. I'm waiting for your brother. You going to sit or maybe I should shoot out a leg?"

Eugene sat down.

Bobby's head felt stuffed. The extra bennies he had taken were having the opposite effect he wanted. Everything was cloudy. He had popped too many too soon, and was both jittery and fuzzy. He tried to shake this off. He focused on Eugene, whose face seemed to expand and contract, and asked, "Where's Jake right now?"

"I don't know. Are you the one who tried to double-cross him? His ex-partner?"

"Me double-cross him?" Bobby had forgotten how this had started. He smiled. "We double-crossed each other."

Eugene rubbed his eyes and let out a tired sigh.

"Where's the stash?" Bobby said. "He came down here with my stash. Where'd he hide it?"

"What?"

"My jewelry, my cash."

"I don't know."

Bobby could tell he was lying, the way he answered so easily. He said, "So Jake tells you about me, but he doesn't say why he ran? You think I'm fucking stupid? He came here with jewels. My jewels. Where is it?" Bobby glanced at the hallway. "Down there?"

"I don't know anything. I just want to be left alone."

Bobby cocked his head, amused. "Don't you care about dying?"

Eugene stared up at him. "I'm not sure."

Bobby pointed to the rooms. "Get up. We're going to do a little looking around. What's in all these boxes?"

"My stuff. My wife's stuff. We're moving out."

"Where's Jake's?"

"The guest room. Straight ahead."

"Move," Bobby said. He pointed the gun, and Eugene stood up slowly and shuffled towards the guest room. Bobby followed, and when he saw two metal briefcases on the floor, he pushed Eugene aside and quickly opened them. They were empty except for molded foam padding. "What was in here?"

"Tools of some kind."

"What kind?"

"I'm not sure."

Bobby opened a paper bag and found drill bits, tape, epoxy, and packaging for putty. He looked up, and said, "You got to be shitting me."

"What?"

"Is he doing another job?"

"Job?"

"Hitting another place? Breaking into some place?"

"I don't know."

Bobby checked the outline of the foam padding and recognized a hand-held drill. The other briefcase held something with a cylinder and narrow hose. Definitely break-in shit. But Bobby wasn't sure what kind. Jake was going to hit another place. What else could it be? Bobby searched through Jake's clothes, but found nothing. He motioned Eugene back to the living room and pushed him onto the sofa. He said, "Where'd he put my stash?"

"I don't know."

"How're you with pain, doughboy?"

"Huh?"

Bobby used the handle of the gun, and hit Eugene on the side of the head—hard but not too hard. Eugene covered his ear and yelled,

"Shit! That hurt!"

Bobby smiled. "No kidding. Now, I want to know a few things, and I got all night."

"I told Jake not to tell me anything. I told him to keep straight while he stayed here."

"Why would you do that?"

"I didn't want him to bring any trouble here."

"What, you think if you close your eyes and cover your ears nothing bad will happen? What are you, five years old?"

Eugene sunk into the sofa. "Just leave me alone."

Bobby smacked him in the face with an open hand. "Rule number one: when I ask you a question you answer it. My question is, What are you, five years old?"

He held his cheek, and shook his head. "No, I'm not."

"Good. Now, let's begin."

78

Jake had gone through six drill bits, and was making slow progress with the hole. He had half an inch left, and his sweaty shirt clung to his back. His hands and arms were sore from the constant pressure, and his ears rang from being so close to the motor. He had to raise the volume on the two-way radio. His fingers quivered.

The bits heated up and became blunt after ten minutes of drilling, so he had to blow on the chuck and collar before loosening the bit for a replacement. This slowed him down. When he had practiced on the safe at Dormer's, he had done this at a leisurely pace, so the bits cooled down before he changed them. Dormer should've warned him. His latex gloves felt sticky from the heat.

"There's a couple about to walk by," the radio cracked.

Jake stopped. He picked up the radio. "Okay." He gave his hands a rest, wiping the sweat off his forehead with his arm. Earlier Rachel had said she could hear the faint drilling from the street, though it was unrecognizable. Still, it had surprised him, so he decided to stop if anyone approached.

"They're gone," Rachel said.

"Got it."

He continued. By the tenth drill bit, he was almost done. He saw the piece of tape approaching the surface, and pushed harder. The bit snapped and flew up, barely missing his ear. It pinged against the cement floor. He refit a new drill bit.

The eleventh bit broke through. He said, "Finally." He pulled out the drill, unlatched the press, making sure he carefully stowed away all the pieces. He didn't want to leave anything behind. He blew on the hole, metal dust falling away. He unpacked the scope and attached the light to the viewer.

"Jake," Rachel's whisper radioed through. "Jake, there's a cop car turning the corner."

He asked, "Did anything come through on the scanner?"

"Nothing in this area."

"Stay down. It's just a patrol."

Jake hurried to the light switch and flicked it off. He opened the door a crack and looked out. From his angle he saw a sliver of the street, and when the cop car drove by, he waited to see if it slowed. It didn't. He closed the door and turned on the light. The longer he spent here, the more exposed he'd be. Inserting the thin tube into the hole, then turning on the light and strapping on the eyepiece, Jake slowly adjusted his vision to the fish-eye view of the interior wheel pack. He pulled, pushed, and twisted the tube until he saw a glimpse of the combination plates, then began maneuvering the scope until he had a direct view of the top, and found four plates instead of the three he had practiced on at Dormer's. No matter.

He spun the combination dial a few times to start the sequencing, and began turning the dial to the right, waiting for the last plate to move into alignment, but he noticed that the second to last plate was moving instead. He tried this again, and the same thing happened. He stopped, unsure why this was happening. Then, thinking about the four plates instead of three, he wondered if the sequence began with the left turn, instead of the right turn, and restarted the combination, spinning the dial a few times to the left. He watched the plates, and saw the notch in the last plate moving into view. Okay. Another thing Dormer hadn't mentioned: not all safes begin with the right turn.

He jotted down the number on the dial that corresponded to the notch—85—and began to spin to the right. The notch on the second plate moved into position: 46. Then the third plate: 59. Finally, the fourth plate: 61. He pulled out the scope, and took off the eyepiece.

85-46-59-61.

The faint ringing in his ear seemed to grow louder as he stared at the numbers he had written on a scrap piece of paper. He thought, Jesus, I'm actually doing this.

He checked the dial and estimated a difference of about twenty to thirty numbers, and began trying the combinations, starting with thirty subtracted from the starting ratios, and moving up from there. His first set—55-16-29-31—didn't work, and he moved it up by one.

Dialing carefully, not wanting to miss a number and screw up the sequencing, Jake exhaled and focused. The notches on the dial were tiny. He went through the combinations, noting on the piece of paper whenever he moved up a number. He tried not to think of what he'd do if this didn't work. He'd go through the entire dial if he had to, but if nothing happened, then what?

"Jake," Rachel radioed. "Some guy is walking towards the store."

Shit. He finished this sequence, which didn't work, and radioed back, "Alone?"

"Yes."

"Keep me posted," he said. He wasn't going to stop. He went through three more series, and on the fourth, the initial ratios minus twenty-one, he felt something click in the handle.

He stopped. The ringing in his ear subsided.

He pulled down on the handle, and it gave way with a satisfying *thunk.* He slowly pulled open the safe door, and saw the trays of jewelry and watches on the top shelves, stacked neatly. A cash register tray sat on the middle shelf, the twenty, ten, five, and one-dollar bills still in their slot. A wad of fifties and hundred-dollar bills were stacked next to the tray.

The bottom shelf held two felt neck displays, slender purple necks with diamond necklaces around both of them. Stunned, he leaned forward and reached for the first diamond necklace. It was an antique, the white gold setting looked handmade, and the entire necklace was covered with small round cut diamonds, leading to a large Marquise cut. A very large Marquise, maybe four carats.

He pulled out a small canvas bag from his backpack and began filling it with the jewelry, starting with the diamond necklaces. He emptied the top trays of all the rings, brooches, earrings, bracelets, and lesser necklaces. He calculated quickly, seeing some of the inferior pieces he had noticed the first time he had come into the store. He needed to appraise these, but this was everything in the store. Everything. He then dumped the cash on top of the jewelry, flipping through the wad of fifties and hundreds before dropping them in. At least ten thousand in cash alone, probably more.

His breath came out unsteadily. He wiped the sweat out of his eyes. His heart was leaping into his throat. Here was everything in the store.

After emptying the safe, he doublechecked the back, then closed and relocked it. Then he pulled out the last two remaining goodies from his backpack, putty and epoxy. Dormer had mentioned covering the hole to buy more time, but Jake had thought of something better. The epoxy came in a double syringe, the two liquids kept separate because once they mixed, the solution would soon set into a strong glue. He had found a brand with a narrow double head, and he opened the ends now. He inserted it into the drilled hole. He slowly pressed the plunger, watching the black stopper push the liquid from two cylinders out, injecting the glue into the wheel pack of the safe. He emptied as much as the wheel pack would hold, and then it began leaking from the drilled hole. He wiped it clean.

Once this set, the wheel pack would be frozen.

Jake began rubbing the putty into the hole, smoothing and pressing, smoothing and pressing, until it met the surface of the escutcheon plate. There was a color difference, the putty was lighter than the old metal plate, so he ran his fingers along the concrete floor, picking up dirt and drill dust. He rubbed this over the putty until it darkened. It wasn't a perfect match, but it looked pretty damn close.

He packed all his tools. He returned the extension cord to its original location. He pocketed the broken and worn drill bits, picked up every bit of garbage he had dropped. He scanned the room for clues.

There. The drill bit that had flown out of the jaws. It had fallen and rolled under the desk. Jake grabbed it. He shouldered his back pack and carried the canvas bag out of the back room. He turned off the light and shut the door tightly.

His radio squawked. He stopped.

"Someone's walking up," Rachel radioed.

He turned down the volume, and radioed back, "Okay."

Lowering himself behind a counter, he waited. After a minute he saw through the front window a man shuffling forward, his shoulders hunched. The man glanced at the empty displays in the front window and stopped. Jake kept still. The man peered through the grilling. He seemed to be squinting at something. Jake followed his line of vision and saw that it was an Omega sign, lit up by the reflection from the street. The man surveyed the store. Jake froze.

After a minute, the man continued walking. Jake waited a minute, then radioed, "Gone?"

"Gone."

He took a deep breath. He felt the blood pumping through his temples.

Examining the alarm, he found that it was triggered by a contact at the top of the front door. To reset it, he'd have to use the key and then make sure the door was shut within the timed delay. He wanted to relock everything, if possible.

He pulled out his snapping wire and tension wrench, as well as the tubular cylinder key. He re-engaged the alarm, hurried out of the door, then shut it tightly. He snapped the deadbolt after a few tries, then found the shear line. He re-locked the deadbolt. Then he worked on the lower lock, doing the same thing. He stopped, checked his handiwork. Everything would be as it was.

He pulled open the grilling, crawled out, then closed it. He rehooked the padlock on the metal loops, and locked it. He saw Rachel moving into the passenger seat. He walked casually across the street, looking up at the windows. Quiet.

He climbed into the car and started the engine.

She said, "The headlights are off."

He turned them on. He pulled out of the parking spot and headed down the street, past Union and back to Pacific Heights. She said, "Well?"

He turned to her and whispered, "Yes."

79

They couldn't wait until they returned to the apartment. They drove into the underground garage of the building, pulled into a guest parking spot, and Jake showed her the stash. As she looked through it, her mouth falling open and her eyes flicking up at him in amazement, he found her incredibly sexy, and needed to touch her. He reached over and lay his hand on her shoulder. She stared at him. "I can't believe this. You did it."

He leaned towards her. She hesitated. They had never kissed outside of Jake's room. He moved closer. She laughed quietly, and kissed him, squeezing his hand. She said, "Mmm," and pulled away. She smiled, and rubbed his leg. "Well, well," she said. "What's this? A celebration?"

They kissed again, groping each other, and she motioned to the back.

They climbed over each other and fell into the seats. There wasn't much room, but Rachel leaned back and pulled him on top of her, and they kissed. Rachel laughed and said, "Like teenagers." They rubbed up against each other, Jake pushing himself between her legs. Rachel gently moved him aside, sat up, and unhooked her bra. She pulled up her shirt, holding her breast out to him, and he kissed her, tugging lightly with his lips. He slipped his hand down her tights, feeling her curly hair, and then her wetness. She inhaled, and said, "Well."

"I want to be in you," he said.

She thrust her pelvis up and yanked down her tights, struggling to pull one leg completely free. Jake unbuttoned and unzipped his jeans urgently, banging his elbow against the roof, and as she settled back into the seat, he pressed up against her and slid in. They fell together into the corner, their heads angled awkwardly against the cushions, their legs and arms tangled, but they didn't lose contact, and thrust against each other, rocking the tiny car and Jake just wanted to get deeper into her. He realized for a moment that this was the first time he was on top, and then this thought snapped away as Rachel dug her nails into his neck. They moved faster, wildly. Her other hand pushed him away, and she said, "Wait, wait, I don't want to come yet—" but he couldn't slow down, and he pushed harder, burying his mouth against her ear, and he whispered, "Go with me to Seattle," but she didn't hear him as she let out a small cry and tightened her grip on him. He then felt himself nearing it, and he threw himself against her and heard the ringing in his ear piercing all other sounds out.

They lay panting, sweaty, cramped. Jake said, "Man."

She was breathing heavily against his shoulder. The car was muggy and smelled of their sweat. He felt her strong heartbeat through his chest. They calmed down. She said quietly, "I can't."

"What?"

"I can't go with you to Seattle."

Jake paused. "Oh."

"Thank you, though."

"Okay."

Their breathing eased. The world seemed to slow around them. Neither of them wanted to move, and Jake had trouble focusing after all the excitement tonight.

Rachel was staring at him. He said, "Yes?"

"You never told me how you cut yourself."

"What?"

"Your scar."

He smiled. "I got in trouble at school for stealing lunches, and my father started beating me up. I lost it. I went a little crazy. I grabbed a kitchen knife and wanted to kill him. But he was too fast, too strong. He threw me aside and I ended up cutting myself pretty badly."

"Cutting yourself?"

"I fell and the tip got me across the cheek," he said. "I wasn't very coordinated."

"Where was Euge?"

Jake let out a quiet laugh. "Right there, frozen. I yelled for him to help me, but he was so fucking scared he just stood there." Jake pictured his brother with his arms rigidly at his sides, his face contorted in fear. "He couldn't have done anything even if he tried, but I was kind of pissed at him."

"You two were so young, though."

Jake shrugged. "I know." He sat up slowly. "We should get moving."

She asked, "What's next?"

"Take this stuff up to the apartment. I want to dump the drill bits, the key, some of the incriminating garbage."

"Where?"

"I saw a few public garbage cans outside."

They dressed. In the silence, Jake said, "Sorry about bringing up Seattle."

"No. It's fine."

"It's just that—"

"It's okay."

"It's just that this worked out so well..,," he trailed off, then shrugged.

She turned to him, and looked him in the eye. "Thank you."

They spilled out of the car, and Jake handed her the canvas bag with the jewelry. He said, "Careful with this. Put it in my room. When I get in, we'll talk about how to give you your share."

"My share."

"I have to go over it again, but it looks like you can get maybe thirty grand in a mix of cash and jewels."

"Thirty grand."

"You'll have to sell the jewelry slowly, and only after everything's cooled off. If you want I can buy some of it off you."

"Thirty thousand?"

"We got a lot," he said. "This is really good."

She touched her forehead, and said, "Oh my God." Her cheeks were flushed.

"Not God." He looked around. "Go. All this stuff out here is making me nervous. I'll be up in ten minutes."

She clutched the canvas bag to her chest. She stared at him, and said, "Thank you, Jake. Really."

"We did a good job—"

"No, I mean about Seattle."

He nodded, but looked away. She walked to the elevator, and once she was inside, he left the garage.

On the street, he headed down the block, throwing out the key in one garbage can, his latex gloves in another, spreading it all out. His neck stung from her nails. Did he just ask Rachel to leave for Seattle? Did he actually do something as stupid as that? He didn't allow himself the possibility that he could be falling for her. Don't be an idiot, he thought.

He emptied his back pack of everything except the tools, which he wanted to keep, and walked back to the apartment building.

In the elevator, he smelled something, and realized it was him. He smelled like sex. He worried that Eugene might be awake, and he said aloud, "Did I just ask my brother's wife to run away with me?"

He sighed. The elevator bell rang his floor. He walked down the hall to the apartment. He checked the knob. Unlocked. Rachel was waiting for him. He felt a small sadness, because he knew they would be splitting up soon.

He opened the door and saw Rachel and Eugene sitting on the sofa, their faces pale, tense. Eugene had a black eye and bloody lip. Jake froze, wondering if he had caught them in a fight. A fist fight? Rachel stood up, and said, "Get out! Get out!"

Jake said, "What?"

Then Bobby Null appeared from behind the door. He aimed a revolver at Jake, and said, "There you are, you son of a bitch." Bobby leapt forward and tried to knock Jake in the head with the gun, but Jake ducked instinctively, and Bobby's gun grazed his ear and bounced off the wall. In one quick motion Jake stepped down, going low, and punched Bobby in the stomach, aiming towards his groin but hitting slightly higher. Bobby let out a choked yell, clutched at his stomach and fell. He raised his gun while holding himself with his other hand, his face contorted in pain, but Jake had already jumped away and was running down the hall. He threw himself around a corner near the elevator, and heard Bobby cursing loudly and slamming the door. Jake scrambled through the emergency exit and flew down the steps. The dead come back to life.

80

Bobby doubled over and wheezed, almost vomiting in pain. He saw movement near the sofa and raised his gun, spitting, "Don't do a thing, goddammit," and stumbled against the table. Jake had hit him right in the stitches and the agony forced him to his knees, coughing, his eyes watery, his scalp tightening. He wanted to curl up on the floor, but he had to watch the two on the sofa and had to figure out what to do about Jake. Fucking missed him by a inch. He sputtered curses and felt a sheen of prickly sweat breaking out over his body. His teeth chattered. He kept still, waiting for the pain to subside, but it didn't; it spread throughout his midsection and up into his chest. He groaned.

When he looked down and saw the dark area around the button of his jeans, he touched it. Wet. Blood. He gritted his teeth, and pulled himself into the chair. Doughboy and his wife were watching him.

"He's bleeding," the woman said to Eugene.

"Shut the fuck up, wifey." Bobby knocked over the lamp next to him and pulled out the electrical cord. He threw it to wifey. "Tie his hands behind his back. Tight. I'm gonna check." He stood up slowly, limped to the kitchen, and shoved paper towels down the front of his pants, bandaging the ripped stitches. He moved back to the living room and waved wifey away. He said, "On your stomach, hands behind your back."

She hesitated, and then he noticed the canvas bag she had brought it. She was keeping it close to her. He pointed his gun at Eugene and said, "Down on the floor, on your stomach. Both of you."

They lay down in front of the sofa, and Bobby checked Eugene's wrists. The cord wasn't that tight, but it'd do for now. He found a roll of speaker wire next to the stereo, and knelt over the wife, placing his foot on the small of her back. He held his gun under one arm, ready to grab it if she tried anything. She didn't. He bound her wrists together.

He realized he was breathing loudly through his mouth, almost panting. His shirt was sticking to his sweaty back and chest. He had trouble concentrating, and pulled out his bag of bennies. He popped two more, swallowing with a dry mouth, and tried to calm himself. Jake had run, but he wouldn't go far. Not with his brother here. Unless he didn't care.

He moved toward the canvas bag and saw the wife turn to him. He kicked the bag, testing its weight, then brought it to the table. The pain in his stomach dug at him. He sat down and unzipped the bag. He heard the wife sigh.

He stopped at the sight of glittering diamonds. "What the…"

"Oh, damn," the wife said.

Bobby glanced at her, then looked further into the bag. He saw the wads of cash and pulled them out. "Well, looky here. What the fuck is all this?" He quickly emptied the contents onto the table, the jewelry clattering, gold and silver rings and necklaces, diamonds, and watches clanking over each other. He first thought this was the Seattle stash, but remembered there being much less cash. Where the hell…

He turned to her. "Jake just did a job? With the equipment from his room?"

Eugene said, "What?"

The wife didn't move.

"Hey! Wifey! I'm talking to you!" He stopped. His stomach flared. He lowered his voice. "Is this from tonight? Did you help him or something?"

She turned away.

"You'll answer me or next time I won't ask so nice."

"Go to hell," she said.

He rubbed his forehead. "Fucking Christ. You people are a pain in the ass." He stood up and walked slowly towards them. He lowered the gun and aimed it at the back of her knee. He said, "Do you think I really care if I blow out your knee and watch you bleed to death?"

"Now, wait a minute," Eugene said.

Bobby turned to him. "I thought I told you to be quiet." He slammed the butt of the gun into his neck. Eugene cried out in pain.

"Stop!" the wife said.

Bobby felt the rush of the bennies, and this time it was clear and cool, washing over the pain. He sighed and stood up. He pressed his foot into Eugene's neck. Soothing fingers tickled Bobby's throat. He let out a small laugh and pressed his foot harder. Eugene gurgled, and tried to say something but Bobby pressed down, choking him.

He said to the wife, "Where is that stuff from?" He put all his weight on his foot and Eugene gasped.

"You're hurting him!" she cried.

"Tell me."

"A jewelry store."

Bobby nodded and eased his foot. Eugene sucked in air. Bobby said, "Tonight?"

"Yes."

"You and Jake?"

"Yes."

"Anyone else?"

"No."

"Where is Jake's Seattle stash?"

"I don't know what you mean."

"If you're lying to me," he said, lowering his foot onto Eugene's neck.

"I don't know what you mean!"

Bobby backed away, and returned to the table. He couldn't believe how lucky he was. Brand new goods, right here, with a shitload of cash. This, with the Seattle stash, would set him up for years. He could settle his debts and buy whatever the fuck he wanted.

The phone rang. He smiled and picked it up, watching Eugene and the wife. "Hello?" he said.

"If you fucking touch them, you little piece of—"

"Hey, Jake. Long time no. I guess I came over at the right time. Nice little haul here. Man, you don't take a break, do you? Even after fucking me over with the other stash. You're a fucking worker bee, you know that?"

"Shit."

"Shit is right. She tried to hide it, but I know the signs. Man, all this cash. What'd you hit, Jewels 'R Us?"

"You killed Chih."

Bobby said, "You heard about Chih? Yeah, that son of a bitch asked for it. I made him beg a while before I offed him. But where's my Seattle stash?"

"I left it all with Chih. I thought you got it."

Bobby's stomach lurched, then stopped. He said, "Don't fucking give me that. He didn't know crap. You took everything and came down here. The stuff is *mine* now. I earned it, you hear me? Where the fuck is it?"

"I'm telling you I left it in Chih's safe—"

"That's how you gonna play it? Maybe your partner here can tell me. All she needs is a little good loving—"

"Stay the fuck away from her."

Bobby pulled the phone from his ear and laughed. He hung up. He moved to Eugene, grabbed his shirt and told him to sit up, propping him against the sofa. When the phone rang again, Bobby pressed the talk button and shoved the handset against Eugene's ear. Eugene tilted his head, "Jake?"

Bobby went to the wife and also propped her up. He put the gun against her cheek and said, "Tell your brother what I'm doing."

"Wait! Wait!" Eugene yelled. "Jake! He's got a gun on Rachel!"

"Where is the Seattle stash?" Bobby asked. "Tell him I've got wifey—Rachel—here."

Eugene listened on the phone, then said, "Fuck your bargaining chip. This kid's crazy. Just tell him—I don't give a shit! You brought this here! I told you—"

Bobby gripped Rachel's throat, and began squeezing. She struggled, and he pressed the gun harder into her cheek. She kicked her legs to try to pull away, but Bobby held tightly.

"He's choking her, goddammit!" Eugene yelled. "Tell him—"

"Better hurry," Bobby said. "She's gonna pass out soon."

Rachel let out a choked, "Don't tell…"

Bobby tightened his grip and she gasped.

Eugene shook the phone off, letting it fall to the ground and said, "I'll tell you. It's in the bank. Jake put it in a safe deposit box."

Bobby let go, and Rachel gasped in air. He grabbed the phone and said, "All right. Now we're getting somewhere. The bank opens when, nine? At nine-thirty in the morning, you're going to come here with everything you took from me—the jewelry and the cash. I remember what was in the box. Don't fuck with me. You got it?"

"You little asshole—"

Bobby hung up. He limped to the table and sat down, holding his stomach. He saw Rachel glaring at Eugene and laughed. "It'll be a while. You better relax."

81

Jake thought about pulling the fire alarm, hoping to force Bobby to appear, but suspected that Bobby would just shove Eugene and Rachel into a closet and wait it out. It was a mess, no matter how he played it. As for the police, they'd be learning about the Lomax job in the morning, so they were out. Jake had no choice. He had to deal. He had hoped to lie to Bobby and separate him from Eugene and Rachel, but Eugene's confession scrapped that.

Christ, he didn't even have a gun. He had his safe cracking tools and the thin hunting knife.

But that was five hours away. There were a couple things he could do: he could check on them, make sure they were all right. He had called the apartment from the laundry room, and now took the stairs up to the twelfth floor. He moved quickly down the hall and stopped at the door, listening. He pulled out his knife and held it by his side. He heard the TV on low. Another sound, something metallic clinking on the glass table. Jake realized Bobby was going through the jewelry piece by piece, something that Jake hadn't done yet.

"Fucking jackpot," Bobby said, his voice muffled.

Rachel said something that Jake couldn't hear.

"Are you kidding? The cops? What's he going to say? My name's Jake and I tried to kill my partner, but now he's stealing the shit I just stole?" Bobby laughed. "He'll bring the Seattle stuff. He's not stupid."

The clinking continued. Bobby said, "Both of you stop moving. I'll do your legs if I have to."

Jake checked the doorknob. It was unlocked, but he was pretty sure the deadbolt was engaged. He turned the knob all the way and pushed in the door slowly. It didn't move. He let go of the knob carefully.

He heard scraping. Bobby was probably testing some of the diamonds, damaging the facets.

Jake thought about waiting this out. At some point Bobby would be away from the table, away from the line of sight of this door. Then Jake could try to go in quietly, maybe jump him. He could try to get his brother and Rachel out. At some point he'd have to go to the bathroom. Jake tried to think of a distraction, something that would give him time to get to Eugene and Rachel. Once they were free, Bobby would probably take what he had and leave.

What would happen if Jake just disappeared? What if he didn't show up in the morning? But he thought about Chih. Bobby wouldn't hesitate to kill.

Jake brought his key to the deadbolt. How the fuck did Bobby survive that gunshot wound? He could still see Bobby unconscious, his body sliding into the dumpster. And how did he find Jake? Chih hadn't known anything. This rattled Jake. Bobby was stronger than he had thought, and he hesitated with the key in his hand. Maybe Bobby expected Jake to return. Maybe he was sitting right in front of the door, gun in hand, waiting.

Movement. The sound of the kitchen faucet. Bobby getting a drink. Jake heard Bobby curse, and say, "Your brother is a dirty fighter."

Jake began pushing his key in, using his fingers as a brace around the lock. He went in one notch at a time, stopping and easing off on the pressure with each movement. Once the key was flush, he started to rotate it, but knew the bolt would click loudly once it disengaged. He turned the key until he felt the bolt catching, and then he stopped. He waited. He listened.

82

Bobby had trouble taking pleasure in fucking Jake over with this new haul because something was wrong inside his stomach. That goddamn punch had messed things up in there, and Bobby could feel the pain worsening. Blood spots appeared between the torn stitches, soaking the paper towels he kept replacing. He had to hold out until tomorrow, and with the new cash he could see a good doctor, not one of those county shits that gave him a fucking infection. The pain flared and he bent over the sink, making sure the two on the floor didn't see him. He breathed hard, hoping the new bennies would kick in soon. He was turning them over faster and faster. He lifted his shirt, wiped away some of the blood and promised himself to kill Jake slowly once he got the Seattle stash.

Not a bullet to his gut, because it was too noisy. Bobby checked the knives in the wooden block on the counter. He'd use the long one with a serrated edge. Let's see how he likes it, Bobby thought. A torn gut. Let's see how long he can survive his fucking intestines chopped up. Thinking about this made him happy. Seeing the jewelry and cash on the table made him happy. He drank more water, since the cold seemed to help, and returned to the jewelry. Goddamn. With this and the Seattle stash, he could retire. He could buy a motor home and live on the beach. Maybe one day he'd drive up to Seattle and show off to his mother, let her know he wasn't a total fuck-up like she thought.

Kevin never had a motor home. Kevin never even left home, that pussy. At least Bobby looked out for himself and didn't depend on Mommy's money to live. What a loser. He found himself getting annoyed. He focused on the jewelry.

The two on the floor were talking. Bobby said, "Shut the hell up.

Am I going to have to lock you guys up in different rooms? You want that?" He stood up too fast, and felt more pain, but he tried not to show it. He walked slowly towards them. Eugene said, "You don't need both of us. Let her go."

Bobby laughed. "Give me a fucking break. Where'd you learn that? TV? Asshole, two of you means double insurance."

"Why don't you just take that and leave?" Rachel said.

Bobby stared at her. She was really pretty, and he looked down at the outline of her legs in her black tights. He said, "Why the hell would you help Jake?"

Her eyes narrowed.

He said, "You supposed to get a cut?" He turned to Eugene. "Why didn't you know about it?"

He said, "I told him not to involve me."

"But she's your wife?"

"Will you just let her go?" he said.

Bobby leaned forward and pushed aside her jacket, checking her breasts. She slid away.

"Hey," Eugene said. "What the hell."

Lifting his gun and aiming it at him, Bobby said, "Quiet." He felt himself getting hard. He hadn't screwed around in months. He wondered if he still could, with his stitches coming out. His groin began hurting, though, from the punch. Everything was connected. He said to Rachel, "Maybe I should put you in the bedroom."

She said, "You can go fuck yourself."

Bobby smiled. "That's what you're here for." He pointed the gun at her and said, "Come on. Get up."

"No fucking way," Eugene said, trying to sit up.

Bobby kicked him in the side, and he went down. The sudden movement sent a jolt of searing pain through his stomach and groin, and he doubled over, holding his stomach. Rachel jumped up and began running towards the door. He cursed and hobbled after her, ignoring the feeling of something tearing inside him. She bent over and backed up, trying to open the door with her hands tied behind her, her fingers wiggling towards the knob. She found the doorknob, but Bobby reached her, grabbed her neck and threw her against the wall. She cried out.

The door clicked, and suddenly flung open. A figure lunged towards him, and he realized it was Jake. Bobby brought his gun up, but Jake sliced his hand with a knife and kicked him hard in the groin, the shock so violent that Bobby actually saw flashes of white light across his vision, and his grip loosened on the gun, but he didn't let go. Jake yanked Bobby's arm up and tried to stab him again, but Bobby fell back, avoiding him. He watched the knife and managed to aim the gun at Jake's midsection. He pulled the trigger and the loud crack seemed to shake the building. Jake clutched his waist, looking down, then up at Bobby in shock. Bobby tightened his grip on the gun, closed the door quickly, and said, "That was very stupid." Jake went down on one knee, holding his side with one hand and staring at the knife in his other hand, his mouth open. Bobby could barely move with the pain in his groin. He said, "You lose." He advanced and hit Jake's head as hard as he could with the gun, connecting cleanly over his ear, Bobby's arm jolting and bouncing off. Jake's head snapped to the side, his eyelids fluttered, and he collapsed.

83

The blur of sounds around him, the haze of lights slowly growing brighter, Jake felt a damp cloth on his forehead, the soothing coolness pulling him out of his confusion, the quiet, threatening voice of his brother drawing him awake. His brother was saying, "…you can't go to the bank now. You should just go and take what you have…" and Jake tried to lift his head, but Rachel whispered, "Keep still."

"Is he up?"

Jake opened his eyes. The top of his skull felt squeezed, a vice tightening as he looked around. He saw Bobby at the table, hunched over, his face red and sweaty. His eyes seemed to be bulging. Waving Rachel away, Bobby said, "All right. He's fine. Get away from him."

Jake tried to sit up, but found his hands and feet tied together. His shoulder joints ached, and he wondered how long he had been out. He had trouble formulating thoughts. He noticed that Bobby had put the jewelry and cash back into the canvas bag, and kept the bag close to his feet.

"Face down on the floor," Bobby told Rachel. "Hands behind your back. I'm tying you up again."

"What about his side? I should replace the bandage soon."

Jake thought, My side? He slowly looked down and saw that his shirt was stiff with dried blood. Red gauze and tape poked out from underneath. Then he winced, his side crackling and throbbing, and he remembered being shot. He became dizzy and had to rest his head back onto the floor, but the sudden movement sent blood rushing to his head, doubling the squeezing pain. His thoughts jumbled together.

Bobby said, "Fuck him. Get away. Hands behind your back."

She lay down and clasped her hands behind her. Bobby walked

over to her, his legs unsteady. He made a loop with extension cord, and while still holding his gun, bound Rachel's wrist together. He then put the gun down and made a knot, tugging and testing it. He quickly picked up the gun and returned to the chair. He sat down with a grimace and fixed the bandage on his hand. To Jake he said, "Stupid fuck. All you had to do was wait until the bank opened."

"I'm hurt," Jake said. "My side."

"Yeah, well, you're lucky I missed. I was aiming for your gut."

"The bullet...?"

"Right through. You must have a fucking guardian angel."

Jake saw his brother sitting on the floor, his back against the sofa; his left eye was puffed closed, purples and yellows coloring the bruise. His lower jaw was also bruised. He seemed dazed and kept staring at Bobby.

"I need a hospital," Jake said.

"The fuck you do. We're gonna wait until the bank opens, and you're going to get my stuff."

"Your stuff."

"That's right," he said. He stopped, and held his stomach, sucking air through his teeth. He lowered his voice and said, "I'm going to open up your insides just like you did to me."

"If you're going to kill me, why should I bother going to the bank?"

"There's still them to worry about," he said. He aimed his gun at Eugene and said, "First him, because he's your brother." He moved the gun towards Rachel. "Then her, but maybe I have some fun with her before."

Jake said in a strong, clear voice, "How did it feel in the garbage?"

Bobby sat up.

"How did it feel to be dumped in with the rotting vegetables?" Jake said.

"You fucking—"

"I threw you in there like a sack of shit."

Bobby stood up, winced, then walked quickly to Jake, winding up and giving him a kick in the stomach. Jake's midsection exploded, and he felt the adhesive tape around his wound tearing off. He cried out and began coughing, the pain blinding him. Bobby laughed. Jake didn't see the second kick coming, but felt his chest collapsing, his breathing caught in his throat. He gasped for air, and tried to turn away from another kick. Rachel yelled something. Jake was trying to inhale but could only wheeze and cough. He felt like he was choking on air, his lungs refusing to expand, and he struggled for what seemed like a long time without breathing. Then, slowly, a breath came through, and he heard his throat rasping as he quickly inhaled.

"You're going to kill him," Rachel said.

Bobby laughed again. "That's the idea."

Jake felt saliva dripping down his chin. He blinked, his vision clearing as he took more deep breaths, and he met Rachel's eyes. He croaked, "I'm sorry about this."

She didn't reply, but nodded. She glanced at Eugene. He was watching them.

"That was fun," Bobby said. "But you're right. He can't die until after I get my stuff."

Jake thought, So this is what it's like to see your death coming. He felt a mix of panic and calm, the struggle to grasp what was happening mingling with the searing pain. He could no longer feel his hands. If he could survive until morning he could try something on the way to the bank. Was Bobby going to wait for him? Jake could get a gun.

His vision was tingling. He saw star bursts and multi-colored static, and tried to blink them away. He felt something dripping along his stomach and looked down. He said, "I'm bleeding."

"The bandage came off," Rachel said.

"Fuck it. Let him bleed."

"He's already lost a lot of blood."

"I said fuck it."

"He'll die."

Bobby let out an annoyed sigh. "Let him bleed, understand? Let him bleed."

"You're an asshole," Rachel said.

Jake thought, Oh, shit.

"What?" Bobby slowly turned in his chair to face her. "What did you just say to me?"

"Stop," Jake said to Bobby. "You're taking her share."

Bobby looked down at the canvas bag. To Rachel he said, "You don't like that, do you. That's how it fucking feels. At least I'm not giving you a gut shot and leaving you in the goddamn dumpster."

Jake said, "You tried to screw me over."

Bobby ignored him and continued staring at Rachel. He said, "You're pretty hot. What're you doing hanging around losers like him?"

She didn't reply.

Bobby was about to say something else, but his face seized up, and he bent over, holding his stomach. "Motherfucker!" he said. He stood and limped to the kitchen. Jake couldn't see what he was doing, but heard the faucet running. He glanced at Eugene, who was staring towards the kitchen and moving his hands behind his back. His shoulders rocked as he struggled with the knots. When Bobby returned, Eugene stopped moving. He turned to Jake.

Jake, startled, saw in his brother's eyes an anger directed at him. Eugene stared coldly, then turned away.

Jake realized his brother knew about Rachel.

Bobby noticed Eugene watching him, and said, "What the fuck's your problem?" Bobby breathed in shallow, short bursts, because anything too deep sent spasms of pain though his groin and stomach. His vision blurred. If it weren't for the bennies giving him a small lift, he'd be spread on the floor. Something burning worked its way up through his insides, and he imagined it was another one of those strong infections, the bacteria multiplying and spreading. He had finished his antibiotics days ago and now felt naked, open to attack.

He plotted his moves. He'd wait this out until the morning, then walk Jake over to the bank, the only way to make sure everything went well. Then he'd take the Seattle stash, add it to what he had now, and disappear. He'd have to find a hospital soon. He'd have to kill Jake quickly.

The walls seemed to pulsate. He looked around. The room breathed. He shook his head and focused on the jewelry in front of him. A fever coming on. He recognized the sluggish air. It was almost five, and he hoped he could hold out.

Jake said, "Why didn't you clean out Chih's store?"

Who? Chih. Felt like another lifetime. Bobby turned to Jake, who was hogtied on the floor, his shirt bloodied from the bullet wound. Damn lucky. Clean. Not like the bullet in his own fucking gut. He said, "He used the alarm." The air moved around Jake, a blurriness surrounding him like heat rising from the highway, and Bobby squeezed his eyes shut, then opened them. He looked at his gun. The barrel puckered its lips and blew a kiss. He kissed it back and smelled the cordite and oil.

They were all watching him now, and he said to Jake, "You knew

Kevin?"

"Your brother? Met him a couple of times."

"What'd you think of him?"

Jake shook his head. "He was a loser and very stupid."

Bobby stiffened.

"And," Jake said, "he was pretty ugly. All that weird shit on his face."

"From steroids," Bobby said.

"I figured. He looked like a freak."

"Our neighbors probably heard the gunshot," Eugene said. "They might be calling the police."

Bobby turned to him. "Was I talking to you? Why are you so fucking dense?"

"It's true," Jake said. "That was loud."

"Maybe. But they'd probably call here first. Find out what it was. Funny thing about neighbors. Most don't give a shit."

"You mind if I get another bandage?" Jake asked. "If I bleed too much I won't be able to make it to the bank."

"Doesn't look like it's bleeding."

"But it hurts like hell."

Bobby stood up. "Oh, does it?" He ignored the flash of heat rising from his stomach. He felt the bugs in him clawing their way up to his chest. The apartment shrunk around him as he walked to Jake and said, "Does that little scratch hurt?"

Jake said, "Never mind."

"Does it hurt?" Bobby raised his foot and lowered it onto Jake's side, right over the wound. "Tell me if this hurts." Bobby stamped down and Jake yelled out.

Bobby said, "Hm. That didn't seem to hurt enough. It wasn't like when I was in the fucking garbage can and had fucking bugs crawling into my body. No, you little fucking goddamn son of a bitch." Bobby stamped on Jake again, then moved back and kicked him hard in the stomach. The sudden jerking twisted something in Bobby's stomach and he stopped, backing away and holding himself. The pain was too much, and he vomited on the floor. He knelt over, and spewed green bile. Remnants of the bennies, maybe. He spat out the taste and stood back up.

"Fuck, I ought to just kill you now and leave."

At first he thought Jake was crying, but then saw that he was laughing. Bobby said, "What the fuck?"

Jake raised his head and turned to Rachel. He said, "All things happen through strife and conflict."

Bobby said, "Hey, asshole. I'm talking to you."

Jake closed his eyes and rested his head. "Death and life are one."

Bobby wiped his mouth and moved to Rachel. He said, "I wasn't done with you before."

Jake opened his eyes. "Stop."

Bobby said, "Oh, that bother you? What's the fucking deal here? I thought she was his wife."

"She is," Eugene said.

"Share and share alike? What a nice brother you have," Bobby said to Jake. "Maybe you all can share her with me."

"Fuck you," Eugene said. He struggled, and tried to stand. Bobby moved towards him, but hesitated. Instead of kicking him, Bobby picked up a small statuette and swung it at Eugene's head. It hit above his ear and Eugene fell over. "Doughboy, you're nothing. You're a piece of shit to me."

"Leave him alone," Jake said. "He's got nothing to do with this."

"He's your brother. He's got everything to do with this. What a piece of work." He glanced at Eugene, whose face was scrunched up. "Oh, no. You're gonna cry? You're gonna call out for your mommy? Pathetic fat piece of shit."

Eugene turned his head away.

Bobby laughed and moved back to Rachel. He touched her hair, and she flinched. He ran his fingers down her neck, and brushed across her breasts. She tried to back away, but he just stepped forward.

"I'm warning you," Jake said.

"*You* are warning *me*." Bobby shook his head. "You're classic."

"Leave her alone," Eugene said.

Rachel gritted her teeth. He touched her breast again, rubbing slowly. He said, "Maybe I take you to the other room."

She stared straight ahead.

"Or maybe I get a little right now, right here," Bobby said, moving closer and unzipping his pants. A paper towel with dried blood spots fell out. "I tell you what. You give me a blow job in front of them, and I let you live." He saw Eugene struggling, breathing hard. He was crying.

Rachel sat up, knelt on one leg. Bobby raised his gun. He said, "And if you don't, I shoot doughboy." He pulled out his penis, slowly getting hard. She turned her head. He saw Jake try to roll over. He aimed his gun at Eugene, and looked down at Rachel. "What do you say?"

She closed her eyes, looked down, and shot up on one leg. Her head moved up so fast that Bobby didn't have time to react, and she head butt him in his chin, knocking his head back and stunning him. He flailed his arms, trying to regain his balance and she butted her head into his chest and he fell back, hearing Jake yell "Get his gun!" and then the brother screamed something and jumped on Bobby.

Jake watched his brother rip his hands out of the knots behind his back and lunge for Bobby, his fingers clawed. Rachel fell back, while Jake writhed across the floor towards the gun. He rolled painfully over his bloody side and tried to grab the gun from behind, pulling on the cord that dug into his flesh, his fingers groping. But then he realized that Eugene had body-slammed Bobby and was choking him with both hands, using his weight to keep Bobby down, and ignoring Bobby's hands as they flailed and tried to punch and scratch Eugene's arms. Eugene's face was frenzied, his teeth bared, and he shook Bobby's head back and forth as he choked him, almost getting kicked off at one point, but then straddling Bobby and slamming his head back into the floor. Eugene was muttering, "Look what you've done look what you've done look what you've done…" as he gripped Bobby's throat tighter, and Bobby's arms stopped flailing, and Eugene pushed more of his weight into Bobby neck and shook him back and forth, up and down, slamming him, and saying, "Look what you've done look what you've done," and Jake watched, frozen.

Bobby was already blinded from the head butt, but now as everything became fainter, as his breathing halted and his body crumpled, he heard the underwater echoes of yells around him, the voices warping. He feebly tried to fight off the hands on his throat. He raked his long fingernails against them, but everything only tightened. He was fading. The sharp pains in his groin and stomach disappeared, all the sensations lapsed except for the distant feeling of descent, and this, too, seemed to edge away as he thought of his jewelry and cash and everything he had worked for that would be gone when he awoke. He would no longer be able to buy a motor home and drive up to Seattle to flaunt it to his mother and tell her, See, I'm not what you think. And then Bobby heard his brother laughing at him, saying, At least I went down fighting. Bobby tried to curse him, the acid burning through his thoughts, and the last thing that flashed through him in the last glimmer of consciousness was an image of Kevin covered with bullet holes and blood with a cat in his arms, and then Bobby died.

Jake told his brother to calm down, but Eugene kept slamming Bobby's head against the floor, Bobby's limbs dancing and jerking with each crash, until Eugene had no strength left to lift him, and collapsed. Eugene was panting, Bobby lay still. Eugene rolled away, and covered his head with his arms, mumbling to himself. He said in a cracking voice, "Can't fucking take this."

Jake saw bloody pieces of hairy scalp on the floor, and pulled himself up, motioning to Rachel to untie him. Rachel stood, staring at Eugene, and backed up towards the dining room table. She picked up Jake's knife, and crouched next to him. Looking over her shoulder, she carefully cut the wire tying his wrists and ankles together. He took the knife and sliced the rest of their knots free.

They approached Eugene cautiously. Bobby's neck was purple. His eyes were open, blank. Jake searched for a pulse around Bobby's crushed throat, and found nothing. His fingers just sank into the soft, collapsed neck. He moved to Eugene, who was still covering his face, and said, "Hey, you okay?" He saw the scratches along Eugene's arms and hands.

Eugene tried to sit up, but couldn't. His left eye was now swollen shut. His right eye, a deep scratch directly over it, was bloody. Eugene blinked pink tears. He held his scratched arms up, and said in a broken voice, "Can't...see."

"Don't move," Jake said. "Let me get something for those cuts." He limped to the bathroom and grabbed bandages, disinfectant, and cotton balls from the medicine cabinet. He returned and saw Rachel still staring at Bobby. As Jake leaned over his brother, he felt his back and ribs tighten in pain. He stopped. He asked Rachel to help.

They cleaned and bandaged the cut over Eugene's eye, and helped him sit up against the sofa. He blinked more tears out and looked down at his scratched arms. Eugene looked at Bobby, his expression moving from incomprehension to anger. He watched Jake and Rachel bandage up his arm. Bobby had dug his nails deep into Eugene's forearm. Then Rachel put a new bandage on Jake's side.

She whispered to Jake, "What should we do?"

"Are you okay?"

She nodded.

Jake glanced at Bobby. He needed to check again to make sure he was dead. He said, "We clean up."

"How?"

"I'll get rid of him," Jake said. He saw Eugene turn to them. Jake asked him if he was okay.

Eugene said quietly, "You take care of him, and then you leave."

"What?" Jake asked, surprised by the clarity of his brother's voice.

"You clean this up, and then you get the fuck out of here."

"Wait," Rachel said. "We—"

"You're leaving me." Eugene stood. "You're leaving me and you're fucking my brother. You're not allowed to say a word."

Rachel froze.

"You are, aren't you," Eugene said.

Jake tried to move away, but Eugene whirled towards him. "And you. How could I be so stupid? I can't even begin to…" He shook his head. "I warned you about bringing your shit here. I warned you about involving us. And what do you do? You bring death here."

"I didn't mean to—"

"And you screw around with my wife? How…why…I don't understand you."

Jake couldn't respond. He felt a pulsing pain in his side.

Eugene said to Rachel, "You take care of this with him. When you get back, I'll be gone."

"Where?"

"If you want your divorce, you take care of the paperwork. And you sell this place. I don't know why I have to do all the goddamn paperwork."

"Where will you go?" she asked.

"Why'd you do it? Why'd you sleep with him? Didn't you know that would hurt me?"

She squeezed her eyes shut for a moment, then opened them. "I don't know."

"It didn't have to end like this."

She said, "You're not thinking clearly."

"Don't tell me what to think."

Jake said, "Where will you go? Do you need cash?"

Eugene turned to him. "I never want to see you again. Do you understand? I don't want to hear from you. I want you out of here. Out of my life. That's it."

"You can't mean that—"

"Don't tell me what I mean."

"I'm sorry, Eugene. I didn't know—"

"Sorry?" Eugene said, raising his voice. "You don't understand. You don't even know what that means. You have no conscience. You scare me. You can't tell the difference between right and wrong."

"Of course I can. Look, I'll fix everything—"

"No. That's it."

"I'll take care of everything," Jake said, uneasily. He had never seen his brother like this. "Really."

Eugene looked sad. "You don't really care. You don't really feel. It's like…it's like you're not alive inside."

Jake shook his head.

"How could you do this to me?" Eugene said. "I looked out for you. I took care of you."

Jake stared at his brother. "Sometimes you did." He nodded.

Eugene's glance went to Jake's cheek, and Eugene said quietly, "I tried to take care of you. I really did."

Jake said, "I know."

Eugene turned to Rachel. "I'm taking a cab to the hospital. When I get back I want this thing," he pointed to Bobby, "out of here. By the time you get back I'll be gone."

"To where?"

"I don't know. I need to start over. I need to start fresh."

Jake thought of their mother, but didn't say anything.

Eugene left the apartment. Jake went to Bobby and checked his wrist pulse, then put his ear near Bobby's mouth, listening for breathing. Nothing. He looked up at Rachel and said, "I'll need help."

"What kind?"

"My car is in the garage. I'll need you to check ahead of me to make sure no one is around while I carry him down there. Then I'll follow you in your car."

"To where?"

"Someplace quiet, maybe one of those long highways near the coast."

Rachel stared at the door.

"Can you help me?" Jake asked.

"I can help you," she whispered.

88

Jake drove his Honda down 19th Avenue, following Rachel. Bobby's body was in the trunk. She led Jake onto Highway One along the Pacific, and he followed her down the coast, heading towards Half Moon Bay. He drove for long stretches of empty highway, with only the ocean to his right and rolling hills covered with brush to his left. The bleeding in his side had stopped, the pain a low, steady throb that spread through his midsection. He'd have to see a doctor, but not until all this was finished.

Before leaving the apartment he had stacked all the cash from the Lomax job on the dining room table for Eugene. Fifteen grand with a note: "Sorry. This is for you." Jake had already decided what he would do. After they finished with Bobby, he would give Rachel the Seattle stash, including the twenty grand, and Jake would take the Lomax jewelry up north. It would be too hot around here. He'd sell off the Lomax jewelry slowly.

Jake secretly hoped Eugene would continue his search for their mother. He knew that this time if his brother went looking, he would find her. This time his brother would be determined and focused and methodical, and would move steadily, and plot his steps as a technician. And their mother would be alive. Oh, certainly she was a survivor, just like they were, and she would have lived a quiet, solitary life somewhere with only the vaguest memories of her former self. Jake knew that this time all Eugene's questions would be answered, and maybe in a few years Jake would hear from him, and Eugene would tell Jake all about this first meeting, with the tentative and cautious pleasantries, the circling, the words masking the fear and urgency beneath both of their fake smiles. Jake knew for certain that Eugene

would not stop until he found her, and then would not stop until he
learned what he needed to learn, until those puzzles that shaded their
lives were solved, or, if not solved, at the very least acknowledged.
What would they say? What would she look like?

Jake had never seen his brother so angry, and he tried not to think
about it. Eugene couldn't have meant what he said. How could you
never see your brother again? They were family. Jake wasn't sure
what he'd do. Lie low. Maybe he would move to the mountains and
live off grasses and plants.

Jake pressed his hand over his heart and felt it beating. He heard
his brother's bitter words. Jake shook his head; he wasn't like that. He
knew right from wrong. He had a conscience. He wasn't dead.

His side throbbed. He pulled up his shirt. The bandage, brown
with dried blood, was holding. Zombies don't bleed. Zombies don't
feel pain.

As he passed Moss Beach and El Granada, the sky glowing with
the impending dawn, he saw a small shoulder with a dirt road leading
into the brush. He honked at Rachel and pulled off the highway. He
drove slowly along the dusty road until they were a few hundred feet
from the entrance. He wanted to be sure they were far enough in, and
then he parked. Rachel pulled up behind him. She stayed in the car.

In the trunk Bobby was rolled into a rug, and Jake dragged him
out, ignoring the pain in his side, and set him down next to the driver's
side. Jake unrolled him, then hoisted him into the car, shoving him
over the gear shift. Rigor mortis was setting in, and Bobby was half
standing. Jake folded up the rug and threw it in the back seat. He
unrolled the windows, and unscrewed the gas tank cap. He walked
towards Rachel's car and motioned for her to pop the trunk. She did.

He pulled out the one-gallon gas can that Rachel had filled
before they had left. He walked back to his car, poured the extra gas
throughout the interior, soaking Bobby, and making sure there was a
heavy dose of gas on the exterior leading to the gas tank opening. He

threw the gas can into the front seat, next to Bobby.

He motioned for Rachel to turn the car around. She did.

He opened her passenger door and said, "When I get in, we head home. Drive normally."

She nodded.

He walked back to his Honda, lit a book of matches and threw it into the back seat. The upholstery flared up, and he walked quickly to Rachel's car and climbed in, and she drove off.

He glanced back and saw the flames leaping up, soot blackening the rear windshield. He thought he saw Bobby's hair on fire, and for a moment it seemed as if Bobby was shaking his head, writhing in pain. He blinked and the image disappeared. He turned around and settled in for the long ride back. His fingers smelled of gasoline. The world is fire.

89

Late, late night. His brother had fallen asleep at the foot of the steps. Jake's father was in the living room upstairs, mumbling to himself, arguing in Korean, descending into a drunken haze. Jake had stopped shaking, and touched his face lightly. He checked the dressing his brother had applied over his cut cheek, a mix of butterfly bandages and gauze, studying the contours of rising bruises. After Jake had cut himself, his father had ordered Eugene to clean the wound and then sent them downstairs.

Jake noticed movement in the corner of the basement, something rippling in the darkness. He heard his brother grinding his teeth.

He focused and thought he saw a goblin hurrying by.

His brother groaned in his sleep.

Jake kept still, hugging his legs and listening to the click of the furnace, the sign of the flame kicking in. His skin prickled with anticipation.

Jake couldn't believe his own actions. He had taunted his father. Speak English! Speak English! And he had seen the purplish veins popping out on his father's forehead, knowing what was going to happen, and yet Jake hadn't been able to stop himself. The first backhand sent Jake flying across the kitchen floor, and after a stunned moment, Jake pulled himself up unsteadily, and said in a tight voice, You can't do that to me! Then, Jake wasn't sure what happened. He started charging his father again and again, only to be swatted away and then pummelled and kicked. He couldn't get up from the quick kicks and yelled for his brother's help, but Eugene stood motionless, staring. Help me, Jake yelled again, but his father pointed his finger at Eugene and said something in Korean, and Eugene shook his head and cried, his arms at his side. Speak English, Jake yelled, and felt that last blow to his chest turn everything off, and rolled away and grabbed the knife from the counter. His father crouched down, arms ready, and Jake dove at him, knife poised, but his father moved quickly, effortlessly, and the next thing Jake knew he was suddenly on the floor, his face bleeding, the wind knocked out of him. He couldn't remember how he had arrived there. He wasn't even sure where the knife had come from. It had appeared in his hand.

His father barked an order to Eugene, and then looked down at Jake with a dull, even gaze and lumbered out of the kitchen. Eugene hurried over and whispered, Why'd you do that? Why'd you push him? But Jake had only said, You didn't help me.

As he listened to his brother asleep on the steps, he checked the bandages on his face. His cheek stung. Eugene's breathing slowed and deepened. Jake felt a release, a freedom he didn't understand. He wasn't afraid.

Soon, their father stopped mumbling upstairs. The house became quiet, the stillness punctuated by a creak in the floor, a doorway settling, the wind outside. Jake was wide awake, unused to the silence. He stared out into the darkness, warmed by the furnace. He listened to everyone breathe, and was lulled by the cadence of sighs. The furnace clicked off. He rose up, used the screwdriver to pick open the basement door, then wandered silently through the house, heading to his bedroom, broken lamps and overturned furniture strewn along the floor. He stopped and stared at his sleeping father. He thought of all the things he could do right now. He could get the knife if he wanted to. He felt stronger. He *was* stronger. He studied his father, then turned away. For a moment he saw the ghostly image of his mother in the corner, watching him. She clapped her hands lightly, applauding. He rubbed his eyes. She disappeared. He focused, and soon saw clearly through the night, and glided down the hallways in the peaceful aftermath.

ABOUT THE AUTHOR

Leonard Chang was born in New York City and studied philosophy at Dartmouth College and Harvard University. He received his M.F.A. from the University of California at Irvine, and is the author of seven previous novels. His books have been translated into Japanese, French and Korean, and are taught at universities around the world. His short stories have been published in literary journals such as *Prairie Schooner* and *The Literary Review*. He lives in Los Angeles. For more information, visit his web site at www.LeonardChang.com.